W9-CDX-247

Praise for *The Paris Architect*

"I love that in *The Paris Architect*, a mercenary, talented man's passion for his creative work leads him down moral roads he never could have envisioned. The ingenious hiding spaces and the people in them infiltrated my imagination for weeks. I *dreamed* about this novel."

—Jenna Blum, *New York Times* bestselling author of *Those Who Save Us* and *The Stormchasers*

"A vivid, suspenseful story that keeps you gripped to the very last page. Charles Belfoure writes with great warmth, conjuring up an intriguing cast of characters and painting a fascinating picture of Paris under the Occupation, with all its contradictions—the opulence, and the fear."

—Margaret Leroy, author of *The Soldier's Wife*

"Belfoure writes like an up-and-coming Ken Follett."

—*Booklist*

"All novelists are architects. But are all architects novelists? Charles Belfoure in his impressive debut seems to have brought us the best of both worlds. Here is a novel to read alongside the latest Alan Furst. I hope there will be more."

—Alan Cheuse, NPR book commentator

"Belfoure's portrayal of Vichy France is both disturbing and captivating, and his beautiful tale demonstrates that while human beings are capable of great atrocities, they have a capacity for tremendous acts of courage as well."

—*Library Journal*, Starred Review

"Belfoure's characters are well-rounded and intricate. Heart, reluctant heroism, and art blend together in this spine-chilling page-turner."

—*Publishers Weekly*

"Architectural and historical details are closely rendered... a satisfyingly streamlined World War II thriller."

—*Kirkus*

"A gripping page-turner, *The Paris Architect* brings to life the dark and merciless streets of German-occupied France. Through elaborate designs of his characters' making, Charles Belfoure shines a light on the human heart—a complex maze of love, hope, and the yearning for redemption—and in doing so, provides a riveting reminder of sacrifices made by history's most unlikely heroes to triumph over evil."

—Kristina McMorris, author of *Bridge of Scarlet Leaves*

"Charles Belfoure's historical thriller delivers the suspense of *Schindler's List* and the German-occupied Paris of Alan Furst in this tense tale of an architect hiding Jews from the Nazis."

—Julie Kramer, author of *Shunning Sarah* and *Stalking Susan*

"Lucien Bernard, an up-and-coming French architect, is teetering on the edge of debt in German-occupied Paris in 1942. When a wealthy industrialist offers him an unusually large amount of money to design a hiding place for his Jewish friend, Lucien immediately refuses. But when an offer is added for Lucien to design a large factory where Germans will manufacture weapons for the war effort, Lucien soon finds himself caught up in a collaboration he cannot back away from. What is it then that changed the course of Lucien's life? This novel, which tells about a desperate time in the lives of Parisians affected by the Nazi's takeover of their city, is an emotionally stirring story about choices and sacrifices. Highly recommended."

—Carol Hicks, Bookshelf at Hooligan Rocks, Truckee, CA

The
PARIS
Architect

A NOVEL

CHARLES
BELFOURE

Copyright © 2013 by Charles Belfoure
Cover and internal design © 2013 by Sourcebooks, Inc.
Cover design by Catherine Casalino
Cover photography © Jitka Saniova/Arcangel Images, riekephotos/Shutterstock,
Ala Alkhouskaya/Shutterstock, Alchena/Shutterstock

Published by Sourcebooks Landmark, an imprint of Sourcebooks, Inc.
P.O. Box 4410, Naperville, Illinois 60567-4410
(630) 961-3900
Fax: (630) 961-2168
www.sourcebooks.com

Library of Congress Cataloging-in-Publication Data

Belfoure, Charles
  The Paris architect : a novel / Charles Belfoure.
    pages cm
  Includes bibliographical references and index.
  (hardcover : alk. paper) 1. Architects—France—Paris—Fiction. 2. World War,
1939–1945—Underground movements—France—Paris—Fiction. 3. Jews—
France—History—Fiction. 4. France—History—German occupation, 1940–
1945—Fiction. 5. Paris (France)—History—1940–1944—Fiction. 6. Historical
fiction. I. Title.
  PS3602.E446P37 2013
  813'.6—dc23
                              2013017034
        Printed and bound in the United States of America.
           WOZ 10 9 8 7 6 5 4 3 2 1

The
PARIS
Architect

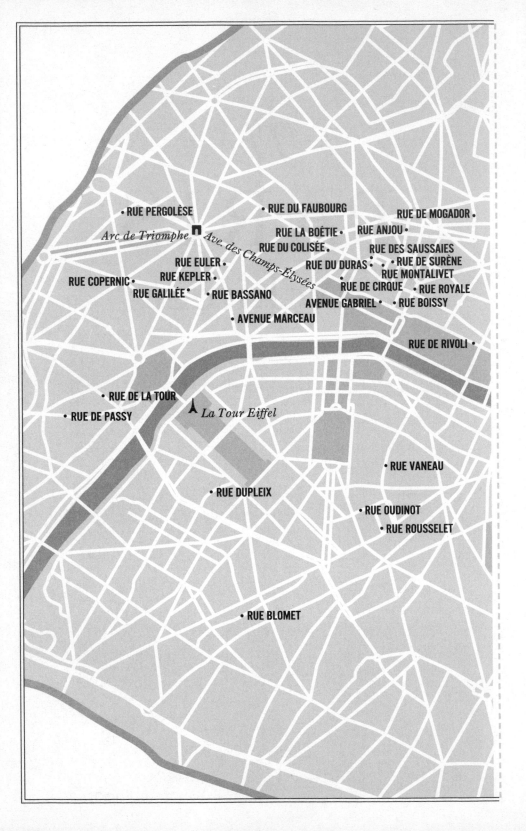

Paris, France

• RUE DE CHÂTEAUDUN

• RUE MONTSIGNY

RUE DU CAIRE •   • RUE SAINT-MARTIN   • AVENUE PARMENTIER

• AVENUE DE L'OPÉRA

   • RUE DU LOUVRE

• RUE SAINT-HONORÉ   • RUE DE BRETAGNE   • RUE DE HUBERT

   • RUE SAINT-DENIS

Musée du Louvre   • RUE SERVAN

   • RUE DU RENARD

   • RUE PAYENNE

   • RUE DU ROI-DE-SICILE

Notre Dame

• RUE DANTE

• RUE DE TOURON

la Seine

• RUE D'ASSAS

J UST AS LUCIEN BERNARD ROUNDED THE CORNER AT THE RUE LA Boétie, a man running from the opposite direction almost collided with him. He came so close that Lucien could smell his cologne as he raced by.

In the very second that Lucien realized he and the man wore the same scent, L'Eau d'Aunay, he heard a loud crack. He turned around. Just two meters away, the man lay face down on the sidewalk, blood streaming from the back of his bald head as though someone had turned on a faucet inside his skull. The dark crimson fluid flowed quickly in a narrow rivulet down his neck, over his crisp white collar, and then onto his well-tailored navy blue suit, changing its color to a rich deep purple.

There had been plenty of killings in Paris in the two years since the beginning of the German occupation in 1940, but Lucien had never actually seen a dead body until this moment. He was oddly mesmerized, not by the dead body, but by the new color the blood had produced on his suit. In an art class at school, he had to paint boring color wheel exercises. Here before him was bizarre proof that blue and red indeed made purple.

"Stay where you are!"

A German officer holding a steel-blue Luger ran up alongside him, followed by two tall soldiers with submachine guns, which they immediately trained on Lucien.

"Don't move, you bastard, or you'll be sleeping next to your friend," said the officer.

Lucien couldn't have moved if he'd wanted to; he was frozen with fear.

The officer walked over to the body, then turned and strolled up to Lucien as if he were going to ask him for a light. About thirty years old, the man had a fine aquiline nose and very dark, un-Aryan brown eyes, which now stared deeply into Lucien's gray-blue ones. Lucien was unnerved. Shortly after the Germans took over, several pamphlets had been written by Frenchmen on how to deal with the occupiers. Maintain dignity and distance, do not talk to them, and above all, avoid eye contact. In the animal world, direct eye contact was a challenge and a form of aggression. But Lucien couldn't avoid breaking this rule with the German's eyes just ten centimeters from his.

"He's not my friend," Lucien said in a quiet voice.

The German's face broke out into a wide grin.

"This kike is nobody's friend anymore," said the officer, whose uniform indicated he was a major in the Waffen-SS. The two soldiers laughed.

Though Lucien was so scared that he thought he had pissed himself, he knew he had to act quickly or he could be lying dead on the ground next. Lucien managed a shallow breath to brace himself and to think. One of the oddest aspects of the Occupation was how incredibly pleasant and polite the Germans were when dealing with their defeated French subjects. They even gave up their seats on the Metro to the elderly.

Lucien tried the same tack.

"Is that your bullet lodged in the gentleman's skull?" he asked.

"Yes, it is. Just one shot," the major said. "But it's really not all that impressive. Jews aren't very athletic. They run so damn slow it's never much of a challenge."

The major began to go through the man's pockets, pulling out papers and a handsome alligator wallet, which he placed in the side pocket of his green and black tunic. He grinned up at Lucien.

"But thank you so much for admiring my marksmanship."

A wave of relief swept over Lucien—this wasn't his day to die.

"You're most welcome, Major."

The officer stood. "You may be on your way, but I suggest you visit a men's room first," he said in a solicitous voice. He gestured with his gray gloved hand at the right shoulder of Lucien's gray suit.

"I'm afraid I splattered you. This filth is all over the back of your suit, which I greatly admire, by the way. Who is your tailor?"

Craning his neck to the right, Lucien could see specks of red on his shoulder. The officer produced a pen and a small brown notebook.

"Monsieur. Your tailor?"

"Millet. On the rue de Mogador." Lucien had always heard that Germans were meticulous record keepers.

The German carefully wrote this down and pocketed his notebook in his trouser pocket.

"Thank you so much. No one in the world can surpass the artistry of French tailors, not even the British. You know, the French have us beat in all the arts, I'm afraid. Even we Germans concede that Gallic culture is vastly superior to Teutonic—in everything except fighting wars, that is." The German laughed at his observation, as did the two soldiers.

Lucien followed suit and also laughed heartily.

After the laughter subsided, the major gave Lucien a curt salute. "I won't keep you any longer, monsieur."

Lucien nodded and walked away. When safely out of earshot, he muttered "German shit" under his breath and continued on at an almost leisurely pace. Running through the streets of Paris had become a death wish—as the poor devil lying facedown in the street had found out. Seeing a man murdered had frightened him, he realized, but he really wasn't upset that the man was dead. All that mattered was that *he* wasn't dead. It bothered him that he had so little compassion for his fellow man.

But no wonder—he'd been brought up in a family where compassion didn't exist.

His father, a university-trained geologist of some distinction, had had the same dog-eat-dog view of life as the most ignorant peasant. When it came to the misfortune of others, his philosophy had been tough shit, better him than me. The late Professor Jean-Baptiste Bernard hadn't seemed to realize that human beings, including his wife and children, had feelings. His love and affection had been heaped upon inanimate objects—the rocks and minerals of France and her colonies—and he demanded that his two sons love them as well. Before most children could read, Lucien and his older brother, Mathieu, had been taught the names of every sedimentary, igneous, and metamorphic rock in every one of France's nine geological provinces.

His father tested them at suppertime, setting rocks on the table for them to name. He was merciless if they made even one mistake, like the time Lucien couldn't identify bertrandite, a member of the silicate family, and his father had ordered him to put the rock in his mouth so he would never forget it. To this day, he remembered bertrandite's bitter taste.

He had hated his father, but now he wondered if he was more like his father than he wanted to admit.

As Lucien walked on in the glaring heat of the July afternoon, he looked up at the buildings clad in limestone (a sedimentary rock of the calcium carbonate family), with their beautiful rusticated bases, tall windows outlined in stone trim, and balconies with finely detailed wrought-iron designs supported on carved stone consoles. Some of the massive double doors of the apartment blocks were open, and he could see children playing in the interior courtyards, just as he had done when he was a boy. He passed a street-level window from which a black and white cat gazed sleepily at him.

Lucien loved every building in Paris—the city of his birth, the most beautiful city in the world. In his youth, he had roamed all over Paris, exploring its monuments, grand avenues, and boulevards down to the grimiest streets and alleys in the poorest districts. He could read the history of the city in the walls of these buildings. If that Kraut bastard's aim had been off, never again would he have seen these wonderful buildings, walk these cobblestone streets, or inhale the delicious aroma of baking bread in the boulangeries.

Farther down the rue la Boétie, he could see shopkeepers standing back from their plate-glass windows—far enough to avoid being spotted from the street but close enough to have seen the shooting. A very fat man motioned to him from the entrance of the Café d'Été. When he reached the door, the man, who seemed to be the owner, handed him a wet bar towel.

"The bathroom's in the back," he said.

Lucien thanked him and walked to the rear of the café. It was a typical dark Parisian café, narrow, a black-and-white-tiled floor with small tables along a wall, and a very poorly stocked bar on the opposite side. The Occupation had done the unthinkable in Paris: it had cut off a Frenchman's most basic necessities of life—cigarettes and wine. But the café was such an ingrained part of his existence that he still went there daily to smoke fake cigarettes made from grass and herbs and drink the watered-down swill that passed for wine. The Café d'Été patrons, who had probably seen what had happened, stopped talking and looked down at their glasses when Lucien passed, acting as if he'd been contaminated by his contact with the Germans. It reminded him of the time he'd been in a café when five German enlisted men blundered in. The place had gone totally silent, as if someone had turned off a switch on a radio. The soldiers had left immediately.

In the filthy bathroom, Lucien took off his suit jacket to begin the cleanup. A few blobs of blood the size of peas dotted the back of the jacket, and one was on the sleeve. He tried to blot out the Jew's blood, but faint stains remained. This annoyed him—he only had one good business suit. A tall, handsome man with a full head of wavy brown hair, Lucien was quite particular about his clothes. His wife, Celeste, was clever about practical matters, though. She could probably get the bloodstains out of his jacket. He stood back and looked at himself in the mirror above the sink to make sure there wasn't any blood on his face or in his hair, then suddenly looked at his watch and realized his appointment was in ten minutes. He put his jacket back on and threw the soiled towel in the sink.

Once in the street, he couldn't help looking back at the corner where the shooting had taken place. The Germans and the body were gone; only a large pool of blood marked the spot of the shooting. The Germans were unbelievably efficient people. The French would have stood around the corpse, chatting and smoking cigarettes. Full rigor mortis would have set in by the time they had carted it away. Lucien almost started trotting but slowed his pace to a brisk walk. He hated being late, but he wasn't about to be shot in the back of the skull because of his obsession with punctuality. Monsieur Manet would understand. Still, this meeting held the possibility of a job, and Lucien didn't want to make a bad first impression.

Lucien had learned early in his career that architecture was a business as well as an art, and one ought not look at a first job from a new client as a one-shot deal but rather as the first in a series of commissions. And this one had a lot of promise. The man he was to meet, Auguste Manet, owned a factory that until the war used to make engines for Citroën and other automobile makers. Before an initial meeting with a client, Lucien would always research his background to see if he had money, and Monsieur Manet definitely had money. Old money, from a distinguished family that went back generations. Manet had tried his hand at industry, something his class frowned upon. Wealth from business was considered dirty, not dignified. But he had multiplied the family fortune a hundredfold, cashing in on the automobile craze, specializing in engines.

Manet was in an excellent position to obtain German contracts during the Occupation. Even before the German invasion in May 1940, a mass exodus had begun, with millions fleeing the north of the country to the south, where they thought they'd be safe. Many industrialists had tried unsuccessfully to move their entire factories, including the workers, to the south. But Manet had remained calm during the panic and stayed put, with all his factories intact.

Normally, a defeated country's economy ground to a halt, but Germany was in the business of war. It needed weapons for its fight with the Russians on the Eastern Front, and suitable French businesses were awarded contracts to produce war materiel. At first, French businessmen had viewed cooperation with the Germans as treason, but faced with a choice of having their businesses appropriated by the Germans without compensation or accepting the contracts, the pragmatic French had chosen the latter. Lucien was betting that Manet was a pragmatic man and that he was producing weapons for the Luftwaffe or the Wehrmacht. And that meant new factory space, which Lucien could design for him.

Before the war, whenever Lucien was on his way to meet a client for the first time, his imagination ran wild with visions of success—especially when he knew the client was rich. He tried to rein in his imagination now, telling himself to be pessimistic. Every time he got his hopes up high these days, they were smashed to bits. Like in 1938, when he was just about to start a store on the rue de la Tour d'Auvergne and then the client went bankrupt because of a divorce. Or the big estate in Orléans whose owner was arrested for embezzlement. He told himself to be grateful for any crumb of work that he could find in wartime.

Having nearly forgotten the incident with the Jew, Lucien's mind began to formulate a generic design of a factory that would be quite suitable for any type of war production. As he turned up the avenue Marceau, he smiled as he always did whenever he thought of a new design.

————————————— ⊙⁊⸛ **2** ⸛⁊⊙ —————————————

L UCIEN CHECKED HIS WATCH AS HE OPENED THE MASSIVE WOOD door of 28 rue Galilée. It gave him a great sense of satisfaction that he was one minute early for his appointment. What other man could walk all the way across town, almost get shot by a German, clean a dead man's blood off his jacket, and make it in time? The experience reinforced his belief that one should always budget an extra fifteen minutes to get to a client appointment. His prized Cartier watch, which his parents had given him upon his graduation from college, said 2:00 p.m., which was actually the time in Germany. The Germans' first official act had been to impose the Reich's time zone on occupied France. It was really 1:00 p.m. French time. After two years of occupation, the forced time change still annoyed Lucien, even more than the swastikas and ugly Gothic-lettered signs the Germans had plastered on all the city's landmarks.

He stepped inside and was relieved to be in the dark, cool shade of the foyer. He loved these apartment blocks, created by Baron Haussmann when he tore down medieval Paris in the 1850s to re-create the city. Lucien admired the stonework and the strong horizontal lines created by the rows of windows and their metal balconies. He lived in a building on the rue du Caire that was similar to this one.

Since 1931, Lucien had abandoned all historical and classical references in his work to become a pure modernist architect, embracing the aesthetic of the Bauhaus, the style created by the German architect Walter Gropius that pioneered modern architecture and design (the one instance in which Teutonic taste definitely triumphed over the

Gallic). Still, he admired these great apartment blocks that Napoleon III had championed. His admiration had grown when he'd visited his brother in New York before the war. The apartment buildings there were junk compared to those in Paris.

He walked to the concierge's apartment, directly to the left of the entry. The glass door yawned open, and an old woman smoking a cigarette was sitting at a table covered with a garish yellow-flowered cloth. Lucien cleared his throat, and she said, without moving a muscle and still gazing into space, "He's in 3B…and the lift's out."

As Lucien climbed the ornate curving stair to the third floor, his heart began to race—not only because he was out of shape, but also because he was so anxious. Would Manet have a real project for him, or would this meeting lead to nothing? And if it was a project, would it be a chance to show his talent?

Lucien knew he had talent. He'd been told by a couple of well-known architects, whom he had worked for in Paris after graduating from school. With a few years' experience and belief in his ability, he then went out on his own. It was hard to build up a practice, doubly hard because he was a modernist and modern architecture was just beginning to be accepted. Most clients still wanted something traditional. Nevertheless, he was able to earn a steady living. But just as an actor needed a break-out role to become a star, an architect needed a career-making project. And Lucien, now thirty-five, hadn't managed to land that one all-important project. He'd come close only once, when he'd been a finalist for a new public library but had been beaten out by Henri Devereaux, whose uncle's brother-in-law was the deputy minister of culture. Ability wasn't enough; one needed the right connections like Devereaux always seemed to have—that and luck.

He looked down at his shoes as they scraped the marble treads of the great stair. They were his client shoes, the one good pair he wore to meetings. A little worn, but they still looked shiny and fashionable, and the soles were in good shape. With leather in short supply, once a Frenchman's shoes wore out he turned to wooden soles or ones of compressed paper, which didn't fare so well in winter. Lucien was glad he still had a pair of leather-soled shoes. He hated the sound of wooden soles clattering on the streets of Paris, which reminded him of the clogs worn by peasants.

Lucien was startled when he looked up and found a pair of very expensive dark brown shoes on the third floor landing right in front of his face. Lucien's gaze traveled up the sharply creased trouser legs to a suit jacket, then to the face of Auguste Manet.

"Monsieur Bernard, what a pleasure it is to meet you."

Before Lucien reached the top step, Manet extended his hand.

Lucien pulled himself up the railing until he stood next to a lean, white-haired man in his seventies, with cheekbones that seemed to be chiseled from stone. And tall. Manet towered above Lucien. He seemed even taller than de Gaulle.

"The pleasure is my mine, monsieur."

"Monsieur Gaston was always raving about the office building you did for him, so I had to see it for myself. A beautiful job." The old man's handshake was strong and confident, something you'd expect from a man who'd made millions.

They were off to an excellent start, Lucien thought as he took an instant liking to this elderly, aristocratic businessman. Back in 1937, he'd done a building on the rue Servan for Charles Gaston, the owner of an insurance company. Four stories of limestone with a curving glass-stair tower. Lucien thought it was the best thing he'd ever designed.

"Monsieur Gaston was very kind to refer you to me. How can I help you?" Most of the time, Lucien was open to the usual small talk before getting down to business. But he was nervous and wanted to see whether a real job would come out of this.

Manet turned toward the open doors of 3B and Lucien followed. Even the back of Monsieur Manet was impressive. His posture was ramrod straight, and his suit was expensive and fit him impeccably—the German major would've wanted the name of his tailor.

"Well, Monsieur Bernard, let me tell you what I've got in mind. A guest of mine will be staying here for a while, and I wish to make some special alterations to the apartment to accommodate him," Manet said as they walked slowly through the place.

Lucien couldn't imagine what the old man would want. The vacant apartment was gorgeous, with high ceilings and tall windows, ornate wood paneling, huge columns that framed the wide entries into the main rooms, beautiful fireplaces with marble surrounds, and parquet floors. And all the bathrooms and the kitchen looked up to date with porcelain-on-steel sinks and tubs with chrome fixtures. The unit was large by Parisian standards, at least twice as large in floor area as a normal apartment.

Manet stopped and faced Lucien.

"I've been told that an architect looks at a space differently from the rest of us. The average person sees a room as it is, but instinctively the architect envisions how it could be changed for the better. Is that true?"

"Absolutely," replied Lucien with pride. "A man would view a run-down, out-of-date flat as very unappealing, but an architect, in his imagination, would renovate that space into something quite fashionable." Lucien was getting excited. Maybe the old man wanted him to redo the place from top to bottom.

"I see. Tell me, monsieur, do you like a challenge? To solve a unique problem?"

"Yes, indeed, I love to come up with a solution for any architectural problem," said Lucien, "and the more challenging, the better." He hoped he was telling Manet what he wanted to hear. If Manet asked him to fit the Arc de Triomphe in here, he'd say it was no problem. You didn't turn down work in wartime. Any fool knew that.

"That's good." Manet walked across the salon and put his hand on Lucien's shoulder in a fatherly way. "I think it's time to give you a little more background on this project, but first let us talk about your fee. I have a figure in mind—twelve thousand francs."

"Twelve hundred francs is most generous, monsieur."

"No, I said twelve thousand."

There was silence. Digits formed in Lucien's mind as if a teacher were writing them methodically on a blackboard—first a one, then a two, a comma, and three zeros. After he mentally verified the number, he said, "Monsieur, that…that is more than generous; it's ludicrous!"

"Not if your life depended on it."

Lucien thought this was such an amusing comment that he was obliged to let out his great belly laugh, the kind that annoyed his wife but always delighted his mistress. But Manet didn't laugh. His face showed no emotion at all.

"Before I give you a little more information about the project, let me ask you a personal question," Manet said.

"You have my full attention, Monsieur Manet."

"How do you feel about Jews?"

Lucien was taken aback. What the hell kind of question was that? But before giving Manet his gut response—that they were money-grubbing thieves—he took a deep breath. He didn't want to say anything that would offend Manet—and lose the job.

"They're human beings like anyone else, I suppose," he replied feebly.

Lucien had grown up in a very anti-Semitic household. The word *Jew* had always been followed by the word *bastard*. His grandfather and father had been convinced that Captain Alfred Dreyfus, a Jewish officer on the staff of the French Army headquarters back in the 1890s, was a traitor, despite evidence that a fellow officer named Esterhazy had been the one who'd sold secrets to the Germans. Lucien's grandfather had also sworn that Jews were responsible for France's humiliating defeat by the Germans in the Franco-Prussian War of 1870, although he could never provide any real proof to back up this charge. *Whether one hated them for betraying the country, for killing Christ, or screwing you over in a business deal, all other Frenchmen were anti-Semites in one way or another, weren't they?* Lucien thought. That's the way it had always been.

Lucien looked into Manet's eyes and was glad he'd kept his true feelings to himself.

He saw an earnestness that alarmed him.

"You've probably noticed that since May all Jews over the age of six are now required to wear a yellow Star of David," said Manet.

"Yes, monsieur."

Lucien was well aware that Jews had to wear a felt star. He didn't think it was such a big deal, though many Parisians were outraged. Gentiles had begun to wear the yellow stars or yellow flowers or hand-kerchiefs in protest. He'd even heard of a woman who'd pinned a yellow star on her dog.

"On July 16," said Manet, "almost thirteen thousand Jews were rounded up in Paris and sent to Drancy, and nine thousand were women and children."

Lucien knew about Drancy. It was an unfinished block of apartment buildings near Le Bourget Airport that an architect friend, Maurice Pappon, had worked on. A year earlier, it became the main detention camp for the Paris region, though it had no water, electric, or sanitary service. Pappon had told him that Drancy prisoners were forced onto trains to be relocated somewhere in the east.

"One hundred people killed themselves instead of being taken. Mothers with babies in their arms jumped from windows. Did you know that, monsieur?"

Lucien saw Manet's growing agitation. He needed to redirect the man's conversation to the project and the twelve thousand francs.

"It is a tragedy, monsieur. Now what kind of changes did you have in mind?"

But Manet continued as though he hadn't heard a word.

"It was bad enough that Jewish businesses were seized and bank accounts frozen, but now they're banned from restaurants, cafés, theaters, cinemas, and parks. It's not just immigrant Jews but Jews of French lineage, whose ancestors fought for France, who are being treated in this way.

"And the worst part," he continued, "is that Vichy and the French police are making most of the arrests, not the Germans."

Lucien was aware of this. The Germans used the French against the French. When a knock came at a Frenchman's door in the middle of the night, it was usually a gendarme sent by the Gestapo.

"All Parisians have suffered under the Germans, monsieur," Lucien began. "Even gentiles are arrested every day. Why, on the way here to meet you, a…" He stopped in mid-sentence when he remembered that the dead man was a Jew. Lucien saw that Manet was staring at him, which made him uncomfortable. He looked down at the beautiful parquet floor and his client's shoes.

"Monsieur Bernard, Gaston has known you a long time. He says you are a man of great integrity and honor. A man who loves his country—and keeps his word," said Manet.

Lucien was now completely confused. What in the hell was this man talking about? Gaston really didn't know him at all, only on a professional level. They weren't friends. Gaston had no idea what kind of man Lucien truly was. He could've been a murderer or a male prostitute, and Gaston would never have known.

Manet walked over to one of the huge windows that overlooked the rue Galilée and stared out into the street for a few moments. He finally turned and faced Lucien, who was surprised by the now-grave expression on the old man's face.

"Monsieur Bernard, this *alteration* is to create a hiding place for a Jewish man who is being hunted by the Gestapo. If, by chance, they come here looking for him, I'd like him to be able to hide in a space that is undetectable, one that the Gestapo will never find. For your own safety, I won't tell you his name. But the Reich wants to arrest him to find out the whereabouts of his fortune, which is considerable."

Lucien was dumbfounded. "Are you insane? You're hiding a Jew?"

Normally, Lucien would never speak so rudely to a client, especially an enormously rich one, but Manet had crossed into forbidden territory here. Aiding Jews: the Germans called it *Judenbegunstigung*. No matter how wealthy he was, Manet could be arrested and executed for hiding Jews. It was the one crime a Frenchman couldn't buy his way out of. Wearing some dumb yellow star out of sympathy was one thing, but actually helping a Jew wanted by the Gestapo was sheer madness. What the hell had Lucien gotten himself into—or rather, what had that bastard Gaston got *him* into? Manet had some set of balls to ask him to do this for twelve thousand or even twelve million francs.

"You're asking me to commit suicide; you know that, don't you?"

"Indeed I do," said Manet. "And I'm also committing suicide."

"Then for God's sake, man, why are you doing this?" exclaimed Lucien.

Manet didn't seem put off by Lucien's question at all. He almost seemed eager to answer it. The old man smiled at Lucien.

"Let me explain something to you, Monsieur Bernard. Back in 1940, when this hell began, I realized that my first duty as a Christian was to overcome my self-centeredness, that I had to inconvenience myself when one of my human brethren was in danger—whoever he may be, or whether he was a born Frenchman or not. I've simply decided not to turn my back."

"Inconvenience myself" was a bit of an understatement under these circumstances, Lucien thought. And as for Christianity, he agreed with his father: it was a well-intentioned set of beliefs that never worked in real life.

"So, Monsieur Bernard," continued Manet, "I will pay you twelve thousand francs to design a hiding place that is invisible to the naked eye. That is your architectural challenge. I have excellent craftsmen to do the work but they're not architects; they don't have your eye and couldn't come up with as clever a solution as you could. That's why I'm asking you for your—help."

"Monsieur, I absolutely refuse. This is crazy. I won't do it."

"I'm hoping you'll reconsider my proposition, Monsieur Bernard. I feel it can be a mutually beneficial arrangement. And it's just this one time."

"Never, Monsieur. I could never agree…"

"I realize that making a decision that could get you killed is not one to be made on the spot. Please, do me the favor of taking some time to think about this. But I'd like to hear from you today by 6:00 p.m., at the Café du Monde. I know you need to make a closer examination of the apartment for you to decide, so take this key and lock the door when you finish. And now, monsieur, I'll leave you to it."

Lucien nodded and tried to speak, but nothing came out.

"By the way, at 9:00 a.m. tomorrow, I'm signing a contract to produce engines for the Heinkel Aircraft Works. My current facilities are much too small to handle such a job, so I'm planning an expansion next to my plant at Chaville. I'm looking for an architect," said Manet as he walked toward the door. "Know of one?"

3

THE ROOM STARTED SPINNING AROUND, AND LUCIEN BECAME SO
disoriented that he couldn't keep his balance. He sat on the floor
and thought he was going to vomit.

"Christ, what a day!" he muttered.

Normally, Lucien would do anything to get a job, no matter how
despicable. Like the time he slept with the very overweight wife of the
wine merchant, Gattier, so that she would persuade her husband to
select Lucien to design his new store on the rue Vaneau. It had turned
out beautifully—not one change had been made to his design.

This, however, was a different matter altogether. Sure, he was
broke, but were twelve thousand francs and a guaranteed commission
worth the risk of dying? The money wouldn't help him if he was dead.
Actually, it wasn't the dying part that troubled him. It was the torture by
the Gestapo that would precede the dying. Lucien had heard on good
authority what the Germans did to those who wouldn't cooperate—
days of barbaric treatment before death, or if the Gestapo was feeling
merciful, which was a rarity, internment in a camp.

Parisians had quickly learned that not all German soldiers were
the same. There were three very different types. The largest branch,
the Wehrmacht, was the regular army that did most of the fighting and had some sense of decency toward the French. Next was
the Waffen-SS, the special elite army unit of the Nazi Party, which
fought in combat but was also used in rounding up Jews. The last and
the absolute worst was the Gestapo, the secret police, who tortured,
murdered, mutilated, and maimed Jews—or anyone, including fellow

Germans, for crimes against the Reich. The Gestapo's cruelty was said to be beyond imagination.

People were even scared to use the word *Gestapo*. Parisians would usually say, "*They've* arrested him." The Gestapo headquarters at 11 rue des Saussaies was just around the corner from the Palais de l'Élysée, the former residence of the French president. Everyone in Paris knew and feared this address.

No, no matter how much he needed money and craved a new project, the risk was unfathomable. Lucien had never fooled himself into believing he was the heroic type. He'd learned that in 1939, when, as an officer called up from the reserves, he'd been stationed for eight months on the Maginot Line, the string of concrete fortresses that the French government guaranteed would protect France from a German onslaught. Since no fighting had occurred in France after the fall of Poland, he'd sat on his ass reading architectural magazines his wife had sent him, designing imaginary projects. One fellow officer who was a university professor had used the time to write a history of the ancient Etruscans.

Then on May 10, 1940, the Germans had invaded, but instead of attacking the "invincible" Maginot Line, they'd swept around it, entering northern France through the Ardennes Forest. Meanwhile, Lucien had been stationed inside a bunker on the Maginot Line, never getting the chance to engage the enemy. Secretly, he'd been glad because he was terrified of fighting the Germans, who seemed like super-beings. They had crushed everyone they had invaded with incredible ease— the Poles, the Belgians, and the Dutch, plus forcing the British off the continent at Dunkirk.

After the armistice was signed on June 22, he was considered officially defeated and captured, but Lucien and other officers had had no intention of being herded into a prisoner of war camp in Germany. Uncle Albert, the brother of Lucien's mother, had spent four years in a German prison camp during the First World War and as a result spent the rest of his life unhinged, doing weird things like chasing squirrels in the park like a dog. Lucien and many other French soldiers had simply taken off their uniforms, destroyed their military papers, and then blended into civilian life with forged demobilization documents. Before the Wehrmacht had reached the garrisons of the Maginot Line at the end of June, Lucien had returned to his wife in Paris.

What he found was a ghost town. Even though Paris had been declared an open city by the British and thus safe from bombing, over a million people—out of a population of three million—fled. Lucien and his wife had decided to stay, believing that it was far less dangerous to face the Germans than the perils of the open road. It had turned out to be the right decision: with millions of other Frenchmen fleeing south, the roads became impassable and many people had gone missing or died of exposure. This mass exodus and the military's quick surrender to the Germans humiliated France in front of the world. Lucien hated the Germans with all his heart for what they did to his country. He cried the day of the surrender. But all that really mattered to him was that he and his wife were still alive.

No, Lucien wasn't a hero, and he definitely wasn't a do-gooder, one of those guys who stood up for the downtrodden. Manet had do-gooder written all over him. And to risk one's life to help a *Jew?* Lucien's father would've laughed in his face. Having grown up in Paris, Lucien had been around Jews all his life, at least indirectly. He'd heard that there were something like two hundred thousand heebs living in Paris, although he'd never met one Jew at the École Spéciale d'Architecture, where he'd studied. There were hardly any Jewish architects. Lucien had always reasoned that Jews had an innate mercantile talent, so they went into business and professions like law and medicine that would make them loads of money. Architecture, Lucien quickly learned, was not the way to go if you wanted to become rich.

But Lucien felt that Manet was right about one thing. The Jews were getting a raw deal. The Germans took away even the most basic everyday necessities—their phones had been disconnected and their bicycles confiscated. And not just the immigrant Jews from Poland, Hungary, and Russia, who lived mostly in the eastern arrondissements of Paris, but the native-born Jews too, the ones who didn't have that "Jew" look. Professional men like doctors, lawyers, and university professors suffered. And it didn't matter how famous you were. Nobel Prize winner Henri Bergson had died from pneumonia that he had contracted while waiting in a line to register himself as a Jew with the French authorities. But what was happening to the Jews was a political matter that was out of his control, even if he thought it was unfair.

For a people that were supposed to be so smart, though, Lucien thought Jews had been acting pretty dumb. Since 1933, there had been reports in French newspapers of how the Nazis treated Jews in Germany. Didn't they realize the Germans would treat them the same way here? Some had made it across the Pyrenees into Spain and Portugal, and others had gotten across the Swiss border early on. They were the smart ones; they'd realized what was in store for them and had saved themselves.

The Jews who had stayed were doomed. Since the fall of 1940, it had been impossible for them to get out of the country. Jews had even been forbidden to cross the demarcation line into unoccupied France. They had to escape the cities to avoid arrest and deportation by the Germans. There must be thousands of them hiding in the countryside, Lucien thought, whole families with kids and grandparents. The Jews who were so used to the good life now had to hide in haylofts surviving on a few grams of bread each day. Compared to a barn, Manet's hideout would be a palace.

Lucien stood up and began walking through the apartment.

Granted, it was suicide to get involved in this.

But…if it was done cleverly, maybe the Jew would never be discovered, no one would know of his involvement, and best of all, Lucien would make a huge amount of money plus get a big commission out of it. Besides, Manet was a very shrewd, successful man. He might take a calculated risk, but he wasn't reckless. The old man would've thought this all out to the last detail.

Then the image of being lashed to a chair at 11 rue des Saussaies, getting his face pummeled to a pasty red lump, came to mind. Lucien turned to walk toward the door. Still, he thought, with a little ingenuity there could be a place to hide a man in plain sight. He placed his hand on the door handle, then looked back into the empty apartment. Lucien shook his head and opened the great wooden door a few centimeters to see if anyone was about, and stepped out in the corridor.

Then again, Lucien reasoned, the commission alone would make the risk worth considering. To get such a huge project to design was an incredible opportunity that would never have come his way before the war. And God knows, he desperately needed the money; he hadn't worked since the Occupation began. His own savings were long gone, and Celeste's money wouldn't last forever. It wouldn't hurt to at least look around, he thought. He reentered the apartment and began walking through the rooms.

First, Lucien ruled out the obvious hiding places, such as behind the bookshelves—a stock cliché of American mystery movies—or in a recess at the back of a closet. As if they were the lens of a movie camera, his eyes swept over every square meter of each room, taking in every detail. At the same time, he intuitively analyzed every surface by contemplating the construction of the space behind it—as if he was thinking with x-ray vision. Though Lucien didn't know how big Manet's "guest" was, his mind placed an imaginary average-size man within each possible space to see if there was enough room. Lucien examined the beautiful wainscoting along the walls. The wide recessed panels could be removed, opening up a space big enough for a man to fit through. But was that too obvious a hiding place? Probably. There had to be a twist. What if the person had to go through the panel opening and crawl down the length of the wall to hide within another hidden compartment? If the Germans found the removable panel, there would be just an empty space behind it. Unfortunately, as Lucien inspected further, he noticed the walls behind the wainscoting weren't deep enough for a man's body.

Then Lucien noticed how unusually tall the baseboards along the floor were. Using the small tape measure he always carried with him, he confirmed they were almost forty centimeters high. Maybe they could be hinged like a flap on a mail slot, so a man could pull them up and slide on his belly into a hollowed-out space. That would've been a solution if the wall had been the right depth. Too bad, the Germans never would've looked down there.

Lucien moved on. There was a wall along a corridor that curved out in the center, creating a semicircular niche where a small bronze statue of Mercury sat on a meter-high base. A man could crouch inside the base, unless he was really tall. The statue and the wood top of the base would have to be lifted up then put back into place in order for the man to hide. That would be quite difficult to do. Even if the statue was fastened to the top from underneath and the top hinged to the base, it would be very heavy. Lucien picked up the statue and guessed it weighed around fifty kilos. Would Manet's guest have the strength to open and close the top?

Lucien walked across the room to get a better look at the niche. Lighting a cigarette, he leaned against one of the very tall wooden Doric columns that framed the opening between the salon and the dining area. He looked it up and down and saw its fluted shaft was made from one piece of exquisite chestnut. If only it sat on a tall pedestal, he thought, a person could fit inside the pedestal to hide. Then Lucien noticed how big the diameter of the column was and measured it—about fifty-six centimeters. An incredible wave of euphoria swept over him. Using his own shoulders as a guide, he calculated that the column was just wide enough to fit a normal-size man upright, even accounting for the thickness of the column wall.

Lucien was giddy with excitement. The two columns, which he knew were nonstructural and merely decorative, must be hollow. Smiling, he ran his hand over the column's shaft; a narrow hinged door could be cut in, with its vertical joints hidden by the fluting. There couldn't be any horizontal joints showing so the bottom joint would have to align with the base. The top joint had to line up with the column capital above. Though the shaft of the column was almost four meters high, a door could be made that tall if he used a piano hinge. Lucien had once designed a door with standard hinges that stood three meters high. If Manet's men were as good as advertised, this could work.

He'd done it! It was such a brilliant, elegant, and ingenious solution. He'd fool those fucking Nazi bastards.

4

TWO HOURS BEFORE MEETING MANET AND LUCIEN WAS ALREADY on his fourth glass of faux red wine. The euphoria of tricking the Germans had worn off, and the reality of being murdered by the Gestapo for getting involved in this scheme returned. A thousand things could go wrong. He knew that Parisians were betraying Jews to the Germans every day. Suppose someone tipped off the Gestapo about Manet's Jew and the column didn't work? The Jew would give up Manet, and Manet would give him up. He'd be crazy to do this.

Before he'd left the apartment on rue Galilée, Lucien had sketched out the details of the column on a scrap of paper. He turned it over now and began sketching out the building for the factory in Chaville, a suburb west of Paris. He imagined a sawtooth roof to let in light, with glass walls separated by steel mullions one meter apart. Every ten meters he added a brick wall. The entry would have a curving brick wall leading to a deeply recessed glass doorway. Maybe the whole thing could be built of poured concrete, with powerful-looking arches on the inside. He smiled as he drew the profile of the arches, each one with its own flaring buttress to resist the outward thrusts. He tried four different profiles until he settled on the one he liked best.

Lucien had visited Walter Gropius's Fagus Factory in Germany in the '30s and had been dazzled by the sleek, clean design. Since then, Lucien had always wanted to design a factory complex. Although it had come to him in a most bizarre way, this commission could be the opportunity he'd been looking for. To prove that he really had talent by designing a large, important building.

He drained the wine in his glass and stared out across the lifeless rue Kepler. The biggest shock he'd experienced when he'd returned to Paris was its surreal emptiness. The boulevard Saint-Germain, the rue de Rivoli, the Place de la Concorde—all were deserted most of the time. Before the war, even the rue Kepler would have had a steady stream of pedestrians in the evening hours. Lucien had loved to gaze out at the city while sipping his coffee or wine in a café, watching for interesting faces and especially beautiful women. But as Lucien sat by the window now, he saw very few people and it saddened him. The Boche had sucked the wonderful street life out of his beloved Paris.

Lucien never got the chance to fight the Germans. Though he hated their guts, he knew he would've been a terrible soldier in battle—he was scared of guns. Honor and service to country were ideals cherished by the French, although he'd always thought of them as a load of patriotic horse manure. But since his return to Paris, he'd had a gnawing feeling inside him that he was a coward. This was reinforced by the fact that there were so many women in Paris and so few men—most had been killed or captured during the invasion. But not Lucien. His neighbor, Madame Dehor, had a lost a son, blown to bits attempting to stop a Panzer tank. Six months after the boy's death, he could still hear her wailing uncontrollably through the thick walls of the apartment building. Secretly, Lucien was ashamed that he was so useless to his country. Sometimes, he felt guilty that he was alive.

And Lucien knew he didn't have the guts to join the Resistance. Besides, he didn't believe in their cause. It was made up of a bunch of fanatical Communists who'd commit some stupid, meaningless act of sabotage that would trigger the Germans to kill scores of hostages in retaliation.

Lucien looked at the sketch of the factory. On the whole, Manet was offering him a pretty good deal—if you removed the possibility of torture and death by the Gestapo. One secret hiding place he designed in less than an hour, in exchange for twelve thousand francs, which could buy plenty of black market goods. Plus the factory commission. He flipped the paper over to the sketch of the column, which immediately brought a smile to his face. The sense of mastery and excitement he had felt in the apartment returned. He'd experienced such intense pleasure when he'd realized that the column would work. Maybe this was something he could do to get back at the Germans. Sure, he couldn't risk his neck by shooting them, but he could risk it in his own way. And besides, given the solution he'd invented, was there really that much risk? The Gestapo would search and search the apartment and never find the hiding place. That image pleased the hell out of him.

This was suicidal. But something within Lucien compelled him to do it.

·!· ·!· ·!·

"You're what the Jews call a *mensch*, Monsieur Bernard," said Manet, who took a sip of wine. Lucien had made sure they had a table off by themselves.

"What the hell does that mean?" asked Lucien. It sounded kind of insulting, similar to the Jewish word *schmuck*.

"I believe it means a human being, a person who stands up and does the right thing."

"Before I do the right thing, there're a few conditions."

"Go on," said Manet.

"I'm not to know anything…I mean anything…about your goddamn Jew," said Lucien, looking around him to make sure no one was listening in on their conversation.

"I understand perfectly."

"What about the workmen who'll be doing the construction? How do I know they won't talk?"

"They are men who have worked for me for over twenty years. I can trust them and so can you."

"The tenants will wonder what's going on when they hear all the noise. Every one of them would be deported if a Jew was found in the building. If they suspected anything, they'd inform the Germans to save themselves."

"There's a risk, I agree, but the concierge has been well paid to lie if need be. All the tenants are at work during the day. Besides, your solution is ingenious because it's so simple—there won't be that much noise."

"What about the owner of the building? What if he gets wind of the work?"

"I am the owner, Monsieur Bernard."

Lucien finally relaxed and sat back in his chair. With those concerns out of the way, it was now time to get down to business.

"You mentioned a fee of twelve thousand francs, Monsieur Manet."

Manet produced a thick hardback book out of the satchel he held on his lap. He placed it on the table and pushed it toward Lucien.

"Do you like to read? This novel by the American writer Hemingway is most entertaining," he said with a great smile.

Lucien never read anything except architectural magazines. But he did go to the cinema and had seen all the American films based on great works of literature, so he could pretend he'd read the books.

"Of course, Hemingway." Gary Cooper starred in *A Farewell to Arms* in 1932. It was a damn good film.

Lucien slowly picked up the book and examined the cover, then began to fan the pages. He abruptly stopped when he saw the first franc note nestled in the hollowed-out book.

"It looks most interesting. I'll start it tonight before I go to bed."

"I know you'll enjoy it," replied Manet.

"Now, did I hear you correctly when you said you'd be needing additional factory space for your new contract?" Lucien asked, holding on to the book with both hands in his lap.

"You did indeed. Why don't you come to my office the day after tomorrow to discuss the project—say about two. I'll have all my requirements written out for you. I'm sure you'll need to go back into the apartment to take a few measurements for a drawing, so hold on to the key."

The smile suddenly vanished from Lucien's face. "But let me make one thing absolutely clear to you, monsieur. I'll never do anything like this again."

"But of course, I understand completely."

An awkward silence settled between the two men. Lucien took another sip of his wine. He wanted to get the hell out of there with his new book. Manet smiled and sipped his drink as if he were in no hurry at all.

"You asked me why I was committing suicide."

"Yes, and you told me you're a devout Christian who wants to help your fellow man," said Lucien.

"Devout? Not at all. I attend mass on Easter and Christmas and that's it. I do believe that as Christians, we have a basic duty to do what's right, but that's not quite the whole story. There's more to it."

"Really?"

"Monsieur Bernard, people think the aristocracy, with their money and privilege, have everything in life, but they're dead wrong. The children of my class lack the most important thing: a mother and a father."

"You were an orphan?"

"Not at all. I had a mother and father, but they, like others of their class, never had time for their children—attending endless social events, entertaining in the city and the country, overseeing their estates and investments. I'll bet in an average week I never spent more than an hour's time with my mother and father. They would often forget my birthday. When I was at boarding school, I didn't see them for months or even receive a letter from them. They were simply too busy for me and my brothers and sisters."

"That's a shame," said Lucien.

"No, I was raised by Madame Ducrot. She was my nanny, but she gave me as much love and affection as the best mother could. And she was a Jew."

"A Jew? How did she…"

"I have no idea how my parents picked a Jew to be our nanny. Maybe they weren't as anti-Semitic as the rest of their kind. Oh, I still got the usual Catholic instruction from priests. But she never hid the fact she was Jewish; in fact, she told us all about it—the holidays, the synagogue, the Exodus—everything."

Lucien found this fascinating.

"Several times before the war, I was a house guest of Winston Churchill's at Chartwell, his estate in England. I once asked him about a photo of an old woman on his mantle, and he told me it was Mrs. Everest, his nanny. He called her 'Woomany.' He said that when she died, he was crushed with almost unbearable sadness and grief, a thousand times worse than when his own mother died later. That's how I felt when my nanny, who was my 'real mother,' died. So you see, Monsieur Bernard, in a way, when I hide these people, I'm hiding Madame Ducrot."

5

L UCIEN COULDN'T WAIT TO GET HOME TO TELL THE NEWS TO Celeste. Well, at least the part about the factory. Telling her about Manet's apartment would put her in grave danger. The apartment job must always remain a secret. As Lucien walked home, he held the book tightly against his chest. He soon realized that any Gestapo agent watching him would think something was up, so he moved the book into one hand and held it loosely by his side, as a person normally would. But because he was terrified that the book would slip out of his hand, hit the sidewalk, and disgorge all of his francs, he kept an iron grip on it.

As he walked by a telephone booth, an idea occurred to him. He picked up the receiver, deposited his coin, and dialed his mistress, Adele Bonneau. It had been a long time since he'd shared the news of a new commission with her, and she would be quite pleased. A successful Paris fashion designer in her late thirties (late twenties, if you asked her), Adele had a genuine interest in his architectural practice. She always wanted to see the designs and wouldn't hesitate to offer her opinion, which Lucien loved, although he rarely took her advice. After they had had sex and were lying in bed smoking and drinking wine, it brought him great pleasure to argue with her when she disliked some aspect of a design. It was as sexually arousing to him as their foreplay. As was often the case with mistresses, Lucien felt that Adele was really the kind of woman he should've married in the first place. Adele also knew of the latest architectural work being done in Paris, whereas Celeste believed architecture was a man's business and thus was of no interest to her.

The phone rang several times before Adele picked up. Lucien was thrilled to hear her deep, sexy voice.

"Adele, my love, I'm going to be doing a new factory for Auguste Manet, the big industrialist," announced Lucien.

"Why, how wonderful, my dear Lucien. That's thrilling news," said Adele. "I just love it when you get a new job—you remind me of a five-year-old on Christmas morning. I'm so happy for you. Remember, you must show me the preliminary designs before you present them to Manet."

"You know I will, my sweet. You're my co-architect, we work together on everything," Lucien said. He always told his clients the same thing, that they would work as a team on a project, but that was pure nonsense. He made all the decisions, because collaboration on any creative work was doomed to fail.

"We must get together to celebrate," said Adele. "Le Chat Roux would be the perfect place."

Lucien grimaced; it was also the most expensive place. "We'll see," he replied.

"I remember whenever my parents said 'we'll see,' it always meant no," said Adele.

"No, we'll go. I promise."

"My love, Bette, my manager, just came in and I must talk to her about the upcoming show. It's been bedlam around here, getting ready for it. Remember, I'll never forgive you if you don't come to my show. Call me tomorrow and I'll let you know my schedule."

"I'm going to use these incredible concrete arches that'll—"

"Precious Lucien, Bette is waiting. Call me tomorrow," said Adele, abruptly cutting him off.

⁘ ⁘ ⁘

After Adele replaced the receiver, she turned to gaze at her nude figure in the floor-length mirror in the hall. For a girl pushing forty, she was quite pleased with what she saw. Not a gram of fat on her body, her breasts still protruded proudly, and her legs, her strongest feature, were still lean, with perfectly formed calves and, most importantly, slim ankles (she had no idea how she got those ankles—her mother's were like tree trunks). Unpinning her long blond hair and shaking it loose, Adele turned to admire her *derrière*, which blended beautifully into her waist. The plain fact that none of her runway models' bodies could come close to hers gave Adele the greatest pleasure of all. Occasionally, just to show who was still the top hen in the roost, she would start to change into an outfit for a fashion show, then parade completely naked in the dressing room where her girls were getting ready. As she stopped to chat with them at their dressing tables, they would get a full view of their boss in the mirror in front of them.

Adele ran her hands down her thighs and walked down the hall to her bedroom. Her apartment had been designed by Lucien in a very *moderne* manner, which delighted her because it was so daring and ahead of its time. Most Parisians, for all their cosmopolitan ways, were old-fashioned, living in apartments that looked like something right out of Versailles. Few had the nerve to try the new style introduced at the Exhibition in Paris in 1925. A leader in fashion had to be at the forefront of all things creative, she believed. The sleek, clean look, with its glass walls and black leather and stainless-steel furniture, was stunningly beautiful, making it the perfect place to hold parties. Before the war, that is.

She paused at her bedroom door, made of black opaque glass, and watched Colonel Helmut Schlegal take off his shirt, revealing a tan, muscular body that sent a surge of excitement through her. He placed the shirt carefully over his tunic, which was hanging on the back of a chair. She loved the Gestapo's black uniform. It was elegant, and so much nicer than the Wehrmacht's ugly muddy green uniforms. Even the Waffen-SS uniforms of black and green were not quite as handsome. Although she did admire the ceremonial chained dagger worn at the waist of Wehrmacht officers—it was a nice accessory, which she could perhaps adapt for a chain belt on one of her dresses. Yes, the Gestapo definitely had the best-looking uniforms, and Adele firmly believed you could never go wrong with black, whether an evening dress or a knee-length winter coat. As Schlegel began to remove his shiny black boots, Adele moved quickly to the thick beige carpet and helped him pull one off.

"And who was that? One of your many admirers?" Schlegel asked.

"A very talented architect, as a matter of fact. He's going to be designing a factory for one of those industrialists who are doing war work for the Germans."

"He's going to be very busy. Many contracts will be awarded in the next few months. The Reich needs all the war materiel it can get to win in Russia."

"Lucien will design the best factories the Germans have ever seen. Beautiful modern glass and steel buildings," said Adele as she yanked off the other boot.

"He's one of those degenerate modern architects, eh? The Fuehrer says modern architecture is a provocation to the German spirit. The Fuehrer's architect, Albert Speer, now *there's* a great architect. You should see his designs for the new Berlin; there's a huge dome that covers a hundred acres. As good as ancient Rome."

"I'm sure it will be, my love," said Adele, removing his jodhpurs in one yank. She loved those pants combined with high black boots. Maybe there was a way for her to introduce jodhpurs into a female wardrobe. She'd definitely have to mention it to Bette.

Adele stood up to admire Schlegal's now naked body.

"But I have other things on my mind besides architecture at this moment."

⚜ ⚜ ⚜

"It's economic collaboration, you simply can't do it."

Lucien felt like throwing his coffee cup at his wife's head.

Celeste was walking back from their balcony with a dead rabbit in her hand. It was impossible for anyone but a baby to live off the officially allowed rations set by the French government, so people had to be resourceful. Even well-to-do Parisians had taken to keeping a hutch of rabbits on their balconies to provide much-needed meat. Who knows what might have happened to cats, but they were spared when the government warned that they were unsafe to use in stews. No one ate their dogs, either, but many had to let them loose because they couldn't feed them anymore. Pigeons and ducks had disappeared from the parks.

There was a shortage of everything. A Frenchman who insisted on an omelet made with at least a half-dozen eggs was hard-pressed to get one egg a month. Rationing had severely limited meat, milk, eggs, butter, cheese, potatoes, salt, and fish. Real coffee didn't exist, so Celeste, like all Parisians, had experimented with acorns and dried apples, with little success. For some reason, carrots and roasted chestnuts were always plentiful so they made their way into every dish one could imagine. Adults had to survive on a measly 1,200 calories a day, with only 140 grams of cheese a month. People in Paris were always hungry. Food was all they thought and talked about.

Lucien's wife, who had just clonked the poor animal on the head with a lead pipe, began to skin it at the sink. For a city girl, Celeste had picked up the skill pretty quickly. The way their marriage was disintegrating, Lucien had feared that she might use the pipe on him while he was asleep.

Sitting at the kitchen table, Lucien stared at his wife's back as she worked on the rabbit. He'd been quite proud of himself for marrying such a pretty, intelligent girl from a good family. Most French girls didn't go to college, but Celeste was trained as a mathematics teacher at the prestigious École Normale Supérieure. She gave up teaching at an elite private girls' school when she married Lucien. After seven years of marriage, Celeste still had a shapely petite figure with a tiny waist. It was her unusual chestnut-colored hair that was so alluring, a beautiful rich reddish brown that contrasted so strikingly with her dark blue eyes. It was only natural that an architect should have an aesthetically pleasing spouse. She'd been an object of great pride when she accompanied him to parties.

Celeste looked the same now, but she had developed a grouchy disposition. In a way, he didn't blame her. Her second miscarriage in 1939 had crushed her, filling her with shame and anger. Her unhappiness hung over both of them like a perpetual fog. To compound their discontent, her father, a wealthy wine merchant, had skipped off to Spain in 1941 without a word. An only child whose mother died when she was six, Celeste had never gotten over this despicable act of disloyalty. She had had great love and affection for her father and had believed that he would always be there for her.

Celeste had been overjoyed when Lucien had returned from the Maginot Line; she'd been scared to death that he would be killed, and she would be left all alone. But her joy had quickly dissipated. Because Lucien's practice had dried up, they'd had to dip into her trust fund to survive. This she bitterly resented, and she let her husband know her feelings on that matter almost daily. Celeste felt a husband should support his wife, war or no war. Lucien was enraged by her attitude, because he'd been a good provider until the surrender. Ashamed that she had to support them, he too became angry and resentful.

And now he had a new commission, and she still couldn't be happy.

"Would you rather that Manet and other Frenchmen have their businesses stolen away by the Germans?"

"That would be the honorable thing, if you ask me," Celeste snapped back. "To produce one single bolt for those bastards is pure treason. You'll see, when this is over, they'll be cutting the throats of all the collaborationists."

For the last two years in Paris, calling someone a collaborator was the worst insult you could hurl. Worse than saying their mother was a whore or they were a bastard. It was a serious charge that could mean death if the Resistance took it seriously. Men had been found outside Paris shot in the head. But the very worst kind of collaboration was a French woman sleeping with a German. They were called the horizontal collaborationists.

As Lucien was about to begin his rebuttal, the lights flickered then went out, engulfing the apartment in total darkness. He didn't bother to go to the window to see if the lights were off in other buildings. Each month, the electrical service in Paris had grown more uncertain, sometimes blacking out the city for hours. Without a word of complaint, Celeste brought out three candlesticks from the cupboard to the right of the sink, lit them, and went back to skinning the rabbit. The yellowish candlelight cast a spooky quivering shadow of Celeste on the kitchen walls.

"Did you ever think that those factories might help France after the war?" asked Lucien.

"Next, you'll be giving me that collaborationist rot—'Let's show we're good losers, get back to work as usual, and work together with the Boche.' Anyway, now that the Americans are in this mess, you'll soon be seeing bombers by the hundreds over France. Your masterpiece will be in ashes."

Lucien chomped down on a piece of very stale bread. He *would* be designing buildings for France that would be used after Germany's defeat, which at the moment seemed far-fetched. But he honestly believed it would happen. The main thing was to manage to stay alive to see it.

"I'm seeing Manet this week about the project," he said.

Celeste turned slowly to face Lucien, a bloody knife in her hands. An evil smile came over her face.

"I bet you'd ask me to sleep with a client for a commission, wouldn't you?"

"I'd never do such a thing!" he shouted. "What a horrible thing to say."

"But you'll design for the Germans."

"This is war, and I'll do anything to keep us alive."

"What about keeping your honor?"

Celeste threw the knife into the sink and walked out of the kitchen as the lights flickered back on.

✢ ✢ ✢

Celeste went into the bedroom and sat in a big overstuffed armchair by the window. It was her favorite place in the apartment. She liked to read there or, in the afternoon, watch the children play in the courtyard below. The chair was soft and comfortable, unlike the furniture in the living room, which was of the modernist style Lucien loved so much. She found the "clean, simple modern lines" of the chairs and sofa uncomfortable and cold. It was Lucien who chose the furniture. A price a woman paid when she married an architect, she learned. Celeste had gone along with his selections because she'd loved him and she trusted his architect's taste in things even though her tastes were far more traditional. Flower-patterned wallpaper and carpets with carved walnut furniture were more to her liking, like the things in the apartment where she grew up.

Celeste pulled out a scarf from the stainless steel dresser inlaid with ebony wood, which rested against the wall opposite the bed. She paused and looked down at the bottom drawer, at what had been resting under the scarf. Baby blankets, dozens of them, in bright colors. She ran her hand over the soft lamb's wool then picked one up and held it to her cheek.

6

W HEN AN ELDERLY PORTER LED LUCIEN INTO MANET'S OFFICE AT
his factory in Chaville, Lucien was shocked to see German
officers sitting in front of the old man's ornate mahogany desk, smoking cigarettes and casually conversing with him. He had imagined a
private meeting with Manet, in which he would learn the particulars of
the project. Maybe a leisurely lunch afterward with a glass of real wine
and roast duck. Manet would be paying, of course.

Manet beamed a great avuncular smile when he saw Lucien and
immediately rose from his chair. The Germans sat where they were,
puffing away without the least bit of curiosity for the late arrival. Lucien
was two minutes early, but being familiar with German punctuality, he
knew they had arrived at least ten minutes early.

"Ah, Lucien. Thank you for coming," Manet said. "Let me introduce you to the members of our team."

Lucien took an immediate dislike to the word "team." Team meant
creative interference and problems.

"This is Colonel Max Lieber of the Wehrmacht."

The stout, barrel-chested German rose, clicked his heels, and firmly
shook Lucien's hand. It was the first time Lucien had shaken hands with
a German, and he was surprised that the officer did not try to squeeze
the blood out of his hand. He imagined that Prussian military men often
did that. Lieber looked like the stereotypical German soldier, with the
short military haircut and bull neck that the French made fun of.

"A great pleasure, Monsieur Bernard," said the German, in a soft
smooth voice that didn't conform with his coarse features.

"And this is Major Dieter Herzog, also of the Wehrmacht. He's a structural engineer and head of construction and engineering of armaments facilities for the Paris region."

This German was in his mid-thirties, of average height, with a face that could have been mistaken for a film star's. He put out his cigarette in the ashtray on Manet's desk and slowly rose from his seat. He had a handshake exactly like Lieber's. Handshaking must have been taught at officer's school. Herzog's clear blue eyes gazed into Lucien's, but he just smiled and did not say anything.

Lucien was still dazed by the presence of the Germans so close to him, in the tight confines of this office.

"Please sit down, Lucien, and we'll begin," Manet said. "I have a plan of the site so we can get an idea of how the building will fit."

Manet unrolled a drawing and placed it on a clear spot on his desk. Lucien thought he should have pinned it up on the wall.

"Monsieur Manet, may I pin this drawing on the wall over there so that we can get a better look?" asked Herzog in a polite manner. "It'll be easier to draw on if we have to."

Lucien was impressed as Herzog took the drawing to the wall opposite the desk and secured it with some tacks. Without anyone saying a word, all four men dragged their chairs in front of the drawing. Herzog stood next to the drawing and studied it intently. He then pulled a small engineer's scale out of his side tunic pocket and placed it on the drawing. Lucien knew that this man would be running the meeting and that from now on he would have to do whatever Herzog said.

"Since the factory will be on one floor, with the exception of some mezzanine space, let's assume a 50,000-square-meter footprint," said Herzog as if he were talking to the drawing. He moved the scale around and then pulled a pencil out of the same pocket, making tick marks on the paper.

"It fits without any problem, plus there's plenty of room for stockpiling materiel outside."

"Excellent, Major," said Lieber.

"Maybe even room for expansion in the future," Lucien said, knowing that this would please the Germans. Expansion would mean the war was going well for their side.

"Exactly, Monsieur Bernard. Room for a separate plant or just an addition," said Herzog.

Herzog started to draw on the map but stopped and looked at Lucien.

"Monsieur Bernard, maybe you could come up and rough out the location and how you think the road would connect to the site. Just a rough concept, you know, to get us going." He handed Lucien the pencil.

Lucien was delighted to take charge. For the next two hours he led a discussion of how the project should be sited, drawing the outline of the building on the map, then erasing it and placing it in another location, and then another, until all four men were in agreement on where the factory should be placed. They talked about entrances and exits, flow of production, and lighting.

While the Germans were talking to Manet about the cost of construction, Lucien, who had sat back down to listen, felt a shiver go up his back. He was so caught up in the planning of the new factory he'd completely forgotten about his extracurricular work for Manet. At this very moment, they both had their heads in the mouth of the lion. The realization made him nervous and prompted fierce perspiring. He took out his handkerchief and wiped his forehead.

Herzog looked over at him with a concerned expression. "Monsieur Bernard, you don't look well. Do you want some water?"

"No. No. I'm fine. It's just hot in here, that's all."

The Germans continued haggling with Manet about the cost, and Lucien continued to perspire. He then heard the magic words that all architects dream of hearing.

"Well, Lucien," said Manet, "if the gentlemen of the Reich are in agreement, you should start the plans immediately."

The Germans nodded their approval, and both stood up from their chairs.

"Monsieur Bernard, because of our time constraints, we're looking for the most basic of drawings," said Herzog.

"Are you available for lunch, Monsieur Manet?" asked Lieber.

Lucien was well aware of what the answer would be. Lieber's invitation was merely a courtesy. Doing business with Germans in private was one thing, but dining with them in public in the middle of the day was crossing a forbidden boundary. The Germans also knew this, and while they didn't care what the French did to collaborators, they didn't want to rock the boat by endangering their French contractors.

"I'm afraid not, Colonel Lieber, but thank you for asking," replied Manet.

Herzog came up to Lucien to shake his hand. "I much admired the building you did for Monsieur Gaston. Wrapping the glass around that exterior staircase was a wonderful detail."

When Lucien heard the word "detail," he knew the man wasn't a layman but one of the architecture fraternity.

"Are you an architect, Major Herzog?"

"I started out to be. In fact, I studied under Walter Gropius at the Bauhaus in Dessau in the late twenties. But when my father came to visit, he thought it was all nonsense and put a stop to it. I transferred to study structural engineering at the Polytechnic in Berlin."

Lucien could sense a great deal of regret in that last sentence and empathized with the German, but all the same he was damned impressed. "Gropius is a genius," said Lucien. "Even to study under him for a short time would be a great experience. It is a shame he had to leave Germany."

"The Fuehrer has different ideas of what architecture should be. To him, Gropius and his work were subversive."

Lucien was about to say that Hitler's taste in architecture was rotten but held his tongue. Herzog may have once been a modernist architect, but he was still a German officer. Lucien could find himself in an internment camp.

"Still, it was quite unfortunate that Herr Gropius had to leave for America," said Lucien sympathetically. "What kind of person was he?"

"Ah, rather harsh and pedantic, but a man of great vision and even greater talent. Have you ever seen the Fagus Factory?"

Lucien was eager to tell Herzog that he had indeed made the pilgrimage to Germany in the mid-1930s to see all the famous German modern buildings. Many snapshots of them were often scattered next to his drafting table for inspiration when he was designing. "I spent two months traveling throughout Germany seeing my favorite buildings, but Gropius's Fagus Factory is a masterpiece. Better than the Bauhaus School, which I also visited."

Lucien saw a smile come over Herzog's face. The major picked up his cap and gloves off a side table and put them on, moving slowly toward the door.

"I'll be looking forward to seeing your design for Monsieur Manet. Maybe it'll be another Fagus Factory," said Herzog with his hand on the door handle.

Lucien grinned and shook his head. "Nothing of mine can ever come close to it, I assure you. But I will produce a building of advanced ideas."

"The Reich will be most pleased," replied Herzog.

7

LUCIEN HAD SOON DISCOVERED ONE OF THE PRICES HE'D BE PAYING for all that money, the commission, and the thrill of designing the hiding place: living in a constant state of fear. He stopped in the doorways of three shops to check if he was being followed. Manet had insisted on a meeting. Lucien didn't think one was necessary; he had done the drawings and that was the end of it. But Manet wanted him to see the finished work. On rue Euler, just a block away from the apartment building, Lucien looked out from another doorway and came face to face with three smiling German enlisted men.

"Pardon, monsieur, could you please tell us the way to Notre Dame? We're totally lost," said a handsome soldier with golden blond hair.

His companions laughed and shrugged their shoulders, admitting their helplessness. Lucien knew his face registered a look of abject terror, but the men didn't seem to notice. The Occupation had brought busloads of German tourist-soldiers like these. Carrying cameras and guidebooks, they hit every main attraction in Paris, including climbing the Eiffel Tower and seeing the Tomb of the Unknown Soldier, where they all insisted on getting their photo taken. Ever since Hitler had taken a two-hour tour of the city right after the armistice, every German soldier had had to see Paris, and the army encouraged them to do so. On one hand, it was kind of flattering to have Germans come to admire the city—they had nothing like it in Germany. Berlin was a second-rate city compared to the City of Light. Giving directions to Germans was a delicate matter, though, as misdirecting them could cause problems if the soldiers ran into you again. Teenagers and the elderly routinely gave them wrong directions—it became a running joke—but many adult Parisians put their hatred aside for a moment and directed the Germans as they would any stranger. Lucien fought the overwhelming urge to bolt. He swallowed hard and smiled.

"Certainly, gentlemen. Go down this street to the avenue Marceau, turn left, and stay on it until you hit the Seine, turn left, and walk along the river for about fifteen minutes, and you'll see Notre Dame. It's on its own little island in the Seine."

A soldier with reddish-brown hair scribbled the directions in a little notebook. The blond one repeated Lucien's directions aloud to make sure he had it right.

"Thank you so much, monsieur. You have a very beautiful city."

"Enjoy yourselves. And remember, we have the best collection of dirty postcards in Europe."

The soldiers roared with laughter, waved, and went on their way. Lucien stayed where he was until they were out of sight. He leaned against a wall of a building and reached inside his jacket pocket for his cigarettes. Could they be Gestapo men disguised as Wehrmacht soldiers who were following him? His hands were shaking, but he managed to light a cigarette and take a few drags before flicking it into the gutter. He waited another five minutes then finally made it to the building, nodded at the concierge, who ignored him, and started up the stairs.

He knew the Gestapo could be waiting for him in the apartment. He'd be tortured and killed, and he hadn't even had the chance to enjoy all that money, having only spent 700 of the 12,000 franc fee on black market eggs and some real wine. At each landing, he felt like turning and running down the stairs, but he continued on. Lucien kept thinking of how fast the construction work had been done—in just a few days. It seemed impossible. Was it a trap?

He had completed the column drawings in a couple of hours then had set to work on the factory. It felt good to be designing again, and

Lucien enjoyed every minute he worked on the building, drawing detail after detail, trying out different ideas for the facades. The building had wonderful skylights, which brought light into the center of the factory floor, and three two-story entries, where the workers would pass through each day. The last thing to do was a perspective drawing of the entire building, as if one were looking at it from an airplane. By Monday, the drawings would be complete, ready for Tuesday morning's meeting. He couldn't wait to present the drawings. Herzog would be impressed.

The Germans had only given him a week to complete the design drawings. If it had been any other client, he would have told them to go to hell. But since this was a client who could have him executed, he didn't protest. He also didn't protest the tiny fee—just 3,000 francs—he was getting for the design. What mattered most was the opportunity to design a good building; he couldn't blow this.

Lucien lightly knocked on the door. He didn't want to draw the attention of any neighbors. The door swung open, and Manet stood before him, looking very contented.

"Come in and see your handiwork, Lucien," he said in a loud voice that made Lucien cringe.

He cast a nervous glance behind him and went into the apartment, following Manet into the salon. At first, Lucien was puzzled that everything looked the same as when he'd first visited the apartment almost a week ago. Then he realized that was a good thing. It seemed as though nothing had been touched. He walked toward the column, but stopped about three meters away to see whether he'd notice anything odd about the shaft. As he circled the column, he kept staring, but everything seemed perfectly normal to him. Moving a meter away, he still saw nothing. Then with his face five centimeters away, Lucien examined the shaft up and down to see if even the tiniest flaw would give the whole ruse away. He could barely see the joints hidden in the square edge of the fluting. He had designed quite a bit of custom cabinetry before the war and had seen work of great precision, but this was amazing. The joints were even less than razor-thin; they almost disappeared. It was the kind of precision one would see in the engineering of high-quality steel machine parts. As an added precaution, the door had been placed on the side of the column closest to the wall to avoid detection.

Lucien took the index and middle fingers of his right hand and sharply tapped the right side of the door about three meters from the floor. The very tall door popped open to reveal the hollow space of the column. He stepped inside and pulled the door shut with a brass handle. He stood in total darkness, looking about him. Lucien couldn't see any light showing through the joints of the door. He stooped down and slowly stretched out his hand, finding a latch at the bottom of the door and fastening it. Running his hand along the door's edge, he found another one a half a meter above it. He continued to do this until he'd fastened five latches.

"Monsieur Manet, I want you to pound on this door with all your might," Lucien shouted.

Manet got a running start and threw his entire body against the door, repeating the motion two more times. With his hand on the door, Lucien felt that the door didn't budge a millimeter. The column itself didn't move at the base either. The workmen had done a good job of securely fastening it to the floor.

"A few more times," said Lucien. Manet walked four meters from the column and charged at it like a bull. After the second time, he began to get winded and tired, but he did it two more times.

"All right, Monsieur, I'm coming out."

Outside the column, Lucien circled it, running his hand along the fluting of the beautiful wood shaft, his face beaming with pride. The feeling of incredible exhilaration was back, and he was off on another high.

"You're certainly a man of your word, Monsieur Manet. The workmanship is extraordinary."

"I'm glad you approve. My men are excellent, but they needed your imagination. They just followed your instructions."

"It's incredible that they could do such fine work in so short a time."

"Because I may have more than one guest staying here at a time, I decided to have the other column done as well," said Manet.

At once, Lucien walked over to the second column to examine its exterior. The work was equal to the first.

"Doubly extraordinary," said Lucien with a smile.

"A clever solution, Monsieur," said Manet, patting him on the shoulder.

"That's if your guest doesn't panic and start crying in there," replied Lucien who knew that the success of the most ingenious design depended on the nerve of the occupant. "I can't soundproof this thing."

"I'm afraid that is something you and I have no control over."

"I'm ready for Tuesday's presentation," said Lucien, shifting the conversation to a more pleasurable topic.

"Major Herzog is looking forward to seeing your work. He called yesterday to see how things were going."

"You…and the major will be very pleased," Lucien said. "It's a very functional design that—"

"Tuesday at 9:00 a.m., then?" said Manet as he walked to the door, gesturing for Lucien to precede him, for they couldn't leave together.

Lucien wasn't insulted that Manet had cut him off. The old man had probably worked with architects before, so he probably knew what bullshitters they were when it came to explaining their work.

Walking down the stairs, Lucien's pride in his columns slowly faded away. When he got to the front door, he stayed there for about two minutes, terrified to go in the street. A black Citroën, the automobile favored by the Gestapo, could be parked at the curb waiting for him. He took a deep breath and opened the door slowly. Looking to the left and right, he stepped out onto the sidewalk and began walking briskly down the rue Galilée. He wanted to break into a run, but he remembered the dead Jew in his blue suit and slowed down to a walk.

8

Y OU WERE RIGHT, IT'S INGENIOUS."

Mendel Janusky popped open the door to the column and stepped inside. He shut the panel, then came out. "The total darkness in there is serenely peaceful."

Janusky walked over to Auguste Manet. "Can your architect be trusted?"

"Without question, my friend. You'll be safe in his hands," said Manet.

"I hope so. I'm so tired of running, Auguste. There are some days I feel like walking into Gestapo headquarters and giving myself up. I'd tell them where all the money is and let them kill me."

Manet laughed. He had known Mendel Janusky for almost twenty years, and he wasn't a man who gave up easily. Janusky would never surrender to the Nazis, let alone let them have his vast fortune. Every sou of it went to buy freedom for his people, not just in France but throughout Europe. Beginning in the late '30s, Janusky had set up a network of agents on the Continent to arrange transit papers and visas to help Jews escape, mainly to Portugal, Turkey, and South America, the easiest places to bribe officials. Money could buy freedom, and he was willing to spend as much as it took. Even as late as 1941, families were being saved by him. Manet knew he'd recently arranged to smuggle sixty Jews into Turkey, where they'd boarded a freighter bound for Venezuela. Warned by his friends that he must get out of France, he'd ignored their advice and now was trapped. The Gestapo was tightening the noose around him. Nonetheless, he told Manet he was determined to escape to continue his work. There were many more to help.

"That's a joke. I'll turn myself in before you ever do, Mendel."

Janusky smiled. "You're a good man, Manet. When most gentile businessmen turned their backs on the Jews, without hesitating you offered to help us, putting yourself and your entire family at great risk."

"Any good Christian would do the same."

"Now *that's* a goddamn joke. You know, I never trusted gentiles. They would smile in your face and call you a dirty kike the minute your back was turned. They would do business with us, but forget about socializing. Did any gentile ever invite me for a weekend in the country except you? Not on your life. France might have been the first country in Europe to grant Jews civil rights, but it's still a country of Jew haters. I was stupid enough to be fooled into thinking they'd finally accepted us."

"I don't believe that."

"That's because you're a true Christian gentleman. But you're a fool to think most men think like you."

Manet was saddened to see the physical change in his friend. Once a tall, distinguished-looking man with piercing blue eyes and a vibrant personality, Janusky's eyes now seemed dull and lifeless, and his face was haggard. His salt-and-pepper hair was completely white. Walking with a pronounced stoop back to the column, Janusky ran his fingers up and down its fluting, clearly enjoying the tactile pleasure of its smoothness.

"You know, I had a dream about my father last night," Janusky said, almost absentmindedly. "That hasn't happened in many years."

"I remember your father. No man worked harder for his family. He rose from nothing."

"Less than nothing. He escaped the pogroms in Russia in 1881. Gathered people's old scrap metal eighteen hours a day and sold it for a tiny profit. A sou here, a sou there. Until he had the biggest scrap metal business in Paris. Then came the steel mill."

"The best in all of France."

"You know, after we made it, we thought we were above all the Jews that came later. But we didn't count for much, Auguste. We were still immigrants, no better than Jews who arrived yesterday. When the Boche started rounding us up, foreign Jews went to Drancy first, no matter when they came to France or how well off they were."

Manet remembered how he'd first met Janusky, when he was bidding on a contract to supply steel for Manet's engines back in the '20s. Each bidder had to show Manet his factory and prove he had the ability to fulfill the contract. Janusky personally took Manet through every part of the plant, explaining how up-to-date and efficient his equipment was. But what struck Manet was that Janusky seemed to know every one of the scores of workers he passed on the tour. Not just their names but personal information—asking them about a health problem a wife was having, how their child's recital went, or did they catch any fish last weekend. He even gave one man a franc piece for his boy's birthday, which he knew was coming up. All of his men perked up when he passed, as if they were glad to see him.

Manet considered himself a decent boss, but he knew little about his men. He'd ended up more impressed with Janusky's relations with his workers than the factory itself. Janusky won the contract and from then on provided all the steel for Manet's automobile engines and other parts. His colleagues had warned him against dealing with Jews because they were natural-born thieves, but Janusky had been the best and most reliable supplier he'd ever had. A man of honor.

"Mendel, you'll stay here for at least a month. But then we'll have to move you. It's never safe to stay in one place."

"I've been moved around like a chess piece," he said with a laugh.

"When the time is right and all the financial arrangements have been made, I can get you into Spain, then Portugal," said Manet.

"Then America. They have to know what's going on."

"America. But now it's impossible to get you out of the country.

My contact in the Gestapo tells me they're killing people right and left to find you. Remember Deligny?"

"Deligny? I thought he got out. They picked him up?"

"I haven't found out if he's talked. Sooner or later they'll pick up some of my people. I want to believe they won't crack, but with what those Gestapo barbarians do, the strongest are made to talk. Men can't betray each other in times like these, but they do."

"Poor Deligny. All on account of me. This isn't right, Auguste."

Manet changed the subject. "You must be quiet as a mouse here— and stay away from the windows even though they're shuttered. We think a hiding place is safe, but they always find out about it. There're informants everywhere."

"Quiet as a mouse."

"Your food will come up on the dumbwaiter in the pantry every three days."

"Well," Janusky said as he looked around the apartment, "this is the lap of luxury compared to being in a barrel in that wine cellar."

"Yes, I noticed the Pinot Noir cologne you're wearing," said Manet, patting his friend on the shoulder.

9

MY DARLING, WHAT A WONDERFUL SURPRISE. BUT THIS MUST HAVE cost you a fortune."

Lucien smiled as Adele held the string of pearls before the small candle on the café table and examined them. He knew many men had bestowed pearls upon her that really weren't pearls but cheap imitations. He was pleased her expert eye could tell these were the genuine thing.

"Real quality doesn't come cheap, but a stylish woman like you deserves only the best," replied Lucien. Actually, he got the pearls for almost nothing. A friend of his told Lucien about a homosexual who was desperate to sell his family heirlooms because he had been ordered to go to Drancy.

"These are magnificent, Lucien." Adele fastened the string around her long slender neck.

Lucien beamed at her. His nightlife in Paris had returned to normal. While the French outside were getting by on scraps and acorn coffee, Le Chat Roux offered a choice of six kinds of fish or oysters, a bouillabaisse, rabbit, chicken, fruit salad, and even pineapple with kirsch. Having money was a wonderful thing, thought Lucien. The necklace looked wonderful against her black dress and her beautiful blond hair.

Lucien was enjoying the fact that other men at Le Chat Roux were stealing admiring glances at Adele. He knew that in a short while, they would be back in her apartment making love and downing the bottle of expensive champagne he'd bought for her.

Adele also saw the looks of envy and admiration and gently fingered the string of pearls. "You're terrible to spoil me so. The pearls,

this wonderful meal. You deserve a reward," she said, shifting her cornflower blue eyes seductively toward the door, then all of a sudden she
started waving her hand like an excited schoolgirl.

"Oh, look, it's Suzy," she said to Lucien. "Hello, my love," Adele
called across the room. "You be sure to come to my salon this week. I
won't forgive you if you cancel again."

Lucien turned around to see the actress Suzy Solidor sitting at
a table with a half-dozen people. She raised her glass to Adele and
smiled. He'd seen other famous actors and entertainers, those who
hadn't fled in 1940, at this restaurant before. Established stars like
Maurice Chevalier, Sacha Guitry, and rising stars like Edith Piaf and
Yves Montand had stayed in Paris and continued their careers. They
enjoyed the nightlife as if there wasn't a war on at all, to the disapproval
of some Frenchmen. Adele loved her connections to the movie world
and crowed about them all the time. She was glad the stars had stayed.
Lucien knew the only celebrity she wished had left was Coco Chanel,
whom she loathed, because Parisians thought Chanel was more talented and chic than Adele, and it drove her mad.

"Suzy's coming in to look at some sketches, and she may bring
Simone Signoret. Isn't that wonderful?" Adele said excitedly. "And
they *both* said they'd definitely come to my show."

Slowly sipping her wine, she ignored Lucien while she took in a
180-degree view of the entire restaurant, admiring the glamorous cli-
entele and surroundings as one would take in a view of the Alps.

"As I said, there's a reward waiting for you to collect at my flat, so
let's get going," said Adele, finishing off the last drop of wine.

On their way out, they passed a table where six German officers
were seated, wolfing down omelets, roast chicken, and lamb chops with
gusto and washing it all down with champagne. Lucien was relieved
that he didn't recognize any of them from his meeting at Manet's factory. They'd be suspicious about how an architect who got paid a pit-
tance by the Reich could afford such a fancy place.

Lucien and Adele took their time as they walked along the rue Monsigny. It was a beautiful July night. Before the war, one of the pleasures of Paris had been strolling its streets and looking at the window displays in all the shops, but now there was no reason to stop and look because they were empty due to the shortages. The wine shops still had displays of bottles, but the bottles were empty. As usual, the streets were practically deserted, with a few people hurrying by to make it to the Metro before the midnight curfew. The Germans were quite clever, thought Lucien. The curfew wasn't just a security measure but a form of psychological control over Parisians, far more powerful than brute force. People were scared to death to be caught outside after midnight. He could see the anxiety in the faces of the people who passed them. There were no cars on the roads. Only a *velo-taxi*, a kind of bicycle rickshaw driven by a young man that carried two women passengers, passed by. It was a very popular means of transport just now in Paris because it didn't need petrol or a horse.

"My friend Jeanne just got an incredible fur coat that once belonged to a Jew," Adele said, touching the necklace. "Pure mink, knee length."

"The Jews have lost everything. I hear many have gone into hiding."

"Ah. They can hide under the smallest rock or in the tiniest crack," she replied, "but the Boche will find them. That's for sure."

"Not many of them made it out of the country before the surrender, so there must be tons of them still around," Lucien said. "I hear thousands were deported last month."

"Now real Frenchmen can control their own economy. I know how the kikes took over the clothing and fashion industries. Dirty swine."

Lucien was surprised at the venom spewing from Adele's mouth. He had never seen this side of her—but the subject of Jews had never come up before. The Occupation, Lucien realized, hadn't just bred hatred of Jews, it had brought out the very worst in human beings. Hardship had bred pure self-interest, setting group against group, neighbor against neighbor, and even friend against friend. People would screw over each other for a lump of butter.

"Just last week, Isabelle, a model from work, found out that her father had been arrested for hiding a Jew in his attic at his home in the country near Troyes," Adele said. "Can you imagine risking your hide like that?"

Lucien looked down at his feet as they walked. "So what happened to Isabelle's father?" he asked.

"Poor Isabelle doesn't know where he is or even if he's still alive. You know damn well he's been tortured to death. She was lucky as hell she wasn't brought in by the Gestapo. A good-looking girl like that could be sent to a brothel in Poland or someplace."

"That's a shame about her father."

Adele stopped suddenly and looked Lucien square in the eyes.

"A shame? Fools who take risks like that deserve to die."

"Still, you have to wonder why someone would do something like that."

"Lucien, my love, you're absolutely hopeless," said Adele, playfully mussing his hair.

They strolled on and Adele chattered away like a magpie, but he didn't hear a word. The wonderful anticipation of making love to Adele he'd felt as they'd left the café now was evaporating into the warm night air. Just for tonight, he'd wanted to put aside his fear of getting caught for what he'd done for Manet, but now Adele had ruined that with her story.

The dread was back. Lucien loved to walk the streets of his beloved Paris, but now he walked them in a state of continuous fear, always looking around to see if a black Gestapo Citroën was pulling alongside him or if plainclothes Gestapo men were sneaking up behind him to make an arrest.

Yesterday, while walking along the rue du Louvre, he'd felt a hand on his shoulder and had come close to fainting, but it had only been his friend Daniel Joffre standing there. Tonight he was so scared he didn't think he'd get it up even with the sight of Adele wearing only the pearl necklace and high heels. Lucien was shaken out of his reverie by Adele's shrill voice.

"Well, my goodness, the streetwalkers *are* out in force tonight, aren't they?" exclaimed Adele. She was talking to a woman walking toward them.

"Mmm, that was exactly what I was thinking when I saw you, my dear," replied the woman.

Lucien was confused by the exchange. The woman, he immediately noticed, was amazingly attractive. Much too beautiful to be a streetwalker.

The three of them now faced one another. "Lucien Bernard, let me introduce Bette Tullard. You've heard me mention her, of course. She's the indispensable right-hand man of my fashion house. I hate to admit it, but if she left me, my business would collapse within twenty-four hours."

"And that's no exaggeration, Monsieur Bernard, believe me. Very pleased to meet you."

"Likewise, mademoiselle," he said, staring like an idiot at Bette's beautiful face.

"I never forget a handsome man. I believe I saw you at our show last spring."

"Why...yes, I was," said Lucien, flattered to be remembered by such an attractive woman.

"I especially liked your wavy hair. Not slicked down like most men's."

"Well, thank you," said Lucien, running his hand self-consciously through his hair.

"Yes, it's one of his many fine qualities. Lucien's an architect, Bette; he designed my apartment."

"Ah, handsome and very talented. I love Adele's apartment, even though I'm barely there five minutes when I visit. Adele's always shoving me out the door," said Bette, frowning at Adele.

"I *am* running a business, my dear."

"Really? I always got the impression that I ran the business," replied Bette.

Lucien had heard Adele talk of Bette many times, but she had never described her. Now he knew why. He was amused by their relationship. Each time Adele insulted her or snapped at her, Bette insulted and snapped back with equal force. Bette seemed to know Adele could never fire her.

"Of course, with the new show coming up, you'll be working through the night on the portfolio?" asked Adele with a smile.

"My, what a beautiful necklace, Adele," said Bette, adroitly changing the subject.

Adele shifted her eyes toward Lucien, and Bette nodded.

"We won't keep you, Bette darling; you have so much work to do tonight."

"Yes," replied Bette, "and I know you'll be plenty busy as well."

10

G OD DAMN YOU, I TOLD YOU NEVER TO LIGHT A CANDLE. YOU CAN see the light coming through the boards at night. What the hell's wrong with you?"

Solomon Geiber jumped to his feet, blew out the candle, and looked up at the ceiling of the pit, which was a crude arrangement of boards nailed together with cross ties. He could make out the figure of Maurier standing above him.

"Please forgive me, Monsieur Maurier; it won't happen again."

"You better believe it won't happen again. You've got to go."

"But you promised we could stay."

"Tough luck. I must've been nuts to hide Jews. You know what would happen to me if they found you?"

"But where will we go?" moaned Miriam, Geiber's wife.

"Who gives a shit? That's your problem, not mine. You can stay until tomorrow night," replied Maurier, who stomped away.

Geiber sat down on the plank floor of the dirt pit and held his head in his hands. About two meters wide, three meters long, and three meters deep, the hole they lived in must have once been a storage place for animal fodder. It had been Solomon and Miriam Geiber's home for the last four weeks. Though it was cold, damp, and always smelled of moldy grain, the pit was a deluxe hotel compared to how they'd lived in the previous weeks.

Warned by a friend in the middle of the afternoon that the Gestapo was on the way to their apartment, Geiber and his wife had grabbed their belongings and savings and escaped into the streets of Paris. After being rebuffed by three friends whom they thought they could count on, the Geibers had had no idea of what to do. In desperation, they'd gone to their longtime pharmacist, a kindly gentile whom they'd hoped would hide them in the basement beneath his shop. But he politely refused and to their horror had offered them free vials of cyanide to take in case they were caught.

Feeling totally abandoned, the Geibers had made their way to the outskirts of the city. After spending a miserable night under a railroad overpass, they'd continued walking west into the countryside, traveling from one farm house to another, begging for a roof over their heads and some food. But knowing the penalty for hiding Jews, the farmers had either slammed their doors in their faces or offered the old couple some scraps of food then shooed them away as though they were stray dogs. Because he'd been so desperate, Geiber had lost all feelings of pride and practically begged on his knees for help. Day after day, they'd wandered with no definite destination, subsisting on handouts and sleeping in the woods or in haystacks at night.

Occasionally, they'd come across some decent people who'd shelter them overnight. They were an odd sight in the middle of the French countryside, an old man in a three-piece English tweed suit and cane, his wife in a fashionable tailored outfit. To avoid capture by the Germans, the couple had steered clear of the highways and only traveled the back country roads. Both were in their late sixties, and the walking soon took a toll on their bodies; Miriam's legs became terribly swollen, and she could barely drag herself along. There had been times when they thought of turning themselves in to end their misery.

The only act of kindness came when a farmer offered them bicycles that had belonged to his sons, both of whom were now prisoners of war in Germany. Though it had been at least ten years ago, the Geibers had gone on many biking holidays with their children through France and Switzerland. To their delight, they discovered that it was true—that once you learned to ride a bicycle, you never forgot. Biking had been better than walking, but they'd still found no one who would take them in permanently.

One evening, they saw a light in a farmhouse set about half a kilometer from the road. Tired and hungry, the couple rode up and knocked on the door. A farmer with a stubbly gray beard and short cropped hair came to the door. He listened to their plea dispassionately. A girl of around sixteen with a beautiful mane of blond hair joined him.

"We know you're Jews. We won't hurt you. Please come in," said the girl. The Geibers, who were amazed by what they heard, actually thought they had found an angel from heaven. But before the Geibers could move, the farmer barred the doorway with his thick muscular arm then slammed the door on them. Behind the plank door, shouting broke out with the girl pleading with the farmer to help them. He screamed back at her, telling her she was a fool. The argument went back and forth. Dejected, the Geibers had walked away, but the door was thrown open, and both the girl and farmer came out.

"I'll hide you if you pay me," demanded the farmer, glaring at the girl, who was about to protest.

"That's no problem, monsieur. I'd be glad to pay for your kindness," replied Geiber. Once the Occupation began, he had taken measures to ensure his vast fortune was safe, but he also knew that cash would come in handy, so he kept a great deal of it in his home to take with them if they had to run. Geiber also had Miriam sew gold coins and her jewels into her dresses.

In exchange for five thousand francs, they lived in a pit in the barn with a bucket for a chamber pot. The smell and the dampness worked its way into their skin and joints, and at night they could hear the rats scampering above them looking for food. But worst of all was the Stygian darkness in which they lived. During the day, the Geibers could barely see each other by the light that filtered in between the cracks of the floor boards, which had a light layer of hay on them to camouflage the hiding place. At night, they couldn't see their hands in front of their faces. Several times, they had lit a Sabbath candle on Friday nights until Maurier caught them.

They passed the time by reminiscing about every single detail of their lives—about their sons and grandchildren, their favorite books, musicals, art, and all the films they'd seen. In an odd way, this ordeal proved what a good marriage they had had for forty years; they could converse about anything and entertain each other for hours, the way friends did over coffee in a café.

Maurier never allowed them out of the pit, but they didn't care. It was better to be alive underground than be a corpse aboveground. Marie, Maurier's niece, brought them food every day and pulled up and cleaned out the chamber pot. She washed their clothes. Marie did turn out to be an angel. Geiber swore that if he survived this, he'd pay back her kindness a hundredfold. Now, the Geibers would be back on the road, begging for help. He laughed to himself. The son of a wealthy businessman who owned an enormous aluminum works, Geiber had never once in his life worried about money or food or where he would live. Now, he wondered if God was teaching him a lesson—this Nazi hell in exchange for the years of privilege and happiness. Thank God his sons had immigrated to England in the '30s. What he'd thought was a curse then had turned out to be a blessing.

Geiber jerked his head up as he heard someone approaching. Every hour of the day, he expected the boards to be yanked away and to see Germans soldiers in their gray-green uniforms, smiling down at him as if they'd unearthed a buried treasure.

"Monsieur Geiber," said Marie.

"Yes?"

"I once worked as a maid in the house of a very rich man. He may be able to help you."

I T'S SO OVERDONE. YOU DON'T NEED ALL THAT GLASS, AND WHAT'S this tower at the front? For chrissake, this is a factory, not a god-damn cathedral."

Lucien was enraged, and without realizing it, he got to his feet. He was about to begin defending his design to Colonel Lieber when Major Herzog walked leisurely over to the drawings, which were tacked to the wall of Manet's office. Lucien sat down, realizing that he had almost done something quite stupid. He had to remember that he wasn't dealing with a normal client but one who could have him deported on the spot. He looked down at his shoes in embarrassment as Herzog began to speak.

"Colonel, the tower contains the mechanical equipment for the plant, plus it's the front entrance, where the workers will clock in. All that glass brings in sunlight. Indeed, the whole design is quite functional; everything you see helps productivity. And isn't that what the Reich insists on—to produce the most in the least amount of time?"

Colonel Lieber didn't look convinced as he pulled out his gold cigarette case from his tunic. "Well, Herzog, if you say so. But a lot of the outside design seems unnecessary. I think we could do with a plain concrete building with a few windows. Something that could survive an attack from the Americans."

"The entire structure is done in reinforced concrete that's been strengthened to withstand a bombing," said Herzog, in a tone of voice one might use with a recalcitrant four-year-old. "And you must remember, Colonel, that this factory will be used by the Reich after the war is won. So it shouldn't be a slapdash affair but a permanent, well-designed building, like all our factories in Germany."

Lieber waved his hand as if he were swatting away a fly, meaning the matter was settled and the design approved. Lucien could tell Lieber knew absolutely nothing about construction or armaments. This surprised him. He thought that the well-organized Germans would make it a point to pick qualified men for positions of responsibility. But, like the French government, they chose dolts who had to depend on men like Herzog to get the job done. Still, Lucien knew he was lucky to be dealing with these men. They belonged to the Wehrmacht, the regular army, not the Waffen-SS.

Lucien was simultaneously embarrassed and flattered by Herzog's defense of his design. He felt both bad and good that someone was sticking up for him when he should've been the one doing the talking. He had failed many times in the past when trying to defend a modern design. It had inevitably been altered into something more classically inspired—either change it or lose the job and the fee. He was committed to the new modernism but not that committed. One had to eat and pay the rent.

The meeting continued with discussions of electrical service to run machinery and the cheapest way to heat the building. Lucien had cleverly run steam pipes behind the horizontal mullions of the ribbons of windows, a fact that did not escape Herzog's notice. Throughout the meeting, Herzog piled compliment upon compliment on Lucien. Praise, Lucien discovered, negated his fear of being in the lion's den.

At the two-hour mark, Lieber cleared his throat and rose from the plush, upholstered armchair Manet had provided for him, signaling that the meeting had come to an end. Everyone then looked over at Herzog, who also stood up. As had become routine, he would do his summation at the conclusion of a meeting.

"Well, if Monsieur Bernard will make these small revisions to the design plans, which we will need in one week," said Herzog, wearing a great smile. "I know that's an incredibly unreasonable amount of time, but I'm sure you can do it."

"Thank you so much, Major Herzog," said Manet. "My men are ready to move on this immediately. The site work can begin at once. You did say you could procure at least one earthmover. It would be so much more efficient than hundreds of men with picks and shovels."

"Of course. In fact, I may get you three. Berlin has given this work a high priority. Do you think the number of workers you listed is adequate? You know I can provide you with a work force if you wish." Herzog spoke in his most charming manner, as if he were offering Manet the use of his umbrella.

Both Lucien and Manet knew that the work force Herzog was talking about consisted of political prisoners from Drancy and the other internment camps around Paris. Emaciated men who were "volunteered" to work for the Reich.

At the beginning of the Occupation, Lucien had been worried that he and all other Frenchmen would be turned into slave laborers, but to his surprise, workers were paid. This, of course, added salt to the wounds of the defeated—most of the French now depended on the Germans for their incomes. Many worked directly for the Germans, especially in construction, where a quarter of a million worked for the Todt organization, which was building fortifications along the Atlantic coast to protect against an Allied invasion. Thousands of French, mainly the scum of the working class, had volunteered to go to Germany to work in factories. The Germans paid higher wages than French employers, but the work was backbreaking—plus, one could get killed by Allied bombing. Manet's men knew they weren't getting paid as much, but they would be treated well.

"That won't be necessary at this time, Major."

"This building is to be constructed in less than two months, Manet. Your men will work twenty-four hours a day, seven days a week. Berlin is expecting no less from you," Lieber stated in a bullying tone. "I don't care how many men it takes."

"Well then," replied Herzog, who turned to Lucien, "this is a very successful start. And I believe Monsieur Manet may have mentioned his new armaments facility for the Luftwaffe?"

Lucien turned to Manet, who gave him a slight smile. Herzog picked up his cap and gloves and followed Lieber out the door. Manet watched them leave. He had a look of disgust on his face that surprised Lucien, given that the meeting had gone so well. "Lieber is a pig," Manet said. "I know he's going to be trouble."

"But our meeting seemed so successful, monsieur. What's your concern?"

Manet looked at Lucien coldly. "Your design may have won the day, but the Boche are squeezing me on my compensation and on the schedule. Lieber won't listen to reason. He wants me to know that the French are under the heel of the Germans and always will be. In the end, I will have to use their labor to finish on time. It turns my stomach to use those poor bastards."

"Once production is under way, they may be more flexible," said Lucien.

"Monsieur Bernard, it's evident that you don't know a damn thing about Germans."

Lucien looked down at the floor.

"And yes, I will be making guns for the Luftwaffe. The Germans have appropriated a large estate in Tremblay to build on. It may be a project you'd be interested in. But I have a small problem I'd like your advice on."

"Why yes, I'd be glad to help."

"An acquaintance of mine has decided to let some friends use his country home in Le Chesnay for a while. But there may be some complications with the Germans. There is a need for some arrangements if the Germans do come to call on them."

The smile on Lucien's face disappeared in an instant.

"This plant in Tremblay will be almost twice as large as the one you just designed. And it will adjoin a small airfield where fighters will be fitted out with the new guns to test fire," said Manet. "So you'll be designing a small airport as well. I hope you'll be interested. I'll send a car for you."

With great reluctance, Lucien reached into his jacket pocket for his notebook to write down the appointment time. But while he was writing, he was envisioning the design of the small control tower for his new airport.

12

L UCIEN SAT BOLT UPRIGHT IN BED AS IF SOMEONE HAD DOUSED HIM with a bucket of ice-cold water in the middle of the night.

He rubbed his face with both hands to make sure he wasn't dreaming, then prodded Celeste, who was sleeping soundly on her stomach.

"Did you hear that?"

Celeste groaned.

"It sounded like a—"

A loud rapping on their apartment door interrupted Lucien. He began breathing heavily. When the rapping started again, he began to tremble uncontrollably. He drew his knees up to his chest and wrapped his arms around them, and started rocking back and forth. He shook Celeste's shoulder violently, and she rolled over on her side.

"There's someone at the door," whispered Lucien.

"What time is it?"

"It's almost three in the morning."

"Who'd be at our door at this hour?" mumbled Celeste, burying her head in her pillow.

Lucien knew the answer to that question. There could be only one visitor who'd come calling at 3:00 a.m.: the French police—or worse, the Gestapo. He had heard that they always raided a house in the middle of the night when their prey was asleep. People woke up confused and disoriented, making it easier for the police to cart them away. He couldn't decide what to do. Face the music or run like a rabbit out the servants' entry in the rear of the apartment? He felt like an idiot for not having an escape plan, but then what about Celeste? He couldn't leave her. Lucien looked down at Celeste, who'd fallen back asleep. If the Germans came through the front door with Panzer tanks, she would sleep right through it.

The rapping began again, this time harder and more impatient. He took a deep breath and finally mustered the courage to jump out of bed. An invisible hand in the middle of his back pushed him toward the door. In the six meters it took to get there, the same gruesome image flashed over and over through his mind: a lead pipe splitting his head open like a melon.

By the time he reached the door, Lucien was shaking with fright. He closed his eyes for a few seconds, then calmly opened the door and stood face to face with a man in his forties wearing a dark gray suit and a black fedora. Lucien was surprised to see an actual Gestapo agent instead of a French policeman who usually made these kinds of arrests. He must be in a shitload of trouble, he realized, if the Gestapo was making a personal call. He wasn't able to see any of the other men out in the corridor with him.

"You must come with me at once," said the man in a very loud voice.

"May I get dressed?"

"Yes."

Leaving the door open, Lucien turned and started to walk back to the bedroom. He didn't really want to wake Celeste and tell her, but he had to. This would probably be the last time he would ever see her, so he had to say good-bye. He began to sob.

"And please bring your bag," shouted the man through the doorway.

Lucien stopped and looked back at the man.

"I need my bag?" So they'd be taking him straight to Drancy, not to rue des Saussaies.

"Yes, bring your instruments. My wife's condition has worsened. You must come right away."

"My instruments?"

"You're Doctor Auteuil, right? I was told you live in apartment 4C. Please, we must hurry."

Lucien felt he was about to faint and steadied himself against a bookcase. His chest started heaving. His first instinct was to curse the man out, but he stopped himself. When his breathing returned to normal, he walked back to the doorway.

"Doctor Auteuil lives in 3C."

A look of panic came over the man's face, and he turned and sprinted down the corridor to the stairs. Lucien slowly closed the door and leaned against it. He gazed down at the olive and crimson rug in the foyer, his mind a complete blank. Suddenly, he felt a warm sensation about his thighs and crotch. Lucien let out a great sigh. He hadn't pissed himself in thirty years.

Incredibly tired and emotionally drained, Lucien shuffled straight to the liquor cabinet in the living room and pulled out a glass tumbler and a decanter of cognac. He stared at the glass, then tossed it onto the sofa and drank straight from the decanter.

When he fell back asleep, he dreamed he'd designed a secret hiding place for Manet. It was a box with a lid sitting in the middle of a room. When a button on the front was pushed, the lid opened, and Lucien's father popped out like a jack-in-the box. He was dressed like one of those orthodox rabbis with a prayer shawl and a yarmulke, and he was laughing hysterically at his son.

13

OOD, THEN I CAN PICK YOU UP AROUND EIGHT. OH NO, NOTHING fancy, just a small private dinner party. Yes, yes, your blue-gray evening dress will be quite appropriate. You'll be the toast of the evening, my Adele. But now you must excuse me; it's been a very busy day, and I have to get back to work. I've got a visitor waiting here who's been very patient. Good-bye, my love."

Schlegal smiled as he put down the receiver. The thought of arriving at the party tonight with Adele on his arm made him quite happy. Every man on the general's staff would be jealous of him, and that's exactly the reaction he wanted. He considered himself very lucky to associate with a woman of Adele's status. Most of the French women Germans came into daily contact with were working-class types— waitresses, shopgirls, and chambermaids, as well as the cooks and laundresses who worked in the homes of Germans.

Even though the high command frowned upon Germans having intimate relations with French women except with registered whores, German soldiers always slept with these working-class French women. Sex became the common language of the Occupation. Still, there were rules. Germans weren't permitted to walk arm in arm with a French woman in public or to take her back to the barracks. A German soldier of any rank would rarely get the chance to sleep with a respectable bourgeois French woman, most of whom would die before having sex with a German. That was why Schlegal considered his finding Adele a miracle.

Schlegal had been sitting on top of a large wooden desk and now swiveled around to face the opposite direction. Stretching out his legs, he clicked the heels of his shiny black boots, then crossed his arms. In front of him sat an elderly man in a wooden chair with his arms tied behind him. The old man's head drooped, and drool dripped from the corner of his mouth.

"Let's see. Where were we? Ah, yes. I asked you to tell me the whereabouts of Mendel Janusky, and you said you had no idea. Then I said you were a filthy lying pig, and if you didn't tell me, I would teach you a very hard lesson. But you're in luck, Monsieur Deligny. Because I'm going out with one of the most beautiful women in Paris tonight, I'm in a very charitable mood. So, I'll give you one more chance. Where is Janusky? You *do* know who he is, don't you? Let me refresh your memory. Janusky is a gentleman of the Hebrew persuasion and very, very rich. Maybe the richest man in Paris. The former owner of the Madelin Steel Works. Where you had been an executive since 1932."

Schlegal held a glossy black-and-white photo in front of Deligny's face. It was a formal portrait of an imposing-looking man in his sixties, dressed in a suit, standing next to a table. His right hand, which had a very large and ornate ring on it, was resting on a book on the table.

"Do you recognize him, monsieur?"

The old man made a gurgling sound.

"This filthy Jew has an estimated fortune of over 100 million francs and possesses one of the greatest art collections in the entire world, one that Reich Marshal Hermann Göring admires very much and wishes to take off Monsieur Janusky's hands. Because once we find Monsieur Janusky, he won't be having much time for art appreciation. We don't consider this man just another rich, thieving Jew but an *enemy* of the Reich. He's used his millions to help hundreds and hundreds of Jews throughout Europe to escape. Janusky found refuge for a bunch of Hungarian Jews in India of all places. It's amazing what your client has accomplished. I'm really looking forward to meeting him. So, please tell me where I can find him."

The old man said nothing.

"I guess it's time for your lesson."

Schlegal picked up a small square box with a lever attached to it and examined it closely.

"When I was a little boy in Leipzig, I had a box like this to run my electric train set. I was mad about model trains then, spent hours playing with them. If I remember right, it had a lever just like this to switch on the electric current, and if I turned the lever to the right…"

An ear-piercing scream rang out that seemed to reverberate for a full minute off the white plaster walls of the office. Schlegal's eyes followed the wires from the box, which ran along the wooden floor, and up to the crotch of the old man, who was slumped over as if someone had punched him in the stomach.

"Heinz," said Schlegal, "are you sure there's enough juice coming from this box?"

"Why yes, Colonel," said a flustered Captain Bruckner, who was sitting on a wooden chair in the corner of the room next to two other officers, Captain Wolf and Lieutenant Voss. "Please, try again. But this time, keep the lever all the way to the right."

Another scream commenced, and it continued for quite a long time. Schlegal didn't look at his guest but just stared at the box during the screaming. The old man's upper body had jolted upright against the back of the wooden chair to which he was tied. When his cries began to produce a ringing in the Gestapo colonel's ears, Schlegal turned the lever to the left, and there was an abrupt silence.

"Where will I find Mendel Janusky, Monsieur Deligny?"

The question was met with silence.

"I'm sorry, I missed that," said Schlegal, who then quickly turned the lever to the right and back to the left to produce a short sharp scream.

"Still didn't hear you." A turn of the lever and another short scream.

The Gestapo colonel then amused himself by producing a whole series of screams of different lengths and pitches in an effort to create a kind of melody, which greatly entertained his staff officers.

"Did that sound at all like *Lili Marlene*?" Schlegal asked his staff.

Bruckner, Voss, and Wolf laughed hysterically and shook their heads.

"Too bad. Let me ask you one more time, Monsieur Deligny, where is Mendel Janusky?"

The old man's full head of long white hair was drenched with sweat and hung down over his eyes. He lifted his head up a little to look at Schlegal, who now walked right up to him holding the box, his fingers on the lever.

The Gestapo officer had interrogated many a man since he'd arrived at 11 rue des Saussaies in 1941. Torture revealed a lot about a man's character or moral fiber, he believed, whether he was French, German, Jew, or gentile. When he'd first started doing this type of work, he'd expected to come across men who wouldn't crack, even under the most barbarous conditions, but that rarely happened. He wanted to meet some really brave men, but to his disappointment, they always broke down and talked. So he knew what was going to happen next.

With great difficulty, the old man took a deep breath, and in a low, almost inaudible voice, said, "Rue de Tournon, at Gattier's, the wine merchant."

"Now that wasn't so hard, was it?" said Schlegal. He tossed the box on his desk. He nodded to Bruckner, who immediately left the room.

"My goodness, what time is it? Lunchtime already?" asked Schlegal, glancing at his wristwatch. "I'm starving. Gentlemen, will you join me for lunch at the Café Daunou?"

His officers exchanged smiles and picked up their gloves and caps. They knew their boss was in a good mood and would be paying. As the three Germans made for the door, Schlegal stopped and reached over for the box on the desk, turning the lever all the way to the right. "I hope you'll excuse us, Monsieur Deligny," he said in a very solicitous tone. "We'll be back in an hour or two to continue our conversation."

The screaming could still be heard as they reached the street four flights below.

14

I FIXED YOU A REAL CUP OF TEA."

Celeste was surprised to see Lucien in the kitchen first thing in the morning. He proudly handed Celeste a cup with a saucer. She remembered her husband telling her that on a trip to England, he'd found out that you never just give someone a cup of tea; it always has to be on a saucer. She smiled at the gesture.

"Real tea?" said Celeste. "Not brewed from catnip leaves?"

"Taste it."

"Good God. It is real tea," she said, holding the first sip in her mouth, relishing the taste. In wartime, Celeste had learned how to be thankful for the smallest pleasures in life. The finest champagne wouldn't have tasted better.

For some time now, Lucien had been bringing home hard-to-get food like cheese, butter, and coffee. She knew it was from the black market but didn't ask any questions. The other thing she learned during the Occupation was that law-abiding citizens now turned a blind eye to the breaking of the law. She could see that Lucien was very proud to provide these things.

"Thank you, it's delicious."

"Now, I must be off. Lots of work to be done at the office," said Lucien cheerfully. He gave her a quick kiss on the forehead and grabbed his suit jacket from the back of the stainless steel kitchen chair. "What's on your schedule today?"

"Nothing much. I heard there's toilet paper at a shop on rue de Bretagne. I'll try my luck." Shopping during the Occupation meant women standing in long lines to try to buy the bare essentials.

"If they run out, I'll see if I can get my hands on some. See you tonight."

Celeste sipped her tea and stared at the gleaming white porcelain and stainless steel kitchen cabinets. Though she would've preferred wood cupboards, at least these were easy to clean. She placed her cup in the sink and went to the vestibule to get her hat, black felt with a pointy Robin Hood brim and white feather. She was glad she and Lucien had the same taste in women's fashion.

It was a cool summer morning, and Celeste enjoyed the breeze on her face as she walked along the boulevard de Sébastopol. The Germans had drained the life out of Paris, but at least they couldn't change its weather, she thought. She continued down to the Pont Notre-Dame and across the Seine. Looking at her wristwatch, she turned east and walked to Notre Dame. There were far more German tourist soldiers than Frenchmen and pigeons in front of the cathedral. Three Wehrmacht officers with cameras stopped snapping away and looked at her as she passed them. They murmured their approval to each other and smiled, but she ignored them. Inside the church were even more German soldiers walking along the aisles, gazing up at the great vaulted ceiling and the tall stained-glass windows. Some were kneeling in pews, praying, which surprised Celeste. She assumed that such people didn't believe in any kind of God.

Celeste sat in a pew but didn't pray. She never attended church on Sundays anymore but still liked the contemplative feel of the place. It was a good place to think and reflect, a tiny oasis of comfort in a disappointing life. What was the use of praying for happiness anyway? It hadn't done her any good. She had been punished with the loss of her child then the abandonment by her father. She couldn't take any more heartbreak. And her marriage had slipped away. Celeste had once truly loved Lucien, but for some reason, that love slowly evaporated like water in a bowl. It was once full, and now there was just a tiny puddle left at its bottom. No one had tipped the bowl over; it just simply vanished over time.

Celeste walked out of the cathedral and across the Petit Pont to the Left Bank. Just before the boulevard Saint-Germain, she turned onto rue Dante and went into an apartment house. On the second-floor landing, she rang the bell of a unit.

The door opened, and a tall middle-aged man with wire-rim glasses faced her.

"Madame Bernard, so wonderful to see you. We're ready for you. This way, please."

"Thank you, Monsieur Richet."

At the dining room table sat a ten-year-old girl with freckled cheeks and brilliant blond hair in long pigtails. She stood up and curt-seyed to Celeste.

"All right, Sandrine, what is your math assignment for this week? Still fractions?" said Celeste, taking off her hat and sitting down next to the girl.

"Yes, Madame, but I still can't quite add wholes and fractions."

"You'll see, my love, in one hour, you'll be doing it with the snap of your fingers, like magic," said Celeste, kissing the girl on her cheek.

When the lesson was over, Richet came back into the dining room.

"I can't thank you enough for your help these past months. Sandrine's old tutor simply disappeared."

"Many, many people in Paris have disappeared," said Celeste.

"Thank you, Madame Bernard, for my lesson," said Sandrine with a curtsey.

"Practice those fraction exercises, and you'll see how well you do on the next exam."

Richet stood behind his daughter, wrapped his arms around her, and kissed her on the top of her head.

"Sandrine, why don't you go to the park for a while," said Richet.

15

MONSIEUR, I TOLD YOU THAT I WOULDN'T BE PART OF THIS anymore."

Manet, who was sitting on a plush red velvet sofa, smiled at Lucien, who was pacing back and forth in front of the enormous fireplace in the hunting lodge in Le Chesnay.

"All I'm asking for is a little advice."

"Advice like that can get me killed. And you, as well."

"Just take a look around and tell me what you think. I'm betting a man with your creative talents could think of another ingenious idea."

Lucien knew the old man was just buttering him up, and it was working. As he gazed around the house, his eyes lit up when he saw that there were far more possibilities here than in the apartment. The building was typical of the great hunting lodges built in the seventeenth century for the nobility. Hidden in a dense forest on a piece of land probably a kilometer square, the house, with its steep slate roof and corner towers, was a good out-of-the-way place to hole up from the Gestapo. Properties like these were kept in the family, passed down through the generations. It must have at least thirty rooms, with a kitchen that was bigger than his own apartment.

Manet walked over to Lucien. Putting his hand on Lucien's shoulder in a grandfatherly manner, he half-whispered, as though there were other people in the room.

"The two guests of this house would be quite grateful for your help—fifteen thousand francs is how grateful they'd be. And I'd be quite grateful."

Lucien's heartbeat raced. The first twelve thousand francs were going fast. There were just too many nice things on the black market. Cheese, eggs, butter, real wine, meat, and even chocolate were all available—for an astronomical amount of money. Most of the black market goods, Lucien discovered, came from the rural areas in northern France. The hicks out in the countryside now had the last laugh; they ate much better than city dwellers, and they sold their produce on the black market for fifty times the normal price. City people with kinfolk in the country were lucky; they were permitted to get family parcels of food through the mail. The Germans made things even worse with their plundering. The official exchange rate between the franc and the mark made them instantly rich, and soldiers descended on Paris like locusts devouring crops. First, they swallowed up luxury goods like perfume, then staples like wine and tobacco. When their tour of duty ended, German officers would board trains with dozens of suitcases filled with their booty. Yes, the fifteen thousand francs, thought Lucien, would come in very handy.

"My guests told me about a property of theirs that looks over the Côte d'Azur," Manet said. "A wonderful place to put a house after the war. With lots of glass and maybe a wide balcony that stretches across the whole back. The view is incredible. And the sea is an indescribable shade of blue. You should see it."

"The Côte d'Azur?" said Lucien. "Well yes, I'd like to see that. But I would need transit papers to travel south."

"No problem, I can arrange it."

"Really?"

Manet threaded his arm through Lucien's and started to guide him gently through the house. Thirty rooms was a lot of ground to cover in an afternoon. They started in the attic and worked their way down, slowly moving from room to room. The floor-to-ceiling paneled walls with high baseboards were a possibility; here, the walls were thick enough to fit a body. Still, Lucien wanted to keep looking. The enormous entrance hall contained a beautiful wood staircase with a thick carved railing. The staircase started from a huge wood-paneled newel post. It reminded Lucien of the base of the statue of Mercury in the rue de Galilée apartment. The top could be hinged, and two people could pull it shut by a strap, but it was too tight for two adults. Lucien gazed up at the ceiling and saw that it was supported by huge exposed wood beams. He immediately knew the second-floor structure could be used.

On top of the main beams was overlaid a series of smaller ones at right angles on which thick plank flooring was attached with pegging. These beams were about thirty centimeters deep, which told Lucien a person could lie down on his back within them. The plank flooring could be removed and hinged to create a trap door of sorts. To prevent a person from falling through the plaster ceiling between the main beams, some board reinforcing would have to be installed. During a search, though, Gestapo boots would be running on top of the guests just a couple of centimeters from their faces. As he'd realized at the rue de Galilée, the cleverest design wouldn't work if Manet's guests panicked and cried out. This seemed too risky.

He discovered a window seat in an oriel window on the second floor at the rear of the house that was deep enough and wide enough to work as a hiding place. As he walked through the house, considering more options, the excitement was building up within him again. He found himself enjoying the challenge of outwitting the Germans, realizing it was a more powerful lure than the fifteen thousand francs. He could see crazed Germans tearing through the house in a hopeless effort to find their quarry. But all the time, the Jews would be right under their noses. Then finally, a Gestapo officer would give the order to leave, saying the Jews weren't there. Thinking about this had the effect of a handful of amphetamines, and Lucien quickened his pace through the rooms, forcing poor Manet to struggle to keep up with him.

"Why not the back of a closet?" asked Manet as they entered the master bedroom.

"That's the first place they'd look," said Lucien impatiently.

He stopped and saw how tired Manet was. Lucien wasn't ready to make his final decision and needed to continue looking.

"Please, monsieur. Go downstairs and wait for me. Let me help you."

"I'm fine. Let's keep going."

Lucien held Manet's elbow as they mounted a short flight of steps that led to a small study. As he put his foot on the first step, it slipped and Lucien fell forward, bashing his knee into the steps.

"Goddamn it!" he cried, clutching his knee in pain.

Manet stooped to help him up.

"Let me be, I'm all right," said Lucien.

Manet sat on the steps to rest.

"Why did they put the steps here?" asked Manet.

"It's just to give the floor a level change and provide more head-room for the library that's right below us."

"I see. It's to separate the study from the bedroom here."

"Yes, just four steps," said Lucien. "It's a nice detail. I would've done the same thing."

As he massaged his kneecap, he gazed at the steps.

"Hold on, I'll be right back." Lucien hobbled downstairs, leaving Manet sitting there with a puzzled look.

Two minutes later, he came back quite excited, with only a trace of a limp.

"It'll work. It'll work!" He was exultant. "They can hide under these stairs."

"How would they get under there?"

"Simple. I'll hinge the steps at the top. They'll lift them open, slip in, and drop them back down. There'll be a latch on the inside so no one could lift it up. I'll keep the carpet runner in place, and it'll hide the joint where it opens up." Both ends of the steps ran into walls so there were no sides; they seemed to melt into the interior of the bedroom. The Germans would probably never notice them. He knew from the fine workmanship on the rue Galilée job that Manet's people could make the stair hinges undetectable. The existing steps would be carefully dismantled then reassembled onto a wooden frame with hinges along its top. The same runner that matched the carpet would cover the steps. Lucien was exultant over his design, brimming with pride as if he'd just won the Prix de Rome. Delighted with his own ingenuity, he experienced the same sense of exhilaration that had swept over him at the rue Galilée.

"That's brilliant, my boy. But what would they lie on?"

"On a thin mattress. And there's just enough room for two people to lie side by side."

"I knew you'd do it," said Manet, clapping Lucien on his back. "I'll need a drawing as quickly as possible."

"Of course, monsieur, right away."

"My guests will be quite pleased to hear the news. They'll—"

"Stop. I don't want to know a damn thing."

"Yes, Monsieur Bernard, I apologize. It's the excitement of the moment."

"And one more thing."

"Yes, monsieur?"

"This is absolutely the last job I'm doing."

"Absolutely," replied Manet.

16

ADELE WASN'T JOKING WHEN SHE SAID SHE WOULDN'T FORGIVE Lucien for missing her fashion show. Nothing in the world was more important to her. That was one of the things he liked most about her. She was as intent on success in her career as he was in his. Even more so, it seemed.

Lucien arrived at her showroom on rue du Colisée twenty minutes to one and stood in the rear. This was the best spot to see any movie stars in attendance. Adele's shows always attracted celebrities; they never failed to come. They loved Adele. Lucien also loved to feast his eyes on Adele's fashion models. So many beautiful women in one place at one time. But this afternoon, Lucien was especially interested in seeing one particular woman—Bette Tullard. Since they met that first evening near Le Chat Roux, he couldn't get the image of that beautiful face out of his mind. Sometimes when he was drawing in his office, he'd begin to daydream about her. He knew she would be here, because without Bette, there would be no show.

The showroom was a two-story high space with white plaster walls and a black marble floor. Although he didn't design it, Lucien still admired its elegant interior. The room began to fill up, mostly with well-dressed women, a few accompanied by men. They sat in black metal folding chairs arranged in a semicircle around a beautiful curving stair with black marble treads and white plaster sidewalls topped by a continuous chrome railing. Lucien noticed some Wehrmacht officers in attendance. After two years of the Occupation, the French now mixed together with Germans in public events like this without shame.

Lucien knew the officers weren't interested in the dresses but what was inside them.

Sure enough, as one o'clock came near, Suzy Solidor and Simone Signoret made their appearance. A buzz of noise rose from the audience like bees around a hive. Everyone craned their necks to see them. Both women were beautifully outfitted in Adele's creations, Solidor in a pretty dark blue outfit with a crimson hat and Signoret in a black suit and matching hat. They waved to everyone and stopped to talk to people they knew. The women took seats that had been reserved for them in the front row. Others joined Lucien in standing at the back since the room was now filled to capacity.

The war had just about extinguished haute couture in Paris, and many fashion houses had closed down. It was to Adele's credit that she kept hers going. The industry's skilled workers who made the clothes, many of them Jews, had escaped south to Vichy or were rounded up and deported. The Germans, who recognized France's leadership in fashion, wanted the fashion industry transferred to Berlin, but later rescinded the order because of its sheer impracticality. They realized Germany had no fashion talent even remotely on a par with France's.

Like food, fabrics were rationed. Wool and leather, along with expensive fabrics like silk, lace, and velvet, became impossible to get. (Because of the restrictions on the amount of cloth that could be used—such as no more than one meter for a blouse—the fashions that Adele and everyone else showed were now simpler and lighter.) Any couture fashions that had remained in Paris at the beginning of the Occupation, Adele told Lucien, had been snapped up by German officers and sent back home to their wives and girlfriends. Despite the shortages and deprivations of the Occupation, Adele said Parisian women had vowed to remain chic and elegant. It was a matter of French pride for girls to look good in front of the enemy, to show them that they couldn't take away their beauty.

Parisian women exercised great creativity because of the shortages. When hairdressers ran out of salon products and could no longer perm hair, women covered their heads with hats and turbans designed from scraps of cloth. Since flowers and feathers were available, they became the main decoration on hats, often to a very gaudy effect, Lucien thought. The greatest coup he had seen was how the women made the heavy, thick wooden clogs into a fashion statement. Not only did they stretch what they were given, but many women also defied the German ban on wearing the colors of the French flag by wearing blue, white, and red buttons and belts.

Jazzy music from a phonograph wafted down from the top of the curving stair, signaling the show was about to begin. People settled in their seats and stopped talking. Then to Lucien's great pleasure, Bette slowly walked down the stair. She was stunning in black high heels and a white dress with black lapels, capped by a black scarf.

She stopped on the next to last step and smiled to the audience. "Welcome, ladies and gentlemen, to the House of Bonneau. Today we're presenting some very chic designs that you will love. They'll show that, despite the times, French beauty and French haute couture still thrive."

Bette raised her arm up toward the top of the stair, and the first model descended. A pretty girl with shoulder-length blond hair, she wore a full black skirt and white blouse with a wide floppy black hat. The audience burst into wild applause. At the bottom of the stair, she walked the semicircle of the first row, pausing in front of Solidor and Signoret, then went behind the stair to a rear door. Bette had moved off to the far right side of the room to watch the parade of models. Down the stairs came more models. Most of them wore blouses and skirts with square shouldered jackets along with floppy hats. A few modeled strapless evening gowns with elbow-length gloves and bright colored sashes around the waist. The other dresses were mostly short-sleeved and knee-length, with scarves and matching cloth handbags. Lucien admired one hat that showcased Adele's creativity—floppy and fun, it was made completely of braided paper.

The models were all attractive and slim, but Lucien couldn't take his eyes off Bette. When he caught her attention, she nodded and beamed a big smile at him. He was quite flattered, as some of the German offi-cers cast a quick envious glance in his direction.

Lucien noticed that the material looked like real silks, lace, and leather. He thought Adele had told him all that stuff had been exported to Germany. He paid close attention to one model's clothes because he needed to tell Adele enthusiastically how much he liked that particular outfit. Once after a show, he had told her he loved her designs and she had asked him which one, but when he couldn't pinpoint an exact one, she got very mad.

After the last model came down, Adele slowly and regally descended the stairs to great applause and cheering. Lucien could see how much she loved the adulation. After waving and throwing kisses, she imme-diately went over to Solidor and Signoret to give them hugs. Everyone circled round them to congratulate Adele and get a closer look at the movie stars. Bottles of champagne were broken out and people imbibed with gusto. Leave it to Adele to scrounge up the real stuff.

Lucien made his way through the mob of people and found Bette.

"Monsieur Bernard, I'm so glad you came."

"I'm flattered you remember me."

"I always remember a handsome—and creative—man," she said, shaking his hand.

"Congratulations on your show, it was magnificent. All those won-derful designs."

"It was hard as hell to put something together that good these days, let me tell you."

"Lucien. Lucien," trilled a voice from afar.

"Ah, I believe the boss is calling you. It was so nice to see you again."

Bette disappeared into the crowd, and Lucien walked over to Adele, who was still surrounded by admirers.

"Now, my brilliant architect, which of my designs did you like best?"

"Definitely was the navy blue skirt with the matching jacket and that wonderful braided paper hat."

17

W HO IS IT?"
"It's Aubier. I've got your food."

Cambon, whose stomach had been growling from hunger for the last two days, was about to unlock the door when he realized it was Thursday. Aubier always came on Fridays. Every Friday evening at 8:00 p.m. for the last six months, the entire time Cambon had been hiding in the apartment on the rue Blomet.

"It's not Friday; what the hell are you doing here?"

"I can't make it on Friday. Open up," whispered Aubier through the thick wood-paneled door. "Do you want your food or not?"

Cambon didn't move. He was thinking how unusual it was for Aubier to change his schedule. But his stomach persuaded him to open the door. Maybe Aubier would have a tin of sardines or a hunk of salami. Sitting alone in the apartment all these months, Cambon thought of little else but food. Once one of France's biggest clothing manufacturers, with palatial houses in the city and country, he could have any kind of food he desired—steak from America, olives from Greece, even walrus from the Arctic Circle if he'd wanted. Now, here he was starving to death, viewing a few morsels of moldy bread as a banquet.

"Hold on," he whispered. He was already planning his meal for the evening while he quietly unlocked the door. A bottle of wine would be wonderful. He'd had his last one four months ago. He opened the door a crack to see the tan leathery face of Aubier, his former servant from his home on the rue Copernic. Aubier flashed him a big smile of yellowed teeth and pulled an apple from a paper bag. Cambon's eyes lit up at that beautiful sight—it was easier to find gold on the streets of Paris than fruit. He opened the door just enough to let Aubier pass through. But the old servant came crashing into the foyer onto his face, pushed from behind by three plainclothes Gestapo officers in brown leather overcoats. Cambon shoved a console table in their path and ran into the rear bedroom, straight to an ornate four-poster bed. He pulled a revolver from beneath the mattress and then sat on the bed. As the first Gestapo man came through the bedroom door, Cambon calmly aimed and fired off a round, hitting the man in the left thigh. The officer dropped to the floor like a sack of potatoes. The officer directly behind him pulled back and ducked behind the wall next to the door. With his revolver in hand, he came out from behind the wall, blasting away, putting four bullets in Cambon, who was still sitting on the bed, making no effort to duck. He fell back, looking as if he'd just lain down for a nap.

✦ ✦ ✦

A few minutes later, Captain Bruckner walked into the room with his hands clasped behind his back and silently surveyed the situation.

"Fuckin' Jew bastard!" screamed the officer writhing in pain on the floor. "Did you see what he did to me? Did you kill the sonovabitch?"

Bruckner walked over to the bed and felt the pulse in Cambon's neck. "One dead Jew. How do you like that? He didn't want to be taken alive."

"I don't blame him after hearing what happens to these kikes once they go east," said the third officer, who was bending over his wounded comrade. "You know, that's the first time one of these kikes put up a fight. He went down fighting. I respect this Jew bastard."

"I sure as hell don't," yelled the wounded man, and the other two laughed at him. They helped him to his feet and dragged him to the door where Aubier was standing.

The wounded man glared at the Frenchman, who looked down at the floor.

"You've done your job, you can go," said Bruckner.

Aubier, clutching the bag of food to his chest, quickly made his way past Bruckner and out the door. Bruckner was always amazed at how easily the French would betray each other. Like Aubier, most did it in exchange for food or a favor, but many did it out of hatred or pure spite. His office would get dozens of letters a day, all of them beginning with some form of the sentence "I have the honor to draw your attention to a person living at…" The letter (usually unsigned) would finger a Jew with wealth: "He has an apartment full of fine objects." Many would ask the Germans to protect Christian families "from the actions of scheming Jews" or to help return a French husband "from the temptations of a Jewess."

And it wasn't always a Jew that was turned in. The French, who were always hungry because of the rationing, despised their fellow countrymen who ate well, so they too would be accused of plotting against the Reich. Was it a flaw in their national character or what? Of course, it served the Gestapo's purpose perfectly, and they encouraged it, but these people had absolutely no pride. The French even had a stock phrase for denunciation: "I'll go and tell the Germans about it." He hadn't expected them to act like this. It filled Bruckner with disgust because he had enormous respect for French culture and history. He wondered whether his own people would be as shameless as the French if they were under Occupation. They didn't understand that these denunciations deepened the contempt the Germans had for them and made it much easier to use brute force on the French.

"Duisberg, bring up the French police and have them round up the neighbors on this floor," said Bruckner. "If they aren't in, get some from the floor below. Bring them downstairs to me. We won't need the children. Becker here can handle Bloem."

Duisberg shouted down into the stairwell, and four police officers came running up the steps. They pounded on each of the wooden doors on the floor, screaming, "Police, everyone downstairs except children! Now!"

Like frightened mice inching out of their hiding places, the neighbors came out from behind their doors. Middle-aged men and women, a sixteen-year-old boy, an ancient man of about eighty-five, a woman around sixty, all silently gathered on the landing next to the lift.

"Move your asses!"

The group ran down the stairs, even the old man. Duisberg was behind them, cursing and shoving them down the four flights. No one uttered a word of protest or tried to make a run for it. As they passed each floor, Bruckner knew that all the residents were behind their doors listening and praying with all their might that there wouldn't be a knock on their door. Duisberg herded them through the beautiful wood-paneled entry foyer and out into the street. Bruckner followed behind and walked to his car parked at the curb and lit a cigarette. When everyone was lined up in front of him, he threw out his unfinished cigarette and paced up and down in front of them.

"I'm thinking of a number from one to twenty. Each of you guess what it is," Bruckner said in a jovial voice. He went to the end of the line and faced the sixty-year-old woman.

"What number?"

The woman was tongue-tied, and this annoyed the captain.

"Give me a number, old woman."

"Eleven."

"No, that's not it." He moved to the next in line, the sixteen-year-old boy.

"One."

"No. How about you, beautiful?" he asked an attractive middle-aged woman.

"Seven."

"You win!" he shouted with glee, like an announcer on a game show on the radio. With lightning-fast reflexes, he whipped his Luger from his holster and shot the woman in the middle of her forehead. She dropped like a rock to the gray sidewalk. Bruckner holstered his weapon, walked to the middle of the street, and looked up at the apartment blocks that surrounded him.

"This woman lived on the floor where a Jew was hiding," he shouted at the windows of the buildings on both sides of the street. "I bet she didn't even know he was there. But that really doesn't matter, my friends. If a Jew is found in your building, every last one of you will be shot. If a Jew is found on the fifth floor and you live on the second floor—you die. It's as simple as that."

Bruckner walked a few meters down the street with his arms folded. His eyes scanned the facades of the elegantly designed apartment blocks. Not a single person was standing at a window, but they were there all right, standing a meter or two away from the sash listening. He understood how the neighbors behind those windows felt. They all were going to look the other way; they didn't want to see what was going to happen to the people waiting in the street. That's the way the French acted during the Occupation—they didn't want to see. All that mattered was that *they* weren't rounded up.

Becker and Bloem came out of the building, and Duisberg helped them get Bloem into a black Citroën by the curb. Bruckner watched impassively and then walked over to the remaining apartment dwellers. They hadn't even looked down at the dead woman but kept their eyes straight ahead. The Gestapo captain resumed pacing directly in front of them, looking each person straight in the eyes as he passed. One of the most fascinating things he'd experienced in his three years of service in the Gestapo was how people acted when they were about to be shot. To his surprise, very few broke down and started sobbing or begged for their lives; most remained resigned to the fact and were quite stoic. The residents of rue Blomet were in the latter group. Like all Parisians, they seemed to accept that death was inevitable and that it could come at any hour of the day. It was odd that the French were so dignified in death but in life acted like shits squealing on each other.

He wondered what they were thinking about. If Bruckner were in their place and were about to die, he'd try to think of the most enjoyable experience he'd ever had. That wonderful summer in Bavaria when he lost his virginity to Claus Hankel's aunt. Seeing Trudy Breker's tits for the first time. Or the time he was awarded his university's highest award for athletic achievement in the long jump.

He stopped in front of a middle-aged man in a rumpled gray suit who stared straight ahead. Maybe he was off in his own world, remembering something fun he had once done. Or was he betting that Bruckner only intended to execute one resident to make his point?

The Gestapo captain kept pacing for another minute, then returned to his car, leaned against the hood, and lit another cigarette.

"Well, ladies and gentlemen, it's getting late and I don't want to keep you any longer. Thank you for your time. Good night to you all."

18

A H, Monsieur Bernard, good to see you. Please, please come in."

Major Herzog looked very odd in civilian clothes. His dark green smoking jacket was quite handsome, and the cuff of his charcoal gray trousers broke just right on his polished chestnut-colored shoes. Lucien, who'd made sure no one saw him slip into the entrance of the apartment building on rue Pergolèse, quickly stepped into the apartment, slamming the door shut behind him.

Lucien saw that Herzog was amused by this. They both knew the French were in a precarious position, and they couldn't be seen in public socializing with their conquerors. That's why Lucien had been invited to dine with the major in his home. Lucien had said absolutely nothing for almost thirty seconds after Herzog had telephoned and extended the invitation. A debate had raged in his head whether to accept. Celeste had also been invited, but that had only been a formality; Herzog must have learned after a few months' duty in Paris that Frenchmen rarely mixed wives with pleasure, a combination of oil and water. Lucien had accepted because, like in peacetime, it was good business to socialize with the client. What the hell, thought Lucien, he'd see Herzog once and that would be the end of it.

German officers were quartered in the affluent western section of Paris, an area that was closed to all French citizens except residents who lived there. Herzog had arranged for Lucien to get a pass to visit him.

Lucien was surprised by the décor of the German's apartment. He'd expected curtains with a swastika pattern, busts of Hitler or at least a portrait of the Fuehrer in a heroic pose, maybe wearing knight's armor. But it was wonderfully decorated with modernist paintings, sculpture, and modern furniture. The rugs were of a dynamic abstract design in bold colors of olive, terra cotta, red, and black. He was instantly drawn to a sleek, streamlined piece of sculpture made of shiny stainless steel.

"This is quite magnificent, Major," said Lucien, careful not to touch the sculpture for fear of leaving fingerprints.

"It's interesting that you're drawn to my favorite piece, my Brancusi. A lot of his work has an almost phallic appearance. The American postal authorities once denied entry to one of his pieces because they thought it was a sex object."

"Puritans," said Lucien, who moved on to a painting of a grid of primary colors. "Is this a Mondrian?"

"A very small one, I'm afraid."

Lucien took a few steps back and gave the German's apartment a 360-degree sweep. It was an elegant dwelling built during Haussmann's reign, with beautiful walnut paneling and a white plaster ceiling done in very fine low-relief work. But it was the juxtaposition of the modern artwork and *moderne* furnishings with the fine nineteenth-century architectural detailing that made the interior so unique. He was impressed and quite envious at the same time, realizing that a German had better taste than he did.

"What an incredible flat. I would've thought that German officers lived—"

"In a cold stone barracks with just a cot, table, and chair with a picture of Hitler on the wall?" Herzog said, smiling. "No, we're allowed to secure our own quarters. This used to belong to a Jewish fellow who wouldn't cooperate with the Reich. So he had to forfeit his property."

"And where is he living now?" Lucien asked, realizing a millisecond after he spoke that it was an incredibly naive question.

"In somewhat less comfortable accommodations," replied Herzog. He poured his guest a glass of cognac.

"Oh," said Lucien as he took the glass from his host, who was pouring one for himself.

"I think you're surprised by my taste in art," said Herzog with a smile. "A bit avant-garde for a soldier of the Reich?"

"Well, I..." Lucien was thinking exactly that.

"I try to keep an open mind when it comes to collecting. Come, let me show you something that I'm especially proud of," said Herzog, leading Lucien down a dark corridor.

Herzog switched on the overhead light and pointed to two small paintings on the wall. One was of a lush green landscape along a riverbank and the other was a portrait of a well-fed man in a black outfit and hat.

"This is my Corot," said Herzog, nodding toward the landscape. "And my Franz Hals. So you see, Monsieur Bernard, not everything has to be decadent and modern."

"They're beautiful. Look at the brushwork on the trees," exclaimed Lucien.

"Two extraordinary masters. No one can capture an expression like Hals."

"They must have been quite expensive."

"Not at all. A gentleman who was about to take a long trip didn't need them anymore," replied Herzog. "And he let me have them for almost nothing."

Lucien could imagine the kind of trip the man was on.

"You've started quite a collection."

Herzog laughed. "Just a modest beginning. But I hope to pick up more bargains in Paris. There's an incredible collection owned by a Jew named Janusky whom the Gestapo is going crazy trying to find. I'd love to get my hands on the two Franz Hals portraits he's supposed to have. But you can be sure Reich Marshal Göring will have first crack at the art. But I am expecting some very beautiful engravings by Dürer any day now."

Lucien said nothing and looked down at his glass. He knew that the acquisition was from another man leaving on a "trip."

Herzog raised his glass. "To great architecture and the architects who create it," he said.

Lucien lifted his glass. He thought this was a good opportunity to kiss his client's ass. After all, the Germans, not Manet, were his real clients. "To great architecture and the great clients who allow architects to create."

Herzog seemed amused by Lucien's toast and took a sip of his cognac. "Come and sit down," he said, beckoning to a Barcelona chair designed by a fellow German, Mies van der Rohe.

The chair was quite comfortable, and Lucien crossed his legs and sipped his cognac. He was beginning to get into the spirit of the evening and relaxed a bit. "Did you get all the furniture here in Paris?" he asked, patting his hand on the seat.

"Just a few pieces, most of them were shipped from Hamburg where I was living before the war started," said Herzog. "Since I'm going to be here for quite a while, I wanted to feel at home." He seemed to expect that Lucien and all the rest of the French accepted this plain fact of life. The Germans were here to stay. Herzog reclined on a chaise lounge and reached for the bottle of cognac to refill his glass.

"Your pony chaise is very handsome. I met Le Corbusier in the '30s. A very important talent," said Lucien, even though he thought the man an arrogant shit.

"Indeed, I've driven out to see the Villa Savoye. I'd always wanted to see it. A tremendous building," exclaimed Herzog. "Where is Le Corbusier these days? Switzerland?"

"He made it over the Pyrenees into Spain, I believe."

"Architects who run away live to design another day, mm?"

"You've got a very fine eye for design, Major," replied Lucien, changing the subject.

"Dieter. Please call me Dieter."

"If you call me Lucien."

"My father may have turned me into an engineer, but he couldn't take away my love of architecture and design, Lucien."

It bothered Lucien that a German could value such beautiful things—like an ape appreciating a string of rare pearls or an ancient Grecian red and black vase. They were monsters without a shred of decency, yet they could hold the same things in high esteem as a Frenchman could. It didn't seem right.

"I brought some things from my time at the Bauhaus, but I purchased most of it over the years. It wasn't that expensive, either. Most Germans think this stuff is decadent trash, and few people want it in their homes."

"They prefer a romantic ticky-tacky landscape on the wall. Or a faux Louis XIV chair," said Lucien with great resignation.

"Exactly. Pure garbage."

"To garbage," said Lucien before he drained his cognac. While the liquor oozed down his throat, he noticed a photo of a woman and child on a glass and steel end table. He had been debating whether Herzog was a family man or not.

"Your wife and daughter?" asked Lucien, nodding toward the picture.

Herzog got up from his seat, went over to the end table, and handed Lucien the photo.

"Yes, my wife Trude and my daughter Greta; she just turned nine."

"Very nice. So does your wife share your modernist tendencies?" asked Lucien, curious because Celeste hated what he liked.

"Oh, yes, she's a very talented graphic designer, but now she only designs propaganda material for the Reich. We're hoping when the war ends, she'll go back to real design."

"You must miss them."

"I haven't seen them in nine months, but I get leave in a few weeks. I can't wait to see my daughter," replied the German with a sad look in his eyes. "I've collected many gifts to bring them."

Herzog put back the photo. Most parents would next start boring the hell out of their guest by relating every school prize their kid had won in the last five years, but Herzog said nothing more.

Herzog held the bottle toward Lucien for a refill. "Your factory design was quite impressive. The horizontal bands of glass and the way they butt into the concrete piers were magnificent."

Lucien emptied his glass and immediately it was refilled. A warm glow within his chest was growing warmer by the minute. "Thank you...Dieter."

"Those wonderful arches just soar through the space, and they can support all those cranes and hoists. Excellent work."

There was nothing that Lucien—or any architect—liked better than flattery laid on with a trowel. Whether it came from a Frenchman or a Nazi, it was just as satisfying.

"I think you'll be pleased with the next building," Lucien slurred.

"I like that your architecture reflects its function with pure form."

"Ah, I hope Colonel Lieber sees it that way."

"Don't concern yourself with Lieber. All he cares about is that the plants get built on schedule. And I'll see to that."

From the far end of the living room, a pair of paneled sliding doors parted, and a young German corporal appeared and stood at attention.

"Major, your supper is ready."

"Thank you, Hausen. You can go back to the barracks. Come, Lucien, a rack of lamb is awaiting us."

With a bit of difficulty due to all the cognac he'd already consumed, Lucien lifted himself from the Barcelona chair and joined his new soul mate for supper.

19

"SOL, I THINK I SAW A LIGHT AT THE GATE."

Geiber knew his wife wasn't the hysterical type. In fact, he admired her for always being so calm and levelheaded. So the minute she said this, Geiber dropped his book and went into action. When Miriam saw him leap out of the leather armchair, she immediately did what she was supposed to do in an emergency. They had only minutes to act. If they hesitated, it would mean certain death for both of them.

Geiber first ran to the kitchen, located on the first floor at the back of the great hunting lodge. He flung open the rear door and tossed an old felt hat on the stone path to the garden. Leaving the door wide open, he then sprinted up the kitchen service stair as fast as a sixty-eight-year-old could. Outside the second-floor master bedroom, he met Miriam, who was holding the small leather bag, packed weeks before with their forged papers, cash, and a change of clothing for both of them. He looked straight into her dark brown eyes and stroked her rouged cheek.

"Are you ready, my dear?"

"God, I hope this works," said Miriam. Her hands were trembling terribly, and her knees threatened to give out at any second.

"Follow me," whispered Geiber.

They hurried through the master bedroom to a flight of four carpeted steps that led to a study, and knelt down as if they were going to offer a prayer before it. Geiber placed his hands on the edge of the bottom step and slowly lifted up the entire stair, which was hinged at the upper floor level. It took all his strength to raise it high enough so that Miriam could slip under it with the bag. She crawled in and placed her frail body at the very back of the cavity, parallel to the steps.

"Are you in?" gasped Geiber, straining to hold up the stairs.

"For God's sake, hurry, Sol."

Geiber slid under the stairway, letting it fall back into place with a heavy thud. Sliding next to Miriam, he fastened two bolts that locked the stairs in place. He was breathing so heavily he thought he would pass out. His back was against Miriam's chest, and he could feel her heart pounding. He moved the bag up by his chest, laid it on its side, and unlatched it. Miriam placed her arm over her husband's body and tightly grasped his hand. She hid her face against the back of his head. For just a fraction of a second, it made him forget about the approaching danger.

Such a warm, comforting feeling, thought Geiber, like they were back in their big bed at home snuggling under the goose down duvet. It was mostly airless and pitch black in the cramped space under the stairs, but the mattress they were lying on was quite comfortable, and because the stairs were almost two meters wide, the Geibers could fully stretch out their legs. The underside of the steps was just centimeters from Geiber's face, so close he could smell the wood. They could do nothing now but wait, seconds passing like hours.

"Our fate's in God's hands," whispered Geiber. "They'll be inside any second, and we can't utter a sound. But there's something I've never told you. And I've got to tell you now."

"Now, Sol?"

"The first time I saw you was at L'Opéra Garnier. You were wearing a light blue gown; I couldn't take my eyes off you. After the opera, I had my carriage follow yours to your house. I bribed your footman to tell me your name, and I sent you a bouquet of roses anonymously the next day."

"*You* sent those roses. My father had a fit."

"Yes, it was me."

"I love you, you old fool."

There was an enormous crash at the front door, the sound of splintering wood, then shouting. Simultaneously, the couple's bodies jerked violently with fear. Men were running through the house yelling and cursing, their boots pounding on the wood planks of the lodge. They could hear furniture being overturned, tables crashing to the floor, bookcases yanked from walls, and cabinets violently emptied of their contents. Then what sounded like a stampede of horses came rushing up the main staircase. Men sprinted down the corridor and into the bedrooms. Miriam was so scared that she couldn't think anymore. Shutting her eyes tight, she began to silently sob.

Soldiers entered the master bedroom, yanking open the closet doors, rifling through the dresser drawers and the armoire, and flipping over the huge bed. After a few minutes, they ran out of the bedroom.

"There's no one here, Colonel," someone shouted.

"Impossible," answered a baritone voice. "Keep looking, they must still be around. Messier's never been wrong yet. Check the backs of the closets for a false wall; that's where we've found some before." There had been a pause in the commotion when the colonel spoke, but now it resumed at an even more furious pace.

Suddenly, someone ran back into the master bedroom and stomped up the flight of steps over Miriam and Geiber. The stairs sagged under the impact of the man's weight, almost touching Geiber's nose. A wave of panic swept over them. With superhuman effort, Miriam stifled a scream, squeezing the life out of her husband's hand. She felt her husband's body tremble uncontrollably as if he were having an epileptic fit. The soldier stayed in the small study, pulling all the books off the shelves that lined the walls from floor to ceiling, sending some of them crashing down on the stairs. The Geibers flinched every time a book came down upon them. When the soldier finished with the books, he started ripping out the wooden shelving. He ran back down the stairs, where he was met by another soldier.

"Did you check behind the bookcase? They hide in spaces behind those shelves, you know."

"What the hell did you think I was just doing?" yelled the soldier.

"Where the fuck are those kikes? I thought this would be an easy detail. Marianne is waiting for me in town."

"Which one's Marianne? You never said anything about her."

"The one with the great jugs who stole that case of wine for me that time. You remember, don't you?"

"What wine? You had wine and didn't tell me?"

One of the soldiers sat down heavily on the steps. Geiber and Miriam could feel the stairs creak and sag directly above them. With a German's body just ten centimeters away, their fright was unbearable. Miriam had almost passed out from fear and wished she would faint dead away to escape this torment. Both clenched their mouths shut with all their might. The tiniest sound would give them away.

"Christ, I'm beat running up all these goddamn steps. These houses are like fuckin' museums. Hold up for a moment."

"Better not let Schlegal see you sitting on your ass."

"Fuck him and all Gestapo bastards."

"You better get the hell up, or your ass will be in Russia."

"Just let me catch my breath. Schlegal's downstairs, anyway."

"Hurry up. I'm going down the hall here to look again."

The soldier didn't move from his spot on the stairs. The Geibers could hear the strike of a match, then smelled the faint aroma of a cigarette. As they waited and waited for the man to leave, the stress was too much to bear. To his horror, Geiber realized that he'd soiled himself. After about a minute, a strong smell filled the space. Then mercifully came the sound of a boot stamping out a cigarette butt on the floor. The steps creaked as the soldier rose from his seat.

"Jesus Christ, are you still here? Schlegal's coming down the hall," said a soldier.

"Do you smell something? Like shit?"

"You're going to be shit if Schlegal sees you."

"No, wait…I—"

"Stauffen, you goddamn moron," a voice yelled out. "Get moving and look for those kikes! Did you check the attic?"

"No, Colonel, I was just—"

"Asshole. You should've done that first. Get the hell up there now."

"Yes, Colonel."

The Geibers could hear more commotion down the hall and in the attic. After fifteen minutes, a group of soldiers congregated outside the master bedroom. The colonel's voice pierced the silence. "The back door was open. They must have gone out through the garden to a car at the rear of the property. But they won't get far. All of you fan out in the garden and sweep the area. Find the cesspool and see if they're in there. And *don't* shoot them, did you hear what I said? I want them alive."

The soldiers trudged down the main staircase and out the back door. There was complete silence, but the Geibers stayed where they were. The plan was to wait two hours before moving. It was like slowly waking up from a terrible nightmare, but it hadn't been a surreal dream created by their subconscious minds but a horribly real event. They were emotionally exhausted, completely drained. As their breathing slowly returned to normal, both could feel that their clothes were soaked through with sweat, as if they had jumped into a lake. Even the mattress was drenched. While they waited, their bodies began to ache from being frozen in the same position. Geiber was lying in his own feces, but he wasn't ashamed; all that mattered was that they had survived. He removed his hand from inside the bag and was relieved they wouldn't be needing the revolver. In hindsight, he wished he'd accepted the pharmacist's vials of cyanide.

20

Y OUR DRAFTSMANSHIP IS EXCEPTIONAL. MY WORK WAS NOWHERE near as good as this when I got out of school."

Alain Girardet looked down at the floor and tried to suppress a smile. Lucien smiled at his response because the young man knew his work was good, but it was important to seem humble at this moment. He would've done the same thing. Architectural work of any kind was virtually impossible to get in Paris, so he knew Alain was determined to walk out of here with a job. They sat across from each other at a table in the corner of Lucien's one-room office that Manet had graciously thrown rent-free into the deal. It was more professional for Lucien to be able to meet with Germans at an office than at his own apartment. Plus Celeste would have had a fit if the Germans had set foot in her home.

"Thank you, monsieur. You're most kind. I worked very hard in school, especially on my drawing. After all, it is the soul of architecture, isn't it?" answered Alain.

The kid could really kiss some ass, thought Lucien, but it won him over.

"Indeed it is," replied Lucien, realizing that at last, after interviewing a half-dozen candidates, here was the guy he wanted. He felt energized—and now asked the question all job applicants wanted to hear.

"If you were offered the job, when could you start?"

"Tomorrow," replied Alain, a little too eagerly. Lucien would've said the day after tomorrow to show that he wasn't so desperate. This kid must be dead broke.

Lucien flipped through the portfolio of drawings again to make sure that he was making the right decision. In the past, he'd hired draftsmen for his firm too impulsively and had regretted it. There was Michel, the middle-aged architect who'd come back after every lunch completely shitfaced. His line work, so beautiful when sober, resembled a four-year-old's in the afternoon. That's if he hadn't fallen asleep on his drafting table. Another memorable hiring choice was Charles, who had turned out to be the laziest bastard in all of France. It had taken him a month to draw a square.

With more factory work coming in, Lucien needed a draftsman to help crank out the drawings. He couldn't do it all himself, so he'd cajoled Herzog into upping his fee so that he could hire someone. Lucien knew he could get someone dirt cheap. And there was another reason a kid this age needed a job. Since the Occupation, thousands of young Frenchmen, who would have been eligible for military service if there had been a French army, were required to perform two years of mandatory labor for France. If a young man did not have a job, he would be "volunteered" into working in the Reich's war industries in Germany.

Lucien looked up at Alain to see if he could detect some visible character flaw. He seemed perfectly respectable, in his early twenties, of average height with sandy-colored hair and light brown eyes. He was also very fashionably dressed and still had nice leather-soled shoes, which made him presentable to the Germans. There was just one more hiring detail that Lucien had to attend to.

"Are your papers in order?"

"Yes, monsieur."

"May I see them?"

At all times, everyone in France had to carry their papers, an identity card similar to a passport listing all the personal details that the French bureaucracy and the German military found so important— date of birth, distinguishing marks, physical appearance, and home address. An "exemption from conscription" certificate was inserted in the boy's identity card, which surprised Lucien—he already was off the hook for compulsory service. That meant only one thing—that Alain knew someone of influence.

He handed the card back to Alain and smiled.

"I can give you two hundred francs a week to start, monsieur."

"That's most generous, Monsieur Bernard. I'll be honored to work for someone of such great talent. I want to learn from one of Paris's up-and-coming modernists," said Alain.

"That's fine," replied Lucien, who believed there was a limit to ass-kissing. "You'll be working on the construction documents for a factory that will make guns for the Luftwaffe." He pointed to the design drawings of the factory pinned to the wall behind him. "So you see, there's a hell of a lot of work coming through the office. And there probably will be a lot more. So you'll become my right-hand man if things go well."

Lucien had always given this spiel to a new man. The whole process of hiring was always full of high hopes. But it had never worked out in his practice before the war. The difference this time was that Lucien was hiring a kid right out of the university. This one could be molded like a lump of clay into what Lucien had always wanted in an employee. Alain had all the skills he needed, especially an understanding of how a building was actually constructed. He could see that in his drawings, showing the construction details of a building. They were as precise and accurate as an experienced architect could have done. Most kids fresh out of school had their heads up their asses when it came to construction. They had no idea how a building was put together.

"I'm most anxious to start, monsieur. Will tomorrow be all right?"

"Of course."

"I'll be here at seven."

"I'll be here at nine. At the end of the week, you'll get a key to the office so you can come in anytime you like." Lucien always waited a week before handing out a key to make sure the new guy seemed honest. He'd learned that lesson from Hippolyte, who'd disappeared with all his drafting supplies the second day on the job.

Alain began to gather his drawings from the table and put them in his brown cardboard portfolio.

"So, I see from your papers you live quite near," said Lucien, hoping to initiate a little informal conversation.

"Yes, monsieur."

"Live with your parents?"

"Yes, monsieur."

Lucien could see this was a dead end, but he was confident that Alain was talented and that was all that mattered. He put his hand on his shoulder and guided him to the door.

"Well, good-bye, Monsieur Girardet. I'll see you tomorrow," said Lucien, shaking his hand.

"Thank you again, monsieur. I look forward to working for you."

‡ ‡ ‡

Instead of waiting for the lift, Alain walked briskly down the four flights of stairs and into the street. As he reached the corner of rue de Châteaudun, a black Mercedes blew its horn and pulled alongside of him. The rear door swung open and a Gestapo officer in a black uniform ordered Alain to get in. Alain stopped and stared inside the car, then did as he was told. He slid into the rear passenger seat next to the officer, who was smoking a cigarette.

"So how did it go?" asked the man, who offered Alain a cigarette.

"He loved my work. I start tomorrow," Alain said with great pride, though he knew beforehand that Bernard would admire his portfolio. His drawing skills were exceptional.

"That's wonderful news. Your mother will be so pleased."

"It wouldn't have happened without you, Uncle Hermann," said Alain, lighting the cigarette.

"Nonsense. It was your talent that got you the position. I only told you about the architect. My boss is screwing his mistress, and that's how I heard about him," said the German, patting his nephew's shoulder with a black-gloved hand. "He's getting a lot of war work, and I thought he might need some help."

"Does your boss know that she's Bernard's mistress?" asked Alain, now more excited by his uncle's talk of sexual liaisons than by his new job.

"Probably, but she won't be the architect's mistress much longer, I bet."

"Well, thank you, Uncle, for all you've done. If there's anything I can do…"

"Think nothing of it, my boy. But now that you mention it, doesn't that man who lives on the fifth floor of your building have a heeb look to him?"

"Monsieur Valery? Mmm, kind of, I suppose. I'll make inquiries for you, Uncle, if you wish."

21

"THIS—IS MINE?"

"All yours, Monsieur Lucien," replied Manet, who handed the architect a set of keys on a shiny new key ring.

Lucien stared dumbfounded at the shiny 1939 navy blue Citroën Roadster parked at the curb. He ran his hands lovingly along the hood, then up onto the sloping convertible leather roof, as if he were caressing a woman's naked body. Lucien hadn't understood why Manet had asked to meet him at 29 rue du Renard. He'd said it was a surprise and it certainly was.

Parisians now rode bicycles to get around. No one drove in Paris anymore; automobiles had practically vanished from the streets. You could stand on the rue Saint-Honoré for twenty minutes at midday and maybe count half a dozen cars. The continuous ribbon of traffic that constantly circled the Place de la Concorde had also disappeared. Permits to drive a car were now issued by the authorities, and only to people in certain jobs, such as doctors, midwives, and firemen. Otherwise, you had to have a lot of pull with the Boche to get a driver's permit, which Manet certainly had. Even if this was a gift, and even if Lucien got a driver's permit, the Citroën would have to stay parked until the war was over because of the shortage of petrol. It was very difficult to find fuel—getting vintage champagne was easier.

"And here are your papers for your petrol ration. You'll need a car to get around to all the jobs you'll be doing. Can't get out to Tremblay on the Metro," Manet said with a great belly laugh.

"You are most generous, Monsieur Manet. I'm speechless. Never in my wildest dreams would I have thought I'd get a car. And such a beautiful one."

"Citroën is *my* favorite car. I knew you'd like it. Your designer's eye appreciates its fine lines. I can see that right away."

Lucien tacitly agreed with that observation. He circled the car, then got behind the wheel. The leather upholstery was soft and comfortable enough to fall asleep on, and the dashboard resembled an airplane cockpit. The engine started instantly and purred like a kitten when it idled. Adele would go crazy when she saw this. He would call her up and tell her to look out her window. He'd pull up and wave for her to come down. She'd cover him with kisses when she jumped in the passenger seat. There was an inn in Poissy in the countryside that they could go to for a long weekend.

Lucien was itching to take the Citroën for a spin. He almost sped off but remembered that Manet was still there on the sidewalk.

"Can I drop you anywhere, monsieur? Or maybe lunch on the avenue de l'Opéra? We can be there in five minutes," said Lucien with a big smile on his face.

"Lunch would be most enjoyable. But could you spare a moment and advise me on a matter? It's just upstairs here in this building."

"Why of course," replied Lucien, switching off the ignition.

They went through the entrance of the apartment building and into the lift. As the metal cage rose, the euphoria of the Citroën suddenly evaporated, and Lucien knew what was about to happen. A cloud of doom engulfed him. He smiled wanly at Manet and stared at the blue and white mosaic floor of the cab. All the horrible images of torture and death that had been tormenting him raced through his mind again. Then the image of him and Adele flying along in the Citroën through the French countryside overpowered the bad thoughts, and he began smiling again. The lift stopped at the fifth floor, and Manet led him to the double doors of apartment number 8. Once inside, Manet placed his hand on Lucien's shoulder in his now trademark grandfatherly manner.

"I'm having a devil of a time finding a hiding place. I just don't have your cleverness for such matters. I hate to bother you again, but where would you put it?"

Lucien remained silent for almost a minute. He walked to the tall narrow leaded-glass window and looked down at the hot August sun glistening on the roof of the Citroën parked in front of the building.

"Let me take a look around. I'm sure I can come up with something, but this will definitely be the last one, monsieur."

"Of course, whatever you say."

It was a very well-furnished six-room apartment with high ceilings and boiserie detailing. Beautiful rugs, plush embroidered sofas and armchairs sat on the honey-colored parquet flooring. Two large crystal chandeliers lit the main rooms. But its most dominating feature was in the salon, an enormous stone fireplace, whose opening was over two meters high and almost three meters wide. It had an unusually thick back wall built into the outside wall that overlooked the central courtyard. After strolling through all the rooms, Lucien came back to the fireplace and stooped down in front of it, gazing at it for a few minutes.

"Is this a working fireplace?"

"Yes, but it's never used," said Manet.

"And this is just to be a temporary hiding place?"

"Just a refuge if the Gestapo comes around. They'll be moved when it's safe."

"For how many?"

"Two."

Lucien smiled.

"They'll hide behind the back wall of the firebox. It'll be a false wall that can be pulled out, and when they're inside, they'll be able to pull it into place. The andirons will be bolted to the front of the false wall so it will look like a real fireplace. It can even have logs set on it," said Lucien, quite pleased with his idea. "The fireplace opening is so huge that they'll be able to get in quite easily and stand upright in the space we'll hollow out. Your guests aren't as tall as you, are they?"

Manet frowned. "No, but isn't that a solid brick wall behind there?"

"Yes, but it's half a meter thick so there will be plenty of depth for two people to stand side by side once we remove the bricks to hollow out a space."

Lucien could tell that Manet was unconvinced about the plan. He looked around. There was another possibility for a hiding place in the apartment, which would be much easier to construct. An interior wall was deep enough to hide two people behind the wainscot paneling. But for Lucien, it was not as clever as using the front of the fireplace. He wanted something especially tricky, even if it meant extra work. The more ingenious the solution, he realized, the greater the thrill. The Germans might look up the flue but never behind the firebox. Lucien began to think of himself as a kind of magician who could make people vanish into thin air.

"Yes, this would work," he said. "The fake wall would be faced with a lightweight brick veneer placed on a steel frame that could easily be moved back and forth in one piece."

To set Manet's mind at ease, Lucien added, "Please don't worry, monsieur. I'll design it so they'll be completely safe."

"Well, if you say so. But it seems so difficult. But if that's what you want, then you shall have it. I trust your judgment."

"I'll deliver a drawing to you the day after tomorrow. Our same arrangement stands."

"Of course, Lucien. No one will ever know. People are most grateful for your help even if they don't know you exist. You have already saved two lives."

Lucien had resumed thinking about the Citroën and Adele but snapped back to attention when he heard this comment.

"I saved someone's life?"

"Yes, indeed. Remember your steps in the hunting lodge in Le Chesnay? The ones that lifted up?"

"Someone actually used them?" Up until now, this had all seemed like a game to him with him designing a pretend hideout that no one would really use.

"The Gestapo tore the house apart but never found the two Jews. They walked over them and even sat on them but never found them."

"And what happened to…"

"They are now in a safe location, rest assured. But they sent word to me that the hiding place saved them and how ingenious I was to think of it. I wished I could've told them who'd really thought of it."

"I'm…glad it worked out."

Lucien walked over to the fireplace and picked up a small jade statuette of a cat and examined it closely. He tried to imagine the two Jews under the stairs, listening to the Germans walking on top of them and searching for them. How terrified they must have been. Then a smile came over his face as he realized that he'd really outwitted the Gestapo with his architectural ingenuity. It had actually worked. They'd been mere centimeters away from their prey, but they hadn't found them. He was quite proud of himself. Once, in an egotistical moment, Lucien had actually hoped the Gestapo would be tipped off so they could rip apart a place to test the cleverness of his hiding space. His mind was starting to race with ideas on how to detail the false wall when Manet yanked him out of his reverie.

"Lucien. Your Citroën is awaiting you."

As he drove off, Lucien was irritated that he wasn't enjoying the ride in his beautiful new car. No, he wasn't enjoying it because he began thinking of the two people he'd saved. That wasn't what this was supposed to be about. This was about fitting an object of certain dimensions into an enclosed space with adequate clearances, rather like placing an object inside a box to be mailed. All for twenty-seven thousand francs and the opportunity to design a huge factory—to show the world that he could really do a great design. And now this wonderful car. And the unexpected pleasure of fooling the Germans.

He almost wished Manet had said nothing about the actual people involved. He didn't want to think of them.

22

AT FIRST, PIERRE THOUGHT IT WAS JEAN-CLAUDE KNOCKING something off the kitchen table again. He was always running around like a little madman, never paying attention to anything. But there came another loud crash, then another, followed by the children's screaming. He could hear men shouting, and Madame Charpointier shouting back at them.

Below him, men like rampaging elephants came tearing up the main staircase of the townhouse, first crashing through the second floor then the third and the fourth, going into one room after another. They were yelling at each other, upending furniture, opening closet doors. Pierre fastened his eyes on the attic door in the floor expecting it to burst open at any second, but the men went back downstairs. He could clearly hear the wailing of Jean-Claude, Isabelle, and Philippe. Pierre's first instinct was to run down the attic stairs and help them. But he remembered what Madame Charpointier had told him and stopped dead in his tracks. His heart pounding, he dropped to his knees and put his ear to the attic door. He could just hear what the grown-ups were saying.

Madame kept telling them that these children were Catholics, baptized in the church in Orléans, and that they knew their prayers. She ordered his brothers and sisters to recite their prayers. In unison, all three started saying a Hail Mary, but a German screamed at them to stop. Philippe, the youngest, was now wailing away, and this angered the German, who yelled at him to shut the hell up. But Philippe cried even louder, and then there was a sudden silence. Madame started screaming at the German for slapping a four-year-old. There was the sound of another slap, which Pierre imagined was directed toward Madame, but that didn't stop her rage. The shouting continued until Pierre heard the front door open and the commotion shifted to the sidewalk. He got up and went to the attic window that overlooked the rue Dupleix. Two French policemen were dragging his brothers and sister into the rear seat of a French police car parked at the curb.

Two German soldiers took hold of Madame Charpointier, who was still screaming at the top of her lungs. A German officer in a black and green uniform came up to her, and the soldiers let her go. His hand rose to the level of Madame's forehead, and there was a loud bang. She dropped to the sidewalk in a heap. The children, who had witnessed everything from the car, screamed out, "Aunt Clare! Aunt Clare!" The officer holstered his pistol and, along with the soldiers, got into another car, which sped off. Madame was lying on her back with her eyes wide open, as if she was quietly watching the clouds roll by.

Pierre backed away from the window in horror, stumbled, and fell onto his backside. He pulled his legs up to his chest and grasped them with all his might, rolling back and forth on the attic floor in anguish, but not uttering a single sound. His eyes shut tight. There was such an intense ache inside his chest, he couldn't stand it. Pierre kept rolling around until he collided with a large steamer trunk piled high with old dusty magazines that fell on top of him. He lay there on his back gasping for breath and finally opened his eyes.

The first thing he saw was an old raincoat covered with cobwebs that hung on a nail on a rafter. As he stared at it, dozens of kind things Madame Charpointier had done for him flashed through his brain. The new football. The beautiful navy blue sweater for his birthday. The money she gave him to take his brothers and sister to the cinema. Helping him with his math homework. He reached to wipe the tears from his eyes and was surprised to find there weren't any. Maybe because he'd been bar mitzvah'd and he was a man now, he didn't cry anymore. Tears were just replaced with this terrible aching feeling in his chest. Pierre wanted desperately to cry but couldn't. Crying, he thought, might not hurt as bad as the pain in his chest.

Pierre sat up and saw the attic window. Below it, he noticed a wisp of grayish-white smoke slowly curling upward into the rafters. Pierre realized it was his cigarette that he'd dropped during all the commotion. He'd come up to the attic in the late afternoon as usual to smoke in secret. It was an excellent place to sit and enjoy his Gauloises. Sitting by the window and looking at the roofs of the houses in the neighborhood and the sky above gave him great pleasure. Madame always gave him hell for smoking, saying a twelve-year-old shouldn't smoke, that it would stunt his growth and yellow his teeth, so Pierre needed his own hideout. He knew she knew he snuck up here to smoke, but she never confronted him about it.

Pierre heard a truck pull up in front of the building, and he crawled on hands and knees to the window and raised himself to peek out. He was sorry he did. Two French laborers hoisted Madame Charpointier's body onto the truck bed. They did it with a casualness that shocked him, like heaving a heavy sack of flour. Sitting against the wall under the small window, he snuffed out the burning cigarette. He closed his eyes and thought of his brothers and sister being thrown into the car. That would be his last image of them forever, screaming and frightened to death. A new wave of sadness even worse than before crushed him. He'd fought, bickered, and sometimes hated Jean-Claude, Isabelle, and Philippe, but he'd loved them with all his heart. They had been the only family he'd had left, and he knew he'd never see them again. Of all his family, he was the only one left. And he didn't understand why.

The horrible images of what had just happened kept swirling around and around in his head. He placed his hands on his skull as if he could squeeze them out. Then the boy realized that all that had just occurred had been predicted by his father. When he'd told Pierre of the plan to pretend to be Christian and stay with Madame Charpointier, he'd explained what could happen to all of them. That one day with no warning, they could be found out. How the Boche would take his brothers and sister and him away and that Madame would be arrested. Everything he'd said had come true. The only difference was that instead of being taken away and tortured to death by the Gestapo, Madame had been shot on the spot. Pierre knew the Boche made examples of all those who hid Jews. The French hated Jews, his father said, even ones who had been in the country for hundreds of years. It didn't matter. They wouldn't hesitate to inform on their neighbors. Gentiles might smile and be polite to Jews, but in the end they'd stab them in the back. Always remember that, he'd said.

Pierre tried to think who could've betrayed Madame. Was it Monsieur Charles, who always argued with her about his dog? Maybe it was just someone who lived across the street and wondered why four children had mysteriously shown up on her doorstep a year ago. Madame's story that they were her niece's children hadn't sounded that convincing even to Pierre.

Pierre waited until it was dark, then he went downstairs to his room and gathered some belongings in a large rucksack. There were so many things he couldn't take, and that made him even sadder. He had to leave his football and model airplane, his books on the Roman Empire. Before he went back up the attic ladder, he went to each of his sibling's rooms and took one small belonging—Jean-Claude's favorite toy truck, Isabelle's stuffed cat, and Philippe's little beach shovel. Just touching these things reminded him of his last image of his brothers and sister, and the pain inside his chest intensified. Maybe this was what grown-ups meant by a broken heart. He'd always thought it was a silly expression.

As he left Philippe's room, he ran into Misha, Madame's calico cat. Although Madame had been incredibly kind to them, it had been Misha who had given him and his siblings the most comfort in those first weeks after losing their parents. He purred and rubbed his head on Pierre's leg. Pierre bent down to rub him under his chin. He looked at the rucksack and decided he could stuff Misha into it. The cat went in without protest and curled up in a ball on top of his sweater, and Pierre gently closed the flap over him.

Pierre went into Madame's room, where her handbag was sitting on the bed. He removed the money from it, then went to her dresser where she kept her savings in a little plaid bag in her stocking drawer. His father had also told him that money could save your life in times like these and the more you had the better. He still had the large roll of franc notes his father had shoved in his pants pocket when they'd parted. Pierre had never expected to see his father and mother again, but even though they'd received no word from them after six months, he and Madame had kept up a charade for the younger children by always saying, "When Papa comes back from his trip…"

He took one more look around and went up to the attic and out through a dormer window. As Pierre crossed the roofs of the adjoining houses, he wondered how long it would be until he was picked up by the Boche.

23

S ERRAULT KNEW THAT THIS WAS MANET'S ARCHITECT.

The light was fading and the rear of the apartment was in shadow so Serrault could watch him without being seen. Serrault had been walking through the apartment when he'd heard someone come in, and he'd quickly hidden. He was surprised the man was tall and distinguished-looking; the architects he had worked with were all mousy and poorly dressed. The architect was on his knees measuring the firebox inside the enormous fireplace, taking great care in noting the dimensions on a pad of paper. This reassured Serrault; the man was making sure everything was accurate. It wouldn't be like the other half-assed hiding places he and his wife Sophie had been stuck in over the last year. An enclosed loft above a stinking pigsty on a small farm south of Paris. A hastily built recess in the rear of a closet that the Gestapo had easily found a week after they had left for a new hideout.

Serrault and his wife hadn't waited for a deportation summons as most Jews did. Well ahead of time, they had known it was time to disappear. But before the Serraults could leave, their three children and four grandchildren had to be saved. They had gone into hiding, moving from household to household, making their way to the south of France, eventually arriving at Marseilles, where he'd arranged passage for them on two Spanish freighters bound for Palestine. It had taken seven months and had cost a small fortune, but now they were safe. Serrault, an immensely rich man, would've gladly spent every sou to help them, even sacrificing his life if he'd had to. His family was his life; without them, nothing mattered.

Everything he had done was for them; from the time fifty-three years ago when he'd arrived in Paris from Nimes with one thousand francs in his pocket to start a business. But the most valuable possession he'd brought with him was his father's construction knowledge, which he had passed on to his only son. Believing he had a gift for constructing buildings, Serrault had quickly set up his own company, and nothing but success had come his way. Especially after he'd specialized in reinforced concrete construction, the new structural method that had transformed building.

He was proud to say that he had helped make France a leader in the field, constructing some of the very first concrete buildings in the world. But every yard of that poured concrete was for his wife and children. He'd reveled in every piece of clothing and morsel of food he'd provided for them, every holiday and gift. That was the essence of life, he sincerely believed, to give his family the best life possible. And it had been the best—a great city mansion, a country estate, a home on the Mediterranean coast, and the finest education for his children. But all that had vanished. Now, he and his wife were like frightened mice running from one crack in the wall to another.

Serrault had met Auguste Manet when they were guests for a weekend at a country estate in the early '30s. A member of a rich aristocratic family, Manet, unlike many of his class, had no problem associating with Jews. Serrault liked the fact that Manet had broken a cardinal rule of the aristocracy and gone into business, an endeavor that most aristocrats thought was beneath them. And he became incredibly successful because of his innate business sense, which Serrault admired. Over the years, he'd lunched with Manet occasionally and once had been a guest at his home in the city. Serrault's social circle consisted mainly of Jews, and Manet was one of the handful of gentiles with whom he had ever socialized. He had not seen Manet in several years, so he'd been shocked when Manet had contacted him about a hideout.

After living in the rear of the closet, Serrault and his wife had moved into an attic in the Saint-Germain district. But the husband of the family who had taken them in had been arrested by the Gestapo and held in prison for weeks. His wife had been convinced the Germans would come to search the house, and if they found the Serraults, she and her children would be arrested. They would have to leave. The husband had taken them in without asking for a sou, showing them incredible kindness, even sharing their family's hot meals with them. Serrault hadn't wanted to place them in any more danger. Then out of the blue, Manet had appeared at the attic and said he could hide them and arrange an escape into Switzerland. The Gestapo, he'd told them, were after them for their fortune and would never give up the search. The Serraults had no idea how he'd learned of their plight.

Serrault continued to watch the architect take measurements. A construction man like himself admired the architect's cleverness in devising such a hiding place. The Germans would look for hours and never find them. He was also thankful that he and Sophie would have a whole furnished apartment to themselves, regaining a measure of the comfort they'd been used to before all this misery had begun. Their ordeal had given them a whole new appreciation of their former life, which he realized they'd taken for granted. Hopefully, he and his wife wouldn't have to stay here that long.

It was quite dark in the apartment now, but the architect wasn't finished. He stepped back about three meters from the fireplace, probably to envision what the false wall would look like. Serrault smiled when he saw this; he liked his thoroughness. After the war, he'd give this architect plenty of work. Now, all he could give the man was his new Citroën. Manet hadn't told him his name, and he didn't want to know it; at seventy-eight, he knew he couldn't stand up to beatings by the Gestapo and would give up his name. The architect put his notepad in his suit jacket pocket and turned toward the door when Serrault, his legs stiff from standing so long, shifted to the right, causing the wood floor to creak beneath him. It was so quiet in the apartment that the

tiny squeak caught the architect's attention. First, he seemed too terrified to turn around, but slowly he faced the darkness that enveloped
the back of the apartment

"Who's there?" the architect shouted, sounding fearful.

Serrault knew it was best to reveal himself.

"Please do not be alarmed, monsieur," replied Serrault, who walked
very slowly out of the shadows.

Serrault was amused to see the expression of relief on the architect's
face when he saw he stood face-to-face with a smiling, well-dressed old
man with a neatly trimmed white beard, not a Gestapo agent pointing
a Luger at him.

"What the hell are you doing here, old man?"

Serrault started walking toward the architect, who raised his hand,
silently ordering him to come no farther.

"It's all right; I know what you're doing here, monsieur."

"You know *nothing*, goddamn it. Now get the hell out of here."

Serrault was unfazed by the architect's reaction. He was still wearing the gentle smile on his grandfatherly face.

"I know what you're doing for us."

"*Us?*"

Serrault pulled his charcoal gray raincoat away from his chest to
reveal a yellow Star of David made of felt on his black suit jacket. He
saw the architect's knees almost collapse under him; he had to steady
himself by holding on to the mantle. He understood the architect's
reaction; this was probably the first time he'd ever met one of the
people he hid. Now facing him was a real and dangerous connection.
Serrault was threatening his very survival by just being in the same
room with him.

"You're a righteous man," said Serrault.

"Me? Righteous? That's a joke."

"No, monsieur, it is not."

"Old fool, why the hell didn't you get out when you could?"

The question surprised Serrault, but it was a fair one that deserved an answer.

"You're quite right. I'd be having dinner in Switzerland right now if I'd exercised better judgment."

"You're all idiots. The chosen people, what a joke."

The old man was amused by this comment. He started pacing slowly back and forth across the far end of the room.

"You ask me why I stayed, and I'll tell you. I feel I should offer an explanation considering what you're risking. My family's been here since the Revolution. All my ancestors have fought for France—the war against the Prussians and myself in the Great War. True, I'm a Jew. But I'm a Jew of French ancestry and very proud to be French. I believed in the glory of France and always will. After the Armistice in '40, I stayed in Paris out of loyalty to my country because it needed me to stand by her."

"You were quite mistaken."

"Yes, I was. No Jew had any idea what life would be like under the German Occupation. But when they made us wear this badge of honor last May, I knew no French Jews would be spared, even those with a French surname. I believed Vichy would protect my family and me, but as you said, I was mistaken. We could never imagine that the French government would be a party to such a crime."

"A French kike or a Polish kike, it's all the same to the Gestapo, old man."

"I'm sorry that I intruded on your work. I'll go," said Serrault.

"Please do."

The old man started to leave but stopped.

"Have you ever heard of an Englishman named Nicholas Owen?"

"No."

"When Elizabeth I was persecuting Catholics in sixteenth-century England, she outlawed all priests and the celebration of the Catholic mass. Catholics had to practice their religion in secret. If discovered, priests were tortured and executed, so they had to hide. Owen designed and built hiding places for Jesuit priests in manor houses all over England. They were called priest holes, and they were so well hidden that the queen's soldiers would tear apart a house for a week and never find them. He saved many lives."

"And what happened to him?"

"He was caught and racked to death in the Tower of London."

"That's a great story," replied the architect. "I knew it would have a happy ending."

"But he was a righteous man—just like you, monsieur," said Serrault as he opened the door to leave.

24

THIS ROOF WILL HAVE TO BE A LOT HIGHER NOW. BERLIN HAS decided to install a permanent crane inside the building. It'll be much easier to have one on-site all the time," said Herzog, puffing away on his cigarette. He'd already gone through a pack in the two hours since he arrived at Lucien's office to review the plans for the armaments factory in Tremblay.

Alain walked over from his drafting table. "The roof could angle up here so it looks like it's blending into the main roof, then it won't look awkward," he said, pointing at the front elevation of the factory. "In fact, there should be an opening in the roof for another crane to lift the interior one out in one piece so it wouldn't have to be disassembled."

"That's an excellent idea, young man," said Herzog, who offered Alain a cigarette. "You've hired yourself one smart kid, Lucien."

Lucien glared at Alain. He was about to make a similar comment about the roofline. He hated it when anyone—especially a know-it-all kid out of school—made any suggestions about how he should design. But he saw that the German was impressed with Alain, and it made Lucien look good for hiring him, so he didn't make a big deal out of it. This wasn't the first time that Alain had stuck his pointy nose into design matters. He'd thought the entry to the plant in Chaville should be stepped down to reduce the scale of the main facade and that the windows should have been vertical in orientation, instead of horizontal. Lucien had felt like telling him to go straight to hell, but he'd held his tongue.

Lucien knew he shouldn't be complaining. After all, Alain was the best employee he'd ever had. His draftsmanship was impeccable, he was extremely intelligent, and best of all, he knew construction inside and out. But it was his know-it-all attitude that Lucien disliked. All kids out of architecture school were full of themselves, believing that they were great designers from day one. Alain would be a model worker, but never someone to take under one's wing to mentor and advise. He didn't think he needed any advice.

"The front doors look a little puny. They have to accommodate a mass of workers on three shift changes a day," remarked Alain.

Lucien could feel the rage creeping up his throat.

"They could be widened, say half a meter for each door," said Herzog, tapping his long, well-manicured fingers on the doors on the plan. "What do you say, Lucien?"

Lucien gave Alain the evil eye. Alain smiled back at him.

"I don't see a problem with that. There's plenty of room to widen them," said Lucien.

"Fantastic. Alain, can you make these changes right away?"

"Of course, Major; they'll be finished by tomorrow."

What a goddamn bootlicker, thought Lucien, who gave a phony smile of approval.

"Would you like the rear door widened as well, Major?" asked Alain.

"That would be good," replied Herzog.

The pencil in Lucien's hand snapped in two. "Alain, could I see you in the storage room for a second?"

Lucien closed the door once Alain was inside, then grabbed him by the lapels of his jacket. "Listen, you little shit; if you ever open your mouth with one of your suggestions, I'll cut off your balls and stuff them up your nostrils."

Alain stared straight into Lucien's eyes but didn't say a word. After a few seconds, Lucien took his hands off him. He immediately regretted what he'd done but offered no apology. They both returned to the studio.

"We make a terrific team, all three of us, eh?" said Herzog. "It's time for lunch. What about the Café Hiver? My treat, gentlemen." Lucien knew the Café Hiver was reserved for Germans only, and no Frenchmen would see him there so he could accept.

"That's most kind, Dieter, but before we go, I'd like to show you a few more sketches for the plant. It'll only take a minute. Alain will get them; they're on my desk."

Lucien was well aware that Alain hated to be treated as a gofer, and sure enough, the boy scowled at him before going over to the desk. He made no effort to find the correct sketches but grabbed a handful of pieces of white tracing paper and stomped back.

One by one, Lucien reviewed the sketches with Herzog, working through the pile until only a single pencil sketch remained. Before Lucien could stop him, Herzog picked up the sketch and examined it.

"Mm, I don't recognize this, Lucien. What is it, something for the mechanical room?"

An ice-cold sensation ran down the middle of Lucien's back, and his eyes widened ever so slightly in fear. He gently took the paper out of Herzog's hand. Alain, who had been looking at Lucien, noticed his reaction.

"It looks like a metal frame around some brick. You didn't tell me about that detail. Is this something I have to add to the drawings?" asked Alain.

"It's for another job, not anything we're doing for Major Herzog," Lucien said. "It must have gotten mixed up with the other sketches on my desk."

"What other job?" said Alain.

"It's…nothing," Lucien said. "We're finished here; let's go to lunch."

Lucien brought the pile of sketches back to his desk, but he slowly folded one of them and put it in the center drawer of his desk and locked it.

25

As Alain was wriggling the blade of his penknife in Lucien's locked desk drawer in the middle of the night, his mind replayed the odd events of the day. He could see that Lucien was quite shaken, barely touching his food during lunch and hardly speaking at all. It was as if Lucien had seen a ghost when that sketch appeared in the pile of papers. Alain definitely knew something was amiss when Lucien told him that he wasn't going back to the office, and he could have the rest of the day off. Alain protested that he had to make the major's revisions, but Lucien yelled at him, telling him he had to enjoy life and not work all the time.

Alain was still furious over the incident in the storage room. How dare that no-talent shit put his hands on him and threaten him? For a fraction of a second, Alain had wanted to punch Lucien in the gut, but he'd thought better of it. It would've queered things with the Germans, and he'd be out on the street without a job, and his Uncle Hermann might not be able to help him. His dislike of his boss had been growing every day with each slight piling one on top of another. Alain might as well have been a nigger servant. Lucien knew *everything* about architecture; you couldn't tell him a damn thing. Every one of Alain's design suggestions was welcomed by Herzog; couldn't his boss see that? Yesterday had been the final straw. But he'd bide his time in getting even.

When he went home after work, he'd tried to figure out what had spooked Lucien so. How could a sketch of some bricks upset him? He couldn't get to sleep thinking about it. He had to see that sketch again. He read until 2:00 a.m., then got up, got dressed, and went to the office. Lucien had given him his own key after his first week, so he could work into the evening if he wanted. He was taking a huge risk being out on the streets after the curfew; the Germans could pick him up. But it didn't scare him. If that happened, it was just a simple matter of calling his uncle to clear up a misunderstanding.

Patiently, Alain kept working the blade back and forth until he heard a click. The drawer slid open, and he rifled through the papers until he found a folded one. Before he pulled it out, he made sure he remembered exactly where he'd found it. It was pitch black in the office, so Alain took the lamp off the desk, set it on the floor, and turned it on. Under the light, he could see the sketch was the one he'd seen that morning—a metal frame one meter square enclosing some bricks. He turned the paper over and found another view of the bricks with what seemed like a fireplace andiron connected to it. Alain kept staring at the drawing, but it made no sense to him at all. Lucien had never mentioned that he was doing any residential work, and this was just an odd detail of something, not a project.

There were also a few notes in pencil on the sketches, giving some dimensions and sizes of the metal frame. One note called out that the new mortar should match the existing mortar. Alain sat on the bare wood floor and rubbed his eyes. He was getting tired, and not having solved the puzzle, he decided to leave. As he was returning the sketch to its proper place, he heard the lift coming up. He quickly slid the drawer shut and replaced the lamp. He stood by the door to the office and listened. When the lift stopped at the office floor, he immediately knew who it was and retreated to the rear of the office into the storage closet. As he shut the door, he heard the key turn in the lock and the click of a light switch.

Through a crack in the door, he saw Lucien walk briskly to the desk and unlock the drawer. With a solemn expression, he carefully pulled out the sketch and unfolded it. He examined it carefully as if this was the first time he'd ever seen it. Then he stared into space for almost an entire minute before he folded it up and stuck it in his inside jacket pocket. He sat in his chair and dialed the phone.

"I know it's late, but I needed to speak to you," said Lucien. "It's important that we hold off on the fireplace...No, nothing has happened; I just think we should wait...I need a little more time...I know how many people are involved in this...I'm one of those people involved in this...Oh, very well, you can have the drawing tomorrow...No, I promise it will be delivered to the usual place...You have my word, Monsieur Manet...I tell you nothing is wrong...I'm just a bit jumpy... *No*, I don't know why," Lucien said and hung up the phone.

Lucien sat down at his desk and began to draw on another sheet of white paper. After twenty minutes, he stood up and lit a match. Holding the first drawing in his right hand, he set it afire and watched it burn into a black crisp, disintegrating into ashes, which floated to the floor. He took the new drawing, folded it, and placed it in his side jacket pocket. After straightening up his desk, he walked to the door and left.

As Alain watched all of this, a great sense of excitement was building up inside of him. He loved reading mysteries and watching them at the cinema. Now here was a real-life mystery to solve. He still couldn't figure out what the detail meant, but in time he was certain he would. Manet was mixed up in this, and that made the whole mystery even more fascinating. After walking to the door to listen if the lift had made it down to the first floor, Alain sat down for a while to ponder the problem. It had to be something quite dangerous to call for all this intrigue. Why all this fuss about a fireplace?

26

I'M GOING TO TAKE OFF THE BLINDFOLD. READY?"

Adele loved this game. It was exciting and decidedly erotic. When she and Schlegal had finished their lunch at the little inn in Savran, he'd blindfolded her after they got back into his car and had told her he had a wonderful surprise to show her. The sensation of being blindfolded while riding in the car was wonderful. Her senses of hearing and smell were intensified. Adele could feel every vibration of the road and smell the cut rye in the fields they passed. Soon, the car came to a stop and her Gestapo lover guided her gently out and onto a stone walk.

"I'm going crazy with curiosity, you evil man."

"Just a few more steps," Schlegal said before yanking off the white handkerchief.

"My God, this is incredible!" Adele said.

"It's all yours, my love. All thirty rooms. Until the Reich decides how to dispose of it."

In front of Adele stood a seventeenth-century hunting lodge with corner towers capped by witch's-hat roofs. Surrounding the building was a dense forest of huge ancient trees, almost blocking out the sky.

"It's as wonderful as Château de Chambord. I was there for dinner once, did I ever tell you that?"

"Yes, a few hundred times, my sweet," said Schlegal. "Now you have your own château to do with whatever you like."

"I can't wait to show Bette, she'll be *so* jealous," she giggled. Her high heels clattered on the stone path as she ran up to the giant front doors and flung them open. When Schlegal walked in, she was racing uncontrollably from room to room on the first floor.

"It's completely furnished," she shouted.

"Down to the last pot in the kitchen, which you'll see is as big as a ballroom."

"I'll be able to entertain two hundred, at least."

"At least," said Schlegal.

Adele could see that her lover was quite pleased with himself, knowing this little present would win her heart.

"Where on earth did you get this place?"

"It belonged to a French nobleman. He was hiding Jews here, but they escaped from us."

"That must have made you quite annoyed, my love," said Adele tauntingly.

"It most certainly did, so the Reich appropriated his home."

"And what happened to the nobleman?"

"He's in Switzerland, so he'll never set foot in his ancestral home again."

"What an idiot, to give all this up for a bunch of Jews," said Adele.

"You'd be surprised, my love, at how many Frenchmen have risked their lives for them. I'm talking about men whose families go back hundreds of years."

Adele was uninterested in this revelation and turned her attention to the grand staircase.

"Let's see the rest of the place. I'll race you upstairs," said Adele, kicking off her shoes.

Schlegal followed her up the grand carved-wood staircase. She ran ahead, going from room to room, exclaiming with delight at every treasure she found.

Adele reappeared at the end of the corridor, leaning seductively against the jamb of a doorway.

"I believe I've discovered the master bedroom, Herr Colonel," she said, while she slowly unbuttoned her white silk blouse, revealing the black brassiere Schlegal so admired.

"Mm, allow me to verify this discovery," he replied.

Schlegal rubbed his body against Adele's as he passed through the doorway. He threw his cap on the bed and took off his black tunic. When he turned around, he was extremely pleased to find Adele completely naked. She was quite proud that he'd once told her that no woman he'd ever known could undress so fast. He took off his uniform and gave her a long, slow kiss. Adele put her arms around Schlegal's neck, hoisting her legs around his waist. He held her aloft while walking around the bedroom, kissing her passionately.

When he got to a flight of carpeted stairs that led to a small study, Schlegal lowered Adele against them and entered her. She had always enjoyed unusual sites for making love—a tour boat on the Seine, the top of Notre Dame—so she was very aroused at being taken on the stairs. Schlegal was also quite aroused and furiously pounded Adele. His feet were firmly planted on the floor to give him extra leverage. But something was wrong that he couldn't quite figure out. To Adele's great disappointment, Schlegal stopped in mid-thrust and looked down at the stairs.

"Did you feel these stairs move beneath us?" he said. "The staircase was moving in unison with us, going up and then down ever so slightly."

"No, my sweet; my mind was elsewhere. And I wish it were still elsewhere."

Schlegal gave Adele a powerful thrust. "The stairs *are* moving," he said. He pulled out of Adele, leaving her sprawled on the stairs.

"So what, for god's sake; get back in here!" shouted Adele.

"Get off the stairs," he barked, and Adele raised herself up and stood next to him.

Schlegal reached down, grabbed the edge of the bottom step, and pulled up on it. With great effort, he raised the entire staircase in one piece, revealing a mattress underneath it.

"What the hell is this?" cried Adele. "Why would anyone put a mattress under a stair like this?"

Schlegal moved the heavy staircase up and down.

"It's hinged at the top, and there's a bolt on the inside of the bottom step," he said.

A smile came over Schlegal's face, and he dropped the stair with a heavy thud. He began to laugh uncontrollably.

"This is most clever," he said. "It was the hiding place for the Jews we were looking for. No wonder we couldn't find the bastards. They were here all the time. And we thought they'd escaped out the back!"

"Then why are you so happy about all this?" asked Adele, who was beginning to shiver.

"I admire such ingenuity. I bet my men walked over them two or three times during the search." Schlegal sat down on the stairs.

"Did the Frenchman think of this?"

"A member of the aristocracy is too stupid to come up with something like this. It had to be someone clever and smart."

"My friend Lucien, he's an architect. Maybe he could sniff around. He can make some inquiries. Lucien knows tons of people in the building trades."

"Your modernist architect lover?"

"Former lover. The one who's doing many important buildings for the Reich."

Adele sat beside Schlegal and wrapped her arms around him and began nibbling his ear, but he pushed her away.

"The question is…is this a unique situation…or are there more of these secret hiding places? All those other apartments and buildings I've searched—were there Jews hiding right under my nose?"

Adele sighed. She walked over to the bed, pulled off the bedspread, and wrapped it around herself. She reached down, took a cigarette out of his tunic pocket, and lit it.

"Jews have lots of money, and they can bribe anyone. Everyone has their price, even if it means risking death, so there have to be more of these things all over Paris. You've made it impossible for the Jews to escape France, so they must be in hiding. I bet you they were right under your nose while you tore those places apart," Adele said with a laugh.

Adele was now lying on the bed with the bedspread over her. She saw her last comment had hit a nerve. Schlegal was now putting on his shirt, clearly angry and embarrassed, and she watched him with great amusement. He'd been bested by Jews, a subhuman species in his eyes, and his Aryan pride was wounded. At least, they were the only ones who knew of his humiliation. He was about to button his white shirt when she threw off the covers and parted her legs.

"Herr Colonel, I believe the Reich has some unfinished business here," Adele said in a soft little girl's voice.

Schlegal turned around to face her and laughed. He pulled off his shirt and dove onto the bed. They made love for hours, but through it all, Adele knew the Gestapo colonel's mind was somewhere else.

27

LUCIEN HAD ALWAYS HATED LIEBER FOR CRITICIZING HIS WORK, but now he loathed the drunken German pig as he guided him through the dark empty streets. Drinking nonstop since 9:00 p.m., Lieber was completely plastered. The café had closed before midnight because of the curfew, so now, along with Herzog and Manet, he was trying to find Lieber another place to drink. Not another soul was on the streets. All the French had to be home and German enlisted men in their barracks, so now the streets belonged to German officers, who had no curfew. There was a complete silence in Paris that lasted from midnight to 6:00 a.m., broken only by the sound of the hobnailed boots of the German five-man patrols walking the streets or a single rifle shot or the spray of machine-gun fire in the distance. A car speeding by meant the Gestapo had picked up some unfortunate soul.

Normally, Lucien avoided Lieber at all costs, but tonight he'd been lassoed into a party by Herzog, who wouldn't take no for an answer because he too had been forced against his will to come. They'd been accompanied by three very drunk young French prostitutes, each carrying a bottle of vintage wine. The girls were from a brothel reserved for German use only, one of seventeen in Paris. The Reich worried obsessively about sex between the French and their soldiers because of VD, so it restricted sex to these whores, who were kept clean as a whistle by constant medical checkups.

Lucien thought the three tarts were part of the wave of girls from the country who came to the city to escape the poverty brought on by the loss of their husbands and lovers. Céline, Jeanne, and Suzy (if those were their real names) all had a wholesome attractiveness quite different from the cheap, painted look of the usual Parisian streetwalker. He was impressed that they had cards that listed their services and prices in both French and German; their business cards were nicer than his. Their cackling and high-pitched laughter caused some residents on the street to switch on their lights and peer out from behind their curtains. Normally, the Germans were highly motorized, but tonight, for some reason, they were without a car, so the whole parade turned down rue de Rivoli. It was an unusually damp and cold night for September, and a light drizzle began.

"Damn it, Bernard, we have to get inside. The girls are freezing their tits off. And we can't have that. Find me a place, now," Lieber ordered. The girls shrieked in agreement, and one kissed Lieber's cheek.

Lucien could see that Herzog, who clearly wanted to be home in bed, was desperate. "What street is this, Lucien?" he asked testily.

"Rue de Rivoli," snapped Lucien, who, with Manet, was holding up Lieber's drunken body.

"Manet, don't you have an apartment on the rue du Renard?" asked Herzog. "That's the next left, isn't it?"

Manet suddenly dropped Lieber's arm, and the German slumped to the pavement, Lucien barely holding him up. Manet looked up and down the street, thunderstruck, as if just realizing where he was. The entire party fell silent, waiting for his response.

Manet then smiled. "How do you happen to know that, Major? Have you been spying on me?" he asked.

"The Wehrmacht thoroughly checks the backgrounds of all its contractors," blustered Lieber. "We have to be sure we're not dealing with a Jew or a Communist. You're not a Jew, are you?"

The girls shrieked with laughter at the question. Suzy planted a kiss on the cheek of the old man. "He doesn't look Jewish to me, Maxie," she said, stroking Manet's nose.

"Well, do you or don't you have an apartment on the rue du Renard?" demanded Lieber.

"Well…Let me see. Yes, this is rue de Rivoli and—"

"Goddamn it, man, don't you know where one of your own proper-ties is? He must have soooo many he can't keep track of them, poor boy."

The girls found Lieber's comment uproariously funny.

Manet shot a glance at Lucien, who now was also quite alert and completely panic-stricken.

"Well, speak up, sir," asked Lieber. "Which one is it?"

"It's…number 29," Manet whispered.

"You said 29, Monsieur Manet?" asked Herzog.

"Yes, follow me," said Manet. Lucien felt like running away down the street, but he kept his wits about him and held on to Lieber, drag-ging the dead weight across the street.

"The night is still young," Lieber shouted into the cold night air. "Ladies, don't drop any of that precious nectar, we'll need every ounce tonight."

The girls pressed the bottles to their bodies and laughed.

When they reached number 29, Manet told them he'd have to wake the concierge and to wait inside the foyer for him. After banging on the door for almost thirty seconds, a drowsy and angry old woman answered the door. She was about to let loose a torrent of obscenities when she saw it was the owner. Manet shoved his way in and closed the door behind him. Minutes passed, and Lieber became upset.

"What the hell is taking him so damn long? All he had to do was get the key."

Lucien knew exactly why it was taking so long. Manet was calling the Jews upstairs to warn them. There was no way he could get up to the apartment before the rest of them. Manet finally appeared from behind the door with key in hand. "I'm sorry for keeping you so long. Madame Fournier had misplaced the key."

"You should fire the stupid bitch," Lieber said. "That's what I would have done."

Herzog rolled his eyes and guided the colonel toward the lift.

Luckily, it was at the fourth floor so they had to wait for it to come down. Lucien was praying that Lieber would pass out, but the fool unfortunately seemed to be getting his second wind.

The group piled in the lift, and it struggled with the excessive load to make it to the fifth floor. Manet unlocked the door, and Lucien held his breath. But the apartment was dark and empty. Maybe no one had used it yet. While taking off his coat, he glanced at the back of the fireplace and couldn't tell if it had been moved. It looked perfectly normal. Lucien smiled to himself. This design definitely topped the stair hideaway at the hunting lodge.

"Ladies, let the drinking commence," said Lieber. "Manet, there must be glasses in so fine a flat. Get us some, will you?"

The apartment didn't look lived in at all. No trace of anyone. But when Manet returned from the kitchen with a tray of glass tumblers, Lucien saw an unmistakable look of fear in his eyes. The Jews were here.

The party made themselves at home on the expensive furniture, with Lieber stretching out on the sofa. Céline sat at the end with Lieber's feet on her knees and she stroked his boots, commenting on the fine quality of the leather. Herzog sat in an upholstered chair at the other end of the room and looked at Lieber with undisguised disgust. When Jeanne came over to sit on the arm of his chair, he waved her away, and she joined Lucien in his armchair. "Manet, there must be some music here," said Lieber.

"I'll try the radio, Colonel," said Manet, who walked over to a fine stand-alone set against a wall and switched it on. Pleasant dance music flooded the large apartment. The French radio station that spewed mostly German propaganda had shut down for the night, but one could always get music from Switzerland and England, even though it was against the rules to listen to overseas channels.

"Manet, your company is doing damn fine work for the Reich. Together, we're going to produce a war machine that will supply our troops for years. Here's to you, monsieur," shouted Lieber, lifting his glass in the air toward Manet, who in turn raised his.

"And you, Herzog, you'll be a colonel by next year for your efforts for the Fatherland."

Herzog barely raised his glass in acknowledgment and resumed leafing through a book he'd gotten from the floor-to-ceiling bookcases. Sitting on the arm of Lucien's leather upholstered chair, Jeanne stretched out her long, slender legs across his lap and refilled her glass with wine.

"How do you like these, lover?" she said patting her thighs.

"Real beauties. Not many girls have silk stockings in Paris anymore," said Lucien.

"You just have to be special…and know the right people," she said, looking in Lieber's direction.

"And I bet you know the right people in your line of work."

Jeanne's raucous laughter hurt Lucien's ears. "The Maison de Chat only allows officers, none of those cheap bastard enlisted men. And they know how to treat a girl," she said, putting her glass to Lucien's lips. This was real honest-to-goodness wine, and he drained the glass in a gulp. He smiled up at her pretty, heart-shaped face. He didn't condemn her for cavorting with the Boche. Girls like her, who were excluded from respectable society in peacetime, exacted a kind of revenge by associating with the enemy, who now held all the power. The women wanted to lord it over those who'd looked down at them before the war.

"Oooohh, someone's thirsty. Want some more?"

"Not just yet, love."

"So, what does a handsome man like you do for a living?" she asked, stroking Lucien's wavy brown hair. He knew she would soon be steering him to a bedroom for services rendered at a very steep price.

"I'm an architect."

"What's that?" Her question brought a bemused look from Herzog.

"I design buildings."

"Like an engineer?"

"Not exactly."

"Like an interior decorator?"

"Forget it, let me have some more wine." What did he expect, thought Lucien, if a respectable member of society didn't know what an architect did, why would a whore? Suzy, in the armchair across from Lieber, vigorously rubbed her hands together and gave him a pouty look.

"You're cold, my love," said Lieber. "Manet, it's damn cold in here. You French don't know shit about central heating. In Germany, our homes are warm and toasty. It's colder than a witch's tit in here."

"It's not that cold in here. It's only the end of September," protested Lucien.

"The building furnace hasn't been turned on yet," said Manet. "The radiators aren't working yet."

"Nonsense, there's some wood in the fireplace," said Lieber. "Light a fire so the girls can warm up."

28

MANET, WHO WAS LIFTING A GLASS OF WINE TO HIS LIPS, FROZE. A look of terror passed over his face then instantly disappeared. He glanced at Lucien, who laid his head against Jeanne's arm and closed his eyes. Drunk as he was, Lieber sensed the tension in the room and set down his glass. He stared at Manet. Like all senior officers, he wasn't used to being ignored.

"Monsieur Manet, didn't you hear me?" he inquired in a surprisingly pleasant tone of voice. "I asked you to light a fire for us."

Manet set his glass down and slowly walked over to the fireplace. He gazed at the logs in the andiron for a few seconds.

"Yes, Maxie, a fire would be so romantic," said Céline, who was giving Major Herzog the eye.

"But, Colonel, it's really not that cold at all in here," offered Manet in a quiet voice. "Maybe once you have some more wine, you'll warm up."

"Bullshit. That is a working fireplace, isn't it?" Lieber said. "So what the hell is your problem?"

"I seem to remember a problem with the flue. I was supposed to get a chimney sweep in, and I don't think he ever cleaned it," said Manet.

Lucien glanced over at Herzog, who had put his book aside and was watching this exchange with great interest. The major, he knew, had grown fond of the industrialist and respected him, so he no doubt hated to see Lieber treat him this way. Herzog jumped up and went over to the fireplace.

"Excuse me, Monsieur Manet. Let me start the fire. I'll check the flue first." Herzog turned the cast-iron handle to the right, squatted on his knees, and peered up the chimney. "I can see the stars, so it must be clean," he said.

He expertly lit some newspaper and kindling and had the fire roaring in seconds. The girls gathered in front of the fireplace, rubbing their hands and legs. Céline lifted her skirt above her waist, to the delighted shrieks of her two coworkers. Manet walked over to an armchair in the corner of the room and sat down in a dejected heap. He stared at the floor. Lucien slumped back in his chair and couldn't bring himself to look at the fireplace.

"That's much better," said Lieber, downing another glass of wine. "The girls can warm up now. Besides, they've got work to do."

All three whores laughed like crazy and began whispering to each other, deciding who would do whom tonight. Each one probably wanted Herzog, with his good looks, thought Lucien.

❖ ❖ ❖

Serrault knew that Manet would never talk the German out of lighting a fire. When he heard the strike of a match, he put his arm around his wife's waist and pulled her tightly against him. Sophie laid her head on his chest and closed her eyes.

"Why, Albert, why?" whimpered Sophie.

"My dear," he replied softly, giving his wife a hug.

It was now a question of time—how long the Germans would stay and how long before the logs were ablaze. They had been fast asleep when Manet had warned them with six rings of the telephone, and they hadn't had time to change out of their bed clothes. Their hiding space was actually quite roomy; they could stand completely upright with enough room in front and behind their bodies. Never did they think they'd actually have to use the hiding space. Only three days from now, they'd be in Switzerland. Serrault could only begin to imagine what was going on in Manet's mind. Just sitting there watching the logs ignite. If he got up and revealed to the Germans that two people were hiding behind the fireplace, then all of them, including the architect, whose voice Serrault recognized, would be arrested.

The inside of the hiding space was pitch black; he couldn't see Sophie's face, only felt the warmth of her body and her pounding heart. Music coming from a radio could be heard quite clearly. With his free hand, Serrault reached in front of him and touched the back of the false fire wall.

"Albert, I'm so frightened. What are we going to do?"

"Do you remember the winter we spent in Morocco—in Rabat? When was that?" whispered Serrault.

"1908—no, 1909."

"Our suite overlooked the beach, and the first evening we were there, we didn't go out. We stayed in and watched the sun drop below the horizon. Do you remember the incredible color it cast on the sea?"

"It was such a beautiful intense shade of red, almost an orange red. Yes, you're right; it was incredible. I'd never seen such a color."

"It's funny how things stay in one's mind. Like it happened just yesterday. That's how vivid a memory it was."

"I think Morocco was the most beautiful place we ever visited, don't you?"

"Even the desert had this magnificent beauty in its desolation. It was breathtaking."

"And at night, there was that blanket of stars, and it seemed to be right on top of us."

"You could almost reach up and pull one down," said Serrault.

"And put it in your pocket and take it home," said Sophie with a quiet laugh.

It was just the faintest of scents, as the smoke seeped through the edges of the false wall, but Serrault recognized it as ash, a wood he had used for his fires at home. After a few minutes, the blackness of the space became dusty with smoke as if someone had beaten out a dirty rug.

"Yes, of all the places we've visited, Morocco may have been the most beautiful," said Serrault, feeling that Sophie was beginning to wheeze. Her breathing became labored, and her chest heaved in and out. Serrault's throat seized up as if he had swallowed cotton.

"I loved walking through…the bazaars, all the wonderful sights and…sounds, right out of the…Arabian nights," replied Sophie with great difficulty. Her speech had become a series of gasps.

"I still carry that Moroccan leather wallet around, can you believe that?"

"Of course, it's so…beautiful with the red leather…and gold inlay."

The air was almost gone now, and thick smoke filled the chamber. Their eyes began to burn and water. Sophie started gagging and coughing, but no matter how hard she tried to stifle her cough with her hand, it came spilling out. Serrault's coughing began and wouldn't let up. He felt for her face and leaned down to give her a long kiss.

"I couldn't have asked for a better a wife."

"And God couldn't have given me a better husband."

Serrault took out the handkerchief from Sophie's dressing gown and placed it in her mouth while she kept her head against his chest. He placed his own handkerchief in his mouth.

❖ ❖ ❖

As the blaze died down, the wood glowed a reddish orange and smoldered away. Meanwhile, the party dragged on for another fifteen minutes, until Lieber vomited all over the beautiful scarlet and tan Persian rug and finally passed out. Immediately, Herzog called his office for a staff car. Then, with Manet's and Lucien's help, he dragged Lieber into the lift, shoving the three tarts in behind. Lucien declined the major's offer of a ride and waited for the lift to descend. Manet had rushed into the kitchen to fetch a pot of water and doused the fire, then, with Lucien's help, dragged out the false wall.

"They'll be all right, monsieur. Don't worry, they'll be fine," Lucien said in a confident tone as they pulled away the wall.

In the opening, they saw two bodies in slippers and nightclothes buckled at the knees.

"Monsieur, madame, we're here," Manet shouted.

"Please hold on; we'll have you out in just a second," said Lucien.

With great difficulty, Lucien and Manet pulled out the two limp bodies by their legs—a very tiny woman in her seventies and an old man Lucien recognized as the Jew he had met in the apartment. Both were dead. To his horror, Lucien saw that both had handkerchiefs stuffed in their mouths. Manet stood motionless above the bodies, but Lucien was dumbstruck at the terrible sight.

"Christ, this can't be," Lucien insisted. "Look, this pipe at the bottom here sucked out any smoke directly to the outside."

Imbedded in the lower half of the back wall of the hiding place was a sheet metal sleeve six centimeters in diameter.

"I'm telling you, the natural draft sucked out the smoke. Hot air will always travel in the direction of cold air. Look." Lucien stuck his arm into the sleeve but ran into something hard and rough.

"What the hell?" Lucien kept hitting the mass with his fist. Manet pulled Lucien's arm out, took out his cigarette lighter, and peered inside.

"It's a bird's nest. It's completely blocking the opening," Manet said.

Lucien looked and, to his astonishment, saw a tight ball of twigs and shreds of cloth mixed with mud clogging the far end of the sleeve. It reminded him of gray papier-mâché.

"A fuckin' bird's nest," said Lucien. "I didn't even think of that when I put in the sleeve. If I'd just thought to put in a little piece of wire mesh at the end…Christ, I'm such an idiot. I killed them. All because of a goddamn bird's nest."

Lucien staggered out from the fireplace opening and stretched his arms out to brace himself against the mantle.

"I should have thought of that. Goddamn it, I should have thought of that."

He turned his head to look down at the dead couple. Suddenly, he collapsed to his knees next to the old lady. Without thinking, he reached out and caressed her soft white hair. Even in old age, she was still uncommonly pretty. He pulled the handkerchief out of her mouth and began to stroke her cheek. Lucien continued to do this for almost two minutes before Manet put his hand on his shoulder, but he did not seem to notice. Manet shook him roughly, and Lucien finally stopped.

"I must make a call to take care of this," said Manet.

Lucien began to sob, his body shaking. "Christ, what have I done?"

"It was Lieber who killed them, Lucien."

"No," said Lucien, looking up at Manet. "I killed them."

"Please don't do this to yourself. It was a cruel accident. God's will."

"Fuck God," Lucien shouted as he pulled the handkerchief from the old man's mouth and held it with both his hands.

"Come, Lucien, you have to get out of here," Manet said. "I'll take care of it. Please go home."

"What were their names?"

"I don't know if that's the best—"

"Goddamn it, what were their names?"

"Albert and Sophie Serrault."

"Who were they? Were they friends of yours?" Lucien shouted. "Tell me, goddamn it."

"Yes, I knew them. He came from Nimes as a kid to start his own construction firm."

"And?"

"The usual story with these people. He works like a dog and becomes a success. At the turn of the century, he was smart enough to realize that reinforced concrete was the new thing, so he specialized in that and made a fortune."

"France was the world leader in reinforced concrete, did you know that?" asked Lucien with pride in his voice.

"I heard he was a war hero. Could've sat out the Great War, but he fought and was decorated for gallantry many times. Foch and Clemenceau personally pinned medals on him."

"He told me he was in the war."

Manet was puzzled. "You met this man? When?"

"When I came back to take some measurements. He was in the apartment. Told me he should've left France. He didn't believe what would happen to him."

"All the old couples, they get their children out, but they wind up staying. It's like they're tired of running. It makes sense in a way; these people have been running for two thousand years."

"Look how pretty she still is. You can tell how beautiful she once was." Lucien started to sob and bent down to kiss her cheek. Manet made no effort to stop him. "I bet they were married a long time. Happily married."

"It's time to leave, Lucien," said Manet, gently placing his hand under Lucien's right arm to bring him to his feet.

"They saved our lives, you know that? If Lieber had discovered them, you and I would be on our way to Drancy. That is, if we hadn't been executed first," said Lucien, looking straight into Manet's eyes.

"Yes, I know that only too well."

"Serrault told me an odd thing. He said I was a righteous man for what I was doing. I told him that was nonsense."

Manet looked down at Serrault's body and smiled.

"He was a shrewd judge of character."

Lucien was in a trance as Manet ushered him to the door. When he found himself outside in the cool night air, he couldn't remember going down the lift. It was well after the curfew and the streets were completely empty. Lucien leaned against the base of the building and looked up and down the rue du Renard for German patrols. He heard no sounds of marching Germans in the distance, so he began walking blindly down the rue du Renard until he came to the quai de Gesvres and almost tumbled down the steps to the Seine. Both the quai and the river were deserted. He knelt by the edge of the Seine and threw up, then sat against the quai wall in the shadows, staring into space. Throughout the night, his emotions swung wildly from unrelenting guilt to blind rage at the Germans. Even if the Jews were the worst of what people called them, they were human beings and shouldn't end up like that. No one should die like that. A German patrol of five men with machine guns slung over their shoulders passed only five meters away from Lucien, never noticing him against the wall. He stayed there until daybreak, clutching the handkerchief he'd taken from Serrault's mouth. Instead of tossing it in the Seine, he kept it in the side pocket of his suit jacket and walked home.

✢ ✢ ✢

For the next week, Lucien could think of nothing but the dead faces of the Serraults, with the handkerchiefs in their mouths. Nothing he did would purge the image from his mind. No hour passed when he did not think of them. His remorse was unending. The couple even invaded his dreams. Every night, the Serraults joined other images from his life to form a surreal film that ran in his mind. In one dream, he was back in his childhood bedroom where he kept his trunk at the foot of the bed, and when he opened it up the Serraults were inside, at the bottom, eating at a dining room table like little doll figures, with hundreds of tiny birds flying around them. He shouted at them, but they ignored him. In another dream, he was in a car he didn't recognize. The Serraults were driving through a landscape that resembled North Africa with him, his father, and Celeste, who was holding a dead rabbit in the backseat. Throughout the ride, his father was screaming something in his ear.

Lucien would toss and turn violently, waking up in a cold sweat, then get up and pace throughout his apartment in the middle of the night, chain smoking away. Even his architecture, which was his whole world, seemed unimportant to him, and he didn't go near his drawing board. He pushed all the work onto Alain and rarely set foot in the office. He couldn't bear being at home so he spent his days walking the streets or sitting by the Seine. Going to the cinema was of no use; he could never keep his mind on the film. And he hadn't had the courage to face Manet since that terrible night. He took the handkerchief with him everywhere and touched it whenever the image of the Serraults came to mind, as if he were rubbing salt in a wound to punish himself for his hubris.

29

THE OLD STONE COTTAGE WITH THE DILAPIDATED BARN NEXT TO IT looked very familiar to Lucien as he steered the Citroën down the winding road. So did the little inn coming up on the right. Lucien knew he'd been this way before but couldn't remember when. It was hard to think with Adele talking nonstop. She hadn't shut up since they'd left Paris. As he'd predicted, she was thrilled to see the car outside her window. In just seconds, she was downstairs and in the passenger's seat, giving him directions where to go. Lucien had planned a romantic afternoon in Saint-Denis, but Adele insisted on going southwest of Paris in the opposite direction. All she would reveal was that she had a new weekend retreat to show him. With a navigator's instincts, she issued directions as they roared down the country roads.

"Make a right here, my love," she ordered. "About five more minutes. You're going to be quite impressed with your little Adele's new house."

Lucien didn't catch the last remark because his attention was focused on the rundown feed store on his left. Where had he seen it before?

"The house came completely furnished with everything, including sheets, if you can believe it. I've already had a party there. It was incredible," gushed Adele.

"And you didn't invite me?" Lucien asked, genuinely disappointed.

Adele instantly realized her faux pas and backpedaled. "Oh, they were just fashion people. Total bores, my love. You'll be coming out quite often—you'll see. And it'll be for a party of *two*," she said, rubbing her hand on the inside of Lucien's thigh.

Lucien was quite aroused by this gesture of affection. He was now glad that he'd worked his way out of his depression and had called Adele up to surprise her with his new car. It would do him good to get out and have some fun and sex. Lucien's good mood vanished when he looked up and saw a grand stone and wrought-iron gate just ahead. Sheer panic gripped him, as if someone were throttling him by the neck.

"Here we are!" Adele exclaimed. "Isn't it magnificent? I bet you thought it was going to be some puny little cottage. Now be honest, didn't you think so?"

Lucien stopped the car just past the gate and stared in disbelief at the house before him. This was the hunting lodge in Le Chesnay—with his secret staircase. It all made sense now. No wonder so many things looked so familiar. He *had* been this way before. Twice in the middle of the night, but he still remembered some landmarks along the way. His first instinct was to turn the car around and speed off. A voice in his brain shouted, "Don't panic, don't panic," and another kept saying, "Run like hell."

Forcing a smile on his face, he turned to Adele. "It's magnificent, my sweet."

To Adele, Lucien's expression of utter disbelief meant abject admiration, and she was beside herself with pride and joy. Bouncing up and down in her seat, she gave him a hug.

"Let's go, I want to show you the inside."

"Of course…" Lucien replied weakly. Adele yanked him out of the car by the sleeve of his suit jacket and led him toward the great house and pushed him through the front door, which was unlocked.

"So what do you think?"

"It's just…incredible," replied Lucien, wondering if anything worse could happen to top this catastrophe.

Taking him by the hand, Adele led Lucien through the first floor and then the second, showing him every room he'd seen before. She saved the master bedroom until last.

"And this, my pet, is where we'll take a slight detour," said Adele, shifting her eyes toward the great bed. "But before the afternoon's festivities commence, let me show you something quite peculiar that I discovered—quite by chance."

Lucien had tried with all his might to avoid looking at the little staircase to the study. Now, to his horror, Adele grabbed his hand and dragged him toward it. He resisted like a child being led to the sink to get his mouth washed out with soap.

"Lift up on the first step and see what happens," said Adele.

Lucien stared at the staircase, silently asking himself why life kept singling him out for such punishment like this. First, the fireplace disaster a few weeks ago, which had devastated him, now this. He stooped down and did what Adele asked. With great effort, he lifted the stair up to reveal the mattress.

"What do you make of all this?" Adele said. "I thought you might know of somebody who could've built something like this."

Lucien let the stair come down with a crash, giving Adele a start.

"Why are you so curious...about this?"

Adele paused for a second or two. "I just thought it was an ingenious hiding place and was impressed by it, that's all."

"It is...quite clever, but I can't imagine who built it. Maybe it's been here since the house was built. Or maybe it was put here during the Revolution."

"I don't think so. The hinges and bolt are quite modern, see for yourself."

"And how did you happen to discover this thing?" Lucien asked.

"A servant was cleaning the carpet and found it."

"I see," said Lucien, then walked over to the bed and sat down.

"And how did you come to possess this modest little cottage? It seems a bit out of your price range."

Adele unbuttoned the side of her black skirt, let it drop to the floor, and pulled off her beige sweater.

"Silly man. One of my clients acquired it and is letting me use it for the rest of the year—completely rent-free. Wasn't that gracious of him?"

"Must be a very special client to be so generous. Do I know him?"

"Oh goodness, no. Just one of those old fools in the clothing business."

Knowing the brief history of this house, Lucien had a suspicion that her client wore a gray-green uniform. He knew he probably wasn't Adele's only lover. She was greedy and opportunistic, willing to use anyone to get ahead. He was intrigued by that mercenary side of her. But if she was literally in the enemy's bed, she was not only a traitor, but also a direct danger to him.

She took off her brassiere, then pushed Lucien down on the bed. Lucien couldn't help looking at the stair the whole time they were making love. But in an odd way, he thought, maybe this was a good thing. This cruel coincidence actually took his mind off the Serraults. It was a case of one horrible thing replacing another. At least he wouldn't think of them every waking hour of the day. Now he'd be forced to face his worst nightmare: could the secret stair be traced back to him? Who else knew about it?

30

A BEAUTIFUL BUILDING. YOU SHOULD BE VERY PROUD."
Lucien was proud. So proud that he was daydreaming at that very moment of winning the French Academy of Architecture's highest award for his just-completed engine factory in Chaville. Standing alongside Major Herzog, he relished every detail—the strong horizontal lines of his ribbon-glass windows, the vertical emphasis of the brick entryway, the beautiful curve of the arched concrete roof, which was strong enough to withstand an Allied air attack. Lucien and Celeste had no children, but he'd always imagined that the completion of a great design would be like the birth of one's child.

"I knew I could do a good building if I had the chance," said Lucien, talking to no one in particular.

"It will be the first of many," said Herzog, slapping him on the back with his elegantly gloved hand. "Your design for the Tremblay factory is even better than this."

Lucien beamed at Herzog. After three months, he had come to regard the German as his friend, a kindred spirit. His unease over being friendly with the enemy had evaporated. Lucien was still annoyed that Celeste thought of him as a collaborator. He was merely an architect who wanted work. And the opportunities to do this happened to be coming from the Germans. Herzog needed factories, and Lucien designed them for him. Technically, he was working for Manet, who cooperated in order not to have his business appropriated by the Germans. It was the smart thing to do. He wasn't some evil profiteer who was raking in millions. And Lucien was in no way getting rich off all this war work for the Reich.

"You really think the Tremblay factory will be better?" asked Lucien, finding himself anxious for Herzog's approval.

"Much better. The concrete structure is even more dynamic than this. A beautiful expression of functionalism."

Lucien's ego was flying into the stratosphere. He had finally proven that he could design. All he had needed was the chance. At this moment, he felt that there was nothing he couldn't do architecturally. He couldn't wait for more commissions.

Lucien and Herzog walked slowly around the building, admiring every detail. Trucks were driving in to unload the machinery for production work, which was to begin next week. Though Manet had driven his crews to finish the building ahead of time, they'd still adhered to Lucien's drawings and hadn't cut any corners. Everything had been done according to Lucien's specifications. That would never have happened in peacetime. Clients always deleted some detail that they thought useless and unnecessary but that Lucien absolutely loved.

"I'll tell you a secret," Herzog said. "A new munitions factory is being planned south of here in Fresnes. When I was in Berlin on leave last week, Reich Minister Speer talked about it. It's only in the early stages, but it will happen, I assure you. And because of your success here, you're a shoo-in for the commission."

"How big will it be?" asked Lucien, almost salivating.

"Over fifty hectares. A huge complex, like a city."

Lucien's mind was racing. He forgot about the building in front of him. In just ten seconds, he was envisioning the site plan. The buildings would all join together to create one grand composition. Lucien was so lost in his fantasy that he didn't notice Colonel Lieber approaching. Herzog cleared his throat and saluted, bringing Lucien back to earth.

"A very adequate building, Herzog," said Lieber. "Some unnecessary flourishes, but very adequate. Congratulations, Major. Berlin is very pleased with my…our work here."

"Thank you, Colonel. But it is Monsieur Bernard's building. His fine design gives us a most efficient facility," said Herzog, nodding toward the architect.

Lieber barely acknowledged Lucien. "Yes, an interesting building, monsieur."

When a client said a building was interesting, it meant he didn't like it but didn't have the nerve to say so outright. He smiled at the colonel and bowed his head slightly. His hatred of the man had increased exponentially since the night at rue du Renard. But as Manet had repeatedly told him, there was nothing to be done about it. Lieber wasn't going away.

"Now Reich Minister Speer, there's a great architect," exclaimed Lieber. "The Fuehrer's *personal* architect. He's designed some incredible buildings. The great dome in Berlin will hold two hundred thousand people. His new Reichstag is an incredibly beautiful structure."

Herzog, who was standing behind Lieber, rolled his eyes, and Lucien looked down at his shoes, trying to suppress a smile. Speer's design for Berlin was an over-scaled, pompous display of egomania. Hitler, who had twice failed to get into the Royal Academy of Art in Vienna when he was a young man, had always harbored the wish to be an architect and took a personal interest in designing the new Berlin. Lucien didn't fault Speer for designing to please the Fuehrer. Maybe Speer secretly hated the neoclassical style that Hitler loved. All architects kissed ass to get commissions; it was part and parcel of the job. Lucien had seen examples of Hitler's art and frankly thought he had an innate talent. He would've hired him to do a rendering of one of his buildings. Just think how the world would've turned out if Hitler had gotten into art school, thought Lucien.

31

"WHAT DO YOU MEAN, YOU'RE NOT INTERESTED IN SEEING MY building?"

Celeste kept her back turned to Lucien, vigorously washing a dinner plate in the sink. Lucien walked up to her and spoke directly into her right ear. There was a time when he would've planted a kiss on that slender neck, but that time had long since passed.

"I said...what do you—?"

"You heard me the first time," Celeste said.

Lucien turned and sat back down at the kitchen table and began to play with the little white enameled scale they used to weigh portions of their food. All Parisians had one, so they could stretch their meals as much as possible. He pressed his finger down on the metal pan and the dial read 200 grams. The rage was building inside of him, but he decided he wasn't going to lose his temper this time.

"All right, you don't have to see it. But can you at least have the courtesy of giving me your reason for not wanting to come with me?"

"I don't want to be seen with a collaborator."

"You're calling *me* a collaborator?"

"You and that Manet, you're profiting from the misery of the French people. Helping Germans to kill our allies. And the worst thing is that you enjoy doing it. You throw your heart and soul into those goddamn projects. And you're always kissing that German major's ass. You spend so much time with that guy that I think you may secretly be a queer."

"Did you happen to notice that we eat three meals a day, have decent clothes, and don't have to scrounge around for the basic necessities of life?" Lucien shot back, still keeping the pent-up rage from spewing out like a geyser.

"But at what price, Lucien?"

"Are you saying I'm a traitor?"

Celeste put down her dish rag and hesitated a moment before answering, which infuriated Lucien. He wanted her to instantly say that it wasn't true.

"No, traitor's not the right word. You're a sort of an architectural Mephistopheles. You know, you've sold your soul to the devil in order to design."

Lucien didn't react but sat there absorbing the word "Mephistopheles," repeating it in his mind. He didn't know what to say to defend himself.

"So don't ask me to go see your buildings again. I won't go."

"Don't worry, I won't trouble you. After all, you never bothered to see my work before the war, so what the hell's the difference."

"You'll be damn lucky if France doesn't find you guilty of being a collaborator after the war. The disgrace…and you could be hanged."

"Knock off the dramatics. No one's going to be hanged because I'm not helping the Germans; I'm doing buildings that will help France recover after the war."

"Nice rationalization—or should I call it fantasy? Your buildings have swastikas on them, never forget that."

"You don't know a goddamn thing, woman. I *am* fighting the Nazis."

"You? That's a joke."

"I've saved French lives."

"The only life you care about is your own."

"Bullshit! I saved two Jews," Lucien said vehemently.

An awful silence enveloped the kitchen. He knew he'd made a horrible mistake. A look of disgust began to form on Celeste's face. She walked over to the table and sat in the chair across from him. Celeste swallowed hard.

"Lucien, have you gone mad? Tell me you didn't help any Jews. Don't you know you've signed our death warrants? Tell me you're lying."

"I can't tell you any more."

"The Gaumont family on the rue Rousselet were all shot for hiding that little Jewish kid. Just for pretending a four-year-old boy was a Christian relative. The mother, the father, the grandparents, and all their kids are dead. All for some stupid self-righteous notion about helping one's fellow man."

"Maybe it isn't so stupid."

"In wartime, Christian brotherhood takes a backseat to saving one's own skin. It's not pretty or noble, but it's the cold hard truth."

"That wasn't why I did it."

Celeste smiled. "I wondered where that money came from. I knew it wasn't from the Nazis. They don't pay their collaborators that well. It must have been a big temptation to have all that money in your pocket. To buy nice things for you, me, and your mistress."

Lucien, who had been holding his head in his hands, looked up at Celeste.

"You idiot," said Celeste. "A wife *always* knows."

"I did it for us, whether you believe it or not."

"I *don't* believe it. But I am impressed that you played both sides. Getting money from the Jews and designing your beloved architecture for the Boche. I guess you can have your cake and eat it too. But leave it to you to screw yourself in both directions. You're either going to be killed by the Gestapo for helping Jews or killed for being a collaborator. I don't know exactly what you've gotten yourself into—I don't want to know. I could put up with that slut you have on the side, but not this. I'm not going to be tortured or deported because of your foolishness."

"So what are you going to do?"

"I'm leaving you."

"You're what?" Stunned, Lucien shot up from his chair and looked down at his wife.

"You heard me. Our marriage was finished anyway. It was a bad match from the beginning. To use one of your dumb architecture metaphors, the marriage was built on a weak foundation, and it just crumbled."

"In war you have to make hard decisions. I—"

"And you made the wrong decisions. No matter how you look at it, you're screwed. Stop fooling yourself, Lucien; you're not a man of high moral fiber. It's just like I said before—an architectural Mephistopheles."

Lucien walked to the tall kitchen window that overlooked the courtyard. Except for a scrawny black cat prowling at its edge, the space was deserted.

"There's something else."

"What?" he answered irritably, his back toward her, bracing for more abuse to be hurled at him.

"I've met someone," she said in a soft quiet voice.

It was as though someone had hit him on the back of his head with a shovel. He almost fell forward. Lucien placed his hands on the sides of the window frame and dropped his head. After a minute, he walked out of the kitchen to the foyer closet and grabbed his tweed jacket. Slamming the door behind him, he ran down the stairs instead of waiting for the lift. He was so beside himself with anger that it took him almost five minutes to notice he'd walked ten blocks along the rue Saint-Denis. Three hours later, when he returned to the apartment, Celeste and her clothes were gone.

32

D ON'T LIE TO ME, GASPARD. YOU'RE NOT LEAVING ME FOR another woman."

"One of my students. We've…"

Juliette Trenet walked up to her husband and looked into his eyes. He immediately looked away.

"I wish it were one of your students," Juliette said. "Then I could bear the heartbreak."

Gaspard said nothing, gazing at the oriental rug in the vestibule of their apartment.

"Professor Pinard called you into his office, didn't he?"

"No, that's not…"

"And he gave you a choice—me…or your job."

"Juliette, please…"

"And you chose your professorship in medieval literature."

Gaspard, a short, handsome man with light brown hair, stepped back from Juliette.

"All because Vichy and the Nazis decreed that because my grandmother—whom I never even met—was Jewish…I'm now officially Jewish."

Juliette went over to the coat rack and held up her forest-green flannel blazer, which had a yellow felt star on its front breast pocket. "Even though I've never set foot in a synagogue or know a single word of Hebrew."

"The way they decide who's a Jew is ridiculous." Gaspard shook his head. "A priest at a parish in Ménilmontant was classified a Jew."

"I was fired from a job I loved because I'm a Jew. And now the only man I've ever loved is leaving me because I'm a Jew."

"It's not…"

"Please, please tell me this isn't happening, Gaspard," Juliette cried out. "That I'm just having a terrible nightmare. For God's sake, wake me up."

Juliette placed her hand on the lapel of his tweed jacket. Gaspard stepped away from her until his back was against the wood-paneled apartment door.

"You know, I fell in love with you the moment I first saw you at Jean's party," said Juliette. "So handsome. And when we started talking, I knew right then how brilliant you were. Remember?"

"Of course, I remember. And *you* won my heart in an instant. For a woman to be so pretty and to have a doctorate in bacteriology doing such important research at the university," replied Gaspard. "I was so happy to find you."

"All the wonderful trips we took and all the good times we've had together in the last five years. The parties we gave."

"Why, yes," said Gaspard with a smile.

"Then please stay, my love. Together, we can get through this," Juliette pleaded with tears welling up in her eyes.

A pained expression replaced her husband's smile.

"I…just can't do it, Juliette. I can't."

"Is it the thought of us being penniless? Or the loss of your position?" Juliette started toward him but stopped. "Do you think *you'll* be sent to Drancy with me?"

Gaspard's reply was an agonizing silence.

Juliette put her head in her hands. "*Please* don't do this," she begged. She wanted to run up to him, put her arms around his waist, and bury her face in his broad chest as she'd done in the past when she was upset or sad.

Gaspard's fair complexion was now flushed with shame. He turned and placed his hand on the door handle. Without saying a word, Juliette grabbed hold of his sleeve, and Gaspard shook his arm to get loose of her as he opened the door. With a furious tug, he finally freed himself and slammed the door.

"Come back," Juliette yelled after him. "Please!"

She stood staring at the door, tears streaming down her face. She walked into the salon where she sobbed uncontrollably and loudly, not caring who might hear her.

God, I married a coward, she thought. *But it doesn't matter. I still love him!*

Juliette sat down in an armchair and tried to calm herself. She gently rubbed her belly. She and her baby were now totally alone in the world.

·❖· ·❖· ·❖·

Six weeks later, as Juliette sat in the empty lion's den, the memory of that terrible day still played over and over in her mind. Every time she thought of Gaspard's shocking betrayal, she felt like crying. Time hadn't lessened the pain in the least. She had loved her husband so much…and then to see this handsome, intelligent man turn into a frightened little boy who ran away.

Everything had come down on them so suddenly. First, Juliette lost her position at the university where they both worked, then came the unexpected pregnancy. Gaspard hadn't seemed truly happy when she told him the news, though for her sake, he'd tried to seem so. Just after the surrender, when they'd seen a couple pushing a pram, Juliette remembered he'd said that no one should bring a child into a hell like the Occupation. She knew it wasn't the best time to have a baby, but she was still overjoyed; being a mother would always trump her career, no matter how successful she became.

Gaspard had loved being a professor. More than a job, it was his whole identity. If he were fired, the loss of the prestige and his place in elite intellectual circles, she realized, would be even more devastating than the loss of income. A full professor at only thirty-two with a highly praised book on twelfth-century epic poetry, he was admired and respected by everyone at the university, even outside the history and literature departments. A shining star in the academic universe. Juliette had really never understood how much it all meant to Gaspard. Much more than his wife…and his own child meant to him.

Because Juliette didn't consider herself a Jew, she found little solace in the fact that thousands of Jews had been kicked out of universities throughout France. Or that hundreds of gentile husbands in Paris had abandoned their Jewish wives when faced with the same situation as Gaspard. They too knew they couldn't bear the hardship, poverty, and threat to their lives that suddenly came with being married to a Jew.

The lingering smell of lion piss on top of her morning sickness had made Juliette even more nauseous. Still, she knew she was very lucky to have found this hiding place. Just a week after Gaspard had left, Monsieur Ducreux, her landlord, had showed up at the door of her apartment and ordered her to get out right then and there. A man who had been friendly and cordial to her every day of the five years she had lived there now treated her like a complete stranger. Waving an official-looking paper in her face, he claimed he could evict her. Juliette didn't argue but just replied in a quiet voice that she needed an hour to pack and calmly shut the door. After being turned out, she had been able to stay with her former lab assistant, Henri Leroy, and his family in their small apartment. After a few days, a neighbor down the hall knocked on the door and started asking questions, and Juliette knew it was time to move on. Henri had been a loyal colleague for seven years, and she had no intention of having his family suffer on her account. When Juliette told Henri she had nowhere else to go, he told her he wouldn't abandon her. In desperation, he had asked his cousin, Michel Dauphin, who also refused. His wife, he said, would never risk her life to help anyone, let alone a Jew. But Dauphin was a kind-hearted man, and he had offered a temporary solution.

He was a zookeeper and told his cousin that Professor Trenet could hide for a while in one of the unused cages in the section of animal houses that were completely shut up. Despite the food shortages, the zoo was kept up during the Occupation, mainly for the benefit of the German soldiers. The animals ate better than most Parisians. Now Juliette was living in a concrete den behind the empty lions' cage at the zoo. It was the enclosed space where the lions slept and ate when they weren't walking around in the cage in front of the public. Even lions want their privacy occasionally, thought Juliette. Out of her savings, Juliette gave Dauphin five thousand francs, even though the man hadn't asked for payment. If Juliette was found, the zookeeper would be arrested too, so she had insisted.

Dauphin, a short, rotund man in his sixties, brought Juliette food and drink every night without fail. She knew he was spending the five thousand to take care of her. Dauphin, she discovered, had three grown daughters of his own and knew what a pregnant woman looked like, so no one had to tell him he was feeding two people. She could see that Dauphin devoted a lot of effort to preparing her meals. Juliette ate meat, chicken, potatoes, carrots, and beets, all thoroughly cooked and served in a covered metal platter. With all of her meals came a large cup of milk. He had also supplied a big thick mattress with a sheet for her bed.

As a bacteriologist, Juliette knew how important it was to keep clean from germs to protect Marie or Pierre (her baby was to be named after her heroine Madame Curie or her husband and, of course, grow up to be a scientist). Dauphin obliged by providing abundant amounts of soap and water so she could bathe. And as a man who was used to cleaning out lion and elephant excrement, he cheerfully dumped out Juliette's slop bucket daily. The problem with the space was that a human could not stand upright in it. Juliette sat the whole day and was only able to walk around in the open cage at night.

One evening, after Dauphin brought her a meal and some clean clothes, Juliette asked him why he was putting his life in so much danger. His answer stunned her. "Oh, madame, you don't know how good it makes me feel about myself to help a human in this time of evil." The zookeeper, who probably had no more than a few years of schooling, had a far more profound sense of morality, Juliette realized, than many of the highly trained scientists she used to work with.

Sitting in her cage by herself, day after day, Juliette sometimes found her loneliness unbearable. She often placed her hand on her belly and talked about her happy childhood in Lyon to Marie or Pierre. Sometimes she sang her baby her favorite songs. During the day, by placing heavy canvas over the den opening, Juliette could burn candles, which enabled her to read and write. She tried to keep her mind occupied by pretending she was on a sabbatical where she could concentrate on theoretical work. On notebooks provided by the good Dauphin, she scribbled formulas and ideas then stared off into space thinking and thinking. She did some preliminary work that she hoped would one day be the basis of a research paper.

Just as Juliette was stretching out on the mattress to read a newspaper Dauphin had brought her earlier that evening, all the lights in the animal house came on. It startled Juliette, and she called out loudly, "Monsieur Dauphin," then stopped because she remembered he had never turned on the lights. He had always used a lantern at night. She heard the drunken mutterings of a man in front of the cage. Then to her horror, the side of the canvas sheet was pulled back and moments later, a Wehrmacht soldier dragging a bottle of schnapps along the concrete floor crawled on his hands and knees through the opening.

Roaring like a lion, the soldier leered at Juliette. "What a pretty lioness—or are you a tigress? Roar!" Juliette slid off the mattress and backed into the corner of the den, but the soldier lunged forward and grabbed her right ankle, pulling her toward him. He fumbled open the fly buttons of his trousers and yanked Juliette beneath him and pushed her dress up. She could smell his stinking breath when, all of a sudden, he rolled off her. Above her she saw Dauphin with a shovel in his hands.

"He broke in by the side door."

Juliette raised herself up on her elbows. "Are there any more?"

"No, it was just him, thank God. I'll dump him into the gutter on the far side of the zoo, and his people will find him in the morning with a very bad headache."

"But will he...?"

"No, madame, he won't remember a thing."

Juliette was shaking with fear, and Dauphin knelt down to hug her. She wrapped her arms around his neck.

"It's not this one we have to worry about, madame," said Dauphin, caressing her brown hair and patting her back. "Yesterday, I got official word that the Germans are transferring some animals from Berlin so they'll need these cages. It won't be safe for you here anymore."

Juliette now felt more frightened than she'd been when the soldier had attacked her. *She had absolutely nowhere to go.*

"My God, what will I do?" she said, panic-stricken.

"My cousin says he knows a man who knows a man who can help you," said Dauphin.

33

I KNEW YOU'D SHOW UP."

Lucien settled on the chaise lounge and reached out to accept the glass of cognac from Manet, then drained it in one gulp. It was almost nine o'clock in the morning when Lucien arrived at the little stone cottage—two floors with a dormered attic set off from a country road just on the outskirts of Paris, near Epinay-sur-Seine. He knew it wasn't Manet's country house, as it was way too modest and plain for a man of his stature.

"Ah, now that's a nutritious breakfast," said Lucien. "Now tell me, how did you know I'd be here today?"

"I just had a feeling," said Manet, "that's all."

"Because I felt guilty about killing Monsieur and Madame Serrault?"

Manet frowned. "Lucien, be reasonable. It wasn't your fault that they died. Who would've thought the Boche would wind up there that evening? And the bird's nest? It was pure rotten luck. Lieber murdered them, not you."

"I was responsible for planning every possible contingency, no matter how absurd. I placed them in danger when I chose to use the fireplace."

"Nonsense."

"I could have found another place for them to hide, but that would've been too easy. I had to be clever."

"I asked you here to see if you would help me again, Lucien. Will you?"

Lucien looked down at the glass in his hands. The last few weeks had been a living hell for him. After the discovery of Adele's stair three weeks ago, the guilt over the Serraults hadn't gone away, as he'd hoped. Then Celeste abandoned him. It was literally tearing his insides out; the last few nights he'd pissed blood. If he wasn't thinking about the Serraults, the stair problem consumed him, leaving him a nervous wreck.

"We have a problem," said Lucien. "The stair in the hunting lodge in Le Chesnay has been discovered. A friend of mine who now has use of the place told me."

"Adele Bonneau," replied Manet.

At first Lucien was startled that Manet knew her name, then slowly nodded his head.

"The Germans must have given her the house."

"The Gestapo," said Manet.

Lucien was visibly shaken at Manet's reply, then became revolted at the thought of her even touching such an animal. To be with a German was bad enough, but to lower oneself like that was unthinkable. How could any French woman do such a thing?

"She could link you to the stair."

"I know."

"It's in our best interest that you avoid Mademoiselle Bonneau."

Lucien had agreed to meet Manet expressly for the purpose of telling him that this was the end of it. He just couldn't take it any longer. Now was the time to get out. Besides, he'd made out okay in this deal—a great deal of money, a car, plus two commissions. While he was driving, he'd rehearsed what he had to say to Manet, revising it and imagining what Manet's response would be. Being a good Christian, the old man would probably make it easy for him and say that it was all right to call it quits, that Lucien already had done more than any man need do. But when Lucien looked up into Manet's eyes and was about to begin his speech, the words stuck in his throat. He lost his nerve. There were a million reasons for walking away from this mess. But not one would come out of his mouth. It was like a dream in which he was on a speeding train that he couldn't jump off. He knew the train was heading for a brick wall at the end of the track, so he *had* to get off, but he couldn't.

The Serraults' death had made Lucien see things in a different light. The sight of the frail elderly couple dead with handkerchiefs in their mouths had jolted him. They'd died saving him, when he was supposed to save them. Like most Frenchmen, he hadn't given a damn about what was happening to the Jews; all that mattered was saving his own skin. But he realized that the sheer hatred and brutality heaped upon the Jews was something he now couldn't ignore. The punishment for being a Jew in the Reich crossed the line into barbarism. They were being hunted down like wild animals. What made it so sickening was that it wasn't perpetrated by a bunch of ignorant half-naked savages, but the citizens of a nation renowned for its culture and intelligence that had produced men like Goethe and Beethoven.

Lucien, the atheist, didn't want to use any religious horseshit, like it was a Christian's duty to protect "God's chosen people," to justify his change of heart. Or have an epiphany and decide to become a Jew. And he didn't believe there was some moral structure to the universe, a set of rules governing good and bad (not like the nonsense of the Ten Commandments). No, he made this decision because he'd seen almost every Frenchman turn his back on these people, and that cowardice now filled him with disgust.

Lucien knew he couldn't be that way and just stand by; he had to continue what he'd been doing. When he asked himself why he was risking his life, the answer wasn't the cash, the factories, or the sheer thrill of the challenge. He was risking his life because it was the right thing to do. He had to go beyond himself and help these people. His father was probably looking up at him from Hell (certainly not Heaven), laughing and cursing at him, but he didn't care.

Finally Lucien swallowed hard and spoke. "What is the business at hand, monsieur?"

"An emergency refuge is needed," Manet said. "My guest won't be here long."

"Let me take a look around," said Lucien. "I'll figure out something for you."

"The guest you'll be helping has offered twenty thousand francs for your services," said Manet as he walked through the first floor with Lucien.

"No."

"How much more do you want then?"

"Nothing. No more money."

Manet stopped and looked Lucien straight in his eyes. "Have you become a patriot, monsieur?"

Lucien laughed. "Not quite, but I can't take the money."

Manet put his hand on Lucien's shoulder in his signature grand-fatherly gesture. "A most noble sentiment, Lucien, but an incredibly stupid one. Twenty thousand francs is nothing for saving a life. And remember the risk you're taking. Please, my friend, take the money."

Lucien was surprised that Manet had such a cold, practical side to him. He wasn't the Christian with the heart of gold he'd thought he was.

"No, monsieur, I can't."

"I'll hold on to the money for you, how about that?"

"Shall we take our usual stroll?"

They went up to the second floor and then to the attic and returned to the first floor via a service stair.

"Does this stair go down to the basement?" asked Lucien.

"Yes, I believe it does. That's where the kitchen is located."

Lucien led the way down, and they found themselves in a very spacious kitchen with an enormous oven against the wall and a huge butcher block table in the center of the space. Pots and pans hung from a rack attached to the ceiling. A door at the rear of the kitchen led out to a garden. Lucien walked slowly around the room, peering into storage closets and cabinets. He put his hands in the pockets of his trousers and paced back and forth along the stone floor.

"That space under the platform where the bathtub sits could work. We could fashion a removable panel, and he could easily squeeze in under there," said Lucien, though he wasn't convinced this was the best solution. He continued to pace, staring at the floor and trying to think of a better hiding place. For each possible place, he forced himself to think of a dozen ways it could be discovered, because he was scared he'd screw up again and get someone killed.

His pacing brought him to a large floor drain about sixty centimeters square set in the stone floor of the kitchen. He knelt down to examine it. He pulled the grating up and discovered a hole that was a meter and a half deep and lined with lead sheet. A pipe was connected at the bottom to carry off the water.

"Here," said Lucien, pointing to the drain.

Manet stooped down to take a closer look.

"We'll hide him in here. It's big enough for him to fit in. He can pull up the entire grating, get in, then put it back in place. A shallow metal pan will be connected to the underside of the grating, and we'll fill it with water so it'll look completely natural."

The old feeling of excitement returned, which surprised Lucien. He thought it had been driven out of him by the Serraults' death. The ingenuity of this idea started him on another high. He felt good about himself again and was smiling from ear to ear.

"That's brilliant, but what about the pipe down there?"

"We'll have to disconnect it. The drain is only used if the kitchen floor floods, so we don't need it." Lucien now began to think of the inhabitants of the spaces as real, breathing human beings and considered their comfort. Before they were just cargo. Instead of putting the imaginary person in to try out the space, he inserted himself to gauge its comfort. The drain was wide enough to fit an adult, but because of its depth, he would have to stoop or sit at the bottom.

"Have your men dig down deep to give him a little more room under the pan. Put some wood planks on the floor and a cushion."

"What about a tunnel out into the garden? As a backup," asked Manet.

"That's a lot of work, and the sides and top of it have to be supported to prevent a cave-in. It has to extend way out in the garden so he can get out undetected." Lucien knew Manet wanted a contingency plan after the fireplace mishap. It was a good idea.

"I can get it done in time."

Lucien stood up and stared at the drain, thinking of every possible way it could fail. After a few minutes, he grinned at Manet. "Let's do it."

Manet patted him on the back "I'm glad you're still on our side. With men like you in the fight, we're sure to win."

"Win? I don't know if I believe that anymore."

"The Germans seemed invincible, but their luck has turned," said Manet with a smile. "The British stopped them at El Alamein in July, and the Allies will probably invade North Africa soon. Rommel and his troops will be driven out because they have no petrol for their tanks. They can be the best soldiers in the world, but it won't matter if they don't have fuel."

"From your lips to God's ears. Isn't that what the Jews say?"

✛ ✛ ✛

As the two men went out the front door, Alain crouched lower behind the hedge inside the stone wall that formed the perimeter of the yard. He had been able to creep up to the first-floor windows but hadn't been able to overhear anything. He'd seen them go into the basement and stay there for a long time. It had been too risky to peek into the windows, so he stayed where he was and waited until they came out. After shaking hands, both men got into their cars and left. Alain came out from behind the hedge and went to the rear of the house, where the basement level led to the yard. He peered through the windows and surveyed the kitchen very carefully, but nothing unusual caught his eye. But considering the time they'd spent there, he guessed the kitchen had been the focus of their attention.

It was all still a puzzle to Alain—the mysterious fireplace detail, now the trip to this out-of-the-way cottage. He was angry with himself for not being able to piece things together. He needed something more to make sense of it all. When he got back to his car, a dark green Peugeot that his cousin had lent him, Alain sat on the hood and smoked a cigarette, mulling over every detail he'd seen.

34

A T LEAST HE DOESN'T LOOK JEWISH," MUTTERED LUCIEN.
Father Jacques chuckled and got up from his chair. "No, he doesn't, and that makes our task a bit easier, but still, we always have to be careful. Every day children are betrayed to the Gestapo."

Lucien continued to stare at the boy sitting in a chair at the table in his office. A large green rucksack with a cat's head sticking out of the top was set next to him on the floor.

"He seems a well-mannered kid. How old is he again?"

"Twelve. Pierre is a good child. From a very scholarly family. His father was a chemistry professor at the University of Paris before the Germans banned Jews from holding teaching positions. His mother was also a scholar. They were rounded up and taken to Drancy and never heard from again. Probably sent east to work in the labor camps. It's the same with all the Jews—deported, and the poor devils vanish from the face of the earth."

"It's just him?"

"His sister and brothers were betrayed last month and taken away by the Gestapo. And his benefactor, a seventy-year-old woman, was executed."

Lucien turned and looked at the old priest. Father Jacques bit his lip as if he realized that he should have left out that last detail.

"And what makes you think I'd hide a Jew?" Lucien said.

"Monsieur Manet vouched for you."

"He did, eh?"

"I know it's a big decision. But you'd be surprised, Monsieur Lucien, how many gentiles have taken in children. Most Frenchmen don't give a damn about deporting adult Jews, but the idea of the Germans rounding up children disgusts them."

"Is that a fact?"

"It would just be a temporary situation until I can arrange passage across the Pyrenees and into Spain."

"Just how temporary do you mean, Father?"

"A month at the most."

"Christ, I thought you meant a couple of weeks. And I bet the cat comes with him."

"It does indeed, monsieur. He loves that cat."

"Who knows you brought him here?"

"Just Monsieur Manet."

"So is Pierre Gau his fake name or his real name?" asked Lucien with considerable irritation.

"It is his new identity. He has all the papers to prove it—false identity papers and a false baptismal certificate."

"And why can't you keep him at your youth center in Montparnasse?"

"The French police are getting suspicious. Two weeks ago, they staged a sudden raid but found nothing. Out of respect, they didn't ransack the house. But if the Gestapo comes, it'll be a much different story. They'll rip the place to pieces."

"How the hell will I explain him being here? I have an employee, and from time to time, Germans visit the office."

"Other families make up a story. He could be the son of a friend killed during the war, or a relative from the south who lost his family."

"Who's going to believe a load of bullshit like that?" replied Lucien, not caring that he cursed in front of a priest.

"You can say he's a war orphan temporarily placed in your care by the Church. In a way, that is the truth. I'm sorry, but I wouldn't have come to you unless you were my last hope. I'm desperate, monsieur."

Lucien was annoyed that Manet was taking advantage of him.

Maybe when he'd refused the money the last time, Manet felt that Lucien now qualified as a true Christian and would take such a risk. And it was a *big* risk. Working anonymously to hide Jews was one thing. There was a buffer that protected him. And it wouldn't just be him in danger. If a Jew was found in an apartment house, every single soul who lived there would be arrested and deported, no questions asked. Last month, a woman in a building discovered a Jew was hiding in an apartment next door to hers, and she started screaming her head off up and down the corridors, warning the other tenants. They'd beaten down the door and turned the Jew in to the Gestapo. They didn't want to die.

Lucien walked over to the boy to get a closer look. He was a good-looking kid with thick, dark brown hair and eyebrows and as scrawny as all the other famished children in Paris. For parents, that was the most heartbreaking thing about the Occupation—to see their kids go hungry. Mothers spent hours queuing and scrounging food for their kids. Pierre was now looking intently at Lucien's old architectural magazines, stopping at certain photos to get a closer look. Lucien watched him for another minute or two as the boy paused to gaze at a picture of a department store.

"How do you do, Monsieur Pierre? My name is Lucien."

The boy rose from his seat and shook his hand firmly. "Pierre Gau, monsieur."

Good manners, Lucien immediately thought, *very well brought up. You have to hand it to the Jews on that count. You never hear of bands of Jewish juvenile delinquents raising hell in Paris.*

"I see that you're interested in architecture."

"How did they make the curve at the corner of this building, monsieur?" asked Pierre, pointing to a photo of a train station in the magazine.

"It's done in concrete. You can make curves out of wooden forms, then pour in the concrete. You can make any shape you want."

"Like this roof of an airplane hangar?" the boy asked, holding up another photo.

"Yes, concrete's especially good for hangars," Lucien said. "So what's your cat's name?"

"Misha."

Lucien rubbed its head, and it started purring as if there were a little motor inside its throat. Lucien had loved cats as a boy. His family had always had one or two as pets. He'd liked getting up in the morning and finding them snuggled against him fast asleep. But after marrying Celeste, he'd discovered she was allergic to them so no more cats. It was nice to see a cat in the office; it gave the place a real homey touch.

"How did they fit such a big piece of glass here?" asked the boy, pointing to the front of an office building that had a store on the first floor.

"They made a beam of concrete above it and put the glass sheet in below." The boy continued to flip through the magazines and said nothing more. This kid was beginning to grow on him.

Lucien continued to observe the boy. For a child who had had everything near and dear to him—mother, father, brothers, and sister—wiped out of his life, he seemed pretty tough and mature for his age. That was because this kid had had to grow up in a real hurry. Lucien wondered how he, as a twelve-year-old, would've reacted to such tragedy. Brave like this child, or a whimpering mess? Because Lucien imagined the latter, he admired the kid. This boy needed somebody to look after him.

He felt as if he was in one of those dumb-ass American movies he'd seen. A character would be in a quandary over what to do. A miniature angel wearing wings and a halo appeared on one shoulder telling him to do what's right, and a devil with a pitchfork was on the other shoulder advising him not to. Sometimes the devil and the angel would argue with each other, and because of America's morality code, the angel would win out even though the devil could easily kill the angel with his pitchfork. Pierre kept leafing through the magazines, and Lucien walked slowly back to Father Jacques.

The priest placed his hand on Lucien's shoulder.

"Monsieur Manet knew I was desperate, and he said you are a good Christian."

"A Christian? I don't even want to tell you how long it's been since I attended mass. You'd throw up." Lucien would never admit to the priest that he was an atheist. In Catholic France, that was worse than admitting one was a rapist.

Father Jacques's smile disappeared and his grip tightened like a vise. "Listen, asshole. Is it yes or no? Will you do it or not? I haven't got all day."

Lucien was surprised to hear such words coming from a priest. But he then smiled. He liked that Father Jacques had balls. Lucien's father had told him that priests were spineless eunuchs.

Lucien looked back at the boy and then down at the floor. The devil sitting on his shoulder—his father—would not win this one. To hell with him.

"A month, right?

Father Jacques's fatherly smile returned, and he shook Lucien's hand.

"I have a storage room in the back of the office, nothing fancy. I'll say I've brought him on to be an apprentice. Maybe he'll learn something if he's such a smart Jew."

"Remember, just say he's a war orphan and that you knew his family," advised Father Jacques.

"What about feeding him? That's going to be a problem."

"Don't worry. His ration card is still valid," said Father Jacques. "It's a sin how the little ones go without food. Last week at the school, the children were asked to write an essay on what one wish they'd want a fairy to grant. A seven-year-old girl named Danielle just wrote, 'Never ever be hungry.'"

"I don't know a damn thing about kids, but I guess I'll learn on the job. You know, we'll both be tortured to death for this," said Lucien with a smile. "We'll ask ourselves why we did such a foolish thing."

"I remember when Monsignor Theas, the archbishop of Montauban, issued a pastoral letter after the deportation of Jews began in '42. It said that what Vichy and the Germans were doing was an affront to human dignity and a violation of the most sacred rights of the individual and the family. It's not a foolish thing, monsieur."

"So will doing this make up for all the Sunday masses I've missed since 1930?"

"Don't push it, my son."

35

LIEUTENANT VOSS, COULD YOU JOG MONSIEUR TRIOLET'S MEMORY?"
Voss was more than happy to oblige Colonel Schlegal, who
was growing very irritated with Triolet. After an hour of pummeling
his face and body, the frog bastard still wouldn't cooperate. Voss had
been ordered all the way out to a hunting lodge in Le Chesnay and
wanted to get this over with and get back to Paris.

Schlegal motioned toward the secret stair, and Voss immediately
knew what he meant. He yanked Triolet from the chair by his collar
and dragged him to the foot of the stair. Captain Wolf, an officer who
was standing nearby, also knew what was to be done. He lifted the
very heavy hinged stair, Voss placed Triolet's arm under the edge, then
Wolf dropped the stair.

The cracking sound it made when it landed on the Frenchman's
arm reminded Schlegal of snapping chicken drumsticks during Sunday
dinner when he was a kid. It always made his brothers laugh like crazy
but caused his father to scream at him at the top of his lungs.

After the echo of Triolet's scream faded, Schlegal walked over to
him and gently kicked him in the ribs.

"Come, Monsieur Triolet, I've got a luncheon date with an
extremely beautiful woman in an hour, can't we wrap this matter up?
You don't want me to a keep a lady waiting. That wouldn't be gentle-
manly at all, would it?"

Triolet just groaned. For a second the Gestapo officers thought
he was dying. But they were experts in this field and knew from vast
experience how far to go before killing a guest of the Reich. They

all looked at each other with exasperated expressions. Voss grabbed Triolet's legs and turned him around so Wolf could drop the stair on his legs. This time, an incredibly ear-piercing scream came out of the little Frenchman with the elegant waxed mustache. Voss smiled from ear to ear; maybe they were finally making some progress with this stubborn fellow.

Schlegal kicked him again, but this time not so gently.

"Please don't make me late for my engagement," he said. "This young lady is especially dear to me. She'd be so disappointed in me. Come on, you French are experts in romance. You know that wouldn't do."

With a surprising burst of energy, Triolet tried to raise himself on his elbows but quickly collapsed, the side of his face smashing to the floor.

"Why don't we try the neck region this time, Lieutenant Voss?" Schlegal said.

Wolf raised the stair and Voss grabbed his legs. Triolet roared in pain. His head was now positioned at the foot of the stair, and Wolf was waiting for the word to let go.

"At the count of three," said Schlegal in a detached tone of voice. "One…two…"

"All right," groaned Triolet.

"So, the question was…who do you think could build such a stair? Come on, monsieur, you've been a building contractor for forty years in Paris. You know everyone in the building trades. Give me a name."

Triolet muttered something that Schlegal couldn't make out.

"I didn't hear that, Monsieur Triolet."

"There's a cabinetmaker in the eleventh arrondissement…who could do something like this."

"His name please, monsieur."

There was a long pause. Schlegal was used to this phase of interrogation. The pause of conscience. His guest was now debating whether to give in to stop the horrible pain or take the high-minded road and say nothing. When the threat of horrible physical pain confronted one's moral conscience, it was Schlegal's experience that pain always won out. With some, the pause was longer, but in the end, most talked if they knew something. Monsieur Triolet was ready to talk.

"His name is Louis Ledoyen."

"Thank you. Now that wasn't so hard, was it?" said Schlegal. "You have the honor of helping the Reich. No shame in that."

Triolet mumbled something, then passed out from the pain. Voss gave him a kick, but he lay motionless. Schlegal looked down at the Frenchman.

"Take him back to the city and hold him until we track down this cabinetmaker. If it turns out he gave us a fake name, finish him," said Schlegal. "Sooner or later, we'll find out who's behind this hiding place. When we do, gentlemen, I bet we'll find many more of these ingenious devices."

Voss went to the hallway and shouted orders at two waiting soldiers, who came in and dragged Triolet away.

"Wipe that blood off the floor," ordered Schlegal. "This is someone's home, you know. I don't want to leave it a mess."

Voss and Wolf escorted their superior down the grand staircase and out to his black staff car, parked in the circular drive. Schlegal had been preoccupied by the discovery of the stair, and he had ordered his staff to round up everyone connected to the Paris building industry. But each time, the Gestapo came up empty. Informants could tell them nothing, and the most ferocious torture produced no results. This was a very secret operation with only a handful of Frenchmen involved. He knew it didn't involve the Resistance. None of his people on the inside knew anything about it. Schlegal had found plenty of Jews hiding throughout Paris, but not in such a tricky place. It still gnawed at him that the Jews had fooled him. What angered him even more was that gentiles must be helping them. When he got his hands on them, they would pay dearly.

A dark blue Renault was parked farther down the drive, and a short, barrel-chested man in his late fifties was leaning against it smoking a cigarette. Schlegal saw him and nodded, letting the man know it was all right to approach him.

"Any news, Messier?"

"Nothing yet, Colonel, but I'll find out something."

Messier was a gangster the Gestapo used to hunt down Jews for a bounty. With a gang of about twenty petty criminals, he had a unique knack for rooting out Jews and Resistance men in Paris and the surrounding suburbs, like a pig sniffing out truffles. It bothered Schlegal that he had to use such scum of the earth, but they were very effective, especially as informants. Messier had provided lots of valuable information that had led to many arrests. All they wanted in return was a cash bounty and the opportunity to loot the apartments and country houses of Jews and other enemies of the Reich.

Although Germany counted on the treasure of the Jews to enrich its war chest, it allowed men like Messier to share the wealth. Messier was said to have raided a house in the sixth arrondissement and stolen two million francs worth of jewels. Schlegal was surprised to find out that Messier was a former policeman who had been forced to resign because of extortion before the war. But it was his policeman's instincts that made him so good, plus he employed other disgraced gendarmes to help him. This came in handy for Messier's additional line of work— impersonating German policemen to rob people or extract bribes from people involved in the black market. The underground economy had blurred the lines between respectable and non-respectable Parisians, making it easy to use blackmail. Schlegal heard that Messier had even extorted money from a priest who was dealing in black-market butter. The Gestapo never asked questions unless it seemed as if they were getting cut out of the loot.

"Keep looking. Someone is building these hiding places all over Paris. Sooner or later, he'll slip up," said Schlegal. "And what about our friend Janusky? We've placed the *highest* priority on this man's capture. It's not only his fortune and that art collection everyone raves about, he's a political enemy as well."

"He's one slippery Hebrew, I'll give him that. He was at a place on the rue Saint-Hubert for a few weeks, then lit out in a hurry."

"How do you know someone inside your outfit isn't tipping him off? The garbage you use would sell out their grandmothers for a franc. This Jew's rich as Croesus."

Messier burst out laughing. "You're absolutely right, Colonel; anyone can sell out anybody."

"Just make sure you don't sell me out."

36

A ND THIS WILL BE YOUR ROOM. THERE'S AN ARMOIRE OVER THERE in the corner, and this will be your own desk."

Pierre sat down on the bed and ran his hand over the embroidered bedspread.

"I used to have a blue bedspread."

Lucien was pleased that the boy was happy with his new room. He had had the spare room cleaned from top to bottom and had bought a secondhand rug for the wooden floor. Now that he was sure Celeste would not return (he had no idea where she went), it made sense that Pierre move into his apartment. It had been almost two weeks since Father Jacques brought the boy to his office, and making him live in the office seemed cruel—such a good kid deserved better than that.

Lucien had wanted this to be a special day for the boy, so on the way from the office to his new home, they'd gone to the cinema. A depressing German newsreel extolled the virtues of the Fatherland and showed pictures of its defeated subjects, all smiling and laughing, thoroughly happy to be slaves of the Nazis. It was such laughable propaganda that if Lucien had been by himself, he would've walked right out. But a cartoon followed the newsreel. Now that America was in the war, Mickey Mouse and Bugs Bunny had been banned from French theaters, so German cartoons filled the void. Even though it was German, the cartoon's plot about a duck outsmarting a hunter was pretty funny. This surprised Lucien. The Germans he dealt with didn't seem to have much of a sense of humor. At each act of cartoon violence, the audience convulsed with laughter. When Lucien looked to his right at Pierre's profile in the dark of the theater, the light from the screen illuminated the boy's face, and Lucien could see him laughing away. Lucien found himself quite pleased by this sight and kept looking over at the boy, completely ignoring the cartoon. During the feature, a second-rate French production about a bank robbery, Lucien continued to watch Pierre enjoying the film. Not once did the boy take his eyes off the screen.

After the cinema, they took a velo-taxi to Le Chat Roux, where they could get all the hot food they wanted—for a steep price, of course. But Lucien enjoyed himself immensely watching Pierre wolf down potatoes, rabbit, fresh bread, and an éclair.

Even though Pierre wouldn't be staying long, a boy his age needed a room of his own. He remembered how important his room in the apartment on the rue de Passy had been to him when he was growing up. Lucien had craved privacy, and the room became his inner sanctum, a place all his own where he could escape. He'd shut the door to get away from his father and his brother's unmerciful teasing. Lucien would sit for hours reading and drawing or listening to all the great programs and music on the radio, stuffing himself with the candy and treats he'd bought at the newsstands and cafés.

He'd open the tall windows and watch the world go by—the hundreds of people who walked the stone pavements every hour, the cars, of which he knew every make, and the loaded wagons pulled by tired old horses. He'd loved to stare into the windows of the apartments directly opposite his, hoping to spot some dramatic event, like a murder or a robbery or a woman undressing, but he never did. Important milestones in his life had taken place there: learning to smoke, losing his virginity. When he was sixteen and his family had left for a weekend trip to Poissy, he'd brought Anne Laffront to his room for his first affair. He could still remember every detail and how much fun they had had that summer, until she dumped him. All through architecture school, he lived there doing his projects and studying. Lucien wanted Pierre to have the same special attachment to his own room.

Lucien knew he couldn't replace the father Pierre had lost, but he could give the boy at least the semblance of a real home. Besides, Lucien might enjoy the company, even though Pierre seemed to be a loner and rarely spoke.

"Now, let's talk about food," said Lucien who sat down next to Pierre. He wasn't on such familiar terms with the boy yet that he could put his hand on his shoulder. "I can't cook worth a damn."

This was true. Now with Celeste gone, he had to make his own meals, and he was indeed a terrible cook. Lucien had also realized that he had to go out and buy the food, which meant standing in long queues with women, something that Celeste had always done. In Paris, the lines formed as early as 3:00 a.m. and snaked around the block from a shop, moving forward inch by inch. Often, when one's turn finally came, the shelves were empty. He was so embarrassed to do this that he paid a woman on his street four francs an hour to queue up and shop for him.

"That's all right, Monsieur Bernard, I can prepare some simple things for us. Or I can fetch some things from the café on the corner, so we don't have to use the stove."

"That might be the best course of action. I don't even know how to turn it on. It uses gas, and I'm afraid I'll blow up the place."

Pierre burst out laughing. Laughter from Pierre was a rare thing, and Lucien was pleased to hear it. It was almost as if Pierre had decided never to laugh again after his ordeal. Lucien vowed to make him do so more often.

"I'll give you your own key so you can come and go as you please—but remember, I don't want you *ever* to be caught in the street after curfew. We'll both be in deep trouble if that happens. You understand that, don't you? And it's Lucien, not Monsieur Bernard."

"Yes, monsieur…Lucien, I'm very careful about that. I've never been out at night," said Pierre.

Misha had already taken a shine to the room by jumping onto the bed and curling up in a ball against the pillow.

"You see, Misha likes his new room," said Lucien, which made Pierre smile. The boy reached over and rubbed the cat under his chin. Lucien was beginning to like playing the part of father. Even though Pierre was a Jew and could get him (and everyone else in the apartment building) tortured and killed, he was the kind of son Lucien would've loved to have—intelligent, polite, and thoughtful.

"So, do you like your room, Pierre?"

"It's very nice, just as nice as the one in my old home, on the rue Oudinot."

Lucien had been careful not to ask Pierre any questions about his past, especially in the office, where Alain was always hovering about. He really didn't want to know. But now in the privacy of his home, he did. At least a little bit.

"So…when did you last see your parents?"

"Just before the roundup in May," said Pierre in a barely audible voice.

Lucien had to lean toward him to catch what he was saying.

"I hear you had brothers and a sister?" asked Lucien, knowing he was venturing into sensitive territory, but he pressed on.

"They're gone. I don't know where, but I guess they're dead too. It happened when the Germans shot Madame Charpointier."

"She took care of you after your parents were taken?"

"Yes, that's when we made up the story about being Christians. My father arranged it even before they took him away. We had to learn prayers like the Hail Mary and the Our Father and even go to mass to understand how it worked. He made us really practice hard because he wanted us to be safe, but it didn't work."

"How did the Germans find out?"

"I never found out. I think someone betrayed us."

"And how did you escape?"

Pierre remained silent, and Lucien now felt foolish for forcing a twelve-year-old to relive such terrible memories. He was about to change the subject when the boy started talking.

"They didn't find me. I was up in the attic, and they never came up there. I don't know why, but they didn't. I was up there when I saw Madame shot."

"You saw her killed?" exclaimed Lucien.

"I looked out the attic window and saw them shoot her. She was arguing with the Germans as they put Jean-Claude, Philippe, and Isabelle in the car. I was saved because I was smoking."

"Smoking?"

"I'd sneak up to the attic to smoke. That's what I was doing when they came to get us and I heard all this…"

To Lucien's surprise, Pierre suddenly broke down crying. After a few seconds, Lucien hesitantly put his arm around the boy and gently pulled him close.

"I shouldn't have been up there," Pierre cried. "I shouldn't have been up there."

Lucien ran his hand through Pierre's hair and patted his back. When Pierre pulled away, Lucien saw that he was ashamed of crying. The boy didn't need unnecessary shame on top of everything else. Lucien walked over to get a package from the dining room table and handed it to Pierre.

"I thought you should have a homecoming gift, Pierre."

The boy wiped his eyes with the sleeve of his sweater and eagerly unwrapped the package. He smiled when he found the set of Roman soldiers he'd seen in the store window on the rue du Roi-de-Sicile.

37

AND WHERE ARE WE GOING SO DAMN EARLY IN THE MORNING?" SAID Lucien, who was annoyed at Herzog for rousting him out of bed at seven in the morning.

Herzog laughed. "To the Hotel Majestic, and I promise you a very large cup of café au lait as soon as we get there."

Lucien stiffened with fear. The Hotel Majestic was the headquarters of the German High Command in Paris. He had heard of people entering the palatial hotel and never being seen again. Looking down at the door handle of the German staff car, Lucien had a sudden urge to grab it, open the door, and leap out of the speeding Mercedes, but he stayed put. Herzog, who was next to him smoking a cigarette, was in a jolly mood, enjoying the ride through the sun-drenched streets of the city, pointing out buildings he especially liked. Lucien knew that the German loved Paris and would wander through the city for hours, admiring even the most commonplace sight. A street sweeper, an old woman selling lace in a market stall—they all fascinated him.

"Are all Germans this cheerful at 7:00 a.m.?"

"Hausen, are you cheerful so early in the morning?" Herzog asked his driver with great glee.

"Hell, no, Major," growled Hausen, who stepped on the accelerator and raced down the avenue.

"Hausen is hung over. He was out late last night entertaining one of his many hussies, weren't you, Corporal?"

"I'm going to get me a hussy, and I ain't going to be fussy," sang Hausen in a cracked voice. "That's my motto, Major."

"I bet you still haven't made it to Notre Dame, Hausen."

"Not yet, but I'll get there, I promise."

"I'm trying with little success to educate the corporal here. But he has been to every whorehouse in the city," said Herzog, nudging Lucien with his elbow.

"So why are you so damn cheerful this morning? Have you acquired another Dürer etching?"

"Maybe you'd be in a cheerful mood if you were going to be promoted for meritorious achievement to the Reich."

"Really? Well, congratulations."

Lucien was genuinely happy for Herzog. A few months earlier, he would've felt ashamed and embarrassed for feeling this way about a German, but as his friendship and admiration for the engineer grew, he no longer minded. It was just his gray-green Wehrmacht uniform that was different, and Herzog only wore that when he was on duty. At other times, when Lucien visited him in his apartment, he dressed like a million other Frenchmen relaxing on their day off.

He and the German could slip effortlessly into a discussion about art, architecture, women, the news of Paris, or any topic except the events of the war. Lucien suspected Herzog never talked about it because he didn't want to offend him, and Lucien never raised the subject either. Over the years, Lucien had let his friends drift away until he had only a handful of professional acquaintances left, and since the defeat, even they had scattered. But he had never really had a close friend in his life. He looked forward to his meetings with Herzog, who often invited Lucien to his place. Lucien assumed Herzog understood that Lucien couldn't invite him to his apartment because Celeste didn't want the enemy in her home. When she left him, he didn't tell Herzog. Partly because he was ashamed, but mainly because Pierre was living there now.

"Still awfully early in the morning to be getting a promotion. You Teutons are all so efficient; is it to make sure you get the maximum use of every hour of the day?"

"I'm not, but Herr Albert Speer is, and when the Fuehrer's personal architect calls, I come at any hour."

"Speer himself is going to be there?"

"The Reich's minister of armaments and war production himself, in all his glory."

"I forgot that he's the minister of armaments."

"When the first minister, Fritz Todt, died in that plane crash in February, the Fuehrer chose him to run the show, and he made a very, very wise choice. One of his very few wise choices. Speer's a brilliant man."

"But as a designer, you think he's quite retrograde," said Lucien, with a sly smile.

Herzog grinned and scratched his head. He tried to evade the question but couldn't.

"I remember how impressed I was with his Nuremburg parade grounds back in '34. The buildings were all knockoffs of Greek architecture, but he used antiaircraft searchlights to create a kind of cathedral of light. There were 150 of them, all pointing straight up into the night sky. It was so breathtaking. Something like two hundred thousand people were there, surrounded by these towers of light."

"You were there?"

"I saw it at the cinema. *Triumph of the Will*, by that woman director, Leni Riefenstahl, showed the whole thing."

"Didn't he design the stadium in Berlin where they held the 1936 Olympics?"

"No, Werner March did that. Speer did Hitler's Reich Chancellery. It's got a hall that's twice as long as the Hall of Mirrors at Versailles. I've been there."

"Did you take a taxi to get from one end to the other?"

"I should have. It felt like I was walking across Russia. Of course, there was his new capital, Welthauptstadt Germania, with a domed building that was going to be seventeen times larger than St. Peter's."

Lucien roared with laughter.

"And there was supposed to be an arch so goddamned big that the Arc de Triomphe could've fit inside its opening. Good thing the war came, and it didn't get built. Speer and the Fuehrer had a little problem with scale."

"Christ, that's for sure," said Lucien.

"But the Fuehrer loves his classical architecture. In fact, he wanted all his buildings built of granite so a thousand years from now there would be these impressive ruins, like the Acropolis in Athens. So people would remember the Reich as they did ancient Rome."

"You've got to hand it to Speer, though, he's got the ultimate client."

"He was in the right place at the right time. Goebbels had hired him to renovate his Propaganda Ministry, so he recommended Speer to the Fuehrer. The two hit it off immediately—became soul mates. He basically had carte blanche as a designer. You do know the Fuehrer once wanted to be an architect?"

"Yes, I knew that."

"Maybe he felt that he didn't have the talent to be a painter, so he settled for being an architect, which didn't require as much talent," replied Herzog, grinning.

"It'll be a cold day in hell when a painter can do all the things an architect can do!" Lucien said. "Those lucky bastards can hide away in a garret and paint whatever they please."

Herzog couldn't suppress his smile.

"When you meet Reich Minister Speer, you can tell him yourself what jerks painters are. I'm sure he'll agree with you."

"I'm going up with you?" Lucien was startled.

"Why of course. I didn't tell you that our minister of armaments has heard of your talent and the buildings you've designed? He wants to meet you."

Hausen sped down the empty streets. He turned onto a narrow street where up ahead on the left a black Mercedes was parked. Two men, obviously plainclothes Gestapo officers in their fedoras and long top coats, were coming out of a building, escorting a man and a woman wearing yellow felt stars. The woman was trying to comfort the crying toddler she was holding.

"Slow down, Hausen."

Herzog rolled down his window and craned his neck to look as they passed by then twisted his body around to look out the back window. He stayed there until the car was out of sight.

Herzog looked down at his lap and absentmindedly fiddled with his gray kid gloves.

"Can you believe the army of Bismarck is reduced to doing that?" he muttered. "Makes me feel ashamed to be in uniform."

The German's jovial mood had vanished, and the rest of the ride continued in silence.

When they pulled up in front of the Majestic, Herzog took Lucien by the arm and led him through the grand entrance of the hotel. Inside the lobby, he growled a few words to a lieutenant, who immediately led them both to an elevator flanked by two well-armed soldiers.

At the sixth floor, Lucien and Herzog were escorted to a set of double doors, which the officer opened without knocking. He announced the visitors and slipped away. A tall, imposing man with heavy, dark eyebrows came out from a room with his hand extended.

"Colonel Herzog, it's a pleasure to see you again."

Herzog bowed his head, clicked his heels, and shook his hand. "Reich Minister Speer, I'm honored to see you. May I introduce Lucien Bernard, an architect whom the Reich has employed?"

"And with very good results. I saw your factory in Chaville yesterday, a most interesting and robust structure."

"You're most kind, Reich Minister," replied Lucien.

"A wonderfully functional piece of work as all utilitarian architecture should be. Those concrete arches are quite beautiful."

Lucien smiled and nodded a silent thank you to Speer.

They followed Speer into a suite of spacious rooms. Lucien, who had never been in the Majestic, was in awe of the opulent surroundings. Rolls of maps and drawings were scattered on tables and the sofas.

"Have a seat, gentlemen. I have coffee and croissants ready for you," said Speer, snapping his fingers. A soldier servant materialized out of nowhere.

Lucien looked at Speer closely as the Reich Minister sipped his coffee and chatted with Herzog about what factories were most critical for armaments production in 1943 and how much they would cost. Speer didn't look evil at all. He was an architect, a respectable-looking, professional man like himself. A man of great intelligence and charm who was responsible for the implementation of the death and destruction of tens of thousands of people in the past six months. He was a cold-blooded murderer, but he didn't personally use a gun or a knife. Instead, he ordered others to use the weapons he planned and produced. And to what end? The pure evil of dominating other nations merely because the Nazis deemed them inferior?

Lucien wondered why such an upstanding man like Speer would serve a madman like Hitler. Were there others like him? As intelligent and capable? If so, Germany would win the war. Lucien began to feel nauseous and wanted to get out of there.

Speer rose to signal the meeting was over.

"Monsieur Bernard is a most creative man. He takes his architecture very seriously," said Herzog, gesturing toward Lucien.

"We all do, Colonel," replied Speer. "It is the most difficult of all the creative arts."

"Far more difficult than the painter's craft, I think," said Herzog.

"Much more difficult than painting," exclaimed Speer. "No comparison."

Herzog had a hard time holding back a smile.

"Colonel, I want to congratulate you on your fine work in France. The facilities you have built are producing a great deal of war matériel for the Reich. We have plans for more plants, and I know you will continue to demonstrate your superior skills and planning. The Fuehrer is counting on you."

"I'm honored to serve the Fuehrer, Reich Minister."

"Did you tell Monsieur Bernard about the Fresnes facility?"

"No, Reich Minister, I was waiting for final confirmation of the plan."

"Well, now you have it. This is a most important building for the Reich," said Speer. "It will produce torpedoes for our U-boat fleet. This must be especially strong to withstand an Allied attack. They'll do everything humanly possible to take it out. It's absolutely critical to strengthen our submarine fleet. It must continue to destroy American ships. The Americans work day and night to produce armaments on a scale Germany can never approach. It seems never-ending."

Lucien looked down at the rug.

"All Germans know the fine job you're doing, Reich Minister," said Herzog in a voice that seemed quite sincere to Lucien.

"The politics, the Gauleiters, the party—you would think they would all work together to bring total victory to Germany. But they fight me and each other tooth and nail. Even the Fuehrer can't help me," said Speer in a tired voice. "The silliest things can hinder production. Like Germany's view of women. In all other countries, women work in factories making armaments, but not in Germany. Most women aren't allowed to work in factories; it's an affront to womanhood," he said in disgust. "We have a new automatic assault weapon ready to go, but we can't produce nearly enough of them, so the army still has to use a bolt-action rifle like it used in the first war."

"Thank you for meeting with me, Reich Minister. I will double my efforts, I can assure you," said Herzog, shaking Speer's hand.

"I know you will. Good luck, my boy."

Lucien extended his hand.

"Monsieur Bernard, I envy you. You're a designer—I'm reduced to being a bureaucrat nowadays."

"It's been a pleasure, Reich Minister."

"You're very fortunate to live in such a wonderful city, monsieur. You know, the Fuehrer once said, 'I'm ready to flatten Leningrad and Moscow without losing any peace of mind, but it would have pained me greatly if I'd had to destroy Paris.'"

Speer walked them to the door of the suite. "The Fuehrer was never interested in any of the cities he defeated except for Paris. I was with him and his sculptor, Arno Breker, when he visited for a few hours in June 1940. We went to the Eiffel Tower and Napoleon's Tomb," said Speer with a smile. "He thought Vienna was the more beautiful city, but I don't agree."

After opening the door for them, he placed his hand on Lucien's shoulder.

"You know, I once did a plan that would redesign Berlin with a five-kilometer-long avenue as a new axis, similar to your Champs-Élysées."

38

A DELE WAS JUST SECONDS FROM REACHING AN ORGASM WHEN SHE heard a loud knocking at the door of her flat.

"Who the hell is that?" yelled Schlegal. With Adele astride him, he was also quite excited.

"Keep going, keep going, just ignore it. Don't stop, damn it," Adele pleaded. But the knocking became louder and faster. Adele felt Schlegal deflate beneath her.

"Goddamn it, I told you I only had half an hour before I had to get back," said Schlegal, who grabbed Adele's arm and tossed her off the bed as if she were a rag doll.

If she hadn't caught hold of the blanket, she would have landed on the floor. Adele scowled at Schlegal. She wasn't used to this type of treatment from a lover.

"Answer the goddamn door," Schlegal said before he put a pillow over his face.

Adele put on her black silk dressing gown and walked to the door. "Yes, yes, I'm coming," she called out. "Or rather, I was about to come," she mumbled under her breath.

She flung open the door to face Bette, who walked through the doorway with a big smile on her face, knowing full well she'd interrupted some serious goings-on.

"And what in God's name do you want?" Adele said.

"I always follow your instructions to the letter, boss, and they were to come here promptly at 12:30 to pick up the sketches and take them to André. 'Don't dare be late. André needs those sketches *now*.' Sound familiar?"

"Don't be such a smartass, okay? I had a little last-minute business to take care of, and I lost track of the time."

Bette walked into the salon and sat on the black art *moderne* sofa and propped her feet on the art *moderne* stainless-steel coffee table.

"Get your feet off my table. By the way, did anyone ever tell you what huge feet you have? Like canoes."

"I'll be out of here in a second. Still time for him to get it up again. So don't despair, my love," said Bette.

Adele came out of her study with a black portfolio under her arm. Bette rose from the sofa and took the portfolio from Adele. "How about a drink? You know—one for the road?"

Adele glanced toward the open bedroom door and nodded. Bette walked over to a black and steel liquor cabinet and helped herself to a generous serving of cognac.

"Save me a molecule or two of that, will you?" said Adele, tightening the belt around her gown.

Bette smiled and smacked her lips, then placed the cut glass tumbler on the top of the cabinet.

"Again, please forgive me for the coitus-interruptus, but like you've said before, business is business."

"Next time, call first."

"I'll be sure to do that. Or maybe a singing telegram."

"Take care," said Adele in a singsong voice as she shoved Bette out the door.

"You will remember to come to the fitting this afternoon, around four? You will be finished with him by then?"

•··•··•

Bette found herself in the corridor and the door slammed shut behind her. She put her ear to the thick paneled door and heard shouting going on toward the rear of the flat. A smile came over her face as she walked to the lift. As she'd walked across Adele's salon, she'd looked into the bedroom and seen a very distinctive black uniform draped over the footboard of the bed. She knew Adele adored anything in black, but that piece didn't belong to her—nor did the Gestapo cap sitting on top of it.

Outside the entrance of Adele's building, in the span of thirty seconds three men smiled and tipped their hats to Bette. This was nothing out of the ordinary. Last February she'd turned thirty-one, but she knew she was even more beautiful now than she'd been at nineteen when she began her modeling career. If Bette had believed in God, she would've thanked him for her long-lasting beauty. She knew that when she hit fifty, she would still be ravishing. Bette was a big believer in luck, and it was pure luck that she had turned out beautiful while her sister Simone had turned out as ugly as a bulldog. Just a freak happenstance of nature, she thought. Bette often shuddered when she envisioned Simone as a beauty and herself resembling something canine. It could've gone either way.

Bette had had to beat off men with a stick since puberty. Almost every day of her life, even Christmas and Easter, a man had called to ask her out. Bette thought it was wonderful to be beautiful. Besides the attention of men, there was no waiting in lines at stores, no waiting for tables in fine restaurants—and no paying for meals in those fine restaurants—and presents showing up unexpectedly on her doorstep. Poor Simone, her only hope of getting a man would be either to have her family pay someone to marry her or to be matched with a blind man. She was a sweet, gentle girl with a heart of gold who would make a wonderful wife and mother, but she was likely doomed to a bleak, unhappy life of spinsterhood.

There was a time when Bette wouldn't go out with a boy unless he arranged a date for Simone. One minute after the boy saw Simone, he always vanished. Simone never showed a shred of jealousy toward her gorgeous younger sister. She would do anything for her. Bette's mother and father had resigned themselves to the sad fact that Simone would never marry and that Bette would be the daughter who would give them their beloved grandchildren. But that would never happen. Three years ago, Bette's doctor had explained that because of an abnormality in her uterus, she could never bear children. He'd tied her tubes and that was that. Offsetting the crushing news was the realization that she could screw as much as she wanted and never have to worry about getting pregnant. It was actually a tremendous burden off her shoulders. Many of her friends who were models had to endure the pain and anxiety of back-street abortions to continue their careers because they didn't want to give up the good life. Not one of them wanted to be a single mother—the shame of that would be too much to bear. They'd be outcasts from their own families, who already viewed them as unrespectable.

Bette turned right onto the rue Saint-Martin, where André, Adele's cutter, had his shop. She dropped off the portfolio, issued precise instructions, and was on her way home to her flat on the rue Payenne. One block before she reached her building, she stopped and knocked on the door of the shop of Denis Borge, a chocolatier. The shop windows were covered with shades, and presently, the edge of a shade was pulled back, then the door unlocked.

"Good afternoon, Denis," said Bette.

"Mademoiselle Bette, so good to see you," gushed Denis. All shopkeepers fawned over Bette.

"I'm here for my chocolates. Are they ready?"

"Of course, they've been ready since yesterday. I'd never forget your order. All the special items are here as you wished." Denis handed her a small brown paper bag to inspect. She reached her hand in and picked through the individually wrapped candies.

"You're an angel, Denis. Chocolates are harder to come by than diamonds these days."

"I'll always fill any order you wish. You're my best customer,

Mademoiselle Bette. Every two weeks for almost the past year. I envy you. You eat so much chocolate and never gain a gram. How do you do it?"

Bette looked down shyly at the floor and smiled. "It's just my metabolism. I can eat a lot. I can devour an entire baguette slathered with butter in one sitting."

"I definitely can't manage that without paying for it, if you know what I mean," said Denis, patting his enormous belly. Bette playfully gave it a poke and Denis laughed delightedly. Because of rationing, shopkeepers, grocers, and butchers in Paris had a newfound power during the Occupation and lorded it over their customers, but they never treated Bette unfairly—another advantage to being beautiful.

"Good-bye, my friend. I'll see you on the fourteenth."

When Bette reached the top floor of the building where her flat was located, she knocked three times on the door, paused, then knocked three more times before she unlocked the door. Once inside, she called out in a gentle voice, "I'm home, my little ones."

Like small animals cautiously peeking out of their burrows, a six-year-old boy and a four-year-old girl appeared at the edge of the doorway to the living room.

"It's chocolate time, come and get it," cooed Bette as she held the bag toward the children.

Slowly, smiles came over their faces, and they took the bag from her.

"Remember what I told you."

"Fifty-fifty," they sang out in unison.

Bette watched with delight as they divvied up the candy. Then, as they always did, the children offered her a piece, which she took from them and popped into her mouth.

She always wondered if she would've raised children as well-behaved and polite as the Kaminskys had. Bette had never paid any attention to the children who had lived on the second floor of her building. She had been on cordial terms with Mr. and Mrs. Kaminsky but had never said more than "how do you do" or "good morning" to them. That all changed over a year ago when Mrs. Kaminsky and another woman knocked on her door late one night. She told Bette that she'd just received a call informing her that the French police were on the way to arrest her family. She was desperate to find someone to hide her children. Bette had nothing against Jews but knew full well that helping them meant certain death. Bette tried brushing them off, saying she knew nothing about raising children, but Mrs. Kaminsky began to cry and plead with her. Normally a refined and well-dressed woman whom Bette admired, she was now reduced to a terrified, miserable supplicant. She wailed loudly and went down on her knees, offering a huge wad of cash to Bette. Just to stop the woman's hysterics, Bette told her to bring them up, along with their clothes.

Minutes later, there were two frightened children in their pajamas holding each other tightly in the middle of Bette's living room. She went over to the window that overlooked the street and saw a police car pull up. Three French policemen got out and ran into her building. She expected to hear shouting and crying from the stairwell, but it was eerily quiet. Ten minutes later, she saw Mr. and Mrs. Kaminsky get in the police car, which drove off. She would never see them again. Bette had turned to face the children, who were still huddled together. She smiled at them and extended her hand. "Come, let's have some chocolate." At that moment, Bette, with her hard-as-nails attitude about the world, had thought this was the worst thing that had ever happened to her.

Very quickly she realized that it had been the best thing.

39

B UT DIDN'T THE JEWS KILL CHRIST, FATHER?"
"That's debatable, my son. But even if they did, I'd still
help them."

Schlegal liked Father Jacques's nerve. He'd always hated the
clergy, Protestant or Catholic. All self-righteous fools. His men
had discovered that the old priest had been running a safe house for
Jewish children in Montparnasse before they were whisked across
the Pyrenees and into Spain. Another priest from Carcassonne who
escorted the children had also been caught. Schlegal was slowly cir-
cling the chair where Father Jacques had been sitting since 2:00 a.m.
The priest didn't show the slightest sign of fatigue. In fact, he seemed
quite cheerful as the morning light streamed through the window of
the interrogation room.

"I thought the Jewish elders forced Pilate to condemn Christ to
death," Schlegal said. "They wanted him out of the way."

"Mm…some theologians make that case. It could be true."

"So why risk your life for a bunch of Christ killers?"

"You don't understand, Colonel, that we're all brothers on this earth."

"Brothers." Schlegal let out a great laugh. "What a load of bullshit."

He had nothing but contempt for the old priest or any gentile
who tried to hide Jews. Yet there were many who risked their lives to
help them. It puzzled him to no end. Why die because of this human
vermin? Frenchmen who had no connection to Jews before the war
all of a sudden hid them in their attics or barns, knowing full well
what would happen if they were caught. To risk one's life for these

thieving scum, who had brought nothing but misery to the world, was incomprehensible. Just last week, during a raid on Rue Saint-Honoré, a gendarme had lent a Jew his cape and hat so he could escape. Both were caught and shot on the spot. And the crazy thing was that the French cop didn't even know the man. No, the planet would be a far better place if all the Jews just disappeared. And in Paris, he and the Gestapo were trying their hardest to make that happen.

"How many children have you helped to escape into Spain, Father?"

"I'm proud to say that it numbers in the hundreds by now." Father Jacques gave him an ear-to-ear smile.

The priest's smug expression angered Lieutenant Voss, who'd been standing in the shadows, and he punched Father Jacques in the side of the face so hard that the old man landed hard on the floor.

"Please, Voss," said Schlegal. "That was quite unnecessary. Father Jacques has outwitted the Reich and is naturally quite proud of it. Let him have his moment of glory."

Voss snorted, yanked the priest by his collar, and threw him back into the chair, then walked behind Schlegal and folded his arms.

"You must forgive Lieutenant Voss, Father. He's grouchy because he hasn't had his breakfast. So, if you could just confess your sins, he could go and eat."

The priest rubbed the side of his face, then defiantly looked directly into Schlegal's eyes. "Then I'm afraid Lieutenant Voss will have to wait until hell freezes over for his breakfast."

This impressed Schlegal, who despised the priest for what he'd done, yet had respect for the old man. He wondered if a younger priest would be as defiant as an old man near the end of his life. With all those years of living ahead of him, would he act the same?

"So I guess if I let you go, you wouldn't stop doing this," asked Schlegal with a great smile.

Father Jacques shook with laughter for a few seconds. Schlegal laughed along with him.

"Colonel Schlegal, you're a most amusing fellow. I could almost like you if you weren't such a Gestapo swine."

Schlegal laughed uncontrollably at this remark. Voss looked on with disapproval.

"Ah, Father Jacques," said Schlegal, tears welling up in his eyes, "you almost make me wish I was Catholic."

"But you do have your own church, Colonel. It's run by Satan himself—Herr Hitler."

Schlegal walked up to the priest and stooped down to face him. He placed his hand on the old man's knee.

"So, Father, you've been working quite hard these days hiding these Jewish brats. It must have been an enormous strain on you. So I'm going to do something special for you."

"Convert to Judaism?"

Voss started to lunge at the priest, but Schlegal waved him off.

"You need to take a trip, Father. You need a rest. So I'm arranging a vacation for you."

"What a nice thing to do."

"Have you ever been to southwestern Poland? Very beautiful country. I think you're really going to like it. Fresh air. Trees. Nature. It's kind of a retreat. One with lots of Jews, and since you like Jews, you'll really feel at home."

"Sounds wonderful. I've got a feeling I'm going to leave right away."

"Indeed you are. In about two minutes you'll be on your way. But one last thing. I suppose you won't tell me if there were any others besides Father Philippe in Carcassonne helping the Jews?"

Father Jacques just smiled. "I can't say it's been a pleasure, Colonel, but I did enjoy talking to you. I even hope that when you die and your ass is burning in the fires of hell, you won't suffer too much. In fact, I'll pray for your soul, my son."

"How very kind of you. It's been a pleasure meeting you, Father. It's not often I meet a brave man. Voss here will direct you to your train. I'm afraid you may find the train trip a bit cramped and uncomfortable."

"Yes, I've heard that German train accommodations are not up to French standards. Rumor has it that you can get two hundred into one car."

"Ah, in war, one must make sacrifices."

Father Jacques knew it was time to go and rose from his seat. He bowed slightly to Schlegal and turned to Voss. "Herr Voss, I'm ready for our trip to Drancy."

"Good news, Father," Voss said with a smile on his face. "You can bypass Drancy and get on your train right away."

"Yes, I've gotten you a berth on an express run," added Schlegal. "It's a long trip, but I hear you can get a nice hot shower when you arrive at your destination."

40

D ID YOU FALL INTO THE POT AND DROWN?" ALAIN YELLED.
He heard Pierre flush the toilet and unlatch the door. Alain
was leaning against the wall as he came out.

"What the hell were you doing in there? Sounded like you were
talking to yourself in gibberish. What language was that, boy?"

Pierre just smiled at Alain.

Alain had disliked him the minute he'd laid eyes on him. Pierre
was just supposed to clean up and fetch things, but then Lucien started
giving him drawing lessons, saying the boy could take some of the
drafting load off Alain, and he did. Once, to Alain's great annoyance,
Lucien said that the kid might have found his calling as an architect.
The truth was that the twelve-year-old was a quick study, and he could
quickly handle increasingly complex tasks. His line work was becoming
quite good, and he was very detail-oriented, an important quality in
an architect.

Pierre went back to his drawing board and began drawing a mezzanine plan for the Tremblay factory. After he'd finished his business in
the WC, Alain walked over to Pierre.

"Your wall lines aren't dark enough," he told him.

"Yes, you're right. They could be a lot darker," answered Pierre
cheerfully. It irritated the hell out of Alain that Pierre was always grateful for his advice. Alain ordered Pierre around and cursed at him on a
routine basis but always out of earshot of Lucien.

"So what were you muttering in the bathroom? Sounded like
Chinese or something," asked Alain, leaning on Pierre's drawing board.

"I was just saying a Hail Mary—in Latin."

"Didn't sound like Latin to me. I was an altar boy, and I know Latin when I hear it."

"Well, it was Latin."

"Do you always pray in the can?"

"It's the only private place to pray in the office, don't you think?"

Alain stared at the boy. There was something odd about the whole situation. Him popping up out of nowhere. Lucien telling him that Pierre was the son of a friend who died in the fighting in 1940. He tried to connect it to the strange goings-on with Manet and the cottage. Alain still couldn't figure that one out. He'd followed Lucien a few times, but he hadn't discovered anything. At least once a week, he'd gone through Lucien's desk to look for any odd scraps of details like the one of the fireplace, but he'd found nothing. It was hard to snoop around with this damn kid hanging about all the time.

"So you're a Catholic?"

"What did you think I was? An Arab?" answered Pierre, with surprising bravado.

"Where did you go to school before you came to Paris?"

"St. Bernadine in Toulouse."

"How did your father know Lucien?"

"They had been friends in Paris and served together in the 25th Division when the Germans invaded."

"The 25th Division? Where was it stationed?"

"On the Maginot Line."

"What was your father's rank?"

"A lieutenant."

"So you have no family left."

"No one. Both my mother and father are dead, and so is my brother, Jules."

"That's tough. What's going to happen to you?"

Pierre shrugged his shoulders.

Alain walked back to his desk. He wanted Pierre out of here but knew that wasn't going to happen anytime soon. Alain had no choice but to put up with him. But he might as well take full advantage of the situation. His family had never had servants, but now he had one.

"Hey, shithead. Go downstairs and get me a pack of cigarettes."

41

I'M GOING TO HINGE THIS PILASTER AT THE TOP SO THAT IT LIFTS UP. It's almost a half a meter wide, which is big enough for a hiding place behind it. I hope your guest isn't fat."

Manet and Lucien stood in the salon of a grand townhouse on the rue de Bassano. It was incredibly lavish, with beautiful white and gold paneling and gleaming parquet floors. The classical pilasters, a kind of flat column only fifteen centimeters deep and almost four meters tall applied to the face of the walls, divided the paneling into wide sections. The moment Lucien stepped into the apartment and saw the pilasters, he knew exactly what to do.

"You can do that?" asked Manet.

Lucien heard the concern in the old man's voice. Ever since the disaster with the fireplace, Manet had begun to doubt him, even though he would never admit it.

Lucien looked the pilaster up and down for a last-minute assessment. "Yes, I can make it work. The pilaster has to be carefully removed then reassembled. The whole thing can be lifted up at the bottom so someone can slip into the space behind it, which we'll hollow out from the brick. Then it can be latched shut from behind, just like we did with the stair. But this work has to be done with great accuracy to get it to hinge right."

"You know you don't have to worry on that account. Just give us a drawing, and we'll get it done."

With Manet's help, Lucien took his measurements of the pilaster and the cornice above it. When he was finished, the men walked toward the front door, and they turned to look at the new hiding place one last time.

"This place is beautiful. Do you own it?" asked Lucien as they got into his Citroën.

"No, a colleague of mine in Paris, who will remain nameless, of course."

Lucien started the car, but then switched off the ignition and turned to face Manet. "I want you to get word to Father Jacques that I'll keep the boy. I can protect him. He's safer with me than trying to smuggle him into Spain or Switzerland. Will you tell him for me?"

"Father Jacques is probably dead by now."

Lucien wasn't surprised. It was just a matter of time till the priest would get caught. "When was he picked up?"

"A few days ago. Along with six Jewish kids. Someone betrayed him, and the Gestapo came. They were hiding in the attic, but one of the children started crying, and they found them."

"Did he tell them anything?"

Manet laughed. "Not Father Jacques. He probably told them to go to hell."

"Are you positive?"

"Please don't be afraid, Lucien. We have contacts inside Gestapo headquarters. He told them nothing, I assure you."

"*We* meaning the Resistance?"

"It's best that you don't ask questions."

"I liked Father Jacques. He had balls for a priest."

"He certainly did," said Manet with a great laugh. "He'd be surprised at what you wanted me to tell him about Pierre. He didn't think you possessed a set of balls."

This comment cut through Lucien's heart like a razor. He looked down at the floorboards of the car.

Manet immediately understood what he'd done and looked ashamed.

"During war, people who were thought to have no backbone at all turned out to be quite brave. Father Jacques might have been surprised that you decided to hide Pierre on your own. But I'm not."

Placated by Manet's remark, Lucien started the car.

"I enjoy having Pierre stay with me. He's a damn fine boy. Smart, hardworking, and well mannered. I wish I'd been that way at his age. And you know, he's got real talent; he could be an architect when he grows up. Every day I teach him something about the profession."

Manet gazed through the windshield into the distance, puffing away on his pipe.

"Interesting how things work out in life. Pierre loses his entire family, then winds up with you, who opens up a whole new life for him. It's amazing how our lives are dictated by accident."

"He's less shy and reserved, and he's become good company. I like to take him to the cinema. You know, watching him smile and laugh at the screen gives me a lot more satisfaction than watching the film."

"I'm glad things have worked out between you two. How has Madame Bernard taken all this? She must be quite pleased to have a child to look after."

At the intersection at the Champs-Élysées, Lucien stopped the car to wait for a small military parade to pass. Every day at 1:00 p.m., rain or shine, the Germans staged a parade, complete with military band goose-stepping down the city's main avenue, to remind Parisians who was in power. It was an effective psychological weapon just like the curfew, thought Lucien.

To save petrol while they waited, he switched off the ignition and turned to face Manet.

"Celeste and I parted ways just before the boy was brought to the office. I always thought the expression that 'things always work out for the best' was a crock. But maybe it is for the best. Look what came into my life."

"A son you never would've had."

"My wife and I had no children, and it cast a dark cloud over our marriage. But yes, I admit that he's the son I never had. I enjoy taking care of him."

"And you've saved a life."

The parade cleared the intersection, and the gendarme waved the traffic through. As Lucien switched on the ignition and placed his hand on the gear shift, Manet placed his hand on his.

"The people you've saved are eternally grateful, but there are many more in danger."

"I'm ready to help, monsieur," said Lucien as he drove off.

42

G ODDAMN IT, I'M TELLING YOU THERE'S SOMEONE IN THERE."

"But, Colonel, we've searched the house from top to bottom, every corner, under every piece of furniture," said Captain Bruckner.

"Idiot. The Jews are somewhere in the structure of the house, behind a wall or under the floorboards," screamed Schlegal, pacing back and forth like a caged animal. "Use your imagination, man."

"Don't worry, sir. We'll find them," said Bruckner, saying what Schlegal wanted to hear.

The captain ran back into the cottage screaming at the top of his lungs. Schlegal always enjoyed watching Bruckner and his men jump at his orders. Fear can make a man do incredible things. They weren't just scared of him, though—they all thought he was unhinged, which was better. Bruckner would be especially compliant for fear of losing the two-week leave in Munich for which he'd waited so long. Schlegal decided to torture him a bit with a threat to cancel the trip. Bruckner came back out of the house to reassure the colonel that he was kicking the men in the ass to search again. Schlegal abruptly stopped his pacing and faced Bruckner nose to nose.

"Captain, send for sledgehammers and some pry bars. Have your men go around to the shed in the rear of the house and bring any tools they find. Then have them go inside and tap on the walls. Anything that sounds hollow, they are to open up the walls. And tear apart any stairs. Get to it, mister, or you won't be seeing the Marienplatz anytime soon. That *is* in Munich, isn't it?"

As Bruckner sprinted away screaming orders, Schlegal went back to his staff car. Leaning against the hood, he lit a cigarette and stared at the house. He scanned its exterior to seek out any possible hiding places. Whoever did the stairs in Adele's house must be quite clever. The secret spaces would be almost impossible to find. The designer probably took great pride in being able to outfox the Gestapo. The ingenuity of the stairs told him that he was up against a formidable foe, one who would not make any careless mistakes. The thought of other Jews safe in this fellow's secret hiding places sent Schlegal's blood pressure skyrocketing. Ever since the discovery of the stairs, that possibility had tormented him. It got so bad that he couldn't screw Adele in that bedroom anymore.

With his hands clasped behind his back, Schlegal strolled into the house. The soldiers started tapping on the walls. With twenty men tapping away, it sounded like a flock of crazed woodpeckers. Some began pounding at the plaster, breaking through wood lath to find empty wall cavities. Dust and plaster flew in all directions. Two soldiers tore away a wall behind the stairs on the first floor. Another soldier found a ladder and was tearing away a ceiling in the parlor. A sergeant pulled the mahogany wainscoting from the reception hall walls. A lieutenant had taken a hammer to a wall in the dining room and exposed some brick and pounded away at it until Bruckner screamed at him, telling him no one was behind there. Schlegal walked through the first floor, inspecting the demolition effort. He strode from room to room.

"Come out, come out, wherever you are, my little Jews. I know you're in here," yelled Schlegal in a singsong tone.

"If you come out now, things will be much easier on you." Schlegal knew this was untrue, but he often promised leniency to his victims for their cooperation. He was never lenient, but it always surprised him to find out how many believed him.

"Come out, come out, wherever you are," he continued to yell above the din. He actually found himself enjoying this whole operation. There was a growing sense of excitement about finding the Jews, just like he had as a child playing hide-and-seek. Schlegal expected any moment to open up a wall and find them. He imagined they would giggle and shriek with delight as his cousins in Mannheim had always done when discovered. Those memories put a smile on his lips. He loved visiting his cousins in the summer and during the Christmas holiday. It was endless fun and good food.

"Keep at it, men. The one who finds them gets a case—not a bottle, but a whole case—of champagne," Schlegal shouted out in delight. The pace of the tapping and demolition increased twofold, and Schlegal doubled over with laughter.

"Bruckner, if *you* find them, you get *three* weeks' leave." At that promise, the captain took hammer in hand and proceeded to tear apart the wall at the rear of a closet, getting white plaster dust all over his uniform. A truck pulled up in front of the house, and a dozen soldiers with sledgehammers and pry bars poured out of the back and into the house. Bruckner told them what to do, and the noise in the house became deafening.

"We're going to find you, my little Jewish mice. Or should I say rats?" shouted Schlegal.

Three hours later, not a Jew had been found, and Schlegal's good cheer had turned to pure rage. Every square centimeter of wall had been examined and sounded. Walls in every room were torn open. Almost all the ceilings had come down. The stairs had been torn apart, step by step. Floorboards were pulled up, exposing dusty bug-ridden spaces between the main timber beams. Kitchen cabinets had been ripped apart. The inside of the great oven had been thoroughly searched. Even the chimneys atop the house were knocked down in case the Jews were hiding in the flues. Bruckner had postponed facing Schlegal for the last hour, but he finally mustered up the courage to do it. It was quite apparent that the colonel, who was standing in the kitchen, was in a foul mood.

"It's going to be a long time before you see Munich again, mister."

"Colonel, they're not here. Unless they magically shrunk down to the size of insects and crawled away, they escaped before we came."

"Bullshit," said Schlegal. He hurled a piece of wood paneling across the room. He kicked a chunk of plaster with his black boot, covering it in a fine white powder. He walked over to the window and gazed out onto the lush green garden.

"I'm telling you, they're still here."

"I'm sorry; I can't find them, Colonel."

Schlegal turned to face Bruckner. He patted his shoulder in a fatherly way and smiled.

"Then burn the house down. The Jews will be forced out because of the smoke—or burn to death in their hiding space. When we pick through the debris, we'll find them. Burnt to a crisp."

The captain wasn't about to protest. It was a quick and easy way to end this mess and get back to Paris where a warm bed and a French prostitute named Jane awaited him. They should have done that in the first place. Soldiers raced to the trucks to get the cans of petrol. In minutes the interior of the entire house was drenched. With Schlegal watching, Bruckner nodded to a soldier standing at the front door, who struck a wooden match and tossed it in the reception hall. An inferno raged through the house in just seconds. Dusk was approaching, and the flames shooting through the roof made an impressive sight against the darkening sky. The soldiers, worn out from the useless demolition, were tired to the bone, and Bruckner allowed them to lounge on the grass or inside the trucks and just watch the blaze. The flames cast an eerie orange light on their faces. Schlegal was expecting at any minute to hear screams of agony, but there was just the crackling of the flames. The blaze wouldn't die out until morning, so Schlegal ordered the men back to Paris.

·◈··◈··◈·

The Germans had surprised Juliette Trenet; she'd been napping when they'd pulled up to the house. Disoriented, Juliette had had a hard time remembering where her bag was, but she'd found it under the huge butcher block table in the center of the kitchen. She had just managed to pull the drain pan and grate in place when they'd broken down the locked front door with what sounded like a battering ram. Even with the metal pan full of water above her head, she could still hear the soldiers filling up the house, smashing things left and right, ripping into the walls and ceilings looking for her. She was amazed that all this effort was on account of her. Maybe they were looking for someone else. The Germans came down into the kitchen and flipped over the huge table; it shook the earth when it hit the stone floor, making Juliette shake with fright. Hearing the sound of boots pounding on the stone floor just centimeters away from her was unbearable; she wanted to scream out and had to jam her fist in her mouth. The recess under the drain was wide enough with a few centimeters to spare on either side of her arms, which hugged her body. But it was only a meter and a half deep so Juliette had to crouch on a pillow. Her fear became so great that she closed her eyes and grasped her legs, curling up in a fetal position, her body trembling uncontrollably.

It was the shock of all this happening to her so suddenly that was so wrenching. She'd been enjoying her stay in the comfortable house; it had almost been like a continuous weekend holiday, a million times better than living in an empty lions' den. She couldn't believe her luck in finding such a place. Now she was about to die. The noise and commotion didn't let up, and the soldiers kept stepping right over the drain. Juliette began to unravel. She started to weep. With herculean effort, she had to fight the powerful urge to stand straight up and ram her head against the underside of the drain pan, making it fly up in the air so she'd rise suddenly above the floor, surprising the hell out of the soldiers. Juliette would yell, "Here I am, you Nazi shits. Kill me and get it over with."

But then she felt a small movement within her, then another. Juliette ran her hand all over her bare belly. What the hell was she thinking of? *There's a scientist inside me*, thought Juliette, *who'll need my help and guidance.* Her joy in giving the kid its first microscope. Seeing her child graduate with honors. And forty-some years from now, she could be in Stockholm to see Marie or Pierre win a Nobel Prize. There were so many good things to come. She smiled and decided that she'd be damned if she'd give herself and her child up to these bastards. Juliette had no intention of dying.

Then Juliette realized that all the noise around her had suddenly ceased. She raised her head and stared at the bottom of the drain pan as if she could see through it into the kitchen. The silence continued for fifteen minutes, and it seemed the Germans had given up. She'd still wait an hour before getting out of the hiding place as Manet had told her. Then in an instant, her nose detected the ever-so-faint smell of smoke. Quickly, the smell became stronger. Immediately, she contorted her body to go head first into the tunnel opening at the bottom of the hiding place. Only a half meter square, Juliette and her rucksack barely fit in it. Trying to keep her belly off the damp dirt floor, she squirmed and clawed in total darkness like a crazed mole through the twenty meters of tunnel. An incredible energy propelled her through the tunnel like a shot. The black earth caked her clothes and hands. She worried that any second the tunnel would cave in on her, burying her alive; she'd be just minutes from safety when everything came down on her. But as she crawled along, she saw that it was a well-built passage with planks supporting its sides and ceiling. She smiled when she literally saw the light at the end of the tunnel, but as she got closer, she wondered if the Germans were waiting for her. Would the hail of bullets kill her outright, or would she suffer a slow, agonizing death?

⋅⧫⋅⧫⋅⧫⋅

In the morning, smoke still rose from the ruins as Schlegal's men poked through the debris. When Schlegal arrived two hours later, Bruckner reported that no bodies had been discovered. Schlegal immediately ordered the men away and walked through the wreckage by himself. He half expected to find a charred body but found nothing. Where the kitchen had once stood, he lit a cigarette. He blew the match out and tossed it into what looked like a floor drain. Schlegal realized there was something odd about the drain. Under the grating was a very shallow, empty metal pan. He tossed his cigarette away, knelt down, and pulled off the grating, which was fastened to the pan. There was a dark empty space below. He threw aside the grating, took off his cap, and stuck his head into the hole. He struck a match and held it down the hole. He saw a tunnel. He pulled himself up, smiling. The pan must have been filled with water all the time the soldiers were searching the house. They'd never bothered with it because it looked like an ordinary old floor drain. The water had evaporated during the fire, exposing the pan. Schlegal suspected the tunnel extended far into the garden, its terminus hidden by the dense covering of flowers. The Jew had escaped while they were in the house.

Schlegal lit a cigarette and walked slowly back to his car.

"This is one very smart bastard," he said with a smile.

⸰⸰⸰

Three kilometers away on a high ridge, Juliette could see the wisp of gray smoke still rising slowly above the forest. There had been no one waiting for her at the end of the tunnel, and in the twilight, she had run through the dense forest, tripping and falling on her face dozens of times. She'd looked back to see an orange and yellow pillar of fire lighting up the forest for hundreds of meters around. Exhausted, she'd squeezed under a fallen tree trunk to rest when she was far enough from the house to feel safe. Juliette had laid her head down on the cool green moss under the rotting trunk and slept right through the night.

Manet had instructed Juliette on a backup plan if she was discovered, and now she must follow it to the letter. She picked up her rucksack, looked down at her belly, and gave it a pat, then walked slowly away. Juliette wasn't at all frightened. She knew they were going to live.

43

So who's this special guy? It's not like you to be carrying on during the day."

Adele shifted uneasily in her black iron café chair. Bette was amused that the question annoyed her boss and waited patiently for a well-thought-out lie. It was always fascinating to watch someone lie, to conjure up a story in a matter of seconds. Some were experts at it. Like Etienne, her lover last year; he could whip out a convincing lie in a fraction of a second. She actually had great admiration for accomplished liars.

Adele took a sip of wine and patted her lips with a napkin. It was a neat way of stalling for time until she had her story straight.

"A government official who has a very severe crush on me."

"That can be quite handy. A lover who has influence."

"It is indeed; he's opened a few doors for me."

"What's he like? Handsome? Tall? Good in bed?"

"Yes, all of those things," Adele said testily. "One of the best lovers I've ever had. Did you see the new sketches?"

Bette wasn't about to let Adele change the subject so quickly.

"Married, I suppose."

"Yes, if you must know, Miss Snoop. Now what about André?"

"André will be finished tomorrow for sure. He promised me. So how long have you known him?"

"Only a brief time," said Adele as she took another sip of wine.

"Now would that be the French government or the German government?"

Adele gave Bette an icy stare. "French."

Bette was no patriot, but she had a real feeling of revulsion for Adele at this moment. The French viewed any woman who slept with a German as a slut. Bette had seen firsthand how the French would treat a woman who got too friendly with the Germans. She'd seen a girl in a café laughing and joking with a Wehrmacht officer. When the German left, a complete stranger came up to the girl's table and slapped her across the face without saying a word. It was thought that no girl from a respectable family would ever bed down with a German.

Adele was a rare exception, someone educated and well off jumping into the sack with the enemy. And she wasn't just sleeping with a German, but with a Gestapo officer. It was like fucking Satan himself. Adele wouldn't be so stupid as to reveal that she was having an affair with a Gestapo officer. That would be suicidal. She smiled when she imagined what Adele would look like with a shaved head. There had been occasional reprisals throughout France against women who consorted with Germans. Last fall, some men went into a café, beat up a German officer, and shaved the head of the girl he was with. No one would sell her a wig, and she was so ashamed that she had to hide out until her hair grew back. Adele was incredibly vain, even for an ex-model, so getting her beautiful blond hair sheared off like a sheep would be worse than death. Adele was playing with fire, and she knew it.

It was now clear to Bette how Adele was able to get all the fabric she wanted during a textile shortage. Adele must have thought she'd picked the winning side, but the Germans hadn't been doing too well lately. They weren't the supermen everyone thought they were. In private, people were talking about Liberation.

Bette was about to launch another attack when Lucien Bernard appeared behind Adele. He started stroking her blond hair, and Adele swung around in her seat to face him.

"Lucien, my darling. Where have you been? You haven't called me in ages."

"I tried calling you many times," said Lucien. From the feeble tone of his reply, Bette knew he hadn't been trying very hard.

Adele looked up at Lucien and took hold of his hand. "Lucien, do you remember Bette? My right—and left hand."

"Of course. We met one evening outside Le Chat Roux...and I saw you at the fashion show," said Lucien as he sat in the chair next to Adele.

Bette did remember Lucien. He had definitely made an impression on her. But he belonged to her boss and therefore was off limits.

"So good to see you again, Monsieur Bernard."

"Lucien, tell me about all your new work," said Adele. "When we last spoke, you were designing an armaments plant or something out in Chatou, wasn't it?"

"In Chaville, my love. Now I'm doing another for Monsieur Manet."

"How exciting," feigned Adele.

Lucien smiled at Bette, who saw that he was having a hard time keeping focused on Adele. She realized that he didn't come to the fashion show to see the latest in floppy hats, and that pleased her.

"My Lucien is one of the most talented architects in France," Adele said. "Even more than that boring old fool Le Corbusier. That chicken shit ran off to Spain, or was it Switzerland? And besides, he's such an ugly man."

"But a very talented ugly man, Adele. When the world thought of French architecture in the '20s and '30s, it was always the work of Le Corbusier they admired."

"Yes, but he's still ugly, with those atrocious round black glasses. Is that supposed to make him look intellectual or something?"

"Adele, let's take a spin this afternoon for lunch out to the country. I know of an inn that is most hospitable. What do you say, my darling?"

"Lucien, you're a sweetheart, but my work calls this afternoon. Let's do it another time, shall we?"

"I can cover for you this afternoon, Adele, my sweet. It'll be no problem. It's just the fitting of those two black velvet outfits," said Bette. "You lovebirds can get away for a while. It sounds terribly romantic."

Adele glared at Bette for what seemed like a full minute. Bette responded with an amused look.

"That's quite kind of you, my darling, but I must oversee those fittings," Adele said. "They have to be absolutely perfect for next week's show. You know what a perfectionist I am."

Bette also knew that Adele never went to oversee a fitting, always forcing her to deal with it. This afternoon, Bette knew, Adele would be busy with a Gestapo officer fitting something inside her.

"Yes, I know you do love things that *come* in black."

Adele ignored the comment and looked over at Lucien and patted his hand.

"I've got a wonderful idea!" she said. "Why don't you take my Bette for a jaunt in the country? She'd love to breathe some fresh air. She's always cooped up in Paris. Aren't you, dear?"

So Adele was giving her some leftovers. But that was okay. Lucien seemed very promising material. And the look on his face said he was quite pleased by this turn of events.

"What time should I be ready? I live at 3 rue Payenne," asked Bette.

"Two o'clock?"

44

LUCIEN WATCHED BETTE AS SHE SLEPT NEXT TO HIM. SHE WAS AN extraordinarily beautiful woman, and it felt like an honor to have made love to her. They had spent a wonderful afternoon together, dining and enjoying each other's company. It was taken for granted that they would wind up in bed together by the early evening. Lucien had been hopelessly inexperienced when he'd first slept with women in his student days. Some of the crueler girls hadn't been shy about telling him either. But with practice he'd improved. There had been a series of affairs of varying lengths before he married Celeste, then seven years of exclusive nondescript sex with her until the past three years' fireworks with Adele. He found it tremendously exciting to have a mistress; it felt very grown-up and cosmopolitan. The secret trysts added electricity to his boring life.

But Bette was a far more passionate lover than her boss, far more aggressive. For the first time in his life, sex was more exciting than getting a new commission.

Lucien propped the pillow against the headboard and lit a cigarette. He surveyed the hotel room. The bright white walls with the dark walnut wainscoting and stone fireplace gave it a homey feeling. When the time had come for sex, Lucien hadn't been able to go back to his flat because Pierre was there. He couldn't tell the boy to get lost for the afternoon. He'd thought they'd be going to Bette's, but she'd told him they couldn't go to her place because she had relatives from out of town staying with her, so they'd just gotten a room at the inn where they had dined. He reached over and stroked her beautiful auburn hair, and she began to stir. Bette yawned and opened her eyes. When she saw Lucien, she smiled sleepily.

"We seem to be off on the right foot," she whispered, as she caressed Lucien's cheek.

"Indeed we are, mademoiselle."

"I think you definitely have possibilities."

Lucien was quite pleased at that turn of phrase and laughed. He snuggled up next to Bette, totally intoxicated by her smell and the warmth of her body. Meeting Bette was a lucky break. Maybe a love interest would take his mind off his problems, which were like a sword of Damocles hanging by a thread above his head, ready to drop at any second. Maybe making love a few times a week would alleviate the strain.

"Well, I'm glad I'm a potential lover," said Lucien.

"Potential? You *are* my lover, my sweet. What are you doing Thursday night?"

"I can clear my busy schedule for you. Your place?" asked Lucien hopefully.

"No, how about your place?"

"Can't," Lucien replied quickly.

"And why's that?"

Lucien became tongue-tied and couldn't think quickly enough to dream up an excuse. Pierre was always in the flat in the evening. In fact, Lucien didn't like the boy going anywhere besides the office during the day for fear of being picked up by the Germans. He was more scared of arrest for Pierre than himself now. Countless Parisians had disappeared, quietly vanishing into thin air without a word, never to be seen again. He wanted to get into the sack with Bette as often as he could, but not if it meant casting out Pierre.

"Ah…relatives visiting. Just like you."

"From where?" asked Bette.

"From Nantes. My Uncle Emile. My mother's brother. A fine man."

"I see. So where should we meet?"

"How about the Café l'Hiver? You know it?" asked Lucien, running his hand through her hair.

"It's a charming place. But what about afterward? All through supper, we'll be thinking of making love to each other, so where shall we go?"

"Mmm…well, there's the Hotel Gagnol on the avenue Parmentier. It's very comfortable and quite convenient," said Lucien.

"You've been there before. With the remarkable Adele, I bet."

"Yes, we went there one time when we were so excited we couldn't wait to get to Adele's flat."

"Ah, those were the days. You're not sorry to lose the great Adele?"

"Our days together were bound to come to an end. I've become an item on the menu she got tired of. How about you, my love? Are you ready for a second serving?"

"It's almost seven, and I've got to get back," Bette said. "My relatives will be wondering what happened to me." She bounded out of the bed and headed for the pile of clothes on the floor.

Lucien was mesmerized by the sight of her body. Incredibly long, beautiful legs, a tiny waist. Instead of being flat-chested like so many Paris fashion models, Bette had a wonderful pair of full breasts. She caught him admiring her body.

"Not too bad for an old woman of thirty-one, eh?"

"Not too shabby at all. Are you sure you won't have some dessert?" asked Lucien as he pulled away the sheet to show Bette he was ready to go.

"That's very tempting, but I can't be late," said Bette as she put on her brassiere, exciting Lucien even more.

"You're forcing me to take a cold shower before I leave, you know that, don't you?"

45

WHAT HAPPENS TO ALL THESE JEWS ONCE THEY GET TO DRANCY, Uncle?" asked Alain as he watched his neighbor Monsieur Valery being dragged by his hair from the apartment house entry into a black Citroën. He was followed by his wife and two children, who were being pushed along by two Gestapo officers in plainclothes. The car sped off, and Alain turned to face his uncle, who was enjoying a cigarette. They had been viewing the whole scene from the rear seat of his personal Gestapo staff car.

Uncle Hermann took a long drag of his cigarette, then smiled at Alain.

"After a short stay at Drancy, they're sent on a wonderful holiday in Poland. Plenty of fresh air and exercise."

"They say they're never seen again. None come back to Paris."

"That's because they enjoy it there so much. They don't want to come back."

"Germans seem to hate Jews even more than the French. Why is that, Uncle?"

"Because we Germans know they're the scourge of the world. Vermin that have to be destroyed before they destroy our civilization."

"Don't the French also think that?"

"The French authorities sit on their asses when it comes to rounding up Jews, especially French-born Jews. They tip them off, and they're gone by the time we get to them. But not Monsieur Valery. He was quite surprised when we knocked on his door. You did a splendid job, my boy. He *was* a Jew. You can always tell that heeb look. Valery paid a load of money for false papers and baptismal certificates for his kids, but it didn't do him any good in the end. Schlegal will be quite impressed with his capture."

"I'm glad to help, Uncle. You've been most kind to me and my family. You can call on me at any time."

"I certainly will. Anyone you suspect, you let me know."

"I've got a couple people in mind," muttered Alain, who started to get out of the car.

"Before you go, I have a little surprise for you. Monsieur Valery won't be needing his Renault on his holiday in the East. He'll be taking the train, so I thought you might want to have it. A good-looking young fellow like you can impress many a mademoiselle with a beautiful car," said Hermann. He jangled a set of car keys in front of Alain's face.

Alain's eyes lit up, and he immediately snatched the keys from his uncle's black-gloved hand. No more begging to borrow his cousin's car.

"You're too generous, Uncle. No one in Paris has a car anymore."

"And you'll be needing petrol, so here's a ration card. Don't waste it; petrol is scarce."

"Don't you worry, Uncle, I'll be quite careful. Where is it parked?"

"It's the dark green one, right next to the corner. See?"

Alain couldn't contain himself and was out the door. On the sidewalk, he called out, "Tell Colonel Schlegal that he can count on me."

"I'll wait to relay that information. Schlegal is in a foul mood, and I don't want to go near him for a few days."

Out of courtesy, Alain feigned interest. "Why's that?"

"Oh, he lost some Jew out in a cottage near Epinay."

"Where?"

"Epinay, about five miles north of Paris. This Jew was hiding out there. Schlegal was convinced that he was concealed in some secret hiding space within the walls of the house, so he had our men tear the place apart, stick by stick. But he couldn't find him. Then he burned the whole goddamned house down, but no Jew. It turned out that he'd been hiding under a big fake floor drain in the kitchen in the basement. There was this tunnel that led from it into a garden. That's how he escaped. Schlegal went crazy."

"This was a cottage in Epinay?"

"It's just a pile of burnt rubble now. Now go get your car and start banging some of these French girls. A Renault's got a nice wide backseat. Put it to good use, nephew." Hermann tapped his driver on the shoulder to get moving.

Alain, left standing on the sidewalk, looked down at the keys in his hand. He stared at them for a few seconds, then walked toward the corner where the car was parked. His romantic efforts would have to wait for a while.

⁘ ⁘ ⁘

Alain examined the false drain pan and lowered himself into the cavity below. The tunnel had been crudely but efficiently constructed, with plank bracing on its ceiling to prevent a collapse. Someone had gone to a great deal of effort to save a Jew. But Alain wasn't interested in the men who'd dug the tunnel but the man who'd thought of this ingenious solution. He discovered that the tunnel ended far into the garden, almost twenty meters away, where the Jew could escape unnoticed by the Gestapo who were busy ripping the house apart. Alain already knew who had designed the fake drain. It was the sketch of the metal frame and the brick that he'd found months earlier that still puzzled him. He decided to walk through the charred ruins of the house, poking around the debris until he reached the fireplace and chimney, the only things still intact. He smiled as he walked up to it because now everything made sense. The sketch was for a false wall at the back of a firebox. A very clever solution. The only thought that came into Alain's mind at that moment was why Lucien would be stupid enough to design these hiding places.

46

"THIS IS MY FAVORITE INTERIOR IN ALL OF PARIS. NO OTHER COMES close," said Lucien, who stood behind Pierre, both hands resting on his shoulders.

"The reading room of the Bibliothèque Nationale is world famous. It's the most important library in France. Look up at those domes. See all the light they let in—aren't they incredible? And see how they're carried on those skinny cast-iron columns?"

Lucien always got carried away when he explained his favorite architecture to Pierre. They had been to Notre Dame, La Madeleine, the Eiffel Tower, and the Paris Opera. In each place he jabbered away, but Pierre listened intently. He never seemed bored by Lucien's lectures. On the contrary, he asked questions and pointed out structural and design elements that impressed Lucien.

"The architect, Henri Labrouste, in the 1860s, was the first to use exposed iron as an architectural element. It took a lot of nerve to do that. People criticized him and said it was ugly. Look at those beautiful iron arches that carry the domes. See how they spring out from the columns? Just incredible."

"Shhh," whispered an old man who placed his index finger to his lips. Lucien had forgotten he was in a library and nodded a silent apology.

They walked through the room between the rows of reading tables, gazing up at the skylights in the middle of the domes. Lucien took Pierre up to one of the columns and rapped his knuckles on it, producing a metallic sound. This brought another *shhh* from a patron.

"See. It's metal, not stone." Pierre did the same and smiled at the result.

Men sat at the tables immersed in their books, scribbling notes and marking pages with little scraps of paper. As Lucien walked by them, he wondered if they found solace in their books in bad times like these or whether they were always lost in their world of scholarship.

"It took them six years to build this library. Those are the stacks over there, where they keep the books. They're behind that incredible glass wall, which is framed out in iron."

Lucien and Pierre walked up to the wall and looked inside at row upon row of brown aged volumes. With his hand on Pierre's shoulder, Lucien guided the boy around the perimeter of the great room, pointing out the detailing.

"All these buildings of Paris are treasures," said Lucien.

"But they're all old," replied Pierre. "I thought you were a modern architect."

Lucien stifled a laugh with his hand. "I surely am, but you can learn a lot from an old building." He was pleased that Pierre could pull his leg.

As they moved on through the silent reading room, Lucien heard a sound in the distance. It became louder and louder, and the patrons, one by one, lifted their heads to listen. Lucien recognized the sound of German jackboots on a marble floor.

"Christ," said Lucien. He looked down into Pierre's eyes, which were full of terror.

Panic seized him, but Lucien kept his nerve and acted quickly. Because he'd been here many times, he knew the layout of the room well. Grabbing Pierre by the arm, he led him to a niche in the perimeter wall behind a column and shoved him into it.

"Keep down. You know where to go, don't you?"

He squeezed the boy's hand and kissed his cheek. Pierre nodded and crouched out of sight. At that moment, the double doors of the main entry to the reading room crashed open and a half-dozen German soldiers led by an SS captain walked in briskly. The officer slowly went down the main aisle followed by his men, all of whom were carrying machine guns. He looked up and down the tables. The patrons all kept their heads down as if they were studying their tomes. Lucien walked directly toward the officer between the tables to draw attention away from Pierre. But as he got closer, the captain walked up to a middle-aged man wearing wire-rimmed glasses and a gray tweed coat.

"Professor Paul Mortier, you're to come with me immediately."

"But I've done nothing."

Two soldiers grabbed him by the arms and dragged him out of the room.

"I've done nothing!" he screamed.

The Germans were out the doors, and the reading room was in total silence again. Patrons slowly returned to their books. Lucien was shaking as he walked back to Pierre. The boy had come out from behind the column and was slowly walking toward him. About three meters away he ran to Lucien and buried his face in his chest.

As Lucien hugged the boy, he knew he should get Pierre out of France, but the thought filled him with an awful sadness. He loved and needed the boy with all his heart and couldn't bear to part with him. He didn't want to do it.

47

G OOD SHABBOS, MONSIEUR LAVAL," SCHLEGAL CALLED OUT IN A cheery voice as he entered the room.

Laval, whose hands were tied behind him, slumped forward in the wooden chair.

"I said good shabbos, Laval. Didn't you hear me?" Schlegal grabbed Laval's chin and yanked his swollen and bloody head up. "It is Saturday, so it is shabbos, isn't it? Your people's sabbath?"

Laval grunted, and Schlegal let his head flop down. Turning to Lieutenant Voss and Captain Bruckner, he threw up his hands in mock indignation.

"So what has Monsieur Laval told us of value?"

"I'm afraid Monsieur Laval has been most uncooperative. He hasn't told us a thing about his business associate Mendel Janusky," replied Voss, with deep regret in his voice.

"That's a shame," Schlegal said. "A real shame, Monsieur Laval. I was so counting on you. You know, I've been looking for you for three long months, and when I finally find you, you're no help to me at all." Schlegal bent over and looked directly into the old man's blood-crusted eyes.

Schlegal placed his hands on his hips and paced back and forth in front of Laval.

"And as his banker, you must know where he deposits his fortune. He is no longer your client, so where did he take it?"

Laval raised his head and croaked out a sound.

"I'm sorry, I didn't catch that."

"He…he hid it so no one would find it. I…don't…even know where it is. He wouldn't tell me."

"I find that a little hard to believe. You must have some idea where he could've stashed his loot. Take a guess."

"I'm telling you, I…don't know," groaned Laval.

"All those paintings, sculptures, gold goblets, and gems. Difficult to smuggle out of France into Switzerland. Is this stuff hidden in the countryside somewhere?"

Laval grunted again and his head rolled from side to side.

"Colonel, may I suggest a new means of interrogation?" asked Voss, taking a bag out of a large red leather satchel on the floor.

"Let me guess: it's something electrical, isn't it? My men love all things electrical," said Schlegal to Laval with great amusement.

"It's a soldering iron," replied Voss as he plugged the electric cord into a wall outlet. "It'll take about two minutes to get ready."

"I'm quite impressed with your initiative, Voss."

"Since I've been posted in Paris, Colonel, I've worked over scores of men and women, and it was taking a toll on me physically. Sometimes I go home at night in great pain," said Voss, like an old woman complaining about her bad knees. "I decided there must be a more technologically efficient way to get the job done."

"Voss, I like initiative in an officer."

"I'm afraid it's not an original idea, Colonel. I saw it demonstrated in Warsaw about a year ago."

"Very well, let's get on with it." Schlegal turned to Laval. "Just two simple questions. Where is Janusky, and where is his money? One last chance."

Laval remained silent. Voss walked over to check whether he had passed out, but after slapping his face, Laval opened his eyes.

The lieutenant stepped forward and placed the soldering iron on the old man's forehead. He gave out a scream that reverberated for what seemed like a minute. Schlegal nodded his head vigorously, greatly impressed with the results of the device. Voss pressed the iron all over Laval's face, then tore open his shirt and went to work on his chest. Each scream was louder than the previous one.

"I think there's one obvious place you're overlooking," said Schlegal as he sat down in a chair and lit a cigarette.

Voss smiled at his superior. He unbuckled Laval's belt and opened his zipper to extract the old man's penis.

"Make sure you wash your hands after all this, my boy. You don't know where that thing has been," said Schlegal in all seriousness.

"It reminds me of a shriveled prune," said Voss. He placed the iron on the head of the penis and held it there. The scream became one long continuous wail.

When the noise became too much to bear, Schlegal signaled him to stop. He got up from the chair and placed his face inches from Laval.

"We have an unlimited amount of electricity, Laval, and there're plenty of places on your fat, disgusting body we haven't touched. So what do you say?"

No answer was given and Voss set upon Laval, but Schlegal suddenly stopped him.

"I think Monsieur Laval can spare one of his eyes, don't you?"

Without a second's hesitation, the lieutenant plunged the iron into Laval's left eye.

"86 rue d'Assas, apartment 5C!" screamed Laval.

Schlegal nodded at Voss, who bolted from the room, shouting orders to soldiers waiting down the hall.

"Who was hiding him there, you bastard? Tell me and you walk out of here alive."

"All I know is that he's a rich gentile. I swear that's all I know. Janusky wouldn't tell me anymore."

"A gentile, you say?"

"He's hidden him in a couple places already."

"Has he helped other Jews or was it just Janusky?" screamed Schlegal.

"There were others," moaned Laval.

Schlegal yanked the old man's head back by his hair. "Does he hide them in special secret hiding places?"

This got a reaction out of Laval. His one good eye widened in fear, and Schlegal knew he was getting somewhere.

"Tell me, Laval, or you'll lose the other eye."

Laval began to cry and wail. "God forgive me," he moaned.

Schlegal lit a cigarette and sat on the desk.

"You're quite lucky you gave me something of value. Or you'd be using a cane and dark glasses begging on the streets for the rest of your life, old boy."

48

Maybe I should've bumped up the arches in the center section? The roof line would've looked more dynamic," said Lucien.

"An architect should never rationalize a change in purely aesthetic terms, you know that. He should give the client a pragmatic reason for doing it."

Lucien nodded when he heard Herzog's advice, then thought for a moment.

"If we raise the center section two meters, then the plant can accommodate a taller crane."

"Excellent suggestion, Monsieur Bernard," exclaimed Herzog. "Labrune, come over here, there's a change I need you to make." Herzog and Lucien met at the construction site in Tremblay almost daily to discuss the progress of the job. The meetings always involved Labrune, the elderly cantankerous contractor who was in charge of the whole project. He had been called out of retirement by the Wehrmacht to work for them, which he resented greatly. A veteran of the first war, he still hadn't forgiven the Boche for using poison gas on him in 1916. Labrune walked slowly over to Colonel Herzog, cursing under his breath. He glared at Lucien and spit on the ground as he always did when he saw the architect. Lucien was well aware that the old goat hated him, but then all contractors hated architects because they made changes all the time. Labrune had had a fifty-year career of hating architects.

"Labrune, you move like an old man, get the hell over here," yelled Herzog. Labrune proceeded at the same speed.

"I am an old man, Colonel. Or haven't you noticed? What's your all-important change?"

"Raise the center four arches two meters. It won't take that much lumber, and it won't put us behind schedule," said Herzog.

"It's no big deal, Labrune, you can easily handle this," added Lucien, which drew the evil eye from Labrune, who snorted like a horse and looked down at the ground as he spoke.

"It's not that easy, Monsieur Bernard. I have to thicken the arches in order to raise them, add more reinforcing. I need a structural sketch."

"Mangin, our engineer, will get you one by tomorrow morning. No problem."

Labrune glanced at Herzog, who nodded, and the old man stomped away in disgust.

"Motherfucker," muttered Labrune.

"What did you say, Labrune?" shouted Herzog.

"I said I'll be glad to make your change," answered Labrune. "What the hell choice do I have? I either make the change or get shot on the spot, eh Mein Fuehrer?"

"I like your reasoning, Labrune," said Herzog, who then turned to Lucien.

"This will be your best building, Lucien. The way the arches spring from the ground is beautiful."

Lucien agreed. The formwork for the first three arches was up, and even in wood they looked great. He loved seeing his buildings get built. That was the most wonderful thing about being an architect—to see your drawings become real, three-dimensional objects that you could walk around and touch. All architects were impatient to see their buildings completed. Normally, it took forever for a building to be finished, but the Germans got things done incredibly quickly. What would have taken months under French control took only weeks for the Germans. He had always heard about the legendary German efficiency and scoffed at the notion. Now he witnessed it firsthand and was quite impressed. Working three shifts seven days a week definitely sped up the process. Threatening the workers with beatings and death also helped.

"This couldn't have happened without your support," said Lucien guardedly. He didn't want to get too mushy about it. When Herzog had been promoted to colonel, his former superior officer, the idiotic Colonel Lieber, had been transferred back to Berlin, leaving Herzog as the sole power overseeing the construction program. With Speer's complete confidence, he got the buildings up and running fast, cranking out materiel for the German war effort way ahead of Berlin's schedule. Now there was even talk of a promotion to general.

Herzog began walking toward the excavation for the foundation, and Lucien followed. Not only did he respect Herzog's design sense, but the German also had a sharp eye for construction, knowing when a corner was being cut and not hesitating to order a subcontractor to tear work out and start again. Of course, they never protested. If one refused, a soldier would be called on to drag the poor devil away, never to be seen again. This happened on one occasion, reminding Lucien that Herzog was still a German officer loyal to the Fuehrer and intent on Germany's total victory. But it was more of a personal mission for Herzog. He seemed determined to leave his mark on France for the Reich. After he was gone, the factories would still stand, evidence that he'd been there. Architects thought the same way. Their work would outlast them. A library would serve generations long after the architect was gone. With Lieber out of the way, Lucien had complete creative freedom. It wasn't just a canard that an architect needed a good client to produce great art. Herzog was the ideal client.

"The bands of glass will really accentuate the horizontality, plus let a lot of natural light in," said Herzog with a smile.

"The workers will be able to see better and produce more," added Lucien, and both men laughed.

"Exactly. Those bands of black brick will definitely help productivity.

I don't know how but they do break down the scale of the front wall," said Herzog with a wink.

They looked down into the excavations to examine the footings.

"I ordered them to be extra wide to distribute the loads to the ground," said Herzog. "Sooner or later the buildings will be under Allied attack and will have to be able to take a pounding from bombers. The factory has to survive and be put back on line to keep producing. That's Speer's order."

Herzog never talked about it, but Lucien saw that the Germans were increasingly uneasy about the progress of the war. Everything had been going their way until this fall, when the Allies had invaded North Africa and were slowly gaining the upper hand. Everyone expected an invasion from England. In anticipation, Herzog examined every detail of the building, especially the structural drawings. He had ordered more steel reinforcement in columns and arches, the thickness of steel window frames was increased, and concrete roof slabs were thickened. The design suggestions he made strengthened the overall building but were so aesthetically pleasing that Lucien could never object. Lucien envied his skills and tried to learn from him. Although he'd never finished his training at the Bauhaus, Herzog was a phenomenal designer, blessed with great structural intuition.

Satisfied with the progress of his building, Lucien bid good-bye to Herzog and walked back to his car, which was parked by the construction shed. Labrune was standing by the corner filling his pipe. Lucien waved at the old man.

"Great work, Labrune; keep it up."

"Stinking traitor," said Labrune, loud enough for Lucien to hear.

His ears burning, Lucien kept walking. The excitement of seeing his creation come to life suddenly vanished.

49

LUCIEN WAS QUITE PROUD HE'D PROCURED A ROASTED CHICKEN FOR tonight's supper. It had cost him a pretty penny—twenty times more than what it would have cost in peacetime. But it was worth it. He knew Pierre would smell the delicious aroma the minute he came through the apartment door and come running. That sight alone was worth the money. The twenty thousand francs Manet insisted again that he take wasn't going as far as he'd thought. By 1942, inflation was eating away one's money at an incredible rate. Things had always been expensive, but now they were exorbitant. Butter, which was officially fifty-nine francs and impossible to get, was over two hundred francs on the black market. Bartering had become the rage in Paris. A kid in his building had bought an hour of violin lessons for half a kilo of butter.

As Lucien walked home through the dark streets, he thought of what to have with the chicken. Potatoes and cabbage? Or just bread and wine? He wrestled with the choices and gave no thought to the footsteps behind him. About six blocks from his building, two men came up on either side of him, and Lucien's knees nearly buckled. Were they the Gestapo, who favored snatching people off the sidewalk and throwing them into a waiting car? Or could they be the gangs who pretended to be the police and confiscated black-market goods? His friend, Daniel Joffre, had had a whole leg of mutton he was carrying in a suitcase taken from him last month. He had to decide whether to bolt down the street coming up on his right. He glanced to his right and left to size up the two men. Both looked quite fit and probably could chase him down with ease. Though he was in lousy shape, he knew he had to run. But they kept walking alongside him for two blocks, which struck Lucien as odd. The Gestapo wouldn't take this much time to make an arrest. Realizing they could be the faux police after his chicken, he instinctively clutched the package tight to his chest and walked faster. Maybe they were just ordinary starving men driven mad by the smell of the chicken. One of the men ran ahead and stood directly in Lucien's path. The other stood directly behind him. Lucien decided not to give up the chicken without a fight.

"Please let me pass, monsieur," said Lucien in his politest tone of voice, but he was ready to kick the man in the groin and run. He was about to say he didn't want any trouble when the man facing him spoke.

"Monsieur Bernard, we wish to have a word with you, if you don't mind. I promise you it won't take long." The man was wearing a stylish hat and a Gestapo-like trench coat. He gestured to a car that pulled up alongside them. Lucien began to tremble and saw the amused expressions on the men's faces. The man behind Lucien put his hand on his shoulder and gently guided him into the waiting car. All three sat in the back, Lucien and his chicken in the middle. Lucien knew they must be the French police working with the Gestapo. They definitely weren't after his food. Nothing was said while the car covered about a kilometer before turning into a garage. Lucien twisted around to see someone shutting the garage doors behind them. This was it. They were going to kill him here. The only thought that came into Lucien's mind as he slumped down in the seat was that Pierre would be alone all night, not knowing what had happened to him. Lucien would join the ranks of Parisians who disappeared without a trace. And Pierre wouldn't get his special chicken dinner.

The man on his right opened the door, and they got out of the car. Lucien followed them to a stair at the rear of the garage, which led to a small office where two other men were waiting. An older man in his sixties, wearing a dark gray overcoat, pointed to a wooden chair at a round table, and Lucien sat down.

"Monsieur Bernard, that's quite a building you designed for the Germans in Chaville. The one that's going up in Tremblay's pretty impressive too," said the old man, who sat down in the chair across the table.

"Thank you."

"It's interesting how you're so willing to design a building better than what the Germans could do for themselves."

"I don't see it that way at all, monsieur. I just try to do my best."

"Your best for the Germans, you mean."

"For myself. I design to my own high standard."

"A higher standard than what the Germans could do?"

Lucien knew immediately where this line of questioning was heading and who was asking the questions.

"You're from the Resistance, aren't you?"

"Yes, monsieur, that is the organization we represent. And we have some questions about your loyalty to your country."

"Hold on, you old bastard. I'll be damned if you think I'm a traitor. I'm loyal to France. I was there fighting to the end when the surrender came. You can easily check that," Lucien shouted.

"We know of your heroic war record sitting behind a desk." The room erupted in laughter. "It's *now* that we're talking about."

"And you're *heroes*?" replied Lucien. "What a joke."

The real reason Lucien hated the Resistance was because it was 99 percent Communist, and he despised Communists and their idiotic dreams of overthrowing capitalism. Their supposed acts of heroism brought nothing but a never-ending cycle of reprisals. Since 1941, when the Resistance started murdering German soldiers, the Reich had fought back by killing hostages. Just last week, after the Resistance threw grenades at some airmen at Jean-Boudin Stadium in Paris, killing eight of them, the Germans murdered eighty-five people. Most of them were Communists, which was all right with Lucien, but some were just helpless bystanders.

"You kill one goddamn German and a dozen innocent Frenchmen are murdered. You do some meaningless act of sabotage like cutting some telephone lines or diverting freight cars in the wrong direction and get more of our people killed in reprisals. What about those poor bastards you got killed the other day? What you do, monsieur, doesn't add up to much. Certainly not worth the life of one Frenchman."

"Let me take care of him," shouted a short bearded man sitting in the corner of the room. "One bullet for one collaborator, and we can go home."

"Emile, please don't interrupt. Let me handle this," said the old man. "Monsieur Bernard, the Resistance does its best under extremely difficult conditions. But we must fight back. To live defeated is to die every day."

"Says who? I heard de Gaulle on the BBC say that killing Germans makes it too easy for them to massacre unarmed citizens. He said you do more harm than good. Anyway, it'll be the British and the Americans who save our asses and you know it, not fools like you."

"Yes, but until then we must fight in our own way."

"Christ, you're nothing but a lot of goddamn Communists. Your boy Stalin isn't any angel either. It got out that he starved a few million to death in the Ukraine. And don't forget he signed a nonaggression pact with Hitler. Remember that?"

The old man didn't reply. Lucien knew this was a sore point with all Communists.

"Let's get back to you. We feel that you're a bit too helpful to the German war effort. We're asking you to be a little less cooperative. Don't be so energetic."

"Goddamn you, I'm not a collaborator. Those factories will be used after the war is won."

The old man lit a cigarette and took a long drag. He smiled at Lucien. "That's a very imaginative way of justifying your actions, monsieur." The other men in the room murmured in agreement.

Lucien didn't like being mocked, especially by working-class types like these. "France *will* need factories to rebuild the country."

"There won't be a country, if shits like you help the Boche," shouted the bearded man. "And those factories you design are ugly as sin."

"You've been warned, Monsieur Bernard," said the old man. "Remember where your loyalties lie. When victory does come, collaborators will pay a terrible price, I assure you."

"Maybe before victory," said the bearded man, pulling a revolver out of his coat pocket.

"And I wouldn't be so friendly with Colonel Herzog either. Doesn't look good," added the old man.

Still holding his chicken, Lucien stood up and looked around at the men in the room.

"Listen, you bastards. I love France, and I'm no collaborator. You all can go to hell if you think I am. Now let me go home."

The old man gestured to the man in the trench coat.

"Take him back. Good night, Monsieur Bernard. And enjoy your chicken dinner."

The same two men who picked him up drove him home, pushing him roughly out of the car when they reached the corner of Lucien's block. Lucien fell flat on his face on the pavement, dropping the chicken.

"Let's take his chicken," suggested the man in the trench coat.

"Fuck him. I hope you choke on a bone, you traitor," yelled the driver as the car sped off.

50

ALAIN HAD SEEN LOTS OF AMERICAN FILMS IN WHICH THE DETECTIVE or the spy had to follow someone, and he had the technique down pat. It was most important to stay far enough away so as not to get spotted, but close enough to keep the man in plain sight.

As he walked along the rue du Cirque, Alain always had Lucien in view. If his boss stopped to look in a store window, Alain would stop and duck into a doorway, then continue the tail, which was what following a person was called in the cinema. Lucien was obviously in no hurry to get where he was going. He stopped to buy a book and had a quick drink at the Café de la Place. Maybe Lucien was taking his time to make sure no one was following him. Alain had seen this technique in the cinema also. The man would know he was being tailed, bide his time, and then try to shake the tail.

Lucien turned down the avenue Gabriel, then left on the rue Boissy d'Anglas and walked at a leisurely pace for another fifteen minutes. The streets were just crowded enough so that Alain could go unnoticed. If Lucien had gone down an alley devoid of people, Alain thought, tailing him would've been much more difficult. Alain had gone through Lucien's desk and files almost every night looking for sketches of hiding places for Jews, but had come up empty. After the blunder with the fireplace detail, Lucien had become very cautious. Alain had wanted to go to his uncle and tell him about the fake drain in the cottage that the Gestapo had burned down, but he realized he had no proof that Lucien had designed the hiding place. He had to catch Lucien in the act, so he had to find a building where another Jew was hiding. If there was no paper trail, then it meant following him. But so far the tails had led nowhere.

A red-hot hatred of Lucien burned within him. He could've brushed off what happened in the storage room and all the other slights, but he just couldn't. Daydreams passed through his mind that had Lucien being carted off by the Gestapo, never to be seen again, and Alain inheriting the firm by default. The Germans needed the drawings for the factories and would—through his uncle's influence—ask him to take over. As for the matter of hiding Jews, Alain had never had any particular hatred of Jews. He had grown up with Jews in his neighborhood in Saint-Germain, and they'd always been friendly to him. When he'd denounced Monsieur Valery, who had also been very nice to him, he was just doing it to gain favor with his uncle.

Lucien stopped and looked into another shop window but then did something that aroused Alain's suspicions. While he was examining the men's suit in the display, his head shifted to the right then to the left to see if he was being followed. It was definitely a cautious gesture. Alain had hidden behind a column that flanked the entry of a building when Lucien had paused. Now he waited before going back onto the sidewalk; he had to be sure Lucien would not turn around again. Alain was certain that Lucien was going to a hiding place. He was beside himself with delight. He had to be close behind Lucien when he entered the building so he could creep up the stairs and spy on him.

He followed for several more blocks until Lucien came to a nondescript café on the rue de Duras and sat down at an outdoor table. Alain was brimming with impatience as Lucien called the waiter over and ordered. He waited in a doorway of a milliner shop across the street, smoking a cigarette. It was good that the shop was closed, and no one would shoo him away from the entrance. After Lucien was served a glass of wine, he asked the waiter a question and was directed to the interior of the café. Lucien rose from his seat and went inside. Alain guessed that he had to go the bathroom, but after ten minutes had passed, he became impatient and worried. Another ten minutes passed, and Alain knew what had happened. He ran across the street but approached the café entrance slowly. He didn't want to run into Lucien if he came out.

Alain peered into the darkness of the café and entered cautiously. He stayed to the right of the inner door, hiding behind the door frame. A waiter came up to him, and Alain asked where the bathroom was. The waiter snapped at him, telling him that he had to order something in order to use the facilities. Alain ignored him and walked swiftly to the rear of the café. He slowly opened the door to the men's room, half expecting to face Lucien, but it was empty. He checked all the stalls, and the window above the sink was closed. Outside the bathroom, he saw a doorway that led to a supply room with a rear door. Alain cursed under his breath as he opened it and saw a tiny courtyard that connected to a passageway. He followed it out onto a street. Looking up and down the street, he found no sign of Lucien.

He leaned against the wall of a building and lit a cigarette. He was positive that Lucien had not seen him. He must have used the café as a precaution to give anyone the slip. If he'd been in Lucien's shoes, he would've done the same thing. He smiled to himself as he thought about it; it was a pretty clever maneuver. Alain liked this game of cat and mouse and looked forward to another opportunity to tail Lucien. As he puffed away on his cigarette, he noticed that he was on the rue des Saussaies, right across the street from Gestapo headquarters where his uncle worked. It was an ornate limestone affair with iron balconies and tall windows. He knew its elegant facade belied what actually went on inside. His uncle had once mentioned how he got his "guests" to cooperate. Alain tossed his cigarette butt away and started home. He was in no hurry so he stopped to look in a secondhand bookstore window and saw a volume on *moderne* architecture that looked interesting, so he went inside.

✛ ✛ ✛

Pierre watched Alain from a doorway across the street. When he left the bookstore twenty minutes later, the boy followed him back to his home. Several weeks ago, he'd noticed Alain rifling through some papers on Lucien's desk at the office. At first, this didn't seem unusual; after all, Alain was Lucien's right-hand man who took care of every detail of the buildings. This happened a few more times, but Pierre thought nothing of it.

But one afternoon when Alain ordered him to buy some tracing paper from the stationers, he went out the door but then came back to get a sample of the paper he'd forgotten to take with him. Because Alain constantly screamed at him for the tiniest mistakes, Pierre let himself back in very quietly. Inside the vestibule of the office, he heard a metallic scratching sound. Alain was working his penknife in the lock of Lucien's desk drawer. As Pierre watched, he unlocked the drawer and went through the papers very carefully. This seemed odd, and so Pierre kept an eye on Alain from then on.

One morning when Lucien was out, and Pierre was back in the storage closet straightening up, he overheard Alain on the telephone asking to talk to a German officer. This sent a bolt of panic up his spine. Did Alain know about his fake identity? He was such a mean boy, perfectly capable of betraying him and Lucien. He knew Alain hated Lucien; he cursed him all the time when Lucien wasn't around. And Alain certainly hated Pierre's guts—he told him that almost every day. Pierre knew that it had been too good to be true that he had found Lucien to take care of him and more importantly treat him like a son. It would all be snatched away from him in an instant, just as he was starting to feel safe in his new life. Why would he be so lucky to get a new home when all his family had been killed? His first thought when he heard Alain on the telephone was to run away, but he had nowhere to go. And he couldn't go to Lucien because he really had no proof of Alain's treachery. He decided to stay calm and keep watch on Alain.

But after secretly listening to a few more telephone conversations in the following weeks, Pierre figured out that Alain was talking to a relative, an uncle, of whom he was very fond. He realized that this had nothing to do with revealing *his* secret identity. Although he'd moved into Lucien's apartment, he knew that Alain probably continued to go through Lucien's papers after hours. One day, on his way back to the office after running an errand, he saw Lucien leave the office. Then he saw Alain come out and start walking about twenty meters behind him. He acted like he didn't want Lucien to spot him. Out of curiosity, he followed Alain and discovered that he was following Lucien. The three of them meandered through the streets of Paris with Alain trailing Lucien, and Pierre trailing Alain. Two more times, including today's excursion, he followed Alain when he left right after Lucien did. Pierre was certain that Lucien had some sort of secret life that he didn't want anyone else to know about. He could see that Alain was determined to find out what it was, which meant Lucien was in danger. And that meant he was also in danger.

On his way back home, Pierre took a detour to look at Madame Charpointier's old house. He had visited it twice before, always hiding in a doorway down the street so none of the neighbors would see him and betray him to the Germans. He never figured out who betrayed them. Staring at the attic window where he'd watched Madame Charpointier get shot on the sidewalk that terrible day made him sick to his stomach. The image of her dropping to the ground would never go away. She had been his protector, and Pierre had been powerless to save her. The shame of sitting there and letting it happen haunted him every day. Pierre vowed that would never be repeated. He had to be a man now; that's what his father had told him at his bar mitzvah.

51

H E THINKS HE'S HIDING UNDER THE FLOORBOARDS, PAULUS."
"Maybe he's in that chandelier up there."

"Could be. Or he could be hiding in the cushion I'm sitting on."

Captain Bruckner and Lieutenant Paulus lounged lazily in the plush armchairs of a townhouse on rue de Bassano, where they'd been ordered to go by Colonel Schlegal. Luckily for them, their superior was off in the countryside with his French mistress, so they could deal with this matter without him breathing down their necks. One of Schlegal's informants told him that a Jew was in this apartment. They had decided to study the problem by relaxing in the luxurious salon first.

"You're not going to have me tapping on the walls, are you?" asked Paulus.

"Hell no. That Schlegal has a screw loose," said Bruckner. "I'm not going through the same shit we did at that cottage in Epinay. I still can't believe that. I ruined a uniform tearing through that place."

"You think that's bad? I stepped on a goddamn nail."

"No, we're going to find our Hebrew in a more logical manner."

"Seems a shame to tear apart such a beautiful flat," said Paulus as he gestured at the walls of the palatial apartment. It had incredibly ornate paneling divided by beautiful floor-to-ceiling pilasters that were covered in gilt. The wood floors were parquet and of a rich golden color that glowed in the midday sun. The ceilings were domed, with huge paintings of angels carrying off nymphs into the heavens.

"You know what we could do?" Paulus said with a great smile. "We rip the place apart a bit, then we pick up a Jew in the street, kill him, and say we found the bastard here. How would Schlegal know the difference?"

"Paulus, you'll make captain yet," said Bruckner, who was genuinely impressed with his subordinate.

"We'll just tell him he was hiding in the back of a closet behind one of those fake walls we found a few weeks ago. And when we were taking him downstairs, he tried to make a break for it, and we let him have it."

"Sounds completely plausible to me," replied Bruckner.

"Don't worry, I'll make it very convincing. I was an attorney before the war," boasted Paulus.

"No kidding, you were an attorney? I didn't know that."

"Just out of law school in '39."

"So why are you working for a nut like Schlegal?"

"I thought I'd take a break from the law, get some action under my belt."

"And you wound up chasing Jews in Paris," replied Bruckner with a laugh.

"Yeah, but better here than in Russia."

"That's for damn sure."

"So what do you say? Do we follow my plan and be able to sit down to a fine lunch by two o'clock?" asked Paulus. He, like most German officers, loved French food. Meals were the highlight of their day, and they planned their menus with the same great care they would take in devising a strategy for a battle.

"I say we do it. But finding a Jew straight off the street's going to be damn hard. They never go out anymore."

"You've got a point there. Maybe if we have a couple men each take a block and just keep a lookout, we'll get lucky. Say twenty men for ten blocks. We're bound to find someone."

Bruckner walked over to the sofa and stretched out, placing his shiny black boots on the burgundy cushions. He gazed up at the ornate ceiling, blowing smoke rings at it. Paulus got up from the armchair and started to examine some objects on the fireplace mantle.

"What an exquisite porcelain piece," exclaimed Paulus, holding up a figurine of a deer. It was painted in beautiful earth tones, and the detailing was so precise one could see the whites of the animal's eyes. "Such incredible workmanship."

Bruckner nodded at his subordinate, keeping his opinion to himself. He couldn't stand dust-gathering doodads like that; his wife had a million of them.

"My wife will love this," said Paulus. He pulled out a handkerchief to wrap up the figurine and stuffed it in the side pocket of his tunic. "It's too fragile to mail, so when I go home next month I'll surprise her with it."

"Well, let's get to it," said Bruckner. "Like you said, we should rough the place up a bit. Go out and get Krueger, will you?"

Paulus opened the double doors to the hallway and found Sergeant Krueger and four of his men lounging idly on the steps of the grand center stair.

"Krueger, get off your ass and come in here," ordered Paulus.

Krueger slowly rose from the stair along with a sallow-faced soldier named Wolfe.

"Krueger, you lazy bastard, I want you and your men to pull apart these rooms like you were looking for someone," said Bruckner.

"Sir?"

"You heard me, stupid; go through the closets and turn over all the beds," said Bruckner.

"Yes, sir. At once," shouted a confused Krueger, who in turn screamed at the top of his lungs at the men in the hall to come in.

"Wait a minute," interjected Paulus, "have him fire some bursts in the walls here, just for special effect. That'll impress the hell out of Schlegal."

"Damn good idea, my boy. Krueger, spray the walls in here."

Krueger unslung his MP-40 submachine gun from his shoulder and, walking around the perimeter of the great salon, blasted away at close range at all four walls, splintering the wide wood pilasters, puncturing the molded plaster panels with holes, and shattering the large gold-framed mirrors.

"All right, that's enough. Just go through the rest of the rooms and tear them up, and no shooting, do you understand, Krueger?" said Bruckner.

"Yes, sir."

Paulus and Bruckner waited in the hall until Krueger and his men were finished. They passed the time chatting about visiting the Louvre, the cognac they'd had at dinner last night, and how much more buxom German women were than French girls. Krueger finally came out, and together, they all descended the stair.

"Come on, let's find us a Jew," said Bruckner.

⁘ ⁘ ⁘

After an hour passed, the base of the pilaster in the center of the wall began to slowly lift up. With great difficulty, Mendel Janusky pushed it upward with both his arms. The top of the pilaster was hinged at the bottom of the deep wood molding that ran along the ceiling. Slowly, Janusky lifted it far enough so he could just slip out from under it. With enormous force, the heavy pilaster slammed back into place behind him. He collapsed onto the floor. He gazed down at his left leg and discovered a trickle of blood oozing through his light brown trousers where a bullet had grazed him. Exhausted and soaked in sweat, Janusky rested his back against the wall. Pulling out a soiled handkerchief, he mopped his face, then dabbed at the blood on his leg.

52

THE SPLASH OF WATER FROM THE SPEEDING MERCEDES HIT LUCIEN right in the midsection, soaking his trousers and coat from the waist to the knees.

"Kraut son of a bitch," he yelled after the car, then immediately regretted it, hoping the car wouldn't stop.

Because he was wearing his favorite light gray suit, the dirty, oily water made a very dark, very noticeable stain below his belt. He knew he couldn't go to his meeting in this state. During his presentation, the Germans would all be staring at his crotch. Lucien had to try to clean himself up. He realized that he was only two blocks from Bette's building. Twice he had let her off in front of it, never having been asked to come up. They never made love in each other's homes. For Bette it was always the excuse about the out-of-town relatives still being there. For Lucien, it was also some feeble excuse, on account of Pierre.

He decided to take the chance on finding her at home. Bette knew fashion and clothes, so he figured she would know how to get rid of stains. Lucien trotted down the street. When he reached the foyer of the building, he realized he didn't know which flat she was in, so he had to ring for the concierge. An ancient man with a cigarette hanging from his lips stuck his head from behind the door and asked him what the hell he wanted. After he got Bette's number, Lucien asked the concierge if Bette's relatives were still staying with her. The old man gave Lucien a puzzled look and then dismissed him with a wave.

Lucien was about to rap on Bette's door when he heard the faint sound of music coming from the apartment. It was a children's tune of some kind. Maybe her relatives *were* still hanging around. In a way he didn't blame them for coming to Paris. They knew that Bette, with her connections, could put food on the table. In France, everyone was always hungry so you did what you had to do to survive, which meant sponging off relatives to eat. He rapped loudly and waited.

After a minute, she hadn't answered, so he knocked again. Finally Bette came up to the door.

"Who is it?" she shouted from behind the thick oak door. "What do you want?"

Lucien was taken aback by her rudeness. "Is this how you greet all your lovers?"

"Lucien, is that you?" Bette replied in an astonished voice.

"Yes, my sweet, it is me. Open up, I've had an accident. I need your feminine assistance."

Instead of flinging open the door, embracing him, and welcoming him inside, there was a long silence.

He knocked again. "Bette, it's me, Lucien; come on, I need your help! My suit got messed up just around the corner, and I need to clean it. I've got a meeting in an hour. Please open up."

Another long silence ensued, and now Lucien was starting to imagine things. Like a lover in her bedroom hurriedly getting dressed and finding a place to hide. He banged on the door with his fist, and an old man next door opened his door and stuck his head out.

"What's all this damn racket?" he demanded.

"Mind your own business."

"Stop this noise this minute."

"Shut up, you old fool."

The old man slammed his door in indignation, and suddenly Bette flung open her door.

"Lucien, what the hell are you doing here? I told you I had people staying with me and you couldn't come up," Bette said. "You're causing a scene."

"Look at my suit," Lucien said. "It's a mess. I just need to clean it up. I thought you could rinse it out and maybe dry it off in front of your oven or something so the stain wouldn't show."

"I told you, you can't come in."

At first Lucien was dumbfounded by her response, then he quickly became angry and hurt. "What the hell is your problem, woman?"

Lucien didn't wait for an answer and pushed past her into the foyer. He was taken aback by how splendid the apartment was. The flat was beautifully decorated in a *moderne* style, with quite expensive-looking furniture. Once his architect's instantaneous appraisal was finished, he returned to being angry. Then he realized that she was acting this way because she had a lover in the apartment, which made him even angrier.

"All right, who are you sleeping with? Is he in the bedroom? Let's meet him. I always like to meet your friends." He started in one direction but realized the apartment had more than one bedroom. "And I thought all the men in the fashion business were fags," he said scornfully.

He dashed headlong into one bedroom and looked under the bed, then behind the drapes and in a large armoire. Then he found another bedroom and proceeded to search it.

Bette followed him through the apartment. "Lucien, have you gone mad? Stop it. I'm telling you there's no one here. For chrissake, stop," Bette insisted, yanking on his arm. "Now get out of here."

"Bullshit, I know he's here. And where the hell are those mysterious relatives of yours?"

"I told you to get the hell out of here," she yelled, now slapping him about the head in a fury.

Lucien resisted the strong urge to punch her in the face and kept searching. His anger was like a torrent of raging floodwater that pulled him helplessly along. He could do nothing to stop it. The sense of betrayal shattered him because he had been so happy with Bette. After all the terrible things that had happened to him—the Serraults' deaths, Adele discovering the stair—she was like a miracle who had come into his life. His time with Bette meant he could forget these bad things for a while and just enjoy wonderful moments of pure pleasure. It wasn't only Bette's great beauty and sexuality that appealed to him, but her wit, sense of humor, and intelligence. It was clear to him that he was falling for her. That one could find love in such horrible times amazed and delighted him, making her betrayal all the more painful.

With Bette still beating him about the back, he came to a huge carved walnut chest at the foot of the bed and threw open the heavy lid. When her punches became faster and more furious, he knew he'd hit the jackpot.

"I believe I've found the buried treasure."

"No. Lucien, please don't," pleaded Bette, trying with all her might to pull him away from the chest.

"He must be the fuck of the century," exclaimed Lucien as he yanked out some heavy blankets from the top of the chest.

"I'm going to choke the life out of the bastard." When he threw off the third blanket, he saw the terrified faces of two children looking up at him. He froze and stared at them in amazement; he might as well have unearthed an Egyptian mummy.

Bette roughly pushed Lucien aside and helped the boy and girl out of the chest. They both clung to her thighs, burying their faces in her white dress. She caressed both their heads and gave Lucien a defiant look that said "go straight to hell."

Lucien was mesmerized by the sight. Bette, a smart, independent, and beautiful fashion model, had never displayed any motherly tendencies at all. Here she was protecting two little children, like a lioness ready to fight anyone who would try to hurt her cubs. He smiled at them, and a feeling of great love and admiration for her swept over him. Lucien knelt down and extended his hand to the boy.

"My name is Lucien, and I'm very sorry I scared you. I was looking for someone else. So what's your name, young fellow?"

The boy looked up at Bette and she nodded.

"Emile."

"And you, young lady, what's your name?"

"Carole," announced the girl, who Lucien could see was not shy like the boy.

"I'm so glad to meet you both. Bette, why don't we get acquainted with some refreshments in the salon while you attend to my suit?"

"You're a mess. Let me get you a robe so you can undress."

Lucien took the children by their hands and led them into the salon. He took off his suit coat and trousers and handed them to Bette, who had brought in some drinks. Dressed in the white robe, Lucien stretched out on the sofa and asked the basic questions one asks of all small children. Their age, their favorite toys and books. Emile and Carole slowly dropped their guard and became friendlier with Lucien, laughing at his silly jokes and funny expressions. He didn't need to be told about their religious affiliation; it was plain to see.

Bette stood in the doorway and enjoyed the scene. Lucien was the first person other than herself whom the children had talked to in a year. He smiled at her and could see that she was happy that they were having a good time and that Lucien, who also never exhibited any parental talent, made them feel comfortable and safe. After a while, Bette shooed the children into their room to play and sat down in the chaise lounge across from Lucien.

"Your suit will dry in about five minutes, monsieur."

"That's wonderful. I'll be on time for my meeting. You know how Germans are about punctuality."

Without any prompting, Bette told Lucien the whole story. He listened without interruption, then walked around the salon in silence. She watched him as he examined the apartment.

"Does the architect approve of my space?" Bette asked coyly.

"It's a magnificent apartment. I'm jealous that I didn't do it. The way one decorates her home says a lot about a person."

"And what does it say about me, Monsieur Bernard?"

"That you have excellent taste. But those two 'accessories' of yours playing down the hall tell me a great deal more about Mademoiselle's character."

"Does that please you?"

"It does indeed," replied Lucien as he knelt down in front of her, held her hand, and kissed it tenderly.

"Lucien, you're sweet, you're wonderful. I'm sorry I had to deceive you."

"But there's one problem, my love. Did you notice how easily I found your secret? You know, the Gestapo will have as easy a time as I did. That can't be. We must fix this immediately."

Lucien got up and walked to the window that overlooked the street. "This is an exceptionally deep windowsill. What's under here?"

Bette walked over. "I don't know; you're the architect, you tell me."

"There must have been an old radiator inside here, then they took it out," said Lucien as he pried up the wooden sill with his penknife and looked into the cavity.

"Ask the children to come here," he said. He tossed some cushions from the sofa into the cavity.

"All little bunnies, come out here please."

Emile and Carole scampered out in glee.

"Children, let's play a game," said Lucien.

The children smiled and nodded their heads excitedly.

"It's sort of like hide-and-seek. I want to hide you under the window," said Lucien. He lifted Emile and put him inside the hole, then Carole. They both fit snugly side by side.

"This will be our secret hiding place," he said as he lifted them out. "All right, back in the bedroom to play, my little ones."

"Suppose the Boche search there; they could lift the lid up and find them."

"The lid will be hinged at the back, and there'll be two locks on the underside of it that you'll have Emile fasten when they're inside. The

Boche won't be able to lift the lid. And you'll place lots of stuff on top, like bowls and vases of flowers."

"What a clever man. You thought of that very quickly."

"I have had a bit of experience in these matters. Now if you'll get my suit, I'll be on my way. But I'll return right after my meeting, because I also have a secret. I think you'll find it quite interesting."

53

"I DIDN'T REALIZE YOU HAD SUCH A PECULIAR SENSE OF HUMOR, Monsieur Manet."

"The fact is, I don't have a sense of humor at all. So my wife tells me. But in the case of this refuge, I had no choice."

"Did you happen to notice that it's right across the street from 11 rue des Saussaies?"

"Yes, Lucien, I did."

"Which happens to be Gestapo headquarters?" Lucien peeked between the curtains to look at the building. Lucien had first visited this apartment a week ago to check it out for hiding places. He'd been so intent on making sure he wasn't being followed, he hadn't realized until he'd left that it was directly across the street from Gestapo headquarters. The sight of the official-looking building nauseated him, as if he'd eaten a bad oyster. He hoped that at this meeting, he could persuade Manet to change locations.

"Of course, every Parisian knows that address," replied Manet with a sly smile.

"And are you still intent on using this flat?"

"Like I told you, I had no choice in the matter. Time is critical, and this is the only apartment I could secure at the moment, so you'll have to be extra clever."

"That, Monsieur Manet, is the understatement of the century. There's no way to find another place?"

"No. And I'm sorry to say that you must be extra quick. I must move in a guest in a few days. He's in great danger at the moment.

He'll be staying here for a while. It's still too dangerous to get to Spain, and Switzerland is out of the question."

"There are horrible things taking place over there even as we speak," said Lucien, half expecting to hear screams of agony coming from across the street.

"If we're not careful, you and I could wind up there."

"Believe me, I've thought about that scenario hundreds of times."

"I'm not surprised," replied Manet.

"Well, I have to admit that this choice of apartment does have a kind of insane ingenuity to it."

"So do you have any ideas, Lucien?"

"Yes, since my last visit, I've come up with one or two possibilities." Lucien began his now familiar walk through the apartment. His eyes surveyed every square meter of wall and floor area again. It was a very ornate apartment, like all the others Manet had provided. He thought how difficult it would be to design a hiding place in a plain low-rent flat. Gilt and white paneling lined the walls, and each room had a huge marble fireplace with a deep stone hearth extending a meter in front of it.

About two meters above the floor in the salon was a deep ledge, which protruded almost thirty centimeters from the wall, stretching around the perimeter of the room. On one wall above the ledge, there were large paintings set into the white plaster wall and surrounded by gilt moldings, each separated by floor-to-ceiling pilasters. After walking through the entire apartment, Lucien made a second trip, scribbling down notes and little thumbnail sketches on a scrap of paper. Occasionally, he took some measurements—the width of the pilasters, the depth of a hearth, the width of some doors, and the thickness of a wall. Lucien sat on the sofa in the salon and scribbled some more notes, then pondered for a bit.

"Would you say your guest is fat or lean?"

"Just as lean as you, maybe more so," replied Manet.

"And how tall would you say?"

"About two or three centimeters shorter than you."

"Is he fit and of normal strength?"

"Yes, I'd say so."

"Good, then we're finished here for now. I'll be back tomorrow to verify a few things and have the drawing for you in the evening."

Manet looked over in the direction of Gestapo headquarters. "We do have a problem of sorts. My best man who's been doing this work is, as we speak, being entertained by the Gestapo across the street."

Lucien walked over to a window and peeked through the curtains as if he thought he could see a man being tortured across the street.

"How is he holding up?"

"He's suffered some terrible injuries. He'll never be able to work again."

"But will he crack?"

"No."

"Does he know about this apartment?"

"Yes."

∻ ∻ ∻

It took six glasses of faux wine to steady Lucien's nerves after he left the apartment. He sat at a table at an outdoor café and stared at a bird perched on a kiosk, wishing that he were that bird. He could just fly off and keep going until he got to Switzerland, leaving all his troubles behind. At this moment, a man who knew about the apartment was being tortured to death and could spill everything. The Gestapo could just watch and wait until Manet moved the Jew in, then pounce. Forget about internment; Lucien would be shot on the spot.

He signaled for another round. The waiter who served him seemed quite impressed that Lucien didn't show the faintest signs of drunkenness, even after drinking the watered-down piss they called wine.

Although this suicidal situation scared him shitless, he had no intention of backing out.

He wanted to do it.

54

I THOUGHT YOU WERE MY MOST RELIABLE OFFICER, SCHLEGAL, BUT maybe I was mistaken."

That comment made Schlegal's blood boil. No one had ever questioned his ability. But he kept his mouth closed and stood at attention before his superior, Kurt Lischka, head of the Paris Gestapo.

To Schlegal, Lischka had the bearing of a clerk in an insurance office rather than a policeman. His balding head and wire-rimmed glasses made him seem weak and very un-Aryan. In reality, he was the perfect Gestapo man—devoid of any feeling of compassion, a born murderer. Many a Frenchman had died within the walls of 11 rue des Saussaies under his watch.

"Did you know that Heinrich Mueller has taken a personal interest in the Janusky matter?" asked Lischka in a quiet voice as he paced back and forth in front of Schlegal.

"No, sir," said Schlegal, knowing that a lecture was on the way. When the head of the entire Gestapo of the Reich was breathing down the neck of a regional commandant, that meant trouble.

"To Mueller, Janusky isn't just another Jew destroying the Fatherland, but a repository of wealth—an estimated one hundred million francs—that can help Germany finance the total victory that our Fuehrer desires. Like a gold filling in the mouth of the lowliest Jew, Janusky's wealth belongs to the Reich, but we can't find it. And that's not the worst of it. Do you know how many Jews this bastard has helped escaped over the years? Probably thousands—and not just in France. He has a whole network of agents—even in

Germany—working for him. He's bribed dozens of officials in Spain, Portugal, and Turkey to provide forged papers for these people. This Jew has paid out thousands for passage on ships in a half-dozen ports to help them escape. Now, we've heard Janusky has bought his *own* ships to do the job. On top of that, Göring wants his art collection. Almost every goddamn day, he calls Mueller about it. So you, Schlegal, *must* find Janusky."

"Every day, we search for him, sir. There is an entire network of Frenchmen who are helping this piece of scum to hide. Each day, we chip away at this conspiracy and we get a little closer."

"I don't want Mueller coming here and personally supervising the search. You don't want that, do you?" Lischka sat down on a chair across the room and lit a cigarette. Schlegal noticed he didn't offer him one, which was a bad sign.

"No, that won't be necessary. In just a matter of days, we'll find him," lied Schlegal. He knew if Mueller came to Paris, Lischka would make his life a living hell.

"I hope so, for your sake, Colonel. Your career has been quite impressive. People in Berlin have taken notice. This is your chance to shine. Find this Jew and his money, and the world will be yours on a platter. We're talking promotion to general."

These words heartened Schlegal. His father and mother would be overjoyed—their son a general. It gave him a new resolve. Lischka picked up a bunch of black-and-white photographs off the desk and shuffled through them. He chose one and showed it to Schlegal, the formal portrait of Janusky with his hand resting on a book.

"Look at the ring on this Jewish pig's hand. That emerald is the size of a golf ball. That one gold ring could pay for an entire Panzer tank. Don't you think?" said Lischka.

"Probably two Panzer tanks," Schlegal blurted out, even though he had no idea what one tank would cost.

"You can stand at ease, Colonel," ordered Lischka, who took a final drag on his cigarette and stood up. "Now tell me about this poor devil here."

Lischka walked casually over to a man lying in the corner of the room and kicked him in the head. "Wake up, monsieur," he said in the cheerful tone a mother would use waking up her six-year-old.

"Aubert is a master carpenter who does the best cabinet work in Paris," Schlegal said. "Everyone we've talked to agrees he's the very best."

"And what does this have to do with the problem at hand?"

"I believe that some Jews are being hidden in ingeniously conceived hiding places throughout the city. To do this, master craftsmen like Aubert are needed to disguise these hiding places so we can't find them."

"That's a fascinating theory, Schlegal. Have you uncovered such a secret place?"

"Two."

"Has Aubert shed any light on this problem for us?"

"He's been most uncooperative, but I'm confident that he'll change his attitude," said Schlegal. He motioned to Voss, who had been standing in the other corner of the room. The lieutenant took out a pair of wire cutters one would use to cut electrical cable from his tunic pocket and knelt beside Aubert.

"Wake up," roared Voss into Aubert's ear. The old man stirred and tried to raise his head, but it dropped back down on the wooden floor.

"Monsieur Aubert, I bet your hands are probably your most valued possessions," Schlegal said. "They do the beautiful woodwork everyone so admires, mm?"

Aubert, whose face was a bloody pulp, only moaned a bit.

"What would happen if you didn't have your index fingers? Make it hard to cut wood, maybe?"

Voss snipped off Aubert's entire right index finger as if it were the stem of a flower. It popped up in the air and landed on the floor. Blood gushed from his hand onto the floor as if it came from a garden hose.

Aubert's screams produced a nerve-rattling reverberation off the gray plaster walls.

Lischka grimaced. "We should pad these walls in here, to soak up the noise, don't you think?"

Without any instruction, Voss snipped off the right middle finger, causing even greater screams of agony.

"Monsieur Aubert will probably want some souvenirs of his visit here," Schlegal said.

"Of course, Colonel," replied Voss as he picked up the severed digits from the floor. He scratched his head with one of them, producing torrents of laughter from everyone in the room, including Lischka. He then put both fingers in the side pocket of Aubert's suit jacket and walked over to Schlegal.

"Let's give Monsieur Aubert time to rest and think things over. We'll meet again. After all, he has eight fingers left," said Schlegal. He motioned to his officers. "Give him something to stop the bleeding. I don't want him to die on us—and get all this blood cleaned off the floor."

Lischka stood. "That was most impressive, Colonel," he said, walking out of the room. "Carry on."

Voss summoned two soldiers from the hallway, then yelled out, "Marie, you old bitch, get your mop and pail and get in here."

The soldiers took Aubert by his arms and dragged him away like a sack of potatoes. A minute later, a haggard old woman in a wrinkled maroon dress shuffled in with a pail and knelt down to wipe up the blood with a rag. The officers watched in amusement.

"I'm truly sorry we made such a mess, Marie. It won't happen again, I promise," said Schlegal.

"You're always saying that, Colonel, and always there's a mess," grumbled Marie.

"Marie, I didn't realize you still had such a nice ass," Voss said. "You must have been a hot number during the Franco-Prussian War."

The soldiers howled with laughter. Voss bent over and gave Marie a hard slap on her rear, but the old woman just squeezed out the blood from the wet rag in the pail and kept cleaning.

"Thank you, Lieutenant. I was quite a beauty in the old days. One day, I'll tell you about the time I fucked Kaiser Wilhelm I. He gave me the Iron Cross First Class."

"Marie, my love, if only you were twenty-five years younger, I'd take you right here, right now on the floor," said Schlegal, tossing some franc pieces in the pail of bloody water.

After the room emptied out, Marie slowly got up off her arthritic knees and went over to a desk in the corner of the room and shuffled through some papers. She read one sheet very closely, then picked up her pail and walked out of the interrogation room.

55

As he was going over a detail on the blueprints with Labrune, Lucien realized something was wrong.

All the usual cacophony of the building site in Tremblay had vanished. Dead silence. No hammering, no sawing, no cranes moving or men shouting. Labrune also took notice and had a puzzled look on his face. Lucien turned around and saw every single man staring in the same exact direction off to the east. He immediately thought they saw approaching bombers. There was no antiaircraft protection or bomb shelters at the site. No one in the German High Command in Paris thought it necessary yet. Where would everyone hide?

Lucien followed the eyes of a laborer who'd stopped nearby with his wheelbarrow and discovered to his amazement what had captured everyone's attention. About thirty meters away, in a navy blue dress and a dark gray scarf, came Bette. She smiled and waved as she drew near. Lucien looked around him and was quite amused. Every man had stopped dead in his tracks to gaze at Bette. It must have been quite odd for them to see such an incongruous sight, as if Martians had landed in a flying saucer.

"Hello," said Bette, as she walked up to him. "I bet you're surprised to see me."

"Yes, I am, and so are two hundred other men," replied Lucien, tilting his head to the construction gang behind him.

Bette seemed puzzled. "What, they've never seen a woman on a building site?"

"Not someone like you, I can assure you, mademoiselle," answered Labrune, who turned to Lucien, expecting an introduction.

"Mademoiselle Tullard, this is Monsieur Labrune, our general contractor."

"A great pleasure," said the old man, who kissed her hand.

"So pleased to meet you. Lucien told me that without you, nothing would get built." Labrune's grizzled old face lit up with delight.

"I thought I'd surprise you. Karin from the office has an old Renault and a petrol ration so she dropped me off," Bette said, turning to Lucien. "I first stopped off at your office but that kid from your office, Alain, told me you were out here. I was hoping you'd be free for lunch."

"Well…you see I'm really busy…"

"Don't be so damn rude to such an incredible-looking woman, Bernard. You must take her out for a fine lunch," protested Labrune, smiling from ear to ear at Bette. "You must go immediately. Don't keep mademoiselle waiting a second longer." Labrune grabbed the drawings out of Lucien's hands, placed his hand in the middle of Lucien's back, and started shoving him forward rather roughly. "We'll be fine without you."

"All right, let's go. My car's over there." Bette said good-bye to Labrune and walked off with Lucien.

"Now remember, don't hurry back on my account. Take the whole afternoon. You young people should enjoy yourselves," Labrune shouted after them.

"What a sweet old man, Lucien. And you said he was a son-of-a-bitch."

Labrune looked about him and screamed. "Let's go, you lazy bastards, get back to work. Haven't you ever seen a woman before?" Some men began working, but most kept staring after Bette.

As they walked, Bette's right high-heeled shoe stepped in a mud hole. "Shit, my best shoes."

Lucien burst out laughing. "Next time, wear work boots."

"I don't have any that match this dress, dummy." She took off the shoe and hopped the rest of the way to the car.

Once in the car, she wrapped her arms around Lucien and gave him a long, passionate kiss. He didn't care if anyone could see them. In fact, he was secretly proud that the men saw what a gorgeous girl he had.

On the way back to Paris, she rested her head on his shoulder. Bette had had many lovers come and go in her relatively short life, reminding her of a single file of men marching endlessly through a revolving door. Handsome men, old men, single men, married men, and many rich men. So she considered herself an expert in this field and had come to the conclusion that men in general were a disappointment. Lafont, an aristocrat who once wooed her, introduced her to horseback riding, which became a passion. She learned quickly that a horse was far more reliable and loyal than any man.

Beginning in her early twenties, Bette made a careful analysis of all her men, past and present. Like an anthropologist conducting a field study of the tribes in French Equatorial Africa, she devised categories and lists of salient characteristics of her subjects. There were the basic categories like wealth, breeding, intelligence, education, physical attributes, marital status, and sexual ability, then more specialized ones for alcohol consumption, thoughtfulness, strength of character, and affection. She filled notebooks with data to analyze it in broad strokes, to see connections between types of men. Bette thoroughly enjoyed conducting her study. She would have liked to become a professor who could specialize in this type of work. Most women in France would go out with one or two men then be forced by society and family to marry. Since Bette had ignored that pressure and had countless men in her life, she had what the anthropologist would term a broad sampling group, which allowed her to discover certain patterns of behavior. Some results were expected—rich men were usually selfish, bored, and demanding; the more handsome a man, the more he treated her like shit.

She had liked Lucien right off; the fact that he was creative was unique. He was one of very few creative men, aside from some painters and sculptors who wanted her to model in order to sleep with her. But he had another unique trait.

The "character" category was the one where men failed most miserably. Her study convinced her that men had no character or backbone. Horses, she felt, had more character. She had enjoyed Lucien's company and his lovemaking, but once she found out about Pierre, Lucien's character rating moved very high. In fact, Bette was bowled over by the revelation. She'd never had a man willing to die for something. This single act of courage was very attractive to her, more enticing than a man with a villa or a Bugatti. She could say she was doing the same thing with her two foundlings, but she had an innate woman's compassion, which was entirely different. Lucien stirred something in her heart that none of the scores of others ever had. As Bette got older, she had a keener sense of what was love and what was not. She knew she was falling in love with Lucien.

"I've got an interesting idea," said Bette, breaking the long silence. "Since Monsieur Labrune was kind enough to give you the afternoon off, why don't you show me all the buildings you've done in and around Paris after lunch? I've already gone to see the wine shop on rue Vaneau."

""You saw it?" asked Lucien, who was shocked and at the same time very flattered.

"Oh, yes. I like the way you curved the storefronts into the entry. It sort of sweeps the customer into the store, doesn't it?"

"That's exactly what I intended."

"The front door has a beautiful metal grate…is that bronze?"

"Yes, so are the door handles."

"The interior's very elegant. I saw the shelves where the bottles were displayed. It was very clever of you to design them that way. They sort of swell in and out. Much better than just ordinary straight shelves."

"Yes, I put a lot of thought into that."

"It's very creative."

Lucien had planned to make love to Bette all afternoon, but now he began to think of all the locations of his projects in Paris and the best routes to get to them.

56

"I T'S A GREAT PLEASURE TO FINALLY MEET YOU, MONSIEUR BERNARD. I've heard nothing but good things about you."

Whenever a German paid a Frenchman a compliment, one had to decide whether it was a backhanded compliment or whether he was being sincere. Lucien sensed Schlegal was being honest, but because he had a weakness for compliments, he could've been mistaken. Finally, Lucien relaxed a bit in his wooden chair; he had been scared stiff waiting twenty minutes for Schlegal to come in. In that time, Lucien couldn't keep himself from looking constantly out the window to the flat at 12 rue des Saussaies—which, to his rotten luck, was just across from Schlegal's window.

When Lucien got the telephone call from Schlegal, he almost fainted, he was that frightened. He would've jumped in the Citroën and driven straight into the English Channel. But the Gestapo officer was effusive and cheerful, saying that he knew what great work the architect was doing for the armament division's construction and engineering section. Lucien immediately thought that Herzog had told Schlegal about him, so he didn't panic. Schlegal asked him to come in, and Lucien assumed it was about some design work. But then again, it could be a trap to lure him in and torture him until he revealed what he knew about Manet's operation. His ego, though, convinced him that this meeting was all about his architectural talents, so he came. He knew he had to. After his encounter with the Resistance, Lucien had convinced himself he wasn't a collaborator. But working for the Gestapo was something different. If he was forced to design for them, there could be some serious repercussions, like being garroted or shot in the head by the Resistance. They'd probably watched him go into Gestapo headquarters. Again, his first thought wasn't about himself, but of what would happen to Pierre.

"Thank you, Colonel." He couldn't really repay the compliment by saying he'd heard good things about the Gestapo's work; that would sound a bit insincere.

"You've done some marvelous buildings for the Reich. I've seen them. They're a bit avant-garde for my taste, of course, but the high command in Paris is quite pleased with the results, and that's what counts. Isn't it?"

"The Reich has been satisfied with my work. If they weren't, they wouldn't give me more work, I suppose."

"Exactly. You're probably wondering why I asked you here today. It's for a professional consultation on a very unusual architectural matter."

The flow of compliments had eased his fear and anxiety, but now Lucien narrowed his eyes and gripped the arms of the chair. This *was* about his Jew work. Lucien knew that the very moment Schlegal asked him about the hiding places, the reaction on his face would give him away. He had to keep a blank expression no matter what. The Gestapo officer's next question seemed years in coming.

"We've come across a hiding place. A very ingenious hiding place under a stair. And we're trying to find out who in Paris could construct such a beautiful piece of woodworking. I guess that's what you'd call it—woodworking?"

"Yes, that's the correct term. Please continue."

"It's a hinged stair that someone can hide under."

So Adele was fucking Schlegal. He could see why. He was extremely handsome and, most importantly, all-powerful. He could do or get everything she wanted. The stair was in Adele's country house, in her bedroom to be exact, which was where she'd been sleeping with this Gestapo officer in addition to him. No doubt, Adele had told Schlegal that he might know something about the stair since he was an architect. If she were in the room right now, he would have strangled her in front of the Gestapo devil.

Lucien was scared, but he knew that the next few minutes could determine his fate, so his performance had to be convincing. He couldn't panic.

"This is a brand-new stair?"

"No, they cleverly reused the old one."

Lucien smiled. He enjoyed being complimented in this roundabout manner.

"That is quite clever. And how does it work again?"

"It's just a flight of four steps leading to a small study. It's hinged at the top and can be lifted up, enabling someone to slip beneath it and hide."

"And how did you discover it if it was so well concealed?"

Schlegal paused, searching for the right words. "I...I came upon it completely by accident. I would never have found it."

"Well, there are a few Parisians who could build such a thing, but two are dead, another I know has left Paris for the south. Those are the only ones I know who could devise what you described."

"Would they be capable of designing or rather coming up with an idea like that as well as building it? Who'd think up such a thing is what I'm asking?"

Lucien wanted to blurt out that a carpenter could never design such a clever hiding place, that only an architect had the talent and brains to do it, but he kept his ego in check.

"A carpenter could come up with a stair like that."

"And you're sure you can't think of anyone else who could do it?"

"No, Colonel, I'm sorry I can't."

"Well, if you ever—"

Schlegal was interrupted by an aide who walked in without knocking. "There's a Colonel Herzog outside to see you immediately. He's from the armaments—"

"Goddamn it, man, I know who he is. Tell him to wait a few minutes."

Herzog pushed through the doorway, shoving aside the aide, who retreated back to his desk.

"What's the meaning of this, Schlegal? Why is my architect here?"

"Calm down, Colonel. Your man is just advising me on architectural business. I'm not taking him away from you. We all know about the fine work he's doing for you. He hasn't been arrested, if that's what you're implying," said Schlegal.

Herzog stared down at Schlegal, who hadn't bothered to get up when Herzog barged into the room. Lucien, who knew Herzog's mannerisms by now, saw that he didn't respect Schlegal at all.

"What architectural business?" said Herzog.

Schlegal hesitated. "There are people who are hiding Jews in secret places throughout the city, Colonel."

Herzog shot a puzzled look at Lucien, then turned on the Gestapo officer.

"Jews hiding in the woodwork, you say? Where did you get that harebrained idea?"

Schlegal rose now and stood nose to nose with Herzog. Lucien was sure fists would start swinging any minute. He couldn't decide who'd win the fight; both were quite fit and the same size.

"I'm sure you're aware that the Reich considers international Jewry a serious and dangerous threat, Colonel. And that they must be swiftly and harshly dealt with. The Fuehrer has made this his number-one priority."

"I thought his number-one priority was winning the war against the Communists and the Allies," Herzog said. "Not scouring Paris for a lot of frightened Jews. The Wehrmacht, which is made up of real military men, doesn't lower itself for such nonsense. So you're wasting this man's time. And that means you're wasting my valuable time."

"I'd be careful about what you're saying, old boy. You're going to make a lot of people angry with that kind of talk."

"Next you'll be calling me a Jew lover, huh?"

Schlegal laughed in Herzog's face. "Not at all. Just someone interfering with Reich business—and that's a very serious charge, Colonel."

"You, sir, can go shit in your hat. Now I hope you'll excuse me, I have a war to win. But in case you want to report me, here's Reich Minister Speer's personal home number." Herzog scribbled a number on Schlegal's desk blotter with a pencil. "Give him a call. Maybe he has some Jews hiding under his bed that you can arrest. Come on, Monsieur Bernard, we're leaving."

57

S O, LUCIEN, CAN YOU THROW SOME WORK TO YOUR FRIENDS—FOR old time's sake?"

Lucien had never considered Henri Devereaux a friend. He was a petty, mean, egotistical bastard who, whenever he won an important commission, would immediately call Lucien to rub it in his face. Although he hated him, Lucien wished he could be like Devereaux, who had all the right influential connections to consistently get big projects.

Lucien was shocked that Devereaux had called him up to go out for a drink. That had never happened before the war. The arrogant prick didn't think Lucien's talent deemed him worthy to sit at the same table. But here they both were at a café, sipping wine and exchanging phony pleasantries. Lucien knew that Henri would eventually get down to brass tacks and reveal why he wanted to meet him.

"I don't know, the Boche have their own methods of choosing their architects," said Lucien.

Both Lucien and Devereaux knew this rang hollow. Other architect friends of Lucien's had been given work by the Germans. To Lucien's great pleasure, Devereaux had no work at all and was livid to see him get big commissions.

"I don't care if it's German war work," said Devereaux. "I'm desperate to design something real. All architects do during a war is design imaginary buildings, and that doesn't count. A design has to get built to be real. I'm going crazy. I've got nothing to do—plus, I'm running out of money."

"What about all those clients and contractors you knew?" asked Lucien, repressing a smile. He was well aware that all of Devereaux's clients had fled the country, and all the contractors he had insulted and demeaned before the war who now had work would never throw anything his way. He knew they hated his guts for his arrogance, and now they had the last laugh.

Devereaux sidestepped the question and asked, "Didn't Raoul Cochin get to do the new barracks in Joinville? I recall that he was a friend of yours."

"Sure, I know Raoul, but I didn't put a word in for him, if that's what you mean."

"So he just got that job out of the blue?"

"Could be. Everybody has some sort of connection, and you know that connections mean work," replied Lucien in his most disingenuous tone of voice.

"These days, I have no connections."

Lucien wanted to laugh in Devereaux's face, but he put on an expression of concern.

"It's tough in wartime to get work. It must be so hard for you, considering the way things used to be. You seemed to grab up every job in the city, didn't you?"

Lucien thoroughly enjoyed rubbing salt into this wound, and he found himself pleased that Devereaux was so desperate.

"Yes, I was quite successful before the war, as you well know. I was one of the city's most prominent architects. I had to turn down work and refer clients to other architects."

"I don't remember any referrals."

"Why, dear Lucien, I could've sworn I sent a client or two your way," said Devereaux, lying through his teeth.

"No, there weren't any referrals from you. Believe me, I would've remembered. An occurrence like that happens as often as Halley's Comet."

"You must be mistaken. A Monsieur Renier. I'm sure he came to you with an automobile repair shop. I told him that would be right up your alley."

It was time to end this nonsense. Lucien was glad that Devereaux was down on his luck. It couldn't have happened to a more deserving person.

"Henri, it's been fun, talking about the old days. I'm sure you remember them with great fondness—all the wonderful commissions you once had. But I must go. I've got a meeting this afternoon about a new commission for an ammunition plant. I'm thinking of doing it all in reinforced concrete, which will give it a real expression of structure, don't you think? When construction starts, I'll take you out for a peek."

That was too much for Devereaux. He slammed his fist on the table, upsetting all the glassware and attracting the glances of the café's patrons. Lucien smiled. His last arrow had struck its target precisely. He expected a hysterical tirade, and he got one.

"You son of a bitch!" Devereaux said. "How does a nobody like you get all these jobs and someone of my talent and stature gets nothing?"

Lucien kept smiling, enjoying this moment enormously. He knew Devereaux was just getting started.

"I've seen that factory you did in Chaville. It's shit. You wouldn't know modernist design if it bit you on the ass. Who the hell do you think you are—Gropius?"

Lucien began to laugh. His face was turning beet red, and he had to take a drink of water. This made Devereaux even angrier. Up until now, he had insulted Lucien in a normal conversational tone, but his voice rose to a shout.

"Let me tell you something, friend. I wouldn't want those goddamn jobs. I'm no goddamn collaborationist, working for the Boche. You're a fuckin' traitor to France. You're going to pay for this after the war. I'll see to it."

"That's an extraordinary case of sour grapes, Henri," replied Lucien, still shaking with laughter. "If the Germans offered you a latrine to design tomorrow, you'd do it in the blink of an eye."

Lucien stood up from the table. "Here, Henri, let me get this. It's my treat." He threw money on the white tablecloth. "It's been worth every sou."

"I'll fix your ass, Bernard," shouted Devereaux as Lucien strolled out of the café.

58

Bette let them pound on the door for almost a minute before she flung it open.

"What the hell do you want?" she screamed at the two Gestapo plainclothes officers, whose expressions changed from menacing evil to outright shock.

Before them stood Bette in a black bra and panties accompanied by a garter belt and sheer black silk stockings. They stood there speechless until the taller one with glasses started stammering.

"What the hell are you trying to say?" said Bette.

"I…I said that we're here to search your apartment by order of the Reich."

"Search for what, may I ask?"

"We've been informed that you may be hiding enemies of the Reich."

"Is that a fact? And who told you that fairy tale? My neighbor downstairs, I bet."

"That's none of your business. Move aside," said the other one, a man with enormous ears. Bette imagined that if he could flap them up and down, he could fly away.

Bette stood her ground with her hands on her hips and long slender legs spread apart. She wanted them to get a good long look at what she knew was one of the best bodies in Paris. She let them stare a few seconds more, then moved away from the door.

"Come on in, boys. I wouldn't want to hinder the duties of the Gestapo. Look around all you like."

The men slowly, almost shyly, came inside the apartment. They reluctantly began searching the living room. She strolled over to the windowsill where Emile and Carole were hiding. She moved a potted plant to the side, sat down on the sill, and crossed her legs, smiling at the man with the oversized ears. Bette began to slowly and carefully smooth out her stockings, one leg, then the other.

The men said nothing as they went into her bedroom and her bathroom. One looked out onto the roof.

"So, give me a hint," Bette said. "What are you searching for? Maybe I can help you."

"Enemies of the Reich, I told you," muttered the man with the glasses as he entered the living room.

"Ah, you mean Jews. Well, there's got to be at least five or six hiding in here right now. Keep looking, you'll find them. I can tell you if you're getting hot or cold, if you like."

The man with the glasses didn't find this amusing.

"You're ice cold, old boy…a little warmer…nope, now you're getting colder."

He started to search the hall closet. Bette kept all the children's toys and books hidden in a compartment at the rear of her closet in her bedroom. Boxes and boxes of junk were piled against it.

"Wait a minute," Bette shouted, and the men stopped in their tracks. "There's one up on top of the chandelier. Look, don't you see him? He's right above you. A Jew with a really big nose." She shrieked with laughter.

Bette could see that the Gestapo officers knew they were wasting their time, but being efficient Germans, they continued a cursory search anyway. The one with the big ears went back into the bedroom and opened the closet door. This made Bette uneasy, and she felt she had to act.

"You know, since you're here, you boys can do me a favor. Wait right here." She went to a stack of boxes in the corner of the living room and pulled the lids off two boxes. The men watched her with great interest as she took out a long burgundy evening gown and a white one of the same length.

"Which one should I wear tonight? I need a man's opinion." Bette placed the white gown against her body. In the swaying motion of a runway model, she walked toward them and stopped then repeated the walk with the other gown. "After all, we girls wear these things to please our men. Well?"

"It's quite elegant, mademoiselle. Of course on you, they both look wonderful," stuttered the man with the glasses.

"Oh, you're sweet. But which one? Red or white?" asked Bette.

"Definitely the red," opined the man with the big ears.

"So, you're both quite certain?" Bette held the burgundy gown at arm's length to give it a final inspection.

"Yes," both men said in unison.

"All right, if you gentlemen say red, then red it is. You've been a great help to me this afternoon, and I'm going to reward you."

Bette was sure that the same fantasy flashed in both of the Gestapo officers' minds and that they were disappointed when she threw the gown aside and walked over to the liquor cabinet.

"Two cognacs coming up. And don't you dare say you don't drink on duty."

Bette delivered the drinks to her guests, who were most grateful.

"I'm so sorry you couldn't find any Jews. Usually, the place is crawling with them—they're reading the Old Testament, counting their money."

The men looked at each other and laughed, gulping down their drinks.

"There must have been a misunderstanding, madame," the one with big ears said. "We're so sorry for bothering you. I hope you're not upset with us."

"Not at all, these things happen all the time. You boys were just doing your job."

"You're most understanding. We'll be on our way. We've taken up enough of your time."

Bette put a hand on each of their shoulders and guided them to the door as if they were blind, their eyes craning desperately for a last look at her. Once the door was shut, she leaned her back against it and let out a sigh. Keeping her ear to the door, she waited until she heard them leave the building. Bette headed straight for the liquor cabinet; she needed a stiff bracer to calm herself down. After someone had called to tip her off about the Gestapo raid, Bette barely had ten minutes to prepare—to hide the children and their belongings and get undressed.

She looked over at the windowsill and smiled. Emile and Carole hadn't uttered a peep. Her heart was brimming with love for them. What brave kids they were. Bette tapped three times on the sill, and Emile, with great dexterity for a six-year-old, unfastened the inside latches. She lifted up the sill to see her children still lying on their sides and holding each other tight. They both looked up at her and smiled. Bette was on the verge of crying, but she held it in and reached down to gently lift Carole out.

"Come, my little bunnies; it's safe now. No one will hurt you."

She cradled the little girl, running her hand through her soft brown hair. Emile crawled out by himself and hugged her thigh, not wanting to let go. Bette gazed down into the hiding place that Lucien had designed. He had saved her children, and she now loved him more than ever. Bette wanted to spend the rest of her life with Lucien.

Finally Emile let go of her thigh. "Aunt Bette, aren't you cold in your underwear?"

ALAIN KNEW THAT LUCIEN WAS HEADING FOR A JEW HIDEOUT. HE was taking an incredibly circuitous route to discover if anyone was following him. Alain would have done the same thing if he had been in Lucien's place. But then, Alain would never do anything as insane as hiding Jews.

Lucien had strolled at a very leisurely pace through the Tuileries Gardens then over to the Place de la Concorde, where he circled the obelisk twice before heading north on the rue Royale. When he got to the Church of La Madeleine, he circled that twice, pretending to admire its neoclassical features, then went west on the rue Saint-Honoré until he turned right on the rue d'Anjou, then left on the rue de Surène. As soon as Alain turned the corner, he remembered that the last time he tailed Lucien, he'd lost him on the rue des Saussaies, which was the next street over. He kept close behind him as he walked down the rue des Saussaies. Two doors before the intersection of rue Montalivet, Lucien stopped and lit a cigarette. He backed into a doorway and looked intently at Gestapo headquarters across the street. Alain had made his way across the street, where he could get a clear view of his boss. With the quickness of a cat, Lucien darted out onto the sidewalk and in through the door of number 12.

Alain sprinted across the street to the side of the entry and opened one of the double doors to peek inside. He caught sight of Lucien's left shoe as it stepped on the first stair riser. Alain slid inside the foyer and hid by the side of the stairway. He was relieved to see that the concierge was not about. He could hear Lucien's quick steps as he ascended the stairs. When Lucien was up to the first floor, Alain started his ascent, hugging the wall, keeping out of sight in case Lucien looked down into the open stairwell. As Lucien reached the second floor, Alain was just a flight below him.

At the third floor Lucien walked over to an apartment door and knocked three times, then three times again. Alain was lying flat against the slope of the stair with his head peeking over the edge of the first riser at the landing when Lucien entered the apartment. He waited a few seconds then went right up to the door. He heard men in the distance talking, but the thick door muffled their voices. Even putting his ear to the panel didn't help. He backed away from the door to take note of the apartment number, 3A, and quickly descended the stairs.

Out in the street, he closely examined the building, counting out where the third floor was. With an architect's eye, he knew that the apartment looked over the street. He walked across the rue des Saussaies to get a better view of the building, but stood back in a doorway just in case Lucien looked out the windows, which were all tightly shuttered.

Alain started to imagine where Lucien would hide the Jew, but without being in the apartment, it was impossible to guess. Was it another fireplace recess? Or under a floor? The Jew probably wasn't in there yet. Lucien had gone there today to check out the hiding place and give his approval before the Jew was brought in, which most likely would happen at night. There was no way Alain would be able to get into the apartment after everyone left. Bribing the concierge was a possibility, but whoever arranged all these things would have made sure he or she was honest. Showing up there and pretending to be on an errand from Lucien's office wouldn't work—all the workmen would know something was amiss. If this was a film, Alain would pick the lock and let himself in at night, but he didn't know how to do that.

He decided to wait until Lucien and the others came out. Because the Gestapo had spies all over the city, he was sure that the men would leave one by one, so as not to call attention to themselves. It was quite clever of them to do this just ten meters from Gestapo headquarters. Who would even imagine such a thing? At least Alain could see who else was involved. But there could be a rear entrance—these big buildings all had one—so it was possible he wouldn't see anyone come out. Stepping out from the doorway, Alain searched up and down the street for a café where he could sit and watch, but there wasn't any. He had to stay where he was and wait. The dusk had now turned to night so he could stay better hidden in the doorway.

Then, after only fifteen minutes, Alain saw Lucien open the door slowly and quickly walk down the street. After another fifteen minutes, Alain was impatient to leave, no longer interested in discovering the conspirators. He was hungry and thirsty and had to go to the bathroom. As long as Lucien was arrested by the Gestapo, that would be satisfaction enough. He'd disappear into thin air like thousands of others in Paris.

He stamped out his cigarette and was about to leave when he saw Monsieur Manet come out of the building. The businessman was evidently the brains of the outfit, as they would say in an American film. Manet walked slowly down the rue des Saussaies, as if he hadn't a care in the world. This fool was throwing away his life and fortune on such a dangerous, foolhardy scheme, Alain mused. To coordinate all these hiding places must be quite an undertaking. Alain had met and talked to Manet many times in the office about the details of his factories. He was a true gentleman from the upper classes, so it mystified Alain why such a person would help a bunch of Jews. It couldn't be for the money, as he was already one of the richest men in Paris. Maybe he was being blackmailed into doing it. He knew damn well that Lucien, who got paid nothing for his work for the Germans, was in it for the money.

As Manet strolled toward the rue du Faubourg Saint-Honoré, he passed a decrepit old truck parked at the curb and raised his walking stick to his shoulder. Two heavyset men in their thirties got out of the truck and walked to the back. They pulled out an enormous steamer trunk, and with one man at each end, they carried their heavy load up the street. Alain laughed aloud; he knew what was packed in the trunk. The Jew must have been a real big one, as the two men labored to get him through the doors of number 12. Elated, Alain could now make the call to his uncle. It would have been senseless to send in the Gestapo if he didn't know that the Jew was actually in there. They would be on a wild goose chase, searching an empty apartment, embarrassing his uncle in front of his superiors. But now when the Gestapo came to call, they would have their Jew. Alain was itching to get to the telephone box on the rue du Faubourg, but he waited. He wanted to give the men time to unload the Jew. Thirty minutes later, the two men and a much lighter-looking trunk came back out into the street.

Alain felt like sprinting down the street, but he fought the urge and walked slowly. He was giddy with joy at the image of the Gestapo beating down Lucien's door in the middle of the night and arresting him. It was almost eight o'clock and people had cleared off the streets, so the rue du Faubourg was deserted when he got to the telephone booth. Because it was getting late, he knew his uncle was no longer in his office at 11 rue des Saussaies, so Alain would try him at home before he went out for his usual night of socializing. He deposited the coins and was so excited he could barely dial the number. To his great relief, his uncle answered the phone.

"Hello, this is—"

Alain stopped in mid-sentence. Less than a meter away from him stood Pierre. He stared up into Alain's eyes with such intense hatred that Alain dropped the receiver and stepped back into the box. Pierre then smiled at Alain but said nothing. Alain looked at him in disbelief, as if he was seeing an apparition. Alain regained his composure, and a wave of anger engulfed him.

"What are you doing here, you little shit?" He felt insulted that this useless orphan was interrupting a joyous occasion. The receiver was dangling in air and a voice kept coming from it, asking, "Who is it, who's there?"

"What the hell do you want? Answer me, asshole," Alain demanded as he grabbed the receiver and brought it up to his ear.

Still looking straight into Alain's eyes, Pierre lunged forward. Alain felt a strange burning sensation in his chest. He looked down at his chest and saw a kitchen knife embedded to the hilt. He gasped and dropped the receiver, grabbing onto the call box for support. He tried to call out for help, but the words couldn't make it out of his mouth. It was as if his throat had seized up. Blood rushed from the wound and soaked the front of his white shirt as he slowly dropped to the ground. Alain's eyes bulged out in shock; he still couldn't call out. Pierre watched in silence, not a shred of emotion on his face. Alain crumpled into a ball on the floor of the booth, dead. Pierre kicked the body with his foot to make sure he was gone, then hung up the receiver. He knelt down to pull Alain's billfold from his jacket and slowly walked away.

As he walked home in the darkness, Pierre knew he had had no choice in the matter. Especially after finding out what Lucien was doing. If Lucien was saving his people, then he had to save Lucien. He was quite proud that he'd protected his protector this time—and he'd done it all on his own like a man should.

60

G OOD EVENING, MONSIEUR BERNARD; SO GOOD TO SEE YOU AGAIN."
From the floorboard in the rear of the moving car, Lucien looked up at his host, whom he recognized as the Resistance leader he'd met weeks ago. A few minutes earlier, while walking down a stretch of alley, Lucien had noticed a dark green sedan pull alongside of him. He knew it wasn't a Gestapo car and paid it no mind until two men jumped out and dragged him by his arms into the backseat. The move was perfectly choreographed, taking only two seconds to accomplish.

"Please, sit up here with me, so we can talk," said the old man, patting the seat.

Lucien pulled himself up and onto the seat. He smoothed out his suit and adjusted his tie. He was brimming with indignation but kept his temper in check. It was a bad sign that the Resistance had contacted him again and in so dramatic a fashion.

"Monsieur Bernard, we have a matter that only you can help us with."

"I'll help you in any way I can," muttered Lucien, vividly remembering that the last time they met he'd been accused of being a collaborator.

"We have instructions from London to intensify our efforts in sabotage."

"That's great. So go cut some telephone lines. I wish you the best of luck. Now let me out at the next corner if you please."

"It's a little more complicated than that. Our instructions direct us to disrupt German war production."

"So have the workers mess up the manufacturing process. A little distortion in the milling or the cutting of a piece of materiel will do the trick. And the Boche will never know until they actually fire a shell or shoot a pistol. It's foolproof. That's the best advice I can give you, so will you let me out?"

"That's not exactly what we have in mind, Monsieur. We're planning something a bit more drastic."

"So what can you do?"

"We'll blow up a factory. The Allies aren't in a position to bomb war production in France yet, so we'll do it."

Lucien burst out laughing. What a bunch of self-deluded fools. Every action they carried out, no matter how small, meant reprisals by the Germans. A munitions train gets diverted in the wrong direction, causing an hour's delay, and twenty innocent Frenchmen are shot.

"You're raving mad. You know how many people will be shot for something like that? At least a thousand," shouted Lucien.

The old man gazed out the window. "Yes, there's a price to be paid for every act of resistance, but in the end it will be worth it."

"For chrissakes, you're not going to give me that line about living defeated is dying every day."

"Still, we must obey orders and do everything we can to fight the Germans. Even though the Allies won in North Africa, the Boche can still win this war. It's far from over. Do you want France to become a province of Germany? Do you always want to be under their thumb?"

"The Americans are in this now. Sooner or later they'll come marching in and win this thing," said Lucien. "You'll see, just like in 1918."

"You may be right. In fact, I hope you are. But I still have my orders."

"How the hell will you blow up a factory? They work twenty-four hours a day; you'll kill all those people. How do you set the explosives with people in there?"

"We plan to blow up the factory in Tremblay that's under construction."

A shock jolted through Lucien's entire body, as though he were being electrocuted. He was completely dazed.

"But that's my factory," said Lucien after he calmed down.

The man in the front passenger seat laughed.

"Armand, did you hear this shit? It's *his* factory."

"You can't blow that up."

"And why is that, monsieur?"

"Because I designed it…that's why."

The three men in the car all began laughing and shaking their heads. Lucien felt as if someone was asking him to kill his child. Like that story about God asking Abraham to sacrifice Isaac. But unlike Abraham, he wasn't about to do it. Abraham, he always thought, was a shit to even consider such a thing.

"You don't understand how hard I worked on it, detailing every inch, or how many sketches I did. It's the best design I've ever done in my life."

"Armand, remember you asked me what I wanted for my birthday? Forget about those sausages. As my present, I want you to let me shoot this goddamn traitor," said the passenger.

"Calm down, Remy. No one is going to kill anyone," ordered the old man. "Monsieur Bernard, it's not *your* factory. It's the *Germans'* factory. A factory that produces objects that kill Frenchmen and our allies."

Lucien at that moment had a very hard time accepting Armand's reasoning on the matter. The image of the detailed pencil rendering of the finished building kept running through his mind. In peacetime it would've won an award, maybe even have gotten international recognition.

"Did you know that many people have died because of your architectural masterpiece in Chaville, Monsieur Bernard?"

"No…I didn't," answered a shaken Lucien.

"I want to show you something you may find interesting."

The old man handed Lucien a stack of snapshots. He had a hard time making out the images in the darkness of the car.

"Here, let me help you see," said the old man, flicking on his lighter and shining it above the photos. "Is that better?"

They were photos of dead bodies in what looked like the desert and alongside a road in the countryside.

"Let me explain. These are dead soldiers in North Africa. Notice the uniforms—Free French. They were strafed by fighter planes with Heinkel engines, which just happen to be made in that beautiful factory of yours in Chaville. And this is a picture of some French civilians who were strafed near the Swiss border, trying to get across. Guess where the engines on those planes came from?"

Lucien sat there in silence, looking out the window.

"Let me stop the car, and I'll kill him," the passenger said. "I know a great place to dump the body out here."

"I told you to shut up, Remy."

The snapshots slipped out of Lucien's hand and onto the floorboard. He continued to look out the window. They were in the countryside somewhere just outside of Paris. As he watched the dark fields and woods whiz by, he began to think about Celeste's parting words— an architectural Mephistopheles. Someone who sold his soul to the Germans in order to design. To design things that killed his countrymen. Celeste was right; he had crossed the line over to collaboration for the sake of his art. And he knew the old man was right. His Tremblay design could win a hundred prizes, but in the end it was his enemy's building, not his.

Lucien rehashed in his mind the same old rationale that he had used after his first meeting with the Resistance. He was so desperate for architectural success, he didn't care who he designed for. The war had come and his career was put on hold; it seemed he might not ever get another commission. To his bitter disappointment, the 1930s hadn't brought the recognition he craved. He couldn't get that breakthrough commission that would set him on the path to professional fame. So when Manet offered him the Chaville job, it was the opportunity of a lifetime he had to take.

The devil to whom he'd sold his soul was Herzog, who wasn't your conventional Nazi devil with horns, a red suit, and a pointed tail. He was a skilled engineer who loved architecture and honestly wanted Lucien to produce great buildings. He *wasn't* a barbarian like the rest of them. Herzog had shared his passion for architecture and urged Lucien to design something good because he saw that he had the ability to do it. Designing the two factories proved that he did have talent. But the rationale no longer convinced him as it had before. He realized that he knew what he was doing was wrong.

He wasn't the least bit scared at this moment—his sense of shame erased all the fear inside him. He reached down and picked up the snapshots and flipped through them again. No soul searching was necessary.

"What do you want me to do?" Lucien asked.

"We have a very limited supply of *plastique* that British Special Operations have given us, so we have to place it where it will do the most damage," the old man said. "That's what you will tell us. But first we'll need a set of blueprints to understand the layout of the place before we go in. We'll turn back to Paris and go to your office. Remy will escort you upstairs to get them."

"And if you run, you get one in the back of the head," said Remy with a big smile.

"And when are you going to do this?"

"Tonight," said the old man. "For a couple of hours, there're only two guards on duty watching the whole place. And you're coming with us to make sure it's done right. We have only one shot."

Lucien didn't have the energy to protest. He was resigned to his fate.

"All right, monsieur, I'm with you."

"That's good. Monsieur Devereaux said you were a true patriot."

"Devereaux, the architect?"

"A mutual friend of ours. He was the one who suggested your building and said you would know the best way to bring it down. 'Bernard,' he said, 'would gladly sacrifice his building for the good of France.'"

"I bet he did," said Lucien.

61

K EEP YOUR HEAD DOWN, YOU GODDAMN IDIOT."

"You know he wants to give us away. You know that, don't you, Remy?"

"I hope he does, Albert. It'll give me a good excuse to put one in his brain pan," whispered Remy into Lucien's ear.

Remy had been peeking over the top of a pallet of bricks when Lucien decided to take a look at the factory for himself. After all, it was his building. But Remy shoved him back down to the muddy ground. Seconds later, Remy crouched down next to him.

"The guard's just finished his rounds; he won't be back inside for another half hour," Remy said to Albert, treating Lucien as if he were invisible, even though he was sitting between them.

"That's not enough time to set these charges," said Lucien.

"I told you to shut your mouth, Monsieur Architect. You're just here to tell us the best place to set the *plastique* inside there," said Albert.

Lucien was indignant; this was no way to talk to a professional man. These guys were just lower-class slum rats from Paris. No education or breeding, and stinking Communists to boot. That was the problem with the war: it had upset the social order.

"Unroll that drawing and show us those columns again," commanded Remy, who pulled a lighter out of his jacket pocket.

Lucien had the drawing flat on the ground and pointed to the four columns he'd already indicated with a red pencil.

"Just these four columns will bring the whole structure down."

"I never could read architectural plans, so you're coming in," said Remy.

"But Armand said I could wait outside."

"Would you listen to this jerk, Albert? What a goddamn coward."

"Some patriot of France. Let's kill him after the job. We can say the Boche guard did it," snarled Albert.

"Listen, asshole," said Remy, grabbing Lucien by his collar. "Armand isn't here, so I'm running the show, and you're going in there."

"All right, all right. I'll go." He wriggled out of Remy's grasp.

"We're wasting time; we've got to get moving," urged Albert.

"Where's the best place to enter?" said Remy.

"We can go to the left around those pallets and get through the door on the south side."

"Is it locked?"

"None of the doors are in yet."

"All right, get moving," said Remy, shoving Lucien forward. The three men crawled on their hands and knees around the pallets, which Lucien thought was overly dramatic. They could have stooped over and still not be seen. Albert carried the canvas bag with the *plastique*, and Remy had the one containing the detonator and the spool of wire. Once inside the plant, Lucien had a hard time getting his bearings; because of the moonless night, it was pitch dark in there. It reminded him of the blackouts in the cinema, where you couldn't see your hand in front of your face.

"Which way?" hissed Remy, irritated at Lucien's hesitation.

"Hold on, hold on," Lucien said as his eyes got used to the dark. "Follow me."

The two men followed him to the last column at the far edge of the plant.

"Right here," said Lucien, pointing to the base of the column. Remy expertly placed the charge and set the wire from the spool into the blob of explosive. Lucien was greatly impressed with his speed and dexterity.

"Hey, you're very good at this," said Lucien.

Remy scowled at him. "What are you? My mother? I don't need your goddamn seal of approval."

"Which one next?" demanded Albert.

"We'll do this in a zigzag pattern," whispered Lucien. "Two rows over at the opposite end."

"You're positive this will bring it down?" asked Remy.

Lucien was insulted by such a question. "I was first in my class in structural engineering. Of course I'm sure."

They ran the wire across the floor to the next column and set the charge, then went two rows over to the next column and then the next until all four were wired.

Albert kept looking at his watch. "Just five minutes left before he comes back, so move it, goddamn it."

Lucien was a little surprised that Albert seemed to be losing his nerve. With Remy running the wire off the spool, they made it through the door and out past the pallets just as the wire ran out. Lucien was out of breath, and his left side began to cramp up.

"We're too close to the building," Albert said in a panic-stricken voice. That thought had occurred to Lucien as well.

"We've got no choice," said Remy. "When it starts to blow, we run like hell toward the woods." He quickly fastened the wire to the detonator and cranked the plunger clockwise until it could go no more.

"Here goes," said Remy as he was about to push the plunger down.

"Wait, this is my building. Let me do it." Lucien spoke with such authority that Remy, without the slightest bit of protest, handed him the plunger. Lucien figured that since he'd conceived the building, he alone had the right to kill it.

When Lucien pushed the plunger down, he expected an immediate bang, but it took a few seconds for the first explosion to come, then in short intervals came the other three. The columns seemed to rise up and twist in pain. Then they began to crumble, bringing down all the beautiful soaring arches Lucien had so lovingly designed. The reinforced concrete structure in turn pulled down all the brick exterior walls, sending shards of glass to the floor. Instead of running for his life, Lucien stood there mesmerized by the sight of the destruction of his creation. His heart ached at the sight of the huge pile of rubble. It was like sacrificing your own child.

"Come on, you bloody fool," Remy screamed at Lucien from the woods. He ran back to get Lucien, yanking on his arm and snapping him out of his trance. "That's all we need is for you to get pinched. You'd squeal your guts out."

Lucien ran so fast that he passed both Remy and Albert on the way to the woods. When they reached the tree line, all three fell flat on their stomachs and looked back at the pile of rubble.

"You know your engineering, Bernard," said Albert, thumping Lucien on his back.

"God, what a beautiful sight," exclaimed Remy. "You know, Monsieur Architect, I'm so pleased with our work, I've decided not to kill you."

62

"I'M SORRY, COLONEL. I DIDN'T MEAN TO DO THAT."

Schlegal and Major Hermann Holweig stood over the lifeless body of Aubert, the cabinetmaker. Holweig prodded him with his boot in the hopes that he had just passed out, but the man was stone dead.

"Hermann, I told you to let up on him," Schlegal said. "He was about to crack. But you kept on beating the hell out of him with that goddamn club of yours."

"I'm sorry; you did tell me to stop using the club. I should've listened," replied Holweig, dropping his head down in embarrassment.

"Christ, you've killed two people with that thing. That's why I have Voss handle these matters. He never goes overboard like you do. What the hell's wrong with you?"

"It's just all the bad things that have been happening to me. Losing Helena, then Alain's murder. I just took it out on the old man," Holweig said.

In an uncharacteristically compassionate gesture, Schlegal put his hand on Holweig's shoulder.

"Yes, I'm sorry about your nephew. He was killed and robbed just down the block, in a call box, right?"

"Some French bastard murdered him, just for a few francs in his pocket. If I ever catch that frog, I'll make him pay a thousand times over for what he did."

Schlegal lit a cigarette and sat on the edge of the desk.

"Your nephew—Alain—didn't he work for Bernard, the architect?"

Holweig sat down in the chair in the far corner of the room and put his head in his hands.

"He was his right-hand man. A talented boy, right out of college. What a future that kid had before him."

"So who found him in the call box?"

"He was found the next morning by someone wanting to make a call."

"So he was killed at night?"

"That's what the coroner said."

"So what was he doing around here so late at night? Coming to see you, you think?"

"I've no idea. I got a strange telephone call that night. When I answered, nobody was on the other end."

This last bit of information piqued Schlegal's interest. He stamped out his cigarette next to Aubert's body and walked over to Holweig.

"No one was on the other end, you say? And you got the call the same night Alain was killed?"

"Yes, the same night."

"Do you think it was Alain?"

"I told you there was silence on the other end."

"Go on home and rest, Hermann; no nightclubs for you tonight. I want you to relax. And don't worry about Aubert."

"He was a tough old bird. Imagine snipping off all ten fingers and still not talking," said Holweig as he stepped over to the body. "You know damn well he was involved in hiding those kikes. To suffer that much pain just for a bunch of filthy Jews. I can't understand it. I just can't understand it, Colonel."

The major walked dejectedly out of the room, leaving Schlegal all alone with the dead body, but he acted as though it wasn't there. Aubert could have been a rug on the floor. He lit another cigarette and walked over to the window and opened it. It was a cool crisp December afternoon, and the sun was beaming down on the rue des Saussaies, covering the buildings across the street with a warm golden glow of light. Schlegal returned to his desk and mulled over his predicament. He had really expected Aubert to finally talk, to give him some lead to follow up. Now, he was back to square one with Lischka breathing down his neck. He had no choice but to round up more suspects from the building trades and interrogate them. The way this was heading, there sure as hell would be no generalship for him. The whole prospect greatly depressed him, and he stared out the open window in front of him.

A bright glint of light from across the street caught his attention. The afternoon sun had struck something very shiny on the balcony railing almost directly in front of him. Schlegal stood up slowly from his chair. He could plainly see that the double windows, which had their curtains drawn, were slightly apart, and there was a hand resting on the wrought-iron balcony railing. On the hand was an enormous ring that was catching the light. He could just make out a wisp of smoke coming from between the windows. Schlegal's back stiffened and all of a sudden there was a tightness in his stomach. His eyes widened in disbelief as he saw the hand pull back and the windows close tight. He sat back down and tried to gather his thoughts. His adrenaline started pumping, and a great feeling of elation rose within him. He began to laugh, slapping his sides in glee. Schlegal ran to the doorway and starting shouting orders to whoever was nearby. Officers came racing down the hall to him. Marie, who was mopping the floor, was almost knocked down. They all gathered around Schlegal, who was now waiting in the hallway.

"Voss, I want you to send a detachment of plainclothes men to the streets behind and to the side of number 12 rue des Saussaies. Hold anyone who exits from the front or the rear of the building. Send some men to watch the roof, but keep them out of sight. Ryckel, get me at least a dozen men and have them wait for me downstairs in the foyer, not outside. They'll need sledgehammers, axes, pry bars, and hand saws. Now, move!" Schlegal still couldn't stop laughing. Voss and Ryckel looked at each in astonishment and ran down the hall. Marie was now flat up against the wall to stay out of their way.

"And, Voss, send a man to pick up the architect, Lucien Bernard. If he's not in his office, then he's over in Colonel Herzog's office at the Wehrmacht armaments section. Whatever you do, find him and bring him to me."

As Schlegal watched Voss tear off, he noticed Marie.

"Marie, you old wench. I'm going to buy you the finest Parisian dress to stuff that beautiful ass of yours in," said Schlegal as he trotted past her.

"A size twelve will do just fine, Colonel. In cornflower blue, that's always been my color," she called out after him. "It goes well with my eyes."

"You got it," he yelled over his shoulder.

Marie watched him disappear down the hall, then, with no one in sight, she slipped into the office. Without raising an eyebrow at the sight of Aubert's dead body, she calmly picked up the telephone receiver and dialed a number, letting the phone ring four times before hanging up. She walked over to the window and stared out at number 12 rue des Saussaies.

63

S CHLEGAL FELT AN INCREDIBLE SENSE OF EXHILARATION AS HE dashed up the stairs of 12 rue des Saussaies, like he was leading a cavalry charge in those American westerns he'd enjoyed so much before the Fuehrer declared war on the United States and banned their movies. He especially missed the ones with John Wayne.

"Voss, bring up the concierge, then round up all the residents in the lobby," he yelled down into the stairwell.

A dozen soldiers with submachine guns slung from their shoulders carried an assortment of tools and were right behind Schlegal. They knew what to do. The lock was smashed to bits, then they all rushed in. One man fired a few bursts from his weapon into the walls of the salon. Schlegal walked in behind them, carefully looking around for any sign of his prey.

"Janusky's here," said Schlegal, holding up a half empty glass of wine. There was an ashtray full of cigarette butts on an end table next to the sofa. He closely examined each one to see if any were still warm, a sure sign that the Jew was still inside the apartment. But to his disappointment, none were. Still, with the rear and the roof of the building covered, there was no way he could've escaped. When he went into the kitchen, he found some bread and cheese in the larder.

Schlegal heard an old woman yelling at the top of her lungs on the landing outside the door. She was cursing at Voss, who had dragged her up three flights of stairs by her scrawny neck.

"You German son of a bitch, you can't make me walk up all those steps. I've got terrible rheumatism. We should've taken the lift."

"The exercise will do you good." Voss laughed in her face and threw her down on the floor in front of Schlegal, who gently prodded her with his shiny black boot.

"Grandmother, who's been using this apartment? Give me some names."

"This apartment's been vacant for years. Monsieur Lamont left the country before the surrender."

"Then who's been drinking out of this glass? And who's been smoking these cigarettes? A ghost?"

"No one was supposed to be in here."

"Someone's been bringing food to this apartment. You must have seen them."

"I swear, I haven't a clue. I saw no one. I never come up here. My rheumatism is so bad," whined the concierge, who now was clutching at Schlegal's boots.

"I have just the cure for your rheumatism. I swear, you'll never be bothered by it again." Schlegal backed away from the old woman and nodded to Voss, who grabbed her by the collar of her brown and yellow housecoat. He dragged her to the railing of the landing and, as if tossing a sack of laundry, threw her over. She made it straight down to the ground floor without hitting the lift that was to one side of the stairwell.

‧‧‧ ‧‧‧ ‧‧‧

As Lucien was being led up the stairs, he heard a scream and saw a brown and yellow blur go by, followed by the sound of a loud thump. He looked over the rail and saw a frail old woman lying on the floor, her head twisted at an odd angle and her left arm bent in two. His hands tightened around the wooden railing to control his panic.

When the plainclothes Gestapo man had showed up at his door, Lucien had assumed it was about Alain's murder. He had found out that the boy's uncle was in the Gestapo and was enraged about what had happened. There would be lots of questions. That the murder happened on the rue du Faubourg just around the corner from the hideout made Lucien nervous. That was one hell of a coincidence. Lucien had been shocked to hear about the killing. He wasn't about to pretend that he had ever liked the kid, but he did lose a valuable employee, one whose shoes would be hard to fill. He also doubted that this was about the bombing of the factory. The Germans chalked that one up to sabotage and had simply executed a hundred people the next day, far fewer than he'd expected. He'd heard that Hitler himself wanted five hundred to die. It was not until they'd pulled up in front of 11 rue des Saussaies and walked across the street to number 12 that Lucien knew he was in big trouble. He was amazed that he didn't start running; instead, he remained surprisingly calm.

After witnessing the brutal murder of the old woman, who he knew was the concierge, Lucien took a deep breath and continued to calmly climb the steps with the Gestapo officer. He knew he was going to be arrested in the next few minutes, but he decided then and there he wasn't going to be taken alive. He would soon be joining the old crone on the ground floor. Lucien didn't worry about would happen to Pierre if he should be killed. He had worked that all out with Bette, and it was a great relief that there was someone to look after him. Lucien wasn't scared. He realized he was quite at peace with himself because he'd finally become something he'd always wanted to be—a father—and best of all, he'd been good at it.

As he neared the third floor, Schlegal came out to greet him. Lucien could hear an enormous racket going on inside the apartment, which he knew was the search for Janusky. He smiled and waved to the Gestapo officer, who, to his surprise, returned the greeting with equal friendliness.

"Monsieur Bernard, I'm sorry to have interrupted your work, but I need your architectural expertise again."

Maybe this wasn't his day to die after all. But Lucien had to keep his wits about him or it would be.

"Not at all, Colonel. I'm glad to serve the Reich. How can I help you?"

Schlegal put his hand on his shoulder and guided him into the apartment. Soldiers using axes were busting through every inch of wall. Another group was prying up sections of parquet flooring. Dust was flying everywhere, and it became hard to see through the haze.

"As you can see, I'm making a very thorough search of the premises for a gentleman of the Hebrew persuasion. I believe he's in this apartment as we speak."

Lucien managed to assume an inscrutable expression, knowing that Schlegal was keeping a close watch on his face, looking for any sign that would give the hiding place away.

"And how do you know this?"

"I actually saw him myself."

"Then he's here."

"Any suggestions as to where to look?" asked Schlegal.

Lucien turned about and stopped. "Look up that fireplace flue, then pull up all the stone hearths in each room. They would make excellent hiding places."

Schlegal immediately screamed at a soldier to do what Lucien suggested. Lucien walked through the apartment with the Gestapo officer following close behind. They went into the bathroom.

"Did you look inside that platform the tub is sitting on? It's just high enough for a man to slip under."

A soldier quickly broke apart the wood platform but the cavity revealed no Jew.

"You know, he could be hiding anywhere under the floor between the floor beams. They're deep enough to conceal a man. Maybe using some sort of trap door. You must uncover every square centimeter," said Lucien in a very authoritative voice.

Schlegal nodded, assuring the architect he was doing just that.

"Don't bother with the bookcases. That's too obvious," added Lucien, knowing that Schlegal would rip them off the walls anyway. "And check the floors of all closets for secret compartments."

Thoughts of death temporarily disappeared from Lucien's mind. He was enjoying walking through the vast apartment watching the demolition. After a while, he sat down on the sofa and watched, yelling out suggestions of where to look next. He got a big kick out of the fact that the soldiers did exactly what he ordered. As he smoked cigarette after cigarette, he was very careful not to look at the hiding place. About an hour later, Lucien's navy blue suit was covered with dust. His hair was gray, giving him a bizarre preview in one of the apartment's ornate mirrors as to what he'd look like as an old man.

He could tell from Schlegal's pacing and constant cursing that he was getting nervous. The Gestapo officer picked up a pry bar and was yanking paneling off the walls. He smashed every one of the incredibly ornate mirrors on the walls, hoping to find a hiding place behind them. There was so much debris piling up in the apartment, it became difficult to move around. Schlegal ordered it thrown down the stairwell where it piled up on the dead concierge. The plaster dust in the air was so thick and swirling that the soldiers became ghostly phantomlike images moving in slow motion. Overcome by the dense fog of dust, soon everyone was coughing and hacking their brains out. But their fear of Schlegal kept them working away, tearing every square centimeter of surface apart.

From his hiding place, Janusky could hear everything around him. The roar of the demolition was deafening, but the worst thing was that it never let up. It was incredible how humans could work nonstop like that, as if they were machines powered by electricity. Because of the narrowness of the space he was in, Janusky had to lie on his right side with his arm tucked under his body, so he could feel the vibration caused by the smashing axes and pry bars in the walls, floors, and ceilings. He grimaced and flinched at every jolt. Having survived months of warfare on the Somme in the Great War, he thought that nothing would ever scare him again—the terrible scream of artillery shells before they landed in the trenches, the sight of men's bodies blown to pieces. But he was wrong; he found himself shaking as though he was delirious with a tropical fever. With his history of heart problems, he was worried that his heart would give out on him, and the Gestapo would find a corpse. They'd laugh like crazy because they'd literally scared him to death. Janusky didn't want to give them that satisfaction.

After hearing the concierge get thrown to her death, he decided he couldn't take it any longer and was going to reveal himself. If he hadn't gone over to the window, none of this would've happened. What a goddamn stupid thing to do, he thought, just to get a peek out the window. But it wasn't just the old woman. Too many people had died protecting him. He wasn't worth it, and he wouldn't have any more innocent blood on his hands. Then in amazement, Janusky listened to the conversation between the German and Bernard, whose name he recognized as that of Manet's architect. Why of all people was he here? Did they finally find out what he'd been doing for Manet? At first, Janusky thought the architect would show the Germans where he was hiding, but Bernard was leading them away from him. This gave Janusky a new resolve; he steeled himself and stayed put. He wanted to live. The soldiers continued to rip apart the apartment in a mad frenzy just centimeters away from him.

Suddenly, above the cacophony all around him, he heard a piercing shout.

"Schlegal, you stupid bastard! I warned you not to bother my architect again."

64

HERZOG SMILED AS HE WALKED THROUGH THE APARTMENT. WHEN he finally returned to where Schlegal was standing by the entry door, he removed his cap and began brushing off the dust.

"Let me guess. No Jew," he said without looking at the Gestapo officer.

Herzog knew that Schlegal was already mad as hell at not finding his man, and his taunts were going to make him madder, which was the whole point.

"We're still looking," came a terse reply.

Herzog burst out laughing. "Christ, man, you've uncovered every millimeter of space in this flat; you know he's not here. And who is it you're looking for?"

"Mendel Janusky."

Herzog stopped walking through the apartment and faced Schlegal.

"The art collector? How the hell do you know he's here?"

"Because I saw him from across the street."

Voss came to the doors where they were standing and saluted both officers.

"Colonel, what should I do with the residents down in the lobby?"

Lucien already knew the answer to that question. In the span of an hour, Schlegal had gone from ecstasy to despair and now, worst of all, embarrassment. Those people were doomed.

"Is there a rear entry? He could've slipped out that way," said Herzog.

"We had it covered. He couldn't have gotten out the back," replied Schlegal, annoyed that Herzog would ask such a question.

Schlegal turned his attention to Voss. "Ask them just one more time where Janusky's hiding." Voss nodded and ran down the stairs.

Herzog slowly walked in a circle in the salon, viewing the destruction. Every square centimeter had been ripped apart.

Herzog shook his head. "You've lost him."

All of a sudden, the sound of several bursts of machine gun fire rose up from the stairwell.

"I guess they didn't know where Janusky was," said Schlegal, shrugging his shoulders.

A sergeant, a slightly overweight man of about thirty-five, hesitantly came up to Schlegal. He saw what was going on and wisely didn't want to be caught in the crossfire.

"Sir, we've ripped everything apart. Except those paintings up there."

Herzog saw Lucien look up at the paintings then quickly avert his gaze.

Schlegal backed away from Herzog and looked up above the cornice to see some very large paintings that covered one of the walls.

"In all the commotion, I forgot about them," said Schlegal with a laugh.

Herzog slowly walked over to the paintings and gazed up at them, examining them closely. They were a series of lush pastoral scenes of shepherds and voluptuous nymphs with lutes and pitchers of water done in a rich array of greens and earth tones. "Wait," Herzog shouted. He suddenly stepped between Schlegal and the sergeant.

"You ignorant bastard, can't you see those paintings are valuable? They're by Giorgione da Castelfranco, the sixteenth-century Venetian painter. He was taught by Bellini, and Giorgione was Titian's master."

"So, who the hell cares?"

"They're incredibly expensive, you ignorant fool. As negotiable as gold for the Reich. You can't rip them down. The Reich wants treasures like that."

Schlegal stared up at the paintings. "I don't see what's so great about them."

"Schlegal, they're as valuable as diamonds!" Herzog said excitedly. "Don't touch them. If you do, I'll have Reich Minister Speer on the line to talk to you in two minutes. He knows who Giorgione is, and you'll be explaining why you destroyed millions of Reich marks of property."

"It doesn't matter. They're coming down anyway. And we won't have to get up on ladders."

"What the hell do you mean?" asked Herzog with a puzzled look on his face.

"Look out the window."

Herzog walked to the open window that overlooked the rue des Saussaies. Across the street on the sidewalk was a field artillery piece directly aimed at number 12, manned by two soldiers, one of whom was loading a shell into its breech.

"You have two minutes to get them down if you still want them," added Schlegal with a big smile. "Sergeant, get all the men out of the building at once."

The sergeant and his detail were glad to oblige.

"And just what the hell do you think you're doing?" Herzog said. "You're going to destroy the entire building just because you didn't find your Jew?"

Lucien went over to the window to see what was going on and his heart sank.

"You're absolutely right. I'm not going to waste any more time ripping up flats. The whole building is coming down," replied Schlegal in a quiet voice. "He's in this building, and he's going to die."

"Have you gone completely mad? You'll set the whole place on fire and it'll spread through the entire block. It'll be a goddamn inferno!"

"You've now got one minute to get your valuable paintings down."

"Schlegal, you idiot. I'm telling you not to do it. The percussion of the blasts will break every window in Gestapo headquarters across the street." Herzog went to a gray marble-topped console table where there was a phone and dialed a number.

"Colonel, may I have your permission to leave?" asked Lucien.

"I'm through with you for now, but you and I are going to have a little talk very soon, Monsieur Bernard."

Lucien understood what "a little talk" meant. Schlegal was worse than mad; he'd been humiliated in front of his men, and he was going to take it out on anyone he could.

"Hold on, sir. I'll get him," Herzog spoke into the receiver. "Schlegal, there's someone who wants to speak to you."

"Tell Reich Minister Speer I'm busy."

"I strongly advise you to talk to your boss, Herr Lischka, or you better start packing some warm underwear for a trip to Russia that you'll be taking tomorrow," said Herzog with a broad smile on his face. Schlegal frowned at Herzog as he walked over to take the receiver from him. He had to hold it away from his ear, Lischka was screaming so loud.

"Schlegal, you crazy bastard. What the hell are you doing?" bellowed Lischka. "I'm standing at the window, and I see a gun aimed at the building directly across the street from my headquarters. You'll break every damn window here if you fire that thing."

Schlegal looked across the street to see an extremely agitated Lischka pounding on a window with the flat of his hand.

"But Janusky's in this building, sir. I'm positive."

"Then why don't you ask the Luftwaffe to drop bombs on the whole block. That way, you'll be sure to get him."

"That seems excessive, sir."

"And what you're going to do isn't? Anyway, we wanted the Jew alive. Forget it, Schlegal. I'm ordering you to withdraw immediately."

"If that's a direct order, then I will obey it. Thank you." Lischka slammed down the receiver at the other end, and without a word, Schlegal put on his cap and walked out, leaving Herzog and Lucien alone in the apartment.

"He'll be freezing his balls off in Stalingrad in the very near future," said Herzog with an ear-to-ear grin.

Herzog looked up at the paintings. "What an amazing find. Giorgione da Castelfranco. Did you know there are scholars who think that some of his paintings could have been the work of his student Titian? So these could actually have been painted by Titian himself. Imagine that." Herzog lit a cigarette and walked around the salon.

"It's such a shame to see these beautiful paintings among all this mess. I may have to come back this week to rescue them," said Herzog with a smile and a wink.

As Lucien looked up at the paintings, Herzog placed his hand on Lucien's shoulder and whispered into his ear.

"Better wait until the middle of the night to get him out of there. And you, my friend, must be gone by tomorrow night."

65

M ENDEL, IT'S SAFE TO COME OUT NOW."
Manet, who had been standing in the middle of the apartment, walked over to a sofa covered with plaster dust and sat down.

"Did you hear me, Mendel? You can come down."

Manet heard a faint movement. There was the sound of a sliding latch bolt, then the bottom of one of the paintings on the upper wall started to lift up, until Mendel Janusky could be seen lying behind it, pushing it forward with his hand. The top of the painting within the gilt molding was hinged along its entire length. The whole thing came up like a flap on a bread box. Janusky had been lying on his side in a narrow cavity, barely forty centimeters deep, which had been hollowed out of the brick wall behind the painting.

"Can you make it, Mendel?"

"Yes, I'm just stiff as a board. Give me a second."

Slowly, he crawled out from under the bottom of the painting and onto the wide ledge in front of it. Then he swung his body over the edge, his foot searching for the top of the pilaster. When he found it, he extended his other foot to the base, but it slipped off. He lost his grip on the ledge and crashed to the floor. Once he was out from under it, the painting dropped back into place.

Manet ran over to Janusky, helped him up, and, with great difficulty, guided him over to the sofa. Janusky was breathing heavily, and his clothes were soaked with sweat. "It's been quite a day, hasn't it, old friend?" said Manet, patting Janusky's knee.

"You wouldn't have anything to drink, Auguste?"

"I most certainly do. I knew you would be thirsty and hungry, so I brought you a bottle of wine and a hunk of bread."

Janusky pulled the cork out of the bottle and gulped down its contents, then bit off a piece of bread with the ferocity of an animal.

"You must forgive my manners."

Manet laughed and patted him on his shoulder.

"Innocent people died today because of me, Auguste. I heard it all. I can't do this anymore. After I finish this wine, I'm walking right across that street and turning myself in. I should've done it months ago," said Janusky in a voice shaking with emotion.

"Because of their sacrifice, you *must* escape. If you don't, everything up until now will have been in vain."

"But I'm responsible for their deaths, Auguste."

"What's done is done, Mendel. People are dying every minute in this war; that's the way it's going to be for a long time before we win this thing."

"You actually still believe we can win? I admire your faith. Mine vanished months ago."

"Good triumphed this afternoon, didn't it?"

"That, my friend, was a miracle."

"And a clever bit of design to hide you up there," said Manet as he gazed up at the painting.

"Even better than at rue de Bassano. Does your architect know what the word *mensch* means?"

"Yes, I once explained that word to him."

"Please tell him again for me that he's a *mensch*."

"I'll never see him again. He's made arrangements to leave the city. But I think he now knows that."

"So what's next, my old friend? Did your architect prepare another hiding place for me?"

"After today, it's become too dangerous for all that. You're going to Spain, tonight. It's extremely risky, but I think we can manage it."

"After today's experience, it'll seem like child's play."

"We must leave now; the building could still be under surveillance from across the street. Do you by any chance happen to know the Lord's Prayer?"

"No, Auguste, they neglected to teach me that in Hebrew school. What, are you going to Christianize me?"

Manet walked over to the side of the door of the apartment and picked up a large bundle wrapped in brown paper and handed it to Janusky.

"That's exactly what I'm going to do. Please put these on," said Manet.

"This is most stylish," Janusky said, holding up a priest's cassock. "At least it's not a nun's habit." He pulled out a hat, shoes, socks, trousers, and white shirt and collar.

"You are joining the priesthood for a while. In fact, tonight you're going on a pilgrimage to Lourdes, which as you know is quite close to the Spanish border."

"Am I stopping there to pray for a miracle?"

"You've already had one miracle today. Don't press your luck."

Janusky undressed and put on the new clothes and hat. He twirled around like a fashion model in front of an amused Manet.

"So? I don't look too Jewish, do I?"

"Yes, you do. We can't do anything about that nose, so keep your hat pulled down tight. And carry these rosary beads on that belt there. But first things first. Repeat after me…Our Father, who art in heaven…"

"*Barukh atah adonai, eloheinu…*"

"Stop."

66

H E'S NOT COMING."

"He'll come."

"Is this the right spot? You didn't get it mixed up, did you? And what about the time?"

"This is the right spot and the right time to be here. His message was very specific. Please don't worry," replied Lucien in a cheerful tone that did a good job of masking his fear.

"I can't help it," said Bette as she looked at the backseat of the Citroën, where Emile and Carole were sleeping next to Pierre, who was wide awake and totally calm. He smiled at her.

"You'll have plenty of time for worrying. We've got a four-hour ride to the Swiss border. Anything can happen between here and there," replied Lucien, looking straight ahead through the windshield into the cold December night.

"That's reassuring, my love."

"That's the truth. And you always told me to tell you the truth."

"How do you know you can trust him? He's a German."

Lucien smiled at this question. It was only 9:45, and he knew Herzog would show up. An envelope had been delivered to Lucien's office instructing him to drive to St. Dizier, a town to the west of Paris. When he got there, he was to take a country road heading southeast from the town center and wait behind the ruin of a stone barn. They had been packed and ready to go all day but had to wait until dark to leave Paris. Waiting in Bette's flat had been unbearable. Any minute they expected Schlegal and his men to crash through the door. The little talk Schlegal had mentioned still hadn't been scheduled, but Lucien knew he wouldn't forget about it. He and Pierre sat by the window to keep watch for the Gestapo to pull up in front of the apartment building. If they came, Pierre and the two children would go into the window hiding place, and Monsieur Manet would fetch them later. Lucien and Bette had arranged with Manet, who was not yet under suspicion, to care for the children and get them out of France. Pierre didn't want to hide, but Lucien, in the only time he ever lost his temper with the boy, ordered him to do what he was told. The hours dragged by and mercifully nothing happened.

"He studied at the Bauhaus, you know."

"So that makes him trustworthy? Because he's an architect?"

"A modernist architect."

"You've got an odd sense of trust, my love. He's still a German, and you can never trust a German. Always remember that."

"Yes, my dear, I'll keep that in mind." Lucien rolled down his window a bit to draw in some of the cool night air. It was a beautiful clear night with a steady breeze that refreshed Lucien, evaporating the sweat that was beaded on his face. He ran both his hands through his hair and rubbed his eyes to keep alert. The silence in the countryside reminded him of the deafening silence of Paris at night after the curfew, where one could hear a pin drop in the next block. The only sound he heard was the wind whispering softly through the trees that flanked the car. It was suddenly broken by the sound of cracking twigs and leaves off to his left. His heart began to pound. He continued to look straight ahead into the night, his hands tightly gripping the steering wheel at ten and two o'clock. A short rap on the side of the car gave him a start. He slowly turned his head to the left and just a few centimeters away was Herzog's smiling face. He motioned for him to get out. Lucien was surprised to see the German dressed in civilian clothes. He didn't know what to make of it and was confused about what was happening.

"Do you know what you have to do?" said Herzog casually, as if he were asking Lucien to pick up his laundry.

"We'll drive to the west of Belfort to the exact point you told us, then we get out and walk across the border."

"It *has* to be that exact position. There'll be no guards on either side of the border there tonight," said Herzog. "You mustn't get lost."

Herzog rested his hand on Lucien's shoulder. "I brought a couple of things for your trip," said Herzog, pulling out two folded pieces of paper from his pants pocket. "It's another official pass from the armaments division authorizing you safe passage at any time with today's date. You won't have any trouble on the road tonight."

"The French police won't get suspicious with the kids in the car?"

"Show them this too. It's a letter from me saying you're going to Montbéliard to start work on a factory, and you have to relocate your family."

"You've thought of everything."

"Not quite. This is a backup plan just in case of an emergency," said Herzog as he pulled a Luger from his other pants pocket. "It can come in handy if an unexpected problem comes up."

"Why…thank you," said Lucien, holding the butt of the pistol uneasily.

"They did teach you how to fire a gun in the French army? I know you people aren't much good at fighting wars, just sitting around smoking, drinking, and bullshitting," said Herzog with a smile.

"Yes, you pull this thing," said Lucien, pointing at the trigger.

"Very good. And the bullet comes out at this end. Important to remember that."

"We have some extra room in the car. You're sure you won't come along, Dieter? You're certainly dressed for the occasion."

"I'm still a German soldier sworn to defend the Fatherland, so I'll be going back to building factories and fortifications. *And* there's still much to add to my art collection. You know, I may even reconstruct your building those bastards in the Resistance blew up."

Lucien turned away and stared off toward a grove of trees. "When all this madness is over, I hope we meet again," said Lucien.

"We will, I'm sure of it," replied Herzog.

"I never thought I'd ever say this to a German oppressor, but I'll miss you. We made an odd team."

"That we did, my friend," Herzog agreed. "But now it's time you were on your way. You've got a long night ahead of you."

"Good-bye," said Lucien, extending his hand.

Herzog shook his hand firmly. "Good luck to you, Lucien."

Lucien turned and walked back to his car. Climbing into the driver's seat, he gave the German a final wave of the hand. Bette said nothing and looked straight ahead. He started up the engine and drove off.

Herzog lit a cigarette as he watched the red taillights of the car get smaller and smaller until they were just tiny specks of light, disappearing over the horizon. He took a deep drag and looked up into the cold night sky and saw a sea of stars above him. He knew nothing about constellations or astronomy, but he enjoyed the beautiful sight. In Paris, he had never even noticed the night sky, but out in the country it was immense, almost drawing you up into the heavens. One couldn't help but be awed by the sight. As he smoked, he continued to stare at the sky, marveling at the vast number and configurations of stars. Finally, he threw down the butt, stamped it out, and turned to look down the road. After about a minute, headlights appeared on the horizon. Herzog took one more look up into the sky then walked slowly into the woods, where he had hidden his car. He opened the front passenger door and pulled out a green canvas bag and a machine gun. Behind some bushes at the very edge of the road, he waited as a car raced toward him. When the car was about fifty meters away, he stepped up onto the edge of the road and fired the machine gun. Bullets ripped through the windshield and side windows, and the car careened to the right and ran off the other side of the road. Herzog walked toward a gray-green German staff car, which came to a dead stop almost directly opposite where he was standing. A soldier was slumped over the wheel, and two officers were moving around in the backseat. Setting the machine gun down on the road, Herzog casually reached into the canvas bag he carried on his other shoulder and pulled out a stick hand grenade. He moved a few steps closer and threw the grenade by its long wooden handle. It skidded under the car and exploded, causing it to rise a meter off the ground and burst into a ball of flame. Herzog watched the inferno for a few seconds then walked back to his car and pulled it out from its hiding place. Driving back to Paris, he smiled to himself. He knew Schlegal would never ignore an anonymous tip.

◆ ◆ ◆

As Lucien drove through the night, he realized he wasn't scared. Despite the danger still ahead of them, they were going to make it. He was certain of it. As he stared at the beams of the headlights piercing the empty road stretching in front of him, he smiled as he imagined what his father would've thought of what had happened in the last six months. His son had been a goddamn fool. For a bunch of Jews! What madness. "Didn't I teach you anything, boy?" Professor Bernard would've sighed and said, "A child's failures are the parent's failures." But Lucien knew he hadn't failed in the least. He thought he didn't have it in him to help another human being. But to his great surprise, he did. He was proud of it. And he had proved his father wrong.

He was amazed that such good fortune had come to him in such terrible times. They say that nothing good comes of war, but that wasn't true. Meeting Bette, his friendship with Herzog and Manet, and above all finding Pierre. Their paths would've never crossed if it hadn't been for the war.

"Do you think everything will be all right?" whispered Bette in a scared voice. She had not said a word since they drove off.

"Everything will be fine."

Bette leaned over and kissed his cheek, then laid her head on his shoulder. Lucien knew she believed him, and that absolute trust gave him a very comforting feeling. He turned the heat up and gently pushed his foot down on the gas pedal so the acceleration wouldn't wake anyone. The Citroën, with its quiet purring motor, was like a warm cocoon protecting them as it sped through the cold night.

It had all been an illusion, Lucien knew. The buildings, the arches, the sweeping, graceful lines. All this time he had been worshipping a façade of concrete and glass.

Lucien could tell from her soft breathing that Bette had fallen asleep. Turning, he looked at the three sleeping children huddled under a blue woolen blanket on the backseat. Curled in a ball in the folds of the blanket was Misha. He smiled at the family. His family.

Reading Group Guide

1. Why did the majority of people in France refuse to help the Jews during World War II?

2. Do you think anti-Semitism influenced a person's decision on whether to help others?

3. What do you think of the people who hid Jews in exchange for money? Was it evil and exploitive or a fair business transaction?

4. In the beginning of the novel, Lucien didn't care about what happened to the Jews. Discuss how his character evolved throughout the novel. How did your opinion of him change?

5. The Germans were disgusted that the French always informed on one another during the Occupation. Would you assume that this is a common war practice? Why? In what ways does war bring out the worst in people? In what ways does it bring out the best in people?

6. Many spouses abandoned each other because one was Jewish. What did you think when Juliette Trenet's husband left her? Is there any defense for what he did?

7. One reason Lucien helped Jews was to get architectural commissions from Manet. Did you agree with the French Resistance?

Did Lucien's love of design and the need to prove his talent cross the line into collaboration with the enemy?

8.   Most fiction and films portray Nazis as monsters during World War II. Do you believe that some German military men secretly hated or doubted what they were doing? Does following the crowd make these men just as bad as those who carried out their duties without conscience?

9.   Discuss the unusual relationship between Lucien and Herzog. Can two men from warring countries be friends?

10.   Lucien was already taking an enormous risk by hiding Jews for Manet; why do you think he agreed to take in Pierre?

11.   What was your impression of Father Jacques? What kind of role do you think faith plays throughout the novel?

12.   Adele had no qualms about sleeping with the enemy. Why would she take such a risk?

13.   Bette could have her pick of men but chose Lucien. Discuss what made him special in her eyes. What are the most important qualities you look for in a friend/significant other? Would you be willing to compromise on any of these qualities? For what?

14.   If you were a gentile living under the Nazis in World War II, do you think you would have had the courage to hide Jews? What consequences are you willing to face to help others?

15.   It's easy to say, knowing what we do about the horrors that occurred during WWII, that we would have helped Jews with nowhere to

hide. How do you think you'd react if a similar situation occurred today? Do you think it's even possible for a similar situation to occur in our age and day? Why? Why not?

16. Suppose you had been taken from your apartment by Captain Bruckner and lined up in the street. If you knew your life was about to end, what would you be thinking about?

17. If you were under the stairs in the Geibers' place during the Gestapo's search, how would you have reacted?

18. Schlegal was disappointed that the people he tortured always talked. What do you think were the motivations behind someone who talked and someone who didn't? If you were in a situation where someone was trying to get information from you, what would be the final straw to make you talk?

Author Q & A

1. **How did you first become interested in writing?**

    When I went back to Columbia University, I had to write a thesis for my master's degree. I found that I really enjoyed doing the research and writing the thesis. I'd never written a word before that. So I decided that I'd like to write a book. I co-authored *The Baltimore Rowhouse*, then went on to write three more books on architectural history on my own. I also became a freelance writer for the *Baltimore Sun* and *New York Times*, which I didn't enjoy as much as writing the books.

2. **Why did you start writing fiction?**

    Once I had some nonfiction experience under my belt, I thought I'd try fiction. John Grisham was my inspiration: a real-life attorney who wrote crime novels based on the legal world. I was a real-life architect who could write fiction based on architecture. And I always admired writers who had dual careers, such as Wallace Stevens, who was a lawyer, Somerset Maugham and William Carlos Williams, who were doctors.

3. **Who are your favorite fiction writers?**

    There's just one, Anne Tyler. She's superb at observing human behavior and emotions. And her novels are based in Baltimore, my hometown, so I enjoy identifying the Baltimore references and geography in her books.

4. What was your inspiration for *The Paris Architect*?

For *The Paris Architect*, I transposed a real-life historical event to a different time. During the reign of Elizabeth I, Catholicism was repressed, and the saying of Mass was outlawed. But priests throughout England refused to obey and continued to worship in secret in manor houses. As a precaution, carpenters designed and constructed "priest holes" for them to hide in if the house were discovered. (If caught, the priests, as well as the people who hid them, would be tortured and executed.) When the Queen's soldiers raided a suspected house, they would look for days and never find the priests who were hiding under their noses.

Using Occupied Paris during World War II as my setting, I turned the Elizabethan-age carpenter into a gentile architect who designs temporary hiding places for Jews escaping the Nazis.

The other inspiration would be that of my mother's experience during World War II. After Germany defeated Poland in 1939, many Poles were forced into labor camps to produce war material for the Germans. My mother wasn't Jewish, but she and hundreds of thousands of gentile Poles had to work in factories under horrific conditions, functioning basically as slaves. She was working in a factory that made chewing tobacco for German soldiers. One day, a German supervisor discovered she could speak German and French and found her a job as a translator at the factory in Nordhausen, Germany, where the V-2 rockets were being produced. She worked as a housekeeper and translator for the contractor who constructed tunnels inside the Hartz Mountains, where the rockets were assembled. She lived with the contractor's family in relative comfort while a few hundred meters away, thousands died building rockets. The German supervisor's one act of kindness saved her. People can't survive terrible times without help from others. So I wanted to include those kinds of behavior in the book.

5. **What research did you do before writing the book?**

I studied as much as I could about life in Paris during World War II. The best reference was Jean-Paul Sartre's essay "Paris under the Occupation."

6. **What's the process you use in writing a book?**

I do it the way a building is constructed. First, I build the foundation and a structural skeleton, which is the basic plot structure of the novel. Then, in layers, I flesh out the structure, adding details that give it description and depth. The last layer would be tiny details like the design of a handrail or the door handle on the front doorway in a building.

7. **Who were your favorite characters in the book?**

Aside from Lucien, the architect, it would be Father Jacques. It's a little known fact that a lot of Catholic priests in France were arrested and deported for helping Jews, especially children. I wanted to portray a really brave person committed to helping his fellow man. The scene with Father Jacques being interrogated by the Gestapo colonel is probably my favorite. He isn't scared or intimidated by the Gestapo in the least and stands up to them. He knows he's done the right thing by helping the children and isn't afraid to die for it.

Acknowledgments

A successful author once gave me a very good piece of advice. He said that one of the most important things in writing fiction is that you need to find someone who absolutely believes in your novel. He was right. And I was lucky enough to find two such special people. The first person was my literary agent, Susan Ginsburg of Writers House. Her experience and guidance were of immense help to me. She gave me confidence and encouragement during a very dark period in my life. I'll always remember how she stood by me. The second person was Shana Drehs, editorial manager of Sourcebooks Landmark, who believed in an architect who was a first-time novelist. Her enthusiasm about the book gave me great confidence, and her editorial skills made my novel sharper and better.

I thank both of these people for believing in my work.

Charles Belfoure
Westminster, MD

About the Author

An architect by profession, Charles Belfoure has published several architectural histories, two of which have won awards from the Maryland Historical Trust. He was also given grants by the Graham Foundation and the James Marston Fitch Foundation for architectural research. A graduate of the Pratt Institute and Columbia University, he taught at Pratt as well as at Goucher College in Baltimore, Maryland. His area of specialty is historic preservation, and he writes a blog on historic preservation and architecture: www.thewicked architect.com. He has been a freelance writer for the *Baltimore Sun* and the *New York Times*.